MURDER BY PILLOW

Poppy's eyes scoured the room until they settled on someone lying on top of the bed. She instantly recognized the cute patterned strapless T-shirt dress Danika had been wearing when they last saw her. There was a pillow over her face, which caused a dreaded feeling of déjà vu deep within Poppy.

Timothy called from outside the trailer, "Is everything okay in there?"

Poppy raced over and removed the pillow.

Everything was not okay.

Because Danika Delgado was unmistakably dead . . .

Books by Lee Hollis

Hayley Powell Mysteries
DEATH OF A KITCHEN DIVA
DEATH OF A COUNTRY FRIED REDNECK
DEATH OF A COUPON CLIPPER
DEATH OF A CHOCOHOLIC
DEATH OF A CHRISTMAS CATERER
DEATH OF A CUPCAKE QUEEN
DEATH OF A BACON HEIRESS
DEATH OF A PUMPKIN CARVER
DEATH OF A LOBSTER LOVER
DEATH OF A COOKBOOK AUTHOR
DEATH OF A WEDDING CAKE BAKER
DEATH OF A BLUEBERRY TART
DEATH OF A WICKED WITCH
DEATH OF AN ITALIAN CHEF

Collections
EGGNOG MURDER
(with Leslie Meier and Barbara Ross)
YULE LOG MURDER
(with Leslie Meier and Barbara Ross)
HAUNTED HOUSE MURDER
(with Leslie Meier and Barbara Ross)
CHRISTMAS CARD MURDER
(with Leslie Meier and Peggy Ehrhart)

Poppy Harmon Mysteries
POPPY HARMON INVESTIGATES
POPPY HARMON AND THE HUNG JURY
POPPY HARMON AND THE PILLOW TALK KILLER
POPPY HARMON AND THE BACKSTABBING BACHE-
LOR

Maya & Sandra Mysteries
MURDER AT THE PTA
MURDER AT THE BAKE SALE

Published by Kensington Publishing Corp.

Poppy Harmon and the Pillow Talk Killer

LEE HOLLIS

Kensington Publishing Corp.
www.kensingtonbooks.com

KENSINGTON BOOKS are published by

Kensington Publishing Corp.
119 West 40th Street
New York, NY 10018

All Kensington titles, imprints, and distributed lines are available at special quantity discounts for bulk purchases for sales promotion, premiums, fund-raising, educational, or institutional use.

Special book excerpts or customized printings can also be created to fit specific needs. For details, write or phone the office of the Kensington Sales Manager: Attn.: Sales Department. Kensington Publishing Corp., 119 West 40th Street, New York, NY 10018. Phone: 1-800-221-2647.

The K and Teapot logo is a trademark of Kensington Publishing Corp.

First Kensington Mass Market Printing: April 2022
ISBN: 978-1-4967-3038-1

First Kensington Ebook Edition: April 2021
ISBN: 978-1-4967-3039-8 (ebook)

10 9 8 7 6 5 4 3 2

Printed in the United States of America

For George and Alex

Chapter 1

It had been over thirty years since Poppy Harmon had stepped foot on an actual Hollywood film set. Granted, this shoot was set up at a high-end resort hotel in the heart of Palm Springs and not some cavernous soundstage on the Paramount lot where her mid-1980s television series *Jack Colt, PI* had been filmed, but there was a feeling of warm familiarity, an infusion of happy memories, because back in her heyday when Poppy was an actress with a regular TV role, she had never once taken it for granted. She had always been hyperaware of just how lucky she was to have scored such a cushy, well-paying gig at the time, especially after so many years in her late teens and early twenties struggling, waiting tables, modeling skimpy swimwear at car shows, and answering phones at a call center for a household appliance company.

Poppy watched as the crew busily set up lights by the

shimmering pool where the next scene was to be shot as a bright-eyed, eager, enthusiastic PA who had introduced himself as Timothy led her and Matt through the resort.

Matt was like a kid in a candy store, excitedly soaking up everything he saw: a makeup woman powdering the face of a vaguely recognizable actor; a forty-something man in a gray T-shirt and red baseball cap, slumped over in his director's chair, perusing a script; some kind of set decorator or production designer painstakingly arranging red bougainvillea in the background of the set as the cinematographer stared through the lens of his camera, working on getting his shot just right.

Poppy knew Matt was in his element. This had been his dream for most of his young life. He had wanted so desperately to become a successful actor, the next Ryan Gosling or Chris Hemsworth, or whoever was the hot superstar of the moment. But life never works out exactly as you expect, and now the talented young man found himself playing the role of Matt Flowers, the public face, the de facto head, of the Desert Flowers Detective Agency. He wasn't on billboards and buses, or in the front row of the Academy Awards, but he was successful and surprisingly good at the part he was playing.

When Poppy, along with her two best pals, Iris and Violet, had first started the Palm Springs–based investigative firm, no one would hire them. Mostly due to people's ageist preconceptions that three mature women in their sixties were utterly incapable of solving cases or handling potentially dangerous situations. Enter Matt. Young, virile, disarmingly charming. He had risen to the challenge of playing a master detective wholeheartedly, and his performance had put their fledgling business on the map.

Now they had more clients than they knew what to do with.

Including Danika Delgado, a rising young actress and social media influencer who had heard about Matt's daring exploits online and had called the Desert Flowers office, which was located in Iris's garage, to inquire about hiring them.

Actually, Danika did not call personally. One of her three personal assistants had left the message on voicemail. Poppy, Iris, and Violet were clueless as to who Danika Delgado even was, but Matt had certainly heard of her, which became quite clear when he whooped and hollered about being a big fan at the first mention of her name in their morning staff meeting. His outburst had startled Violet so much, she spilled coffee all over her new blouse she had just bought on sale at TJ Maxx.

The assistant had not explained why Danika wanted to hire local private detectives, just that she would like to meet with them ASAP. Once Poppy read Danika Delgado's net worth online, she immediately called the assistant back and happily informed her that they luckily had an opening to meet this very afternoon.

Danika was at the Sundial Luxury Resort just outside of downtown Palm Springs shooting a reboot of the early 1960s camp classic *Palm Springs Weekend*. The original had featured the sizzling hot stars of the time including Troy Donahue, Connie Stevens, Robert Conrad and Stefanie Powers. In fact, Poppy had been friends with Stefanie Powers, who was co-starring with Robert Wagner on *Hart to Hart*, about a globe-trotting wealthy married couple who solve murders, at the same time Poppy was appearing in *Jack Colt*. Now, after all these years, Netflix, or Hulu, it was one of those giant streaming services, was currently producing a remake, or reboot, Poppy could never keep the lingo straight, of *Palm Springs Weekend*, with an all-new Gen Z cast.

The production assistant, Timothy, cranked his head around to Poppy and Matt, who was so distracted by a bevy of bikini-clad extras, he tripped over a lounge chair, and asked, "Would you like to stop by craft services for some coffee, or a Danish before I take you to Danika's room?"

Matt opened his mouth to speak, but Poppy cut him off with a curt, "No, thank you, Timothy." She was too anxious to hear what kind of case Danika wanted to hire them for and didn't want to waste time while Matt dithered over whether he should have a cruller or go for a healthier option like a granola bar.

Timothy nodded and they kept moving until they reached a glass door leading inside toward the large corner suites. Timothy opened it and stepped aside to allow them both in ahead of him when the man in the T-shirt and red baseball cap, his script rolled up in his fist, bounded toward them.

"Wait!" he yelled, catching up to them, breathless. He took a moment, his eyes fixed on Poppy before continuing. "I'm sorry, I'm Trent, Trent Dodsworth-Jones," he said in a clipped decidedly British accent.

"Trent's our director," Timothy said, slightly concerned he had done something wrong, bracing himself to be dressed down in some unexpected way.

Trent ignored him and remained focused on Poppy. "Are you who I think you are?"

"That depends on who you think I am," Poppy said dryly.

"You are, aren't you? I'd recognize that smoky, sexy voice anywhere! You're Daphne!" Trent practically exploded.

Matt smirked. He loved it whenever Poppy got recognized for her signature role on *Jack Colt*.

Poppy graciously extended her hand. "Poppy Harmon."

Trent excitedly pumped her hand. "I grew up watching you back in the eighties. I was a huge fan of *Jack Colt* when it finally made its way across the pond! My family comes from a dreary little town called Preston in Northern England. There is absolutely nothing to do there. Our only claim to fame is that we are about an hour's drive from Liverpool where the Beatles got their start. That's it. There is no other reason to ever go to Preston. We were dirt poor, but we did have a color TV which was my only lifeline to the outside world and I would watch you every week!"

Poppy had heard from friends that Preston was a lovely little city, but was not about to argue with someone who had grown up there and had probably harbored dreams of getting out to make it big in the film business.

"I am so happy to have played a small part in your adolescence," Poppy said politely.

"Yes, if anything, you helped get me through puberty!" Trent said, a lascivious smile suddenly plastered on his face.

Okay, way too much information, in Poppy's opinion.

"What brings you to our little set?" Trent inquired.

"They're here to see Danika," Timothy offered.

"Oh, are you friends?" Trent asked, curious.

"No, this is a professional call," Matt chimed in.

Poppy resisted rolling her eyes at him. She did not like to burp out information she didn't have to, but Matt was her exact opposite, exceedingly chatty and unfiltered. It could be a burden sometimes.

"I see. Are you an agent, or a manager?" Trent asked, eyeing Matt.

"Neither," Poppy snapped, staring down Matt, who finally got the message to keep his mouth shut from further comment. She turned back to Trent. "It was a pleasure meeting you, but we should go before we're late for our meeting."

"Of course," Trent said, turning to Timothy. "Tell Danika we should be ready to shoot in ten."

"Got it!" Timothy chirped.

Before Poppy had a chance to escape, Trent reached out and touched her arm. "Please, Poppy, before you go . . ."

She turned and warily eyed his hand on her, but didn't want to immediately shake it off and appear rude. "Yes?"

"Let me just say, in my humble opinion, you never got your due," he said solemnly.

Poppy was confused—what on earth he was talking about? "I beg your pardon?"

"As an actress. I know you probably got cast as Daphne because the show needed window dressing, and you certainly fit that bill . . ."

This was now getting downright creepy but Poppy held her tongue.

Trent sighed, realizing how inappropriately he was coming across and quickly added, "But you were quite good in that role. You gave Daphne depth and heart, and I always thought with the right opportunity, you would have risen to the heights of a Jessica Lange or Sissy Spacek."

"Well, I don't know what to say," Poppy murmured, flabbergasted.

"And she's *rarely* speechless!" Matt cracked.

Poppy threw him a stern look, like a mother trying to drive the car while her rambunctious preteen son caused too much of a ruckus in the back seat. She then returned her attention to Trent. "I appreciate your kind words, Mr. Jones. Good luck with the rest of your film shoot."

"A pleasure, Poppy," Trent said, beaming, before jogging back to the set.

Timothy led them down a long hallway to the largest suite in the hotel and knocked on the door. One of Danika's personal assistants, a harried-looking girl carrying two different phones, whipped it open and ushered them inside. "Hurry, we don't have much time and Danika is *dying* to talk to you!"

Timothy hung back as the girl waved Poppy and Matt inside and tried to get out, "Trent wanted to let Danika know we'll be ready to shoot again in—" but the assistant slammed the door in his face.

Poppy and Matt followed the assistant into the main room of the suite. Sitting in a chair in front of a mirror while an African American hairdresser fussed with her wavy dark curls was Danika Delgado, petite, unblemished brown skin, in a pink robe. She held her phone up in front of her face as she recorded a video for her fans. "So this is day eight of the *Palm Springs Weekend* shoot, guys, and it's going awesome! I love my co-stars! Chase Ehrens is such a sweetheart! And a first-rate kisser, too, if I'm going to talk out of school! I'll share more juicy details from the set in my next post at bedtime! Love you all! Oh, and the lipstick shade I'm wearing is called Flawless, in case you were wondering!"

The assistant turned to Poppy. "Danika has a marketing deal with Color My World products. She's one of the highest-paid social media influencers out there."

Poppy nodded as if she had a clue what this girl was prattling on about.

Danika threw her phone down on the table next to her and glanced at herself in the mirror. "Does it look kind of flat to you, Chanel?"

The hairdresser quickly began fluffing Danika's locks out. "No worries, girl, we'll get it where it needs to be."

The nervous assistant cleared her throat. "Excuse me, Danika . . . ?"

Danika was still staring at herself in the mirror, dissatisfied with her appearance. "I'm not liking this eyeliner at all. We may have to reshoot before we post anything to Instagram."

The assistant apprehensively tried again. "Danika?"

"*What*?" Danika snapped, swiveling her head around.

"The private detectives are here," the assistant whispered, practically shaking.

Danika instantly slapped on an inviting smile. "Oh, good!" She popped up from her chair. She was a short little thing, about five feet two inches. Her eyes instantly fell upon Matt and without even a pause, cooed, "You are *so* much hotter in person!"

Unlike Poppy, Matt had no qualms about soaking up compliments. "Why, thank you. As one of your one hundred and twenty-eight million Instagram followers, dare I say the same?"

"Oh, you are the charmer!" Danika said laughing, eyeing him up and down lustfully. "When my people found you online, I said to myself, this guy's a detective? He should be an actor!"

Matt beamed brightly. "Funny you should say that—"

"Miss Delgado needs to be back on the set soon so why don't we get down to business," Poppy quickly interjected.

Danika's eyes finally strayed away from Matt and over to Poppy. "And who are you?"

Obviously, unlike the film's director, Danika was far too young to ever know who Poppy had been in a previous life.

"I'm Poppy, Matt's . . . *assistant*."

She always had trouble actually saying it.

Especially since it was not true.

"Oh, nice to meet you, Poppy," Danika said pleasantly as she pointed out a lush comfy-looking couch nearby. "Why don't you both sit down while Chanel tries to work miracles on this rat's nest?" She sat back down in her chair as Chanel rubbed some gel on her hands and went about smoothing out Danika's chic hairstyle.

"How can we be of service?" Matt asked.

"I'm having trouble with a stalker," Danika said matter-of-factly.

"Do you know who this stalker is?" Poppy asked, reaching inside her shoulder bag and pulling out a pen and some paper to take down notes.

Danika shook her head, forcing Chanel to stop for a second. "No. I have no idea. I mean, let's face it, I have a zillion crazies following me. Everyone with my kind of online profile does. It's impossible to keep track of them. But this guy, he's different. It started out innocent at first. The usual flowers and chocolates and little personalized gifts he knew I liked just by following me on Instagram and subscribing to my YouTube channel. But lately, things have taken a dark turn. His messages are far less adoring and more worrying."

"How so?" Poppy asked.

"There's a rumor going around that I'm dating Chase Ehrens."

"Your co-star on this film," Matt offered.

"Yes, which I am most certainly not. Chase is a decent enough guy, but definitely not my type. We're just friends."

Poppy cocked an eyebrow. "I'm a bit confused. When we walked in here you were making a video with your phone and talking about him as if there might be something going on between the two of you."

"That's just for show. Keep people interested, you know? It promotes the movie and us as well. It doesn't matter if it's not true. The problem is, this wacko thinks it *is* true and it's making him mad! Like, stalker-y, I'm going to murder you, mad!"

"He's threatened you?" Matt asked.

"Yeah, about five hundred times. He knows I'm here in Palm Springs shooting this movie, and he's made no secret of the fact that he is here too and ready to come after me at a time and place of his choosing. That's a direct quote from his last post, by the way."

"Have you called the police?" Poppy asked.

Danika laughed derisively. "Duh. Of course. But what can they do? Oh, sure, they rushed down here acting all concerned and serious and made some kind of report, but that was it. Until this guy literally guts me with a carving knife, they're totally useless. The studio is paying a fortune for a kick-ass security detail while I'm here, but they're not trained detectives. I want to be proactive about this. I want a local firm, one that knows this city, that can track down this lowlife creep and put him away for good before he throws acid in my face, or worse."

Poppy swallowed hard at the prospect.

This young actress was doing a good job of keeping up her bravado, but it was clear on her beautiful, heavily made-up face that she was scared and feeling vulnerable.

"I have a lot of people looking out for me, with good intentions, but for my own peace of mind, I want some-one who knows about things like this, who I can call day and night, who is not here to protect the movie or my brand, but to protect *me*! That's where you come in, Matt."

Matt sat up straight on the couch next to Poppy.

He nodded confidently. "Trust me, Danika, I'm your man."

"I had a strong feeling you would be," Danika said, smiling seductively.

Poppy wasn't so sure.

Keeping a highly public figure with over a hundred million fans safe and secure seemed like a daunting chal-lenge, not to mention the task of locating one of those millions of fans out in the world who was unstable and possibly homicidal, ready to strike at any time. But once Danika offered to pay triple their usual going rate, Poppy was suddenly feeling slightly more emboldened.

How hard could it be?

If only she had listened to her initial instincts.

Chapter 2

Trent Dodsworth-Jones raised an eyebrow as he took off his red ball cap and scratched his balding head while staring incredulously at Poppy. "Private investigator?"

"Yes," Danika sighed impatiently. "I want Matt and Poppy on the set with me at all times so they're going to both need a permanent security pass."

"Of course," Trent said, still in a state of shock. He then smiled at Poppy, impressed. "I had no idea. You're just full of surprises, aren't you, Poppy Harmon?"

"She's not a *real* detective. Matt's the detective, Poppy's just his assistant," Danika sniffed, almost distastefully, as if Poppy was some kind of cautionary tale of what happens to actresses who age out of leading roles and no longer can find work in Hollywood. Danika's dismissiveness bothered Poppy because that was a very simplistic view of her own story and a far cry from the reality, but she kept mum, staying focused on the task at hand. She couldn't let her pride get in the way.

Trent nodded toward Matt, but kept his eyes glued on Poppy. "I'd be honored to have you on my set."

"Thank you, Trent," Danika said. "Now, where do you want me?"

"Your mark's over there," he answered, pointing Danika to a spot near the pool.

Poppy and Matt stepped back, out of the way.

Trent ambled over to his director of photography, a stout German man with frazzled hair and the long drooping face of a bloodhound. They privately conferred about the shot for a few moments before Trent returned to his director's chair and hopped up on it.

"Okay, let's do this!" Trent yelled across the set.

The makeup and hair people scurried onto the set, flocking around Danika like a gaggle of handmaidens, as the star appeared to be mouthing the lines of dialogue she would soon be delivering on camera.

The German cinematographer peered intently into the lens of his camera. The lighting guys finished their work and ducked out of the way, clearing the set.

A costumer zipped over to carry off the baby blue terry-cloth robe that Danika had shed, revealing herself in a tiny dot of a bright green bikini.

Poppy gasped, stunned by the curvaceous figure of her client as well as the eye-popping, overexposed nature of her bathing suit choice.

The assistant director shouted at the top of his lungs, "Quiet, please!"

The makeup and hair people scattered, leaving Danika

alone by the pool, camera aimed in her direction, all eyes focused on her. She lowered her head, mentally preparing for the scene, or at the very least, pretending she was.

There was silence.

"Camera rolling!" the heavily accented German man called out. "And we have speed!"

Poppy knew enough about film shoots to know that the next line they would hear would be the director yelling "Action!"

But he didn't.

He never said a word.

She glanced over to see Trent Dodsworth-Jones just staring into space, as if lost in thought. He wasn't even looking at the monitor in front of him where he was supposed to watch the scene they were about to shoot.

Danika patiently waited for her cue as a strong desert wind suddenly swept through knocking over the carefully placed flowers in the background. Danika shivered, visible goose bumps on her arms and legs, but gamely ignored the cold, waiting to begin the scene.

Finally, after what seemed like almost a full minute, Trent snapped out of his reverie and shouted, "Cut!"

The German cameraman glanced over, confused.

Danika sighed and hugged herself. "Can we fix whatever is wrong quickly before I freeze to death? I thought Palm Springs was supposed to be as hot as Hades."

"Hold on, everybody, I just had a brilliant thought!" Trent said, leaping out of his director's chair.

"I bet he has a lot of those," Matt whispered to Poppy, still so excited to be on a real live Hollywood film set.

Everyone expected Trent to make a beeline for Danika in order to discuss some change of dialogue, or repositioning of her mark, or some other genius creative idea that would make the scene better. But instead, he marched straight over to Poppy, who took another step back, startled, not sure what was happening.

"I want to cast you in the movie!" Trent declared.

"*What*?" Poppy gasped.

"*What*?" Matt cried.

"There's a small but pivotal role of the resort manager, Nomi, an older woman who has a romance with a football coach from LA and I think you'd be absolutely perfect for it," Trent crowed.

The assistant director carefully intervened. "But Trent, what about Rita Rubio? She's playing that part. We've already shot two scenes with her."

"I know," Trent sighed. "I don't know what happened between her audition and the actual shooting, but she's been consistently wooden and unimpressive since she got here and I think it's time we made a change."

Danika wandered off the set and over to join them in order to find out what was going on, and why she had been left hanging out to dry while her director was presently more interested in her hired help. "Are we going to do this, or should I go back to my room until you're ready?"

Trent turned to Danika and grabbed her by the shoulders. "Trust me on this. I want Poppy to play Nomi."

"*Poppy*?" Danika gasped, utterly gobsmacked, as Trent's people across the pond would say.

Poppy finally found her voice and inserted herself into the conversation. "I'm sorry, that's impossible. I haven't acted in years."

"Oh, come on, Poppy, we both know you'll nail it," Trent said, bursting with confidence.

"I did not hire Poppy to be my co-star, I hired her boss to find my stalker," Danika said evenly.

"I understand," Trent explained patiently. "But I have been hired to make the best movie possible, which by the way, benefits you in the end, and I know she can do this. I have been watching her ever since I was a little boy growing up in the UK."

Danika hesitated. She could not quite embrace the idea yet, but she also wanted to trust her director's instincts. "I don't know. . . ."

"Well, I do," Poppy said pointedly. "My acting days are over. They have been for a long time. I just can't do it. And I am not willing to be distracted from our real mission here."

"Poppy, *please* . . ." Trent begged.

"Shouldn't you talk to Greta about this first?" the German cameraman, who was eavesdropping, suggested.

"No," Trent said, brushing him off. "She and I already had a conversation about Rita's lack of screen presence. I know she'll be okay with this. So will Hal."

Poppy had heard someone earlier mention Greta Van Damm and Hal Greenwood, the producers on the film.

Trent was now in front of Poppy's face, his eyes pleading with her. "What do you say, Poppy? You'd be doing us a *huge* favor!"

"No, absolutely not," Poppy insisted.

"It could be helpful to us if Poppy was on the set in an organic way, you know, so as not to stand out as a detective but as a member of the cast. That way, no one gets tipped off that we're running an investigation, just in case the stalker has some kind of inside connection," Matt offered, grinning from ear to ear, totally buying into the idea.

Poppy kept her cool, but was flaring up on the inside. She opened her mouth to protest, but Danika managed to speak first. "Matt has a good point. And I trust his judgment." Trent looked wounded and Danika noticed, choosing to preemptively massage his bruised ego. "Yours too, Trent."

Trent relaxed, then excitedly hugged Poppy. "So it's settled. You'll play Nomi." He turned to the assistant director, "Ryan, check the call sheet. Poppy may be shooting her first scene tomorrow, so we may have to schedule a costume fitting today."

"What about the scenes we've already shot with Rita?" the assistant director asked.

Trent thought about this for a brief moment and then shrugged. "We can always tack on the reshoots toward the end of the schedule, maybe even on a pickup day."

The assistant director nodded, then hurried off to make it all happen.

Poppy turned to Matt, seething. "You were absolutely no help whatsoever."

"This is so exciting!" Matt whispered gleefully, choosing to ignore Poppy's fury.

Trent checked his expensive Rolex watch. "Take ten, everybody! I need to make a few calls."

Danika gave Poppy an encouraging smile. "I'm sure you'll be wonderful, Poppy. And I will feel safer having you close to me at all times." She then glided off to her room, followed by her loyal entourage.

"I'm going to shadow Danika," Matt said. "You stick around here in case they need you to sign a contract, or discuss your scenes with the director, or the costume designer needs to take your measurements! I have to say, Poppy, I'm a little jealous! Imagine, Poppy Harmon starring in a big-budget Netflix movie!"

"Matt—"

But he was gone before she could get another word out.

Poppy was left alone, her mind reeling.

No, she just could not stand for this.

The idea of her playing a role in the film was utterly ridiculous and completely unacceptable.

She was a professional private investigator now.

Not an actress.

That life had been over for decades.

And it was a life she was not eager to return to anytime soon, even if it was part of the job pleasing their client.

She marched over to Trent to stop this train before it left the station, but he was already engaged in a conversation with an older woman in her late forties, early fifties, with fluffy auburn hair, bright red lipstick, and freckled skin, who had just wandered onto the set.

Poppy decided to hang back but could hear their conversation.

"I don't understand. What are you talking about, Rita?" Trent asked, a concerned look on his face.

"I'm worried I'm not giving you want you want," Rita said softly, worry lines on her forehead that had not been Botoxed recently.

"I would never lie to you," he said, gently stroking her arm. "Don't get too inside your head. No one is talking behind your back. You're doing just fine."

"Really?"

"I promise," Trent said, kissing her forehead in an effort to help make those deepening worry lines go away.

"I feel so much better," Rita said, the tension draining from her body. "I'll see you tomorrow."

She practically bounced off the set, reassured and happy. Before Poppy could approach him, Trent turned to

Timothy, the production assistant, who had suddenly appeared at his side. "Get me Rita's agent on the phone. I want him to inform his client that it's not working out and we're recasting."

Timothy nodded dutifully, snatching his phone from his back pocket and scurrying off.

Poppy shook her head, disgusted.

If there was one thing she did know from her experiences in the past, Hollywood would never change.

And like it or not, she was about to act in front of a camera again for the first time in over thirty years.

Chapter 3

Poppy stood outside on the perfectly manicured lawn of the mid-century home she had just purchased in the Movie Colony, supervising the four hulking moving men who were unloading their truck with her belongings, most of which had been stored at a facility ever since she had been forced to leave the home she had shared with her late husband, Chester, and move into a small apartment with her daughter, Heather, almost three years ago.

It had been a trying time. After his unexpected and tragic death from a heart attack, it had come to light that Chester had essentially been living a double life—loving, doting, financially conservative husband when he was with Poppy, but a wild, irresponsible compulsive gambler when he was not. Ultimately, Chester frittered away their nest egg leaving Poppy nearly penniless on the day she buried him in the ground.

It had been a long fight back, but she had done it, despite a number of setbacks, most notably her only daughter Heather's myriad of legal challenges. Amidst all the drama, Poppy had managed to get her fledgling private investigation firm off the ground, and now it was flourishing, boasting an impressive list of wealthy clients in the Coachella Valley who had discovered the Desert Flowers Agency through positive word of mouth at cocktail parties and on the golf course.

And now, two and a half years in, Poppy had made enough of a profit to finally move out of Heather's humble abode and buy a home of her very own in a nice neighborhood, and boy, did it feel good.

She felt she had finally turned a corner, and was on the road back to her old life, and on this sunny warm day in beautiful Palm Springs, absolutely nothing was going to sour her bouncy mood.

That is until one of the moving men, Hymie, a ruggedly attractive man in his early forties, let a vase he was carrying off his truck slip through his fingers and smash to pieces on the ground.

Poppy's mouth dropped open in shock.

Hymie, a sheepish look on his face, squeaked, "I'm sorry, I hope that wasn't too expensive."

"No . . ." Poppy moaned. "My husband and I bought that from a pottery maker in Istanbul. It just has sentimental value . . . and was one of a kind . . ."

Hymie grimaced. "I'll be sure to take that off your final bill."

Poppy nodded, resigned, while two more of Hymie's guys, younger and even less careful, trotted down the plank set against the back of the truck, one on each end of a flat-screen TV that was heading to the living room.

"You guys be careful with that!" Hymie warned.

One of them stopped and asked, "What?"

The other kept going, still carrying the TV, causing the one who had stopped to let go, as one side of the TV crashed to the ground. Both of the young movers stared nervously at Poppy, who shook her head.

"I'll be sure to subtract the damage from that, too," Hymie promised before quickly disappearing into the back of the truck, probably to hide from his increasingly agitated customer.

Poppy's best friends, Iris Becker and Violet Hogan, also the co-founders of Poppy's detective agency, emerged from the house. Iris had her eyes fixed on the two young moving men who were bent over inspecting the cracked screen on Poppy's TV while Violet was waving a newspaper in her hand.

"Poppy, did you see the real estate section? You're on the front page!" Violet cooed.

"Yes, it's so embarrassing," Poppy groaned. "The last thing I need is for everybody to know where I live! There goes any sense of privacy."

"It is good for business!" Iris barked in a thick German accent. "People will see how successful you are and they will flock to us in droves with all their problems for us to solve!"

"The only reason they're writing about me buying this house is because Ava Gardner lived here in the late nineteen fifties for something like three months after she divorced Frank Sinatra. She didn't even own the place, she was a renter," Poppy said, irritated. "If I had known what a fuss the press was going to make of another actress buying this house, I would have kept looking."

"You cannot buy this kind of publicity, trust me on this," Iris said gruffly before returning her gaze to the two young movers who were still bent over the damaged television set.

"Do me a favor, Iris . . ." Poppy began.

Iris didn't respond. She kept her eyes fixed on the two young muscular movers.

Poppy folded her arms. "Iris?"

Violet sighed, and nudged Iris next to her. "Will you stop ogling the man candy long enough to answer poor Poppy?"

Iris snapped out of her fantasies and threw Violet an annoyed look, then turned to Poppy. "What?"

"Make sure the movers don't break *everything* of value I own."

Iris nodded. "Of course. With pleasure."

And then she happily marched over to the two moving men and began barking orders at them. The two young men scurried back inside the truck to join Hymie while Iris lustfully kept her eyes on their backsides as they fled.

"I can't tell you how proud I am of you, Poppy, how you just picked yourself up by the bootstraps after Chester nearly ruined you. You just plowed ahead, determined to start over, and look at you now, at everything you have accomplished," Violet said breathlessly.

"Thank you, Violet," Poppy said. "That's sweet of you to say. We've all worked hard. You, Iris, Matt . . . Desert Flowers is all our success."

Poppy's phone buzzed.

She checked the screen.

It was her daughter, Heather, calling.

Hymie breezed past them carrying a box labeled "Kitchen Utensils" in black felt marker.

"Violet, could you follow him and start unpacking that box for me, please? I need to talk to Heather."

"Of course," Violet said, and then with a wink, added, "Iris may like the young ones, but that Hymie is more my type, big, rugged, older, calloused hands, a real man's man."

Then she eagerly scampered off after him.

Poppy answered her daughter's call. "Hello, darling, how's New York?"

"Cold," Heather said. "And I'm not used to the noise outside my window all night long, constantly."

"You'll get used to it once you're settled," Poppy promised, having lived in Manhattan briefly when she was a young actress just starting out and fancied herself a budding Broadway star. That lasted about five months before she moved to Hollywood to make her mark in movies.

"Classes start tomorrow, and I'm really nervous about it. I'll probably be the oldest one there," Heather said.

"So what? Age is just a number. Believe me, I should know."

After her release following a stint in prison, Poppy's troubled daughter had bounced around, trying to figure out the best way to rebuild her life. Her time behind bars had keenly illustrated the pitfalls of the justice system, and so it was from this empathetic understanding of what people like her have to go through that Heather decided to try to become a lawyer. She knew it would be an uphill battle, given her record and the fact that she wasn't some hotshot college graduate with a 4.2 GPA and high-powered contacts ready to pull a few strings. She was totally on her own. But Heather studied hard, and got rejected by nine schools before NYU Law finally accepted her based on a moving essay she had written about her own legal troubles and road to redemption. One of the admissions officers had copped to crying when he read it. He had told

Heather the system needed more advocates like her, and he was happy to help find her a place at the school.

After a flurry of loan applications and much needed pep talks from her mother, Heather had finally packed her bags and flown east to begin a new life on her own.

But her mother wasn't the only one she was leaving behind.

Matt had dated Heather long before Poppy recruited him to be the face of her Desert Flowers Detective Agency, to play the estimable pretend owner Matt Flowers. And when Heather was arrested and convicted of a crime and sentenced to a year and a half in prison, he had stuck by her, determined to weather the storm, which he did admirably. They had even continued the relationship after her release, but Heather had fundamentally changed. She was lost and unfulfilled, and only when she was accepted into law school did she finally start to rebound. And when she announced she would be moving to New York, there was no invitation forthcoming for Matt to join her.

Matt had insisted they stay together and try the long-distance thing. Heather agreed to give it a go, but was far from optimistic. It appeared to Poppy that she was humoring him, not wanting to hurt him, until she was gone and could set up her new life in Manhattan.

"Are you moved into your new place yet?" Heather asked.

"In the process."

"Violet e-mailed me photos. It looks beautiful. I, however, am residing in a teeny tiny studio way up in Washington Heights, with a screaming baby in the apartment next door and a forty-five-minute subway ride to school, but it's a start and I'm not going to complain."

Poppy debated whether or not she should inquire, but

ultimately couldn't help herself. "Have you spoken to Matt?"

There was a pause.

"He's left a few messages, but I've been way too busy to call him back yet. I'll probably reach out later tonight."

"Heather, I hope you're not stringing him along, you know how he feels about you. . . ."

"Yes, Mother, I know," Heather sighed. "I'm still trying to figure it all out."

Heather had wondered aloud many times before she left Palm Springs whether the risks and challenges of a long-distance relationship outweighed the rewards. And she had come no closer to making a final decision when she stepped onto the JetBlue plane at the Palm Springs Airport that was going to fly her directly to New York.

"I'd just hate to see him get hurt," Poppy muttered.

"I'm your daughter, Mother, you're supposed to be on my side, not Matt's."

"Yes, of course I know that. You need to do what's best for you right now. It's just that I've grown rather fond of him. No one is more surprised by that than I am, and sometimes I feel protective of him—"

"Matt will be fine, no matter what I decide," Heather said. "Listen, I have to go. I have a big day tomorrow."

"Good luck, darling!"

"Thank you, Mother," Heather said quickly before ending the call, almost sounding relieved the conversation was finally over.

"How is she?"

Surprised by the voice so close behind her, Poppy spun around to see Iris standing there while inspecting the two young movers, who were now attempting to carry a large oak dresser out of the back of the truck and across the lawn.

"It's a big change, but she'll adjust. Heather is very adaptable," Poppy said.

"That's it, boys, slow down, this is not a race, be careful, I don't want to see any nicks or scratches after you get it inside, do you hear me?" Iris warned.

"Yes, ma'am," one the young men said as they hauled the piece toward the open front door of the house.

"I'm right behind you," Iris said before turning back to Poppy. "Has she dumped Matt yet?"

"What? No!"

"Not yet, you mean."

"Iris, we shouldn't write them off just because—"

"Just because Matt is here and Heather is three thousand miles away for the foreseeable future? Of course the relationship is going to end. It is for the best."

"I understand that, but Matt—"

"Matt is an adult. He will get over it," Iris said matter-of-factly. "Heather is starting a whole new life and it is best to be free and unencumbered! Like me! I am always free to do whatever I want!"

And what Iris appeared to want right now was to chase after the two boyishly handsome moving men carrying the dresser inside the house while aggressively barking orders at them.

Which was her German way of shamelessly flirting.

Chapter 4

Sam Emerson always had this rascally twinkle in his eye that could be intoxicating and exciting. He had a certain way about him, locking into you, making you feel as if you were the only person in the world he wanted to be with at that very moment in time. In other moments, he could also be infuriatingly remote, uncommunicative, private, which unfortunately would on occasion put Poppy on her guard. She had known Sam since her Hollywood years in the 1980s when the ex-cop was a consultant on her series *Jack Colt*.

The mustachioed cowboy and sharp-shooter who lived in a beautiful cabin high up in the mountains of Big Bear, California, was an old friend with whom Poppy had re-connected when she began this strange odyssey to become a private detective. And he had stuck around, wining and dining her, casually making himself a part of her life again. She reveled in his attention. There had always been a strong chemistry between them that still crackled, and tonight was certainly no exception.

Sam picked up his bourbon and knocked it back, slamming the glass down on the table and staring at Poppy with those sparkling eyes and laconic smile. "I turned down a job today."

"What kind of job?" Poppy asked, sipping her chilled Sauvignon Blanc.

"Consulting on a new thirteen-episode police procedural they're making for FOX. The script was well written, but way too dark. Another serial killer show where they just try to come up with the most grotesque, gruesome ways to kill people and shock the audience. Been there, done that."

"Was it good money?"

"It's *always* good money," Sam laughed. "I need more than that to come down off the mountain and move to LA, even temporarily."

"You should let people know you are officially retired and not interested in working in Hollywood anymore."

"I like to keep my options open," Sam said with a playful wink.

The waiter arrived with their starters, Hawaiian Ahi Tacos and Miso-Ginger Glazed Cauliflower. They were dining at a Palm Springs staple, Copley's, a rustic chic cottage once owned by Cary Grant in the 1940s that was now a lively, casual but sophisticated desert dining hotspot. Perfect for a date night. Poppy and Sam had been seated outside in the garden as it was a balmy, pleasant evening. The restaurant was only half full, allowing them a more intimate setting at a private table away from the other diners.

Once the waiter set the plates down and scurried off,

Poppy excitedly picked up her appetizer fork and dove into the delicious-looking cauliflower. "So what would bring you down from the mountaintop?"

"You, obviously," Sam said with a grin.

"Besides me," Poppy chuckled, popping a piece of cauliflower in her mouth.

Sam picked up a taco and shoved it into his mouth, chewing slowly, thinking about the question. "I think I'd like to do more traveling before I get too old and I'm grappling with all the health challenges that come with being an old geezer."

"You've got a ways to go before you're there, Sam."

Sam cocked an eyebrow. "Ha, it's closer than you think."

"Where would you like to go?"

Sam shrugged. "I don't know, I've been browsing some Web sites online in my spare time. There's a Viking river cruise to Kiev, the Black Sea, and Bucharest, all places I've never been, in May that sounds interesting. Also, Istanbul is on my list and there are parts of Germany I still haven't seen."

"Sounds exciting."

"Of course, it would be more fun if I had someone to go with," Sam remarked, eyeing her cautiously.

Poppy slowly set down her fork.

She suddenly knew where this conversation was going. Poppy took a deep breath and exhaled. "Sam, you know I would love nothing more than to drop everything and traipse across the globe with you—"

"I feel a *but* coming."

"*But* . . . we both know I can't."

Sam stared at his glass as he jiggled the melting ice cubes around in it. "You should be very proud of what you've accomplished, Poppy," he said quietly before raising his eyes to meet hers. "You're in a much better place than you were when the two of us reunited a couple of years ago. You found yourself drowning in an abyss and you crawled out of it, spectacularly I might add."

"Thank you, Sam," she said.

"I read about your recent purchase in the *Desert Sun*," he said, signaling the waiter to bring him another bourbon.

"Oh, God," Poppy groaned. "So did everybody in the Coachella Valley. If I had known Ava Gardner had once lived in that house, and it would turn out to be such a big deal, I never would have bought the place!"

"I think it's great, you carrying on the tradition of living in a home with a long history of beautiful and talented actresses. . . ."

"Now, you're just teasing me," Poppy scolded.

Sam leaned forward, suddenly serious. "I just think you ought to enjoy the fruits of your labor, take a long vacation, let Iris and Violet and . . ."

"Matt," Poppy reminded him.

"Right, the great Matt Flowers, let them run things for a month or two while you run away with me on a little adventure. Treat yourself. Or better yet, let me treat you. The way you deserve to be treated."

He was convincing.

And she could not deny how kind and generous and, yes, sexy she had found him since they had rekindled their friendship. There was also a big part of her that was afraid if she did not commit just a little more to him, she might lose him. And she didn't want to fathom that thought. But still, she knew it had not been an accident that the Desert Flowers Detective Agency had flourished these past few months. It had been a direct result of their hard work, grit, and determination. And she feared if she relaxed, let up on the gas pedal even just a tiny bit, this ascension could stall and die out. And at least at this point, Poppy was not willing to take that risk.

"I'm sorry, Sam, but this whole private eye endeavor is just too important to me. I need to stay focused. For the first time in my life, I feel as if I'm in control. And it would be too hard for me to give that up, at least right now."

He reached out across the table and took her hand in his. "I understand." But his face couldn't lie. He was disappointed. And she knew it. So he felt the need to add, "Honestly, I do."

Poppy's phone buzzed.

She knew without looking it was a text from Matt.

He had been sending her texts all evening with quick updates. He was currently on the set of *Palm Springs Weekend* shadowing their client Danika Delgado, making sure she was never left alone while they were shooting some night scenes at the resort. Poppy assumed this was one more briefing, just to let her know all was quiet so she could enjoy her Roasted Scottish Salmon entree at Copley's. As she scanned the text, her mouth dropped open in surprise. This was not what she had expected.

Sam picked up on her reaction immediately. "Everything okay?"

Poppy shook her head. "No. My daughter just broke up with Matt by text and he's devastated."

Chapter 5

Poppy, overcome with nausea, fled to the bathroom of her private room in the Sundial Luxury Resort with its sunken Jacuzzi tub and expensive marble sink, and threw herself down on her knees, flipping open the toilet lid and lowering her head over the bowl. She waited, her stomach churning, her head pounding, but she didn't get sick. It was a false alarm.

After waiting another moment just to be sure, Poppy climbed back up to her feet, checked herself out in the wall-length mirror, scooped up a perfume bottle of her favorite Dolce & Gabbana fragrance, and sprayed a light mist onto the side of her neck. Then, she took a deep breath and silently prayed she would somehow get through this.

She had been holed up in her room all morning studying her script, making sure she had all of the lines down for her first scene to be shot. Despite being strong-armed into accepting the role, she had decided to just do her best with the hope that she would not embarrass herself. Matt had told her acting was like riding a bicycle. Once you learned the craft, you would never forget how to do it. Of course, Poppy had not been on a bicycle in over thirty years either so she could not be sure Matt even knew what he was talking about.

The scene was a simple one. Poppy behind the reception desk of the resort checking in a rowdy gang of college kids for a wild weekend of fun, their client Danika Delgado's character, played in the original by Connie Stevens, among them. She had a few easy lines, nothing too taxing or complicated. It should be a breeze. But the fear of freezing up, of drawing a complete blank when her admiring director called, "Action!" was almost too much to bear and it was suddenly taking a physical toll.

There was a knock on her door.

Poppy knew the makeup and hair team would make sure she looked presentable when the time came to shoot the scene, and so she decided to ignore the fear and self-doubt that was making her sick to her stomach, and just get on with it. She left the bathroom and crossed over to the door, opening it to find the bright-eyed production assistant Timothy smiling at her.

"We're ready for you on set, Ms. Harmon," he said in a chipper tone. It wasn't hard to pick up on her nerves and so in an effort to calm her, he added, "You're going to crush it!"

"I don't even know what that means. Is it good or bad?"

"Good! Crush it. Like, nail it, do great."

She squeezed his arm, which she found surprisingly muscular. "From your mouth to God's ears, Timothy."

"Shall we?" He crooked his arm so she could slide her own through it and escorted her out to the set. The kid was certainly a gentleman, not to mention a reassuring presence for which she felt grateful.

"Would you like me to swing by craft services and get you a cup of coffee?" Timothy asked.

"Lord, no! I'm jacked up enough already. The last thing I need is a shot of caffeine!" Poppy wailed. "But thank you, Timothy."

"Okay," Timothy chuckled. "By the way, last night after we wrapped, I looked up some old clips of your show *Jack Colt* on YouTube. Trent was right. You were *awesome*. You totally—"

"Crushed it?"

"Yes! There was a scene of you surfing in Hawaii while helping Jack tail a Honolulu gangster's sister at the beach and you were wearing this cherry red bikini, which was super hot!"

"That bathing suit got more fan mail than I did," Poppy cracked.

They arrived on the set, which was bustling with activity. Danika was joking around with a couple of her younger co-stars who would be appearing in the scene, and Poppy noticed Matt hovering in the background keeping a watchful eye on the client, but also a respectful distance.

Trent shot up from his director's chair and ambled over to Poppy, enveloping her in a hug. "How are you feeling? Ready to do this?"

"I still think this is a monumentally bad idea," Poppy moaned.

"Nonsense. I have no bad ideas. And this one, I promise you, is one of my more inspired."

The makeup and hair people descended upon Poppy, fluffing her hair and slapping powder on her face to get rid of any lingering shine. Poppy zeroed in on a small piece of black tape on the floor, her mark, where she was designated to stand during the scene.

Danika wandered away from the gaggle of young actors she had been chatting with, her head down as she tapped furiously on her phone. She finished posting something on Twitter or Instagram or Snapchat, and bounced over to Poppy. "You look fantabulous!" Danika cooed. "Are you nervous?"

"What? Me? No, not at all," Poppy muttered sarcastically.

Danika giggled. "You're going to be great."

"Everybody keeps telling me that, but I get the feeling you're all just saying that so I don't pass out."

A bell rang and the makeup and hair people scattered, leaving only the actors left on the set.

This was it.

The time had come.

Poppy closed her eyes.

Her mind was a blank.

She suddenly couldn't remember her first line.

She knew the college kids spoke first as they invaded the resort, fresh off the bus from LA, and she knew her first line came sometime after Danika made a comment about how cute the young Latino bellhop was, but she couldn't remember the exact words she was supposed to say.

This was going to be a disaster.

"Camera rolling!"

Oh, God, Poppy thought, *what is my first line?*

"We have speed!" the cinematographer called out.

Trent stared into the monitor that was set up on the far side of the reception area so he could watch the scene play out, and yelled, "Action!"

Right on cue, the gang of college kids poured into the reception area, all babbling at once, Danika among them. Poppy stood frozen, watching them conversing with each other, frantically trying to recall her first line.

She caught sight of Matt, hovering over behind Trent, who was leaning forward in his chair, intently staring at the monitor. Matt was beaming.

The next thing Poppy knew, Danika was standing in front of her at the reception desk, wide smile, flashing her perfectly white teeth, saying, "We're here to check in!"

Yes, that was her cue.

"We're here to check in."

Poppy heard herself say, "Welcome to the Sundial, kids . . ."

Of course.

It was that simple.

A few of the rowdier college boys were ogling a pair of female sunbathers crossing through the lobby, and Poppy then turned her attention toward them, launching into a stern list of strict rules they were required to follow at the resort. This had been a tricky line because it was essentially a monologue about how Poppy had owned this resort for decades and was not about to let an unruly mob of sex-crazed college kids run roughshod on her property. Yes, the lines eased off her tongue. All those hours memorizing them had mercifully paid off. She was going to get through this. She only had a few more words to go and then she would be done and the scene would be over when something off to the side of the camera distracted her.

Someone was waving at her.

Ignore it, she told herself. *You're so close to finishing your first scene and not screwing it up.*

The waving became more frenetic, more distracting until Poppy couldn't help herself and glanced over to see Violet excitedly waggling her hand and mouthing, "I'm so proud of you!"

And then Poppy went blank again.

She couldn't remember the last line in the script.

"Cut!" Trent shouted.

Poppy deflated.

Iris rolled her eyes at Violet. "You ruined the scene, Violet! You broke Poppy's concentration!"

"I was just wishing her luck," Violet cried defensively.

"It is obvious you have never been on a film set," Iris snorted. "Not like me who appeared in many German avant-garde films. I am basically a cultural icon in Europe."

"Yes, Iris, you've told us many times," Violet said, racing over to Poppy. "Poppy, I can't apologize enough. I was just trying to be supportive."

"It's fine, Violet," Poppy said. "Luckily we can do it again."

However, since it was Poppy's first scene, she had hoped to get through it once without messing up.

She could see Matt in the background giving her the thumbs-up even though she knew he was just doing that to make her feel better. She could also tell he was putting on a brave face, pretending not to be affected by the Dear John text he had received from Heather the night before, something he and Poppy had yet to discuss other than a few back and forth texts.

Trent jogged over to Poppy, who was now huddling with Iris and Violet. "Ready to go again?"

Poppy nodded. "Yes, Trent, I am so sorry I flubbed the line."

"It was entirely my fault, Mr. Dodsworth-Jones. I was distracting her. Poppy is a wonderful actress who never forgets her lines. If you want to ban me from the set, I will understand, but please don't take it out on poor Poppy," Violet pleaded.

"No, you're fine," Trent said, confused. "Who are you again?"

"Violet Hogan. And this is Iris Becker. We work with Poppy at the Desert Flowers Detective Agency."

"Yes, that is true, but *I* am also a veteran of the performing arts with extensive experience as a chanteuse, in the theatre, and I worked with Fassbinder. He was a pig and he smelled but he was a dear personal friend," Iris said.

Trent nodded, impressed that Iris knew the well-regarded late German film director. "Well, you ladies are welcome to hang around as long as you want."

"Trent, I just got distracted," Poppy said.

"Don't sweat it. We almost got it. We'll do it until you get it right. The point is, you were marvelous."

Poppy raised an eyebrow. "Seriously?"

"I knew I was making the right call. Wait until you see the dailies. You're a real presence. You bring such gravitas to the scene. I couldn't be happier. Trust me, Poppy, you're everything I hoped you would be." He impulsively grabbed her shoulders and planted a kiss on her cheek. "Keep up the good work."

And then he bounded back over to confer with the cameraman.

Poppy suspected he was just trying to make her feel better and put her mind at ease so he could get through the entire scene at least once uninterrupted.

"See, I knew it was only a matter of time before you'd be a star again," Violet cooed, utterly thrilled.

"I am *not* looking to be a star. I'm just doing this to stay close to our client," Poppy insisted.

Iris eyed her skeptically. "What if you are nominated for an Oscar? What if someone like Antonio Banderas wants to be your date for the awards ceremony? What if Paul McCartney's daughter wants to design your dress? Will you say no to all *that*?"

"That is *your* fantasy, Iris, not mine," Poppy snapped.

"Poppy? Do you need more time?" Trent asked from behind the monitor.

"No, all set to go!" Poppy cried, waving Iris and Violet away.

"Do not worry, Poppy, I will keep Violet out of your eye line!" Iris promised before hauling Violet away by the arm.

Poppy closed her eyes, slowly breathed in and out, mentally preparing herself to try the scene again. When she opened her eyes, she spotted Danika in the corner with a broad-shouldered, scruffy, impossibly handsome man in his late twenties. She recognized him as Chase Ehrens, the male lead, playing the role inhabited by teen idol Troy Donahue in the original. She had yet to meet him. Poppy instantly sensed something was wrong. Danika was backing away from him as he advanced upon her, his hands all over her, apparently coming on way too strong.

Matt stood nearby, not sure what to do, not wanting to intervene if he was not wanted.

But Poppy could tell Danika was unhappy about Chase aggressively coming on to her, and finally, she physically pushed him away, hissing something under her breath. Although Poppy couldn't hear her exact words, she was certain that, in effect, Danika was spurning Chase's advances.

Chase, red-faced and humiliated, spun around and started to stalk away when Timothy scurried up to him with some revised script pages. Chase ripped them out of Timothy's hand and snapped at him, pushing him away, telling him to get out of his face and leave him alone. Timothy, whose sole mission seemed to be wanting to make a good impression on everyone, wilted.

Poppy felt sorry for the poor kid. There was no excuse for Chase to treat him like that, or anyone else on set for that matter.

Poppy watched the brooding actor storm off, and her opinion of him was official.

She did not like Chase Ehrens one bit.

Chapter 6

Poppy finished her first big scene with little fanfare much to her relief, and Trent seemed happy with the footage and her performance. She had quickly made a beeline for Matt, who stood over in the corner of the pool area, near the unmanned bar, eyes downcast. She didn't have to ask what he was upset about because it was obvious.

"Matt, I'm sorry I didn't have a chance to speak to you earlier when I first got here—"

He held a hand up in front of her. "It's cool. I'm fine with it."

But she could tell he wasn't.

Matt was a good actor and was trying to keep on a brave, stoic face, pretending the fact that his girlfriend had unceremoniously dumped him, by text no less, was not really weighing on his mind.

"I don't understand why she would do it that way. That's not the kind of behavior I taught her when she was growing up."

"Well, sure, she could've been classier about it and done it in person, but the result would have been the same, Poppy. Heather doesn't want me anymore."

Poppy gave him a motherly hug. "I know how hard you tried to make the relationship work. After all the troubles Heather's gone through these last few years, you've stood by her, all this time. . . ."

"Heather's a good person, who deserves a fresh start and to be happy. And if I'm not a part of that plan, I just have to accept it," Matt said, forcing a smile.

Poppy was certainly rooting for her daughter. She understood that Heather was desperate to put this rocky period in her life squarely behind her, and that Matt may have been a constant reminder of the past few painful years. Even though as a mother, she had to stand by Heather and respect her decisions, that did not mean she was expected to abandon Matt, her business partner, her friend, and she wanted to make sure he knew that.

"Well, you will always have me, Iris, and Violet," Poppy promised.

"Thank you, I appreciate that," Matt said.

Poppy noticed Timothy carrying a bright pink gift box with a giant red bow tied around it in his hands, as he passed by them.

"Anybody seen Danika?" Timothy asked. "A fan dropped this off for her."

Poppy and Matt sprang to attention, suddenly on guard.

"A fan?" Matt asked nervously.

"Yeah, real creepy guy. I have no idea how he got on set. I figured he conned his way past the guard by saying he was a deliveryman. He tried convincing me that he had to make sure Danika signed for this personally, but I told him no one gets near Ms. Delgado that's not personally connected to the production."

Poppy swiveled around, trying to find any unfamiliar faces in the pool area. "Where is he? Did he leave?"

"Yeah, once I told him meeting Danika was not going to happen, he left. At least, I think he did."

Poppy's heart sank as she spotted the group of young actors Danika was chatting with just a few moments earlier. "Where is she? She was right over there a minute ago."

"They just called lunch. Maybe she's at craft services or eating in her room," Timothy suggested.

"Everyone can relax," Matt assured them. "I've memorized her schedule. She's got a session in the gym with her personal trainer scheduled for now. And I'm reasonably confident that her trainer, who's two hundred and fifty pounds of pure muscle and goes by the name of Thor, can keep her safe."

The blood seemed to drain from Timothy's face. "Um, Thor cancelled today . . ."

"*What*?" Poppy gasped.

"I was with Danika when he called earlier just before we shot your scene, Ms. Harmon. Thor came out of his apartment in West Hollywood and found his tires slashed. He was going to Uber here, but Danika told him to forget it, they would skip today."

"Oh, God! Then *where* is she?" Poppy cried.

"I heard her promise Thor she would lift weights on her own. Maybe she's in the gym," Timothy said.

Matt bolted for the resort gym with Poppy close on his heels. Timothy followed behind them. The door to the gym had been closed, and when Matt yanked it open, they all could see Danika inside, backed up against a wall mirror, as a young man wearing a gray hoodie and jeans, odd for such a warm day in the desert, had her pinned in front of him with a dumbbell loaded down with heavy weights on each side. The man's face was pressed up close to Danika as she turned away with a look of revulsion.

Poppy could see his face through the reflection in the wall mirror. Beak nose. Acne-scarred face, wisps of greasy black hair, and beady, disturbed eyes.

Matt sprinted across the gym toward them and grabbed the young man from behind by the hood, yanking him off Danika with all his might. The young man dropped the dumbbell and it crashed to the floor with a loud thud. Matt spun the intruder around and Poppy could see him erupt in anger, enraged that his private moment with Danika had been so rudely interrupted. He took a swing at Matt, who luckily had enough stage combat training to expertly dodge it. The man threw himself upon Matt hurling wild punches, kicking him in the kneecap, before Matt had the opportunity to strike back. Timothy lunged forward to help, but the man scooped up a free weight and swung it wide, clocking Timothy in the side of the head.

Matt now dove into the man's midsection and they hurtled to the floor, rolling around, punching and kicking each other. Matt finally managed to grab the man around the chest, pinning his arms, but the man lashed out crazily, biting Matt's ear. Matt loosened his grip enough for the man to wriggle out of his grasp, and pop back up to his feet. Matt followed suit, raising his fists, ready to continue the bare-knuckled brawl. But then the young man lifted the dumbbell he had used to pin Danika to the wall off the floor, and with all his might launched it at Matt. The sheer weight of it slammed against Matt's chest, lifting him off his feet and back down to the floor, the wind knocked out of him.

The young man pulled his hood down over his face as he raced out of the gym. Poppy rushed toward Matt, but before she could reach him, Matt was back on his feet and chasing after the hooded intruder. Poppy turned to see Danika still standing against the wall mirror in a state of shock. Timothy was on the floor, writhing in pain, so she went to check on him first.

"Timothy, talk to me. Are you hurt? Should I call an ambulance?" Poppy cried.

"No, please don't. I'll be okay, Ms. Harmon. I'm pretty sure he missed my jaw, he just got the side of my face. Luckily all my teeth are still intact . . . I think."

"You should have a doctor check you out just to be on the safe side," Poppy insisted.

Timothy nodded briefly, but Poppy could tell he had no intention of leaving work to go to the hospital. There was no way he was going to risk another up-and-comer replacing him.

Poppy then turned to Danika, who was resting her head against the mirrored wall and staring into space.

Poppy hurried over to her. "Danika, I am so sorry. We should have been more careful, it's on us that you were left alone—"

Danika seemed to finally snap out of her trance. "Poppy, I'm totally fine, just shaken up a little," Danika said calmly. "There's no need to blame yourself. I made the decision to come work out unaccompanied."

"What can you tell me about the man who attacked you?"

"Not much. Just that he's young, maybe early twenties, he said his name was Byron, like Lord Byron the poet, and he told me he writes love sonnets about me, about us, how he's never felt a love like this, ever since he discovered my videos on YouTube and Instagram."

Already Poppy suspected the kid was of unsound mind.

"I didn't want to make him angry so I kind of played along at first, saying he was so sweet and how I would like to read his poems sometime, but then I tried to run and that's when he grabbed me and threw me up against the wall and pinned me with that barbell and told me to stop fighting what is meant to be . . . and that's when you all showed up."

Poppy grabbed her phone from her jacket pocket. "I'm calling security."

"Don't bother, he's gone," she heard Matt say as he limped back into the gym.

Danika hurried over to him, notably far more concerned with his well-being than that of poor Timothy, the lowly production assistant. "Matt!"

"I twisted my ankle chasing after the little creep so he

was able to put some distance between us until he got out to the street and sped away in his car," Matt said, still slightly out of breath. He held up his phone. "But don't worry, I got a photo of his license plate."

Poppy's hopes were quickly raised that they had a significant clue to tracking the stalker.

Matt stared at the picture on the screen and looked back up glumly. "Half of it, anyway. The half that's not blurred."

And then those hopes were just as quickly dashed.

Chapter 7

Don't scream, Poppy said to herself.

Don't scream, she repeated over and over in her mind, determined to keep a mask of calm on her face and not allow the man sitting next to her in the helicopter to derive any satisfaction from the fact that she was melting down into full-blown panic mode.

No, she would remain stubbornly stoic, not the least bit stirred by the dramatic dips in altitude, the unexpected barrel roll and flip of the chopper as if she was caught in some nightmare air circus stunt show. The only clue the pilot had that Poppy was scared out of her wits was her white-knuckled grip on a strap that was attached to the interior wall of the helicopter next to her seat.

She was still wondering how she had managed to find herself buckled in next to a stunt pilot zipping high above the Coachella Valley desert on this bright, hot, sunny afternoon.

She had begun the otherwise non-eventful day at the Sundial resort, studying her lines for an upcoming scene to be shot in a couple days while Matt was on "Danika Duty," sticking close to their client's side, making sure she wasn't accosted again if the stalker returned.

Meanwhile, back at the Desert Flowers office, Violet's grandson Wyatt, their resident computer whiz, was on his desktop busily running a program with the numbers and letters Matt had given him, hoping against all odds to find the stalker's car with only half the license plate. It was going to be an uphill battle, but definitely worth the time and effort if they got lucky.

Poppy had taken a break from her script and left her resort suite that served as her dressing room to grab some coffee from craft services, which was set up just off the pool area. There she found a man pouring himself a cup from the pot, and so she patiently waited a few feet behind him until he was finished. Sensing her presence, he glanced around and offered a rakish smile. "Good morning."

"Good morning," Poppy said, nodding.

Still blocking the coffee station, the man went about adding some cream and a couple of packets of sugar to his paper cup before picking up a wooden stirrer and swishing it around, his eyes still fixed on Poppy.

"Beautiful day, isn't it?" he said, still stirring his coffee.

"Yes, it most certainly is," Poppy said politely, waiting for him to finally step aside.

"Roy Heller," the man said, tossing the stirrer in a nearby trash can and holding out his hand.

Poppy shook it courteously if not enthusiastically. "Poppy Harmon."

His grip was firm and manly. Poppy tended to judge a man by his handshake. This one was strong and confident, not limp and dismissive. A man with an unimpressive handshake was, in her opinion, a man who could not be trusted or counted on when the chips were down. She had willfully ignored her late husband Chester's lackluster grip, and look where that had gotten her.

The man finally moved out of the way so Poppy could pour herself some coffee. He hovered nearby, watching her. She had noticed he was very handsome. How could she not? His close-cropped white hair, the ruggedly good-looking, sun-tanned face with just enough lines to give him a distinguished air, the macho swagger punctuated with a black leather jacket and aviator sunglasses. He had a James Brolin quality about him. Poppy loved James Brolin and how impressively he had aged and made the mercurial Barbra Streisand so happy. This guy could have been his brother.

Poppy had finished pouring her coffee and turned to leave when the man casually stepped in front of her, blocking her exit, and lowered his sunglasses, revealing a set of playfully mischievous green eyes. "I must say, you have only improved with age, Ms. Harmon."

This caught Poppy by surprise. "Have we met?"

The man nodded with a grin. "A long time ago."

"What did you say your name was?"

"Roy Heller."

"Roy Heller . . ." Poppy repeated, her mind working overtime. "I'm sorry, you don't seem familiar."

"The sound you hear is my ego deflating," Roy joked. "Seriously, you don't remember me?"

His face did seem vaguely familiar. But Poppy was

fairly certain that had she met such a charming, hand-some man she would have probably remembered him, and at the moment, she was still drawing a complete blank.

"We had a helicopter pilot on *Jack Colt* who we used for aerial shots and an occasional stunt, but his name was Tiny and he was about six inches taller than you. Perhaps you saw me on one of those retro cable channels where they play my old show, and so you just think we've met before."

"We've worked together," Roy said confidently. "Back in the eighties. Before you did *Jack Colt*."

Poppy studied him some more. No, she was positive she would have remembered meeting this man, even after forty years. "I think you're mistaken."

"What do you want to bet?"

"Nothing. Now if you'll excuse me—"

"If I can prove it, you go up in my helicopter with me for a ride."

"I can't . . ."

"You afraid of heights?"

"No, I am not afraid of heights. I'm just a very busy woman and I can't be running off with some stranger."

"Technically, there will be no running, we'll be flying."

"I've enjoyed this little chat, but I really have to go—"

"You scared I'm right?"

Poppy scoffed at the notion. "No, I'm not scared of anything, Mr. Heller."

"Call me Roy."

"I'm not there yet, Mr. Heller."

He sipped his coffee, staring at her flirtatiously. "Tell

you what, I promise you it'll be a quick ride, thirty minutes tops, I'll have you back here by noon."

"What if I win?"

"You're not going to win."

"Humor me."

Roy thought about it. "What do you want?"

"All I really want is to go back to my room."

Roy stuck out his hand. "It's a deal."

Poppy hesitated, not sure she should engage with him further, but since she was reasonably convinced this man was a stranger she had never seen before, she shook his hand, accepting the bet.

Roy flashed his winning smile and then grabbed his phone and started tapping the screen.

"What are you doing?" Poppy asked.

"Looking for a video on YouTube."

"What video?"

Roy glanced up at her and gave her a wink. "Just hold on."

He finally found what he had been looking for and handed her his phone with the video playing. Poppy looked at the screen. It was an aerial shot of a pretty girl in her late teens running across a field, her long blond hair flapping in the wind as a beat-up Dodge Charger sped dangerously toward her.

"Recognize that?"

"Of course. It's me. This is a scene from a TV movie I appeared in just after moving to Hollywood. *Diary of a Teenaged Hitchhiker* about young women targeted by a psycho motorist. I'll never forget it because that tiny part got me my SAG card."

"This shot wasn't from the movie. It's behind-the-scenes footage somebody put online," Roy said.

Sure enough, as Poppy continued to watch, the cameraman filming Poppy down on the ground from high up in the air panned the camera over to the pilot flying the helicopter he was in, and in an instant, Poppy recognized the young, sexy pilot from her earliest TV role. She remembered because she had had a huge crush on him during the shoot, but never saw him again after the movie wrapped production. Soon after, she was dating a college football star turned actor, a dead ringer for Mark Harmon, and forgot all about the smooth, sexy pilot.

Until now.

Roy noticed the hint of recognition on Poppy's face.

"I win," he said.

Never one to dishonor a bet, Poppy had reluctantly agreed to accompany Roy Heller on a helicopter ride, and now here they were, zipping along about seven thousand feet off the ground. Roy was proving to be a real prankster, banking left and right, diving down, nearly clipping the tops of a few palm trees, and pulling a couple of heart-stopping stunts in his whirlybird in order to impress or terrify Poppy, she wasn't quite sure which.

But Poppy had promised herself not to react, not scream or beg him to land, or show fear of any kind. And after twenty-five minutes, Roy finally returned and landed on the tarmac of the Palm Springs International Airport. Poppy unstrapped her seat belt and calmly stepped out of the chopper as if she was done riding a slow-moving carousel at a children's amusement park.

Never show fear, she thought to herself.

As they walked toward Roy's truck so he could drive her back to the Sundial, Roy couldn't help but remark, "You are one tough broad, Poppy Harmon."

"You hired me for my vision and so you should defer to it, or do you not remember the box office numbers from my last film?"

"I remember them very well, and they were five million less than your previous film. You need a hit, Trent, and Hal and I are here to help you achieve that goal, so you need to work with us, not shut us out."

"I was afraid Hal would try and stop me from casting Poppy because she's no longer a big name."

"I'm sure he would have," Greta said. "But his opinions count, and he has a shelf full of Academy Awards to back them up."

Trent sighed, frustrated. "Have you seen the dailies of Poppy's first scene? She was wonderful."

Poppy's heart sank. They were talking about her, and here she was, awkwardly standing in the middle of the hallway, just a few feet away, eavesdropping on their conversation.

"Yes, I'll admit, she's fine in the role, but that's not the point. You need to stop acting like you're the one in charge around here."

"And you need to stop micromanaging my film," Trent shot back haughtily. "Or I'll walk."

"Don't make threats unless you're ready to see them through. No one on a film set is indispensable, not even the director . . . unless you're a talent on the scale of an Almodóvar, or Scorsese, or Tarantino, and you, my dear, are *no* Tarantino."

"Thank God!" Trent bellowed. "Overrated!"

Irritated with Trent's bombastic, ego-fueled rantings, Greta swiveled around, stopping short at the sight of Poppy standing fumblingly in the middle of the hallway.

"I-I am sorry, I didn't want to interrupt—" Poppy stammered.

Without missing a beat, Greta plowed forward, pumping Poppy's hand. "Greta Van Damm, I'm the film's producer along with Hal Greenwood. I should probably say, the *legendary* Hal Greenwood."

Trent rolled his eyes, annoyed at Greta buttering up the boss even when he wasn't around to feed off it.

"Tell me, Poppy, how is it you came to us? Did your agent lobby Trent?" Greta asked, genuinely curious.

Poppy's eyes flicked toward Trent to see if he would jump in and expose her as a private detective, but Trent had no interest in filling in any blanks, especially to his perceived archnemesis, Greta, and so Poppy felt free to concoct whatever story she wanted. She decided a simple one was probably the best approach.

"I'm a friend of Danika's, and I was here on the set, and was lucky enough to meet Trent here—"

Trent smiled warmly. "*I* was the lucky one."

Greta wasn't done asking questions, but before she had the chance to continue grilling Poppy, they heard a man shouting in the bar just off the lobby, which was located at the end of the hallway.

"Get your hands off me!" a man roared.

Poppy, Greta, and Trent all hustled back in the other direction, rounding the corner and entering the bar to see what all the commotion was about.

Timothy, the production assistant, was manhandling another man, in his early thirties, on the shorter side, thin, stylishly dressed in a Hugo Boss suit and tie, with close-cropped blond hair and piercing blue eyes. The man was trying to push Timothy away, but the young PA was determined to hold on to him unlike the last guy who crashed the set.

"If you rip this jacket, you're paying for it, you little creep!" the man bellowed.

Poppy did not recognize the well-dressed man but Greta certainly did.

"What the hell are you doing here, Fabian?" Greta snarled. "How did you sneak your way onto this set?"

Fabian ceased grappling with Timothy, who finally let him go, allowing him to brush himself off. "I have my ways. I had to do something. You don't return my calls, you ignore my requests for an interview. I am trying to be fair to you in my story, but you don't make it easy. Why not just cooperate?"

"Because you're a self-serving, muckraking journalist on a single-minded mission to destroy Hal Greenwood with a fake news hit piece."

"I wouldn't call fifteen on the record sources fake news, Greta," Fabian sniffed.

A lightbulb went off in Poppy's head.

Fabian.

Fabian Granger.

Poppy had seen the handsome young reporter interviewed on CNN. He was a bright, up-and-coming investigative journalist known for his hard-hitting stories of egregious behavior in both Hollywood and Washington, DC. His other claim to fame was being the answer to a *Jeopardy!* question. "Who is a distant relative of Hollywood film star Farley Granger?"

Fabian was despised by the Hollywood and DC establishments, but his stories resonated with the public. Corruption, sexual misconduct, everything was fair game. He had recently begun writing about entertainment moguls like Hal Greenwood, who had a history that at best could be described as "bad boy behavior" and at worst, criminal offenses including assault and battery, harassment both sexual and otherwise, and financial malfeasance. Hal Greenwood raged in the press that he was being unfairly targeted, and also made a point of banning all reporters, especially Fabian Granger, from his film sets.

"So will you talk to me?" Fabian asked, hopeful.

Greta didn't blink. She just stared daggers at the appealing young man with expensive taste in suits. "Timothy, escort him out and make sure he doesn't find his way back in, do you hear me? If he gives you any trouble, call security."

Timothy nodded, reaching out to grab Fabian's arm, but Fabian moved away from him. "Don't you dare touch me. I'll go on my own." He then turned back and spit out, "You have twenty-four hours before my story goes up online, Greta. Tick tock."

And then he stormed off.

Greta signaled Timothy to follow Fabian and make sure he actually left and didn't try to double back to get a few more juicy quotes from the cast and crew.

"What kind of story is he writing?" Poppy quietly asked.

Greta was clearly shaken by Fabian's unexpected presence, but tried to brush it off as if she was unconcerned. "Typical character assassination. Hal's weathered them countless times. Granger's angling for a Pulitzer so he'll write about anything provocative, true or not, just to get himself some attention."

Poppy resisted the urge to excuse herself and chase

after the young reporter to find out what kind of trail he was following, but she never had the chance because at that moment Danika burst into the bar, eyes wide with fear, her face pale. "Please, somebody, stop them before they kill each other!"

Danika spun back around to lead the way, and Poppy, Greta, and Trent all followed her back outside to the pool area in time to see the male lead on the film, Chase Ehrens, grappling on the tiled floor with a man whose face they couldn't see because Chase, who was now throwing hard, violent punches at the man's face, was blocking him. The man underneath Chase managed to knee him in the groin, causing Chase to howl like a wild animal, which allowed the man to roll away from him. When he jumped to his feet, Poppy gasped. It was Matt, his nose was bloodied and there were scratches on his neck. Matt wiped the blood away with his shirtsleeve as Chase dove at him, relentlessly pummeling him with more blows.

Trent sprang forward to pull Chase off Matt, and got elbowed in the cheek for his effort.

"Chase, what's going on here?" Greta cried, although she made no move to stop the brawl.

"Somebody do something!" Danika cried.

With Trent moaning, holding his face with his hand, Poppy knew she had to try and break this up. She was about to physically intervene and risk damage to herself when suddenly Matt reached up and planted the palms of his hand on Chase's rock-hard chest and shoved him as hard as he could. Chase stumbled backward, tripping over a lounge chair, and went hurtling into the swimming pool near the deep end. When he emerged, his face was a deep red from the humiliation and embarrassment. Two crew members, who had sauntered in during the fight carrying some klieg lights, dropped everything to haul a soaking wet Chase out of the pool.

Chase waved them away and marched up to Greta. "This lunatic attacked me for no reason! Call the police, Greta! I want him arrested!"

Greta tried adopting a motherly tone. "Let's just calm down, Chase, and—"

"No! He could have messed up my face, put the whole production, my career, in jeopardy!"

Trent whispered under his breath next to Poppy, "He's right about that. His face is his biggest asset. It's not like he can rely on his acting skills."

Poppy resisted the urge to laugh. She raced over to Matt, who was holding a rag over his nose to stop the bleeding and was being attended to by Danika.

"Are you okay?" Poppy asked.

Matt nodded.

"Where's security?" Greta demanded to know. She then pointed at Matt. "I want him held until the cops get here."

"No!" Danika protested. "It wasn't Matt's fault. He was just trying to protect me."

Chase balked, nostrils flaring. "I can't believe you're taking his side, Danika! I was just being playful and this maniac went all Tyson Fury on me!"

Poppy leaned closer to Danika. "Who is that?"

"Boxer," Danika whispered.

"Who started it, Danika?" Greta asked.

Danika stood resolutely next to Matt. "Chase started it."

"I don't have to put up with these lies!" Chase bellowed. "I want that guy out of here, or I'm walking!" He then stormed off, kicking the upended lounge chair for emphasis as he left.

Greta turned to Danika. "What happened?"

"I came out here to swim some laps, get a little exercise in before I shoot my next scene this afternoon. Chase intercepted me and said he wanted to talk to me."

Greta threw her hands up impatiently. "About what?"

"The same thing he always wants to talk about. Getting in my pants. The more I say no, the more he thinks it's some kind of challenge. I tried to explain that I don't think of him that way, but he got aggressive and I was afraid I wouldn't be able to get him to stop. That's when Matt showed up. I had sent him inside to get me a towel, and luckily he was around to come to my rescue. Again."

Poppy swelled with pride.

She thought of Matt as her own son at times.

"Okay, I'll call Hal and the studio, give them the full report, see how they want to proceed," Greta said. "In the meantime, Danika, I think it would be wise if your friend vamoosed so we don't risk another UFC fight and possible lawsuit."

"Wrong," Danika said looking Greta squarely in the eye.

"I beg your pardon?" Greta asked, surprised.

"Matt is part of my security team. I need him here on set with me. In case you've forgotten, there's a crackpot on the loose stalking me. He's already conned his way onto the set once."

"We have plenty of security on this production," Greta assured her. "You have nothing to worry about."

"You're not hearing me, Greta," Danika said evenly. "I've brought in my own people and they have every right to be here. In fact, it's in my contract. I'd be happy to have my agents and lawyers call you to go over that particular clause with you if you're unfamiliar with it."

Greta fumed, not used to being contradicted.

"And I will be filing a complaint with SAG about Chase's unacceptable on-set behavior. He needs to know harassing a co-star has real consequences."

And with that, Danika spun around and marched off in a huff, leaving Poppy trying not to smile in front of a chastened Greta Van Damm, who didn't feel so all-powerful at the moment.

Chapter 9

Violet's grandson Wyatt was resoundingly unimpressed with being on the set of a major motion picture. He had reminded his grandmother, who thought it might be a treat for the boy to see how a real live Hollywood film is made, that if they were shooting a Marvel movie like *Dr. Strange* or *Black Panther,* or even a James Bond film, he might be more enthusiastic, but this piffle was an icky sweet romantic comedy based on an ancient film from way back in the 1960s.

Still, ever optimistic Violet had thought once Wyatt was physically on the set, observing all the action, maybe get to watch an actual scene filmed with two recognizable stars, he might change his mind and get a little more excited. But he didn't. It was an imposition to be here instead of at his computer playing video games. When Matt had presented Wyatt to Greta Van Damm, she had mistaken him for the child actor playing Poppy's grandson in the movie. Matt corrected her, explaining that Wyatt was the Desert Flowers tech whiz. She had erupted in derisive laughter. But when Wyatt began to spool off all the oppo research he had gathered on Chase Ehrens after his inappropriate behavior with Danika, Greta stopped howling and shut up to listen.

Poppy hung back, not quite ready to reveal to Greta that she was, in fact, part of the Desert Flowers team, when Danika called a meeting in her suite to discuss the information Wyatt had uncovered. Poppy explained her presence as being there for her friend Danika as moral support.

Greta stood, arms folded, soaking up the intel as Poppy and Violet sat on a couch while Danika sat in a makeup chair in front of a fully lit mirror while her hairdresser fussed with her mane and Matt stood guard next to her.

"Back in Idaho, Chase Ehrens didn't exist. He legally changed his name from Alvin Hicks once he got run out of Boise. This is what he used to look like."

Wyatt handed Greta his iPad. There was a mug shot of Chase, aka Alvin, and he looked nothing like the muscular leading man he was today. He was rail thin with sunken cheeks and a bulbous nose; the eyes still popped with color and you could see there was a handsome man beneath all the hard living, but he was nearly unrecognizable.

"He definitely had his nose done," Greta noted. "And no doubt joined a gym once he hit town."

Wyatt took the iPad back from Greta. "He's got a long rap sheet back home. Possession of drugs, assault and battery, resisting arrest, I could go on, but you get the picture."

Greta raised an eyebrow. "I'm sorry, how old are you?"

"I'll be thirteen next month," Wyatt said. "I happily accept Amazon gift cards if you'd like to get me a birthday present."

Greta cracked a smile. Poppy could tell she liked the kid's moxie.

"It's obvious to us that Alvin came out here to reinvent himself and escape his violent, thuggish past," Violet piped in. "Isn't that right, dear?"

Wyatt nodded. "Yes, Grandma. But you can change your name and even your nose, but you're still the same person, and it looks like he hasn't changed all that much."

Danika swiveled around in her chair. "I had no idea. . . ."

"And how did you find out all this information?" Greta asked Wyatt.

"We don't reveal our sources and methods at the Desert Flowers Detective Agency," Wyatt snorted.

"I see," Greta said, grinning. "Well, you've done a very thorough job. I am duly impressed."

"This is why they're here," Danika said. "To key us in to this kind of information. And now that we know, I do not feel safe having Chase Ehrens on my set . . . I mean, our set."

Greta nodded apprehensively. Firing the male lead this deep into the shoot wasn't a decision she was keen to make. But Danika was the bigger name, the one carrying the picture, a big reason the movie got green-lit in the first place. And so she had to respect her opinion. "Hal is on his way out here from Bel Air. Let me call him in the car and bring him up to speed." Greta turned and started out of the room, stopping next to Wyatt and smiling down at him. "Nice work, Scooby-Doo."

She left.

Wyatt glanced around the room, aghast. "Did she just compare me to a dog?"

Violet rushed over and hugged him. "I'm so proud of you!"

Wyatt squirmed in her grip. "Grandma, please. Let's try to maintain a little professionalism in front of the client."

Danika burst out laughing. "You are *too* cute, Wyatt."

Wyatt's face lit up. Although he had tried so hard to give off an air of nonchalance, this hot older girl with millions of Instagram followers had just called him "cute" and that was something he just could not simply ignore.

Poppy stood up. "I'm in the next scene so I better report to hair and makeup."

"I'll stay here and escort Danika to the set when they're ready for her," Matt said.

Violet put her arm around her grandson. "I'll drive Wyatt back to school. I told the principal's office I was signing him out for a doctor's appointment."

"Violet Hogan, you *lied*?" Poppy gasped.

"I know, isn't it terrible? Look what this line of work is doing to me!"

And then she quickly ushered Wyatt out.

When Poppy reported to the hair and makeup department, which had been set up in one of the smaller resort rooms, the altercation between Chase Ehrens and Matt Flowers was still the only topic anyone wanted to talk about. Poppy smiled to herself when the women and gay men who were busily applying eyeliner on the actors and rubbing globs of gel through their hair debated who was sexier, Chase or Matt, with most agreeing Matt won hands down.

By the time they had finished with Poppy, and Timothy showed up to make sure she reported to the pool area set, Poppy got her first look at Hal Greenwood in the flesh. And there was a lot of flesh to take in because he had to be tipping the scale at over three hundred pounds. She had seen him on TV, mostly when watching Oscar ceremonies where his films usually won Best Picture. Poppy thought he might be a bit more appealing in person, but he wasn't. He was just as sweaty and piggish with pasty white, pock-marked skin and beady, busy eyes that you didn't really want to make contact with. His short, stout frame was stuffed inside an expensive suit, but with his protruding gut, there was no way he could button the jacket.

At the moment, he was deep in conference with his wing woman Greta. Poppy assumed Greta was bringing Hal up to speed on the Chase Ehrens situation.

Chase was oblivious to all of this, and at the moment was doing push-ups near the bar, shirtless, arm muscles straining as his hands pressed down on the floor, his perfectly round butt rising and falling.

Trent, the director, was huddling with his German cinematographer, and it appeared as if they were close to shooting when Danika and Matt finally wandered in together.

Poppy noticed Danika's google-eyed gaze as she looked at Matt, and wondered if this was a good thing that the client appeared to be so besotted by him.

Finally, Hal broke away from Greta and hustled over near the pool where he could address everyone, stopping briefly to ask Poppy, "Are you the new broad playing Nomi?"

"Yes, Poppy Harmon."

He looked right through her and then turned away.

Poppy assumed Hal had no reason to waste his time on a wide swath of the female population, presumably those over twenty-five years old. She had read in countless articles that Hal Greenwood was a pig. And he did nothing now to dispel that notion. Being called a "broad" by the dashing helicopter stunt pilot Roy Heller had been mildly titillating. Being called a "broad" by Hal Greenwood, not so much.

Hal snatched a handkerchief from his back pocket to wipe the perspiration off his brow. "It's damn hot out here in the desert! I'm melting! How do people live like this?"

No one answered, assuming his question was rhetorical.

"I'm serious! It must be horrible in the summer!"

"It's a dry heat," Poppy found herself saying. "People don't normally sweat so much out here." She refrained from mentioning that the extra bulk he was carrying around might explain all the perspiration he was sopping up from his face.

Hal ignored her. "So let me spell it out for you, people! I'm shutting down production for the day!"

This suddenly got Trent's attention and he ditched his cinematographer to race over to Hal. "Whatever for?"

"We're making some changes and I need some time before we're ready to move forward again."

"I don't understand," Trent said, gobsmacked.

"You don't have to," Hal literally spit out. "This is my film and I decide what's best."

"But I'm the *director*!" Trent protested.

"You know, France did the Hollywood industry no favors coming up with the auteur theory, making directors believe they're the king on a movie set, when in reality they're basically traffic cops!"

Trent reared back, indignant. But he knew Hal was in one of his mercurial moods and he didn't have the backbone to stand up to him. Instead, fear in his eyes, he whispered, "Are you firing me?"

"No!" Hal barked. "I'm not firing you! But don't tempt me! I'm firing *him*!"

Everyone looked over at who Hal was pointing at with his pudgy finger. Chase was just wrapping up his two hundred and fifty push-ups. Sensing something was wrong, he tucked his knees in and sprang to his feet, surprised to find everyone on the set staring at him.

"What's going on? Who's fired?" Chase asked.

"You are!" Hal bellowed. "Get off my set!"

Chase's mouth dropped open in shock. "*What*?"

"Sorry, kid, I don't condone violence of any kind, and I got witnesses who saw you punching out a security guard for no good reason."

Chase's eyes zeroed in on Matt. "He attacked *me*! I was just having a casual conversation with Danika—"

"Come on, Chase, you know that's not true," Danika scoffed.

Chase fumed, rage building, ready to explode like Mount Vesuvius, but he fought hard to keep his quick temper in check.

Hal finished wiping the sweat off his face and then blew his nose into the handkerchief before continuing. "We also received an official SAG complaint about your inappropriate behavior during this shoot, sexually harassing another actor . . ."

"*Really?* You of all people are accusing *me*—?" Chase stopped himself because he knew the power Hal Greenwood wielded in Hollywood.

But the irony of the statement was not lost on anybody.

Hal took umbrage at the implication no matter how dead-on accurate it was. "Plus, you're a lousy actor."

That did it.

Chase could accept the accusations of violent behavior and sexual misconduct, but he would never stand by and allow aspersions to be cast on his acting talent. "I will sue you!"

Hal guffawed. "I would love that. Do you know how many lawyers work for me? How many lawsuits I've fought and won over the years? Go for it, man. I will suck you dry. Now you can walk out of here on your own, or I can have my goons carry you out."

The silence on the set was deafening.

Chase sniffed, wiped his restructured nose, and then stormed off, but not before throwing a threatening look toward Matt, as if they still had unfinished business.

Trent, still rattled by the whole scene, finally spoke up. "All right, you heard Mr. Greenwood, that's a wrap for today."

The crew began to slowly disperse.

Poppy hung back as Danika bounced over to Hal, whose chubby face brightened as she approached.

"Hello, baby girl," Hal cooed as he embraced Danika, rubbing his meaty hands all over her back. She didn't flinch because she was obviously working him.

"I want you to know, Hal, I am behind you one hundred percent on your decision to replace Chase. It was a totally toxic environment with him around."

"I want you to be happy, angel face," Hal said, pulling away, but keeping his hands planted on her hips.

"Do you have any thoughts on who you might bring in to replace him?"

Hal shook his head. "Greta's going to call around to the agencies to see if anyone on our short list is available. We'll find someone great, trust me."

"I trust you, Hal," Danika said, carefully extricating herself from his grasp. "Are you open to any suggestions?"

"Of course, honey, you have to work with the guy, so I'd love to hear any ideas you might have?"

Poppy stepped closer, intrigued.

So did Matt.

"I know it's crazy, way out of left field, and he doesn't have a lot of credits, but I know he could pull it off and he already has a lot of fans on this set."

Hal was hooked. "Who are we talking about?"

"Matt," Danika said.

"*Matt*?" Poppy heard herself say out loud.

"*Me*?" Matt cried.

"Who's Matt?" Hal asked, dumbfounded.

Danika slid an arm around Matt. "This is Matt."

"Your *security guard*?" Hal asked, confused.

"Yes. Hear me out. Matt's also a very good actor. He showed me some of his theatre work on YouTube. He's perfect! You should at least give him a screen test," Danika said, not quite insisting but showing her teeth as the film's true star.

The blood drained from Trent's face. He was not exactly on board with this casting prospect as he had been with Poppy taking over the much smaller resort owner role.

Hal was perplexed as to what to do.

Poppy could see he didn't like the idea, but he had just fired his male lead and didn't want to now alienate his female lead and her millions of Instagram followers so he promised to think about it.

Poppy whipped her head around toward Matt, who was still in a state of shock, not quite sure what had just happened.

Poppy, however, was relatively confident what was about to happen. Matt would have to start preparing for his first Hollywood screen test.

Chapter 10

There had been absolutely no expectation that Matt would assume the role of Jim Munroe in the *Palm Springs Weekend* reboot for Netflix. Matt himself had declined Trent's reluctant invitation to take a screen test three times, explaining that his role on the set was to strictly look after Danika, keep her safe from the stalker who was still out there roaming around, and he should not be distracted in his mission. But Danika had continued to insist. It made sense to her that with Matt in the cast she would feel safer, more secure. Poppy suspected that she had a little crush on him, and knowing he had once been an aspiring actor, Danika wanted to help him out and make him like her more. But to Matt's credit, he had resisted the urge to seize this once-in-a-lifetime opportunity. That is until Danika threw down an ultimatum, strongly suggesting that she might terminate the Desert

Flowers Detective Agency if she didn't get what she wanted.

Left with no choice, Matt had finally agreed to a screen test. What happened next was mind-blowing to everybody, cast and crew, director Trent, producers Hal and Greta, Poppy, Iris, Violet, and most of all, Matt himself.

Matt had emerged from the screen test filmed in the director's suite at the resort convinced he had blown it and relieved that now they could move on and focus on finding this mysterious Byron character who had crashed the set and physically threatened Danika.

But word had leaked out quickly that Matt had nailed it.

Even the supremely skeptical Trent Dodsworth-Jones, who was still reeling from losing his leading man Chase after already filming a number of scenes with him that would need to be reshot, was stunned by Matt's raw talent and undeniable screen presence. The scenes were hastily sent to Hal and Netflix back in Los Angeles, and it didn't take long for word to come down that they were all willing to sign off on Matt. He was a suitable replacement for Chase. There were some rumblings that Matt was a nobody, with little experience, but the test seemed to drown out those voices, and Hal had determined that they had enough star power with Danika. They could afford a few unknowns in the cast. Plus, Matt would come cheap. Like SAG minimum cheap.

The crew had already finished shooting the scenes at the Sundial Resort, although they would have to return later for reshoots, and moved the company to Joshua Tree National Park, startlingly picturesque with its massive rock formations, barren desert landscapes, tangled trees, and long hiking trails through the boulders of Hidden Valley.

Trent was excited about shooting in this stark yet cine-matic setting. There were some complicated sequences that would be filmed here including a desert car chase, which would enlist the services of Roy Heller and his he-licopter. But today, the scene was relatively simple. Two supporting characters in the film, goofball Biff and Plain Jane Amanda, who are predictably repulsed by each other at first but eventually can't fight their attraction. Finally unable to resist their carnal needs, the pair wind up mak-ing love behind some rocks off the beaten path. Unfortu-nately a tour group stumbles upon them.

Poppy, Matt, Iris, and Violet were all on the set be-cause Danika was scheduled to shoot a few pickup shots once the scene was finished, and although security was tight, they were in the vast desert with a number of ways to sneak around the perimeter. Danika agreed to remain in her trailer with the door locked, especially since Matt had promised to keep her company.

"Poppy, I swear, I had nothing to do with Danika de-manding they give me a screen test," Matt promised as he loaded up some fruit into a bag at the craft services table to take to Danika.

"I know, Matt," Poppy said, although she couldn't help notice the spring in his step, how excited he appeared to be over his big break.

"It was her idea, *totally*!" Matt insisted.

"Yes, she made that perfectly clear to everyone," Poppy said.

Matt reached in the bag, grabbed an apple, and took a big bite. "And I want you to know I have no intention of trying to parlay this into more acting roles. I am commit-ted to Desert Flowers. Remember last year when that manager heard me sing and told me he might take me on as a client?"

"Yes, I do," Poppy said, nodding.

"And I didn't go with him. I stayed here, and look how far we've come."

Poppy refrained from commenting on the fact that shortly after that manager considered taking on Matt, he filed for bankruptcy and shut down his whole agency, but why quibble?

"I mean, even though Danika thinks I could be the next Chris Pine or Ryan Gosling . . ." His eyes twinkled as he considered the possibilities, but then caught himself. "And maybe down the road I might get more serious about my acting goals again, who knows, but I promise you, for the foreseeable future, I am Matt Flowers, private investigator. Head of the Desert Flowers Detective Agency."

Poppy gave him a tight smile.

He wasn't blowing smoke.

Matt was a big key to their recent success.

But in her mind, she was the one in charge.

This was her baby.

And she was not going to let anyone forget that.

With each case, she was becoming more confident in her own abilities as an investigator, and perhaps with time she would ask Matt to scale back his part as "the face" of the agency and allow her to take a more central role publicly, but she was not completely prepared for that, at least not yet.

"Danika's waiting, you better go," Poppy said.

Matt gave her a quick peck on the cheek and scurried off toward Danika's trailer. Poppy wandered over to where they were shooting the scene with the two young actors who get caught in flagrante delicto having sex in public by the astonished tourists. Both Iris and Violet had been recruited as extras for the scene. When Trent asked them to be a part of the tour group since he felt he needed a few more people to make up the crowd of onlookers, Violet had refused, explaining she was too self-conscious to appear on camera. But Iris told her she was being silly, it's not like she had to recite any lines, and strong-armed her into participating alongside her.

As it turned out, Trent was duly impressed with Iris's shock of white hair, bright red lipstick, keen fashion sense, and demonstrative confidence and commanding presence. And so when the tour group rounded the big boulder to see the young couple in each other's arms stark naked, he decided to add the comedic line, "This was not in the brochure!"

And he wanted Iris to deliver it.

Iris was beyond excited.

Poppy just shook her head with a sigh.

The point of them being on set was to stay in the background and observe, make note of anything suspicious, and now, in addition to herself, both Matt and Iris had speaking parts in the movie.

Trent called, "Action!"

The young couple began to do their fake gyrating and the tour group, led by Iris, wandered around the corner and all stopped. Everyone waited for Iris to speak.

Finally, Trent, who was sitting in his director's chair watching his monitor, glanced over. "Iris?"

"Yes?"

"Say your line."

"I forgot it."

"The line is, 'This was not in the brochure!' " Trent reminded her.

"Yes, of course. I am sorry."

"No worries, let's go again. Keep rolling. Back to one," Trent instructed.

The tour group disappeared back behind the boulder. Trent yelled, "Action!" and the couple began simulating sex again. The tour group appeared on cue, with Iris in front. Everyone waited expectantly, Iris opened her mouth to speak, hesitated, but then got out "This was not . . ."

And her mind went blank.

There was an agonizing pause.

Violet finally whispered in her ear, "In the brochure."

"I know, Violet!" Iris snapped. Iris sheepishly turned toward Trent. "I will get it this time."

But she didn't.

Four more takes.

Four more flubs.

Finally, desperate, Trent asked Violet to say the line and much to Iris's chagrin, Violet delivered it effortlessly and with some bite, which made the crew snicker off-camera.

Poppy couldn't believe it.

Violet was a natural.

"Cut! Moving on!" Trent declared with much relief. The scene was mercifully in the can.

Iris was not happy. As she and Violet marched over to her, Poppy could hear Iris berating her. "I was just a little nervous! You didn't have to steal the part right out from under me!"

"I didn't *steal* anything," Violet protested. "I was just trying to help get the scene done."

Iris was not assuaged in the least. "Who knew we had an Eve Harrington amongst us?"

Poppy was about to come to Violet's defense when she suddenly noticed one of the extras she had heard introduce herself as Lulu to Iris and Violet earlier, over by video village, the area set up for the director and his monitors, conferring with Greta Van Damm. Lulu was a colorful character to be sure, bouncy, big blond hair, tiny frame but jiggling some huge assets that Poppy swore must cause the poor girl painful back problems. She had muscled her way to the front of the crowd of extras in the tour group securing a place right next to Violet, who was sure to be on camera. Surprisingly, Trent did not object to Lulu placing herself so prominently in the shot. Perhaps he was impressed with Lulu's assets that she so proudly flaunted, and it was some kind of artistic choice.

Poppy chuckled to herself.

But now, what was so strange, was Lulu's intense conversation with Greta. Poppy had worked on enough sets to know how unusual it was for an extra, probably the lowest rung on the film set totem pole, to be hobnobbing with one of the movie's powerful producers.

Poppy casually meandered over to video village, hoping to eavesdrop on their exchange when Greta, who still did not see Poppy approaching, reached into her bag, extracted a wad of cash, and surreptitiously handed it to Lulu, who quickly and covertly stuffed it down the front of her shirt. Lulu winked at Greta, who gave her a withering, dismissive look, and then Lulu happily bounced away to join the rest of the extras eagerly lining up at the craft services table for today's dinner of short ribs and macaroni and cheese.

Greta sighed, checked her watch and turned to go, then

suddenly noticed Poppy staring at her. "I didn't see your name on the call sheet for today. What are you doing here?"

Poppy still had not copped to the fact that she was part of the Desert Flowers team, at least not to Greta or Hal yet, and apparently no one else in the know had blown her cover either. "My friends Iris and Violet were part of the scene you just shot, so I came for moral support."

"I see," Greta said warily.

"It's been a long time since I've appeared in the movies, a lot has changed over the years," Poppy remarked.

"Yes, it's a whole new world," Greta sniffed, already bored with her.

"But I never thought I'd see the day when a producer paid an extra with cash out of her own pocket."

Greta bristled.

"From everything I know, most professional productions have payroll companies to handle all that," Poppy said pretending it was simply an innocent observation.

But Greta didn't take it as innocent.

Poppy was clearly prying and she didn't appreciate it.

"Well, luckily it's not my job to explain to you how I run my business," Greta snorted before storming off.

Poppy watched her go, curious as to why Greta was suddenly so rattled and anxious to get away from her.

Chapter 11

Danika Delgado ran across the wind-swept desert terrain, past a towering yucca palm toward the burning
car wreckage. She stopped, shielded her eyes from the
blazing hot sun with her hand, and stared at the lifeless
body sprawled on the ground, having been thrown from
the vehicle upon impact.

"No!" Danika wailed, as if she refused to believe her
own eyes, and stumbled forward, sobbing, shrieking,
until she reached the prone body and dropped down to
her knees to see if he was still alive.

It was Matt, his body twisted and apparently broken
from the crash, a nasty gash down the side of his face,
barely breathing. Danika scooped up his hand and held it
to her heart. "Don't you die on me! I won't let you leave
me! Not after all we've been through!"

Danika squeezed his hand, but he didn't squeeze back.

She sobbed some more, unable to accept that he was gone. "No, no, no, no . . ."

She raised his limp hand to her face, softly caressing it against her cheek, then gently kissing it.

She closed her eyes, barely able to breathe she was so distraught, when suddenly, unexpectedly the index finger on the hand she was clutching twitched ever so slightly. Danika's eyes popped open in surprise.

Matt was still unconscious, most of his bruised and battered body not moving, but his fingers slowly began to wrap weakly around the palm of her hand, and then she felt a gentle squeeze.

Danika gasped. Hope had not been lost. He was still alive. She threw herself upon him, overcome with relief, and sniffed, "Hold on, baby, help's on the way!"

"And . . . cut!" Trent Dodsworth-Jones called out from video village.

Matt finally opened his eyes and smiled. "How'd I do?"

"Joaquin Phoenix better watch his back!" Danika crowed. She leaned down and kissed him on the side of his face that hadn't been caked with the fake bloody gash.

Poppy and Iris stood off-camera excitedly observing all the action as Trent trotted over to his two actors and heaped praise upon them for their searing performances. Danika asked if they should do another take just for safety, but Trent assured her they had gotten what they needed for the scene and could move on. This was the second scene shot with Danika and Matt today. The first, a romantic walk along the dramatic rock formations of Joshua Tree, had indisputably proven there was a crackling chemistry between the two, which stretched well past when the cameras stopped rolling.

Poppy had been impressed by Matt's effortless ability

to jump right in and make the role his own. After all, he had been waiting his whole life for this opportunity, and there was little chance he was going to risk blowing it now. It also helped that he had such an encouraging scene partner in Danika, who came across as quite smitten with her new co-star.

Trent held out a hand, which Matt took, and hauled him to his feet, slapping him on the back. "You just might wind up a big star if you play your cards right, Matt."

"Thanks, Trent, you're too kind," Matt said shyly although Poppy could tell he was doing cartwheels inside his head.

"You two take a break while we set up for the car chase scene. But we probably won't get to it until after lunch," Trent said.

Danika nodded, and Trent raced back to video village to watch a playback of the scene they had just wrapped. The schedule had called for them to film the dramatic scene post–car crash in the morning while shooting the actual car chase and crash later in the day. There had also been a major change in the new script that deviated from the original movie. The characters Danika and Matt were playing, Jim (Troy Donahue) and Gayle (Connie Stevens), never became romantically involved in the 1963 version, but this more free-wheeling, gender-bending Gen Y reboot had everyone hooking up with everyone else, boys with girls, girls with girls, boys with boys. It truly was a modern take on an old classic, and so the writer paired them up, and it was paying off in dividends with the obvious sparks between Danika and Matt.

Danika kissed Matt softly on the cheek and whispered, "I'm so proud of you. You were so good in that last scene."

Matt grinned and shook his head. "Come on, all I had to do was just lay there pretending to be dead. You did most of the heavy lifting."

As they playfully argued over who was most effective in the scene, Poppy's phone buzzed.

It was a text from Violet.

Poppy read it and turned to Iris. "Wyatt's still working on tracing the stalker's car. He got access to some DMV records, don't ask me how, and he's cross-referencing the half a license plate we got with the name Byron hoping to find a match. Violet says it's slow going, but they're optimistic."

"It is good Violet is back at the office and not here trying to steal the role you are playing in the movie!" Iris sniffed, still smarting from being replaced at the last minute in her big scene.

Poppy rolled her eyes, refusing to engage with her.

Iris would get over her hurt feelings eventually.

As Danika was surrounded by her people—agents, manager, stylists and social media advisors—Matt bounded over to Poppy and Iris.

"What did you think, Iris?" Matt asked hesitantly.

"You were . . . *fine*," Iris said curtly.

"Wow, coming from you, that means I just might win an Oscar!" Matt said, laughing.

"Do not get too big for your britches!" Iris warned. "I do not tolerate an overinflated ego!"

"Yes, ma'am," Matt promised.

"I want to get a cream-filled donut before all those teamsters clean them out," Iris announced, hustling off as the crew wandered toward the tent that housed craft services.

Matt waited for her to be gone before turning to Poppy. "And you? What does the professional actress say?"

"You were wonderful, in both scenes," Poppy said, trying not to gush too much.

Matt stared across the set toward Danika, who was snapping selfies with her pals. "It helps to be playing opposite someone like her."

Poppy noticed the sparkle in his eye as he gazed adoringly at Danika. He quickly caught himself and tried to get back to business. "Any progress tracking down the stalker?"

"Violet and Wyatt are still working on it."

"If anybody can do it, the whiz kid can," Matt said.

Matt glanced over again at Danika, who made eye contact while chatting with her stylist and winked at him.

"You two seem to be getting along rather well," Poppy remarked. "People are starting to talk."

Matt's guard went up. "What people? No, I'm just sticking close by her side because it's my job."

Poppy wondered why he was suddenly defensive.

She was simply stating the obvious.

"But watching you two together, there's certainly a chemistry . . ."

"We're *acting*, Poppy, we're playing characters who fall in love, it's as simple as that."

"Why are you downplaying this? I've been around long enough to know genuine attraction when I see it."

"Because . . ." Matt began but something got caught in his throat and he stopped.

"It's Heather, isn't it?" Poppy guessed.

Matt sighed. "Maybe. I don't know. I literally just got dumped a few days ago so I'm not exactly eager to jump into something new. . . ."

Poppy could tell Matt felt uncomfortable talking about this. Poppy, after all, was Heather's mother and he obviously did not want to appear like a player, hopping from one girl to the next.

"You're a good man, Matt. Believe me, I had my doubts when we first met. But as I got to know you, I got to know your heart, and I see how much you care deeply for us, me, Violet, Iris, and yes, Heather . . . But Heather has made her decision. So you should feel free to pursue whatever relationship you like."

Matt glanced furtively back over in Danika's direction. Although people were squawking at her from every side, her attention was directed at Poppy and Matt, curious to know what they were talking about.

"I appreciate you wanting to put my mind at ease, Poppy, but I truly did love your daughter, it's going to take some time for me to get over it. Danika is our client, and I plan to keep it that way," he said firmly.

"Got it," Poppy said, although she was not entirely convinced this edict of Matt's would last the rest of the week, let alone the remainder of the film shoot.

Chapter 12

When Poppy approached Roy Heller he was listening to a heated discussion between the director Trent Dodsworth-Jones and the film's stunt coordinator, Frank, a short, squat, red-faced Irishman with a loud voice to make up for his diminutive stature. Frank was gritting his teeth at the moment as Trent quietly explained his reasoning for a decision he had made.

Roy shook his head disapprovingly.

"What are they arguing about?" Poppy asked, curious.

"Trent wants Matt to drive the car so he can get some clear shots of him behind the wheel and Frank thinks they should use his stuntman Eddie."

Poppy's mouth dropped open. "But doesn't the car crash into the tree at the end of the scene?"

Roy nodded. "Yes. Trent says Matt can stop the car before he reaches the tree and then he can film the actual crash with Eddie driving, but Frank's worried Matt won't know when to stop in time to avoid the tree and thinks it's too dangerous."

"Well, then it's a risk not worth taking," Poppy concluded.

"Trent's insisting, and he's got Matt on his side," Roy said. "The kid wants to do it."

"*What*?" Poppy gasped. "Where's Matt?"

Roy pointed over to where Matt was getting touched up by hair and makeup, Danika closely at his side.

"Huge mistake, if you ask me. But nobody's asking me," Roy said, shaking his head, disgusted.

Poppy marched straight over to Matt.

He looked up at her and immediately could tell she was fuming and he also had a hunch why. "I know what you're going to say, Poppy, but really, it's no big deal. I got this. Trent says it will be perfectly safe—"

"I don't care what Trent says. The stunt coordinator is the only person anyone should be listening to on this subject and he strongly disagrees."

"The stunt team always wants to use their own guy in the shot, but we have to make it look believable. The audience needs to see me driving the car," Matt said.

"I simply will not stand by and allow you to do this," Poppy cried.

"You're not his mother," Danika said dismissively.

Matt cringed slightly but Danika did not seem to notice and continued. "Matt's a big boy. He can make his own decisions and if he thinks he can do it, then I for one trust him."

Matt saw Poppy's nostrils flaring and jumped in to do a little damage control. He bounded over and gave Poppy a hug. "Trust me, everything will be fine. I'll hit the brake in plenty of time, and then I'll hop out and the stunt guy can hop in and do it for real."

Poppy was still unconvinced but she was clearly outnumbered. Especially when she turned to see the stunt coordinator throwing his hands in the air, giving up and walking away. Trent waved at Matt and gave him the thumbs-up that they were good to go as the crew finished attaching a camera to the hood of the car and locking in the shot.

Short of tackling Matt and physically restraining him from climbing into the red sports car, Poppy knew she was powerless to stop him. She walked back to Roy.

"Can you talk to Trent? You have the most experience on this set. He might listen to you."

Roy shrugged. "I tried. He doesn't care. He's got a single mission in mind and that's getting the best shot for his movie."

Poppy sighed, frustrated.

"By the way, you look ravishing today," Roy said with a roused grin.

"Please don't do that, not right now," Poppy snapped as she began to panic. She scanned the set for Matt again, hoping to try one more time to convince him not to do the stunt himself, but the makeup and hair people had already dispersed and neither he nor Danika were anywhere to be seen.

"Poppy!"

It was Violet's voice.

Poppy turned around to see Violet and Wyatt hustling up to her. "What are you two doing here?"

"Well," Violet panted, out of breath. "Wyatt has been working very hard on locating Danika's stalker, this Byron person, and we finally had a breakthrough! I am so proud of him! How on earth did our family manage to produce such a *genius*?"

"We can speculate later," Poppy said impatiently before focusing on Wyatt. "What did you find out?"

Wyatt appeared bored as he detailed his information. "I used a cross-referencing program, one that I personally designed, by the way, to sort through DMV records. . . ."

Poppy did not want to know how a twelve-year-old boy got access to DMV records so she didn't ask.

"I input the first name Byron and the last half of the license number from that Instagram photo of the car the stalker drove away in after he ambushed Danika in the gym and—"

"He's *so* smart!" Violet gushed. "Isn't he smart? His teachers think he could be the next Steve Jobs or Mark Zuckerberg or—"

"Violet, let the poor boy speak!" Poppy said sharply.

Violet buttoned her lips.

"Anyway, it took a while but I found the car! A 2008 Toyota Corolla. It's registered to a Byron Savage who lives in Desert Hot Springs." He handed Poppy a piece of paper. "Here is the address."

Poppy turned to Violet. "You're right. He is a genius."

"Wait, I'm not done," Wyatt huffed. "I have more."

Now it was Poppy's turn to button her lips.

"Once I got his full name and home address, I was able to check out his social media presence. He didn't post much on Twitter or Instagram about what was going on in his life, and for good reason, but his friends and contacts sure did. Everybody was wishing him luck at Desert Oasis."

"What's that?" Poppy asked.

"A psychiatric hospital. And it wasn't his first time there. Apparently Byron has a long history of mental illness. I got ahold of an evaluation report after his first visit. . . ."

"How on earth did you—?" Poppy stopped herself. "Never mind. Just tell me what it said."

"He's a danger to himself . . . *and others*."

Poppy exhaled and swung around to Violet. "Okay, now at least we know what we're dealing with." She paused, then glanced back at Wyatt. "Why didn't you just call me with all this? Why did you and your grandmother drive all the way out here to Joshua Tree?"

Wyatt broke into a wide grin, markedly more excited than he was on his first visit to the set. "Because Matt texted me and told me he was getting ready to do a really big action scene and that he was going to be racing a sports car himself like a NASCAR driver, and it was going to be really cool, and that I should come out and watch!"

"This is insane! What is he thinking putting himself in danger like that? We have to stop him!" Poppy fretted.

"It's too late," Violet said. "I think they're ready to start."

Poppy whipped around to see Matt already behind the wheel of the sports car, the stunt team finishing up their last safety checks and Trent glued to the monitor ready to go.

"And . . . action!" Trent called out.

"No!" Poppy screamed, but her voice was drowned out by the sound of the revving engine.

She was helpless to do anything to stop him now.

With Matt in the driver's seat, the mounted camera on top of the hood capturing his fierce intensity, his fingers tightly gripping the steering wheel, a bead of sweat dripping down his left cheek, Matt slammed his foot down on the accelerator and the sports car shot forward at lightning speed.

Poppy watched, horrified, as the red car sped across the dusty desert terrain in a red blur, clocking what must have been nearly a hundred miles an hour. The lone Joshua tree stood ominously in the distance.

As the car got closer and closer to the tree, Poppy expected Matt to finally slow down as he was supposed to do.

But he didn't.

He kept going.

The car was on a direct collision course with the tree.

"Matt, hit the brakes!" Poppy yelled, knowing there was no way for him to hear her.

The car was now moments from impact with the tree.

"Hit the brakes!" Poppy cried, a sense of dread consuming her.

Violet and Wyatt both stood frozen in place, unable to move as they stared, stunned at what was about to happen.

Poppy wanted to cover her face but she couldn't tear her eyes away.

Suddenly, in a flash, the car swerved violently to the left as if Matt jerked the wheel at the last possible second, and the vehicle flipped, rolling over and over and over four, five, six times, metal crunching violently, before landing upside down in a heap.

The stunt team, seven men in all, ran to the scene of the crash and worked feverishly to pull Matt from the burning wreckage. They dragged him away from the vehicle as far as they could before it exploded in a burst of flames.

But Poppy didn't care about the state of the car.

She was too busy staring at what looked like Matt's lifeless body as several crew members ran frantically toward him, one lugging a first aid kit.

Chapter 13

It was a miracle, but due in no small part to the car's safety features including air bags and seat belts as well as his young age and healthy, in-shape body, Matt survived the crash. Despite his loud protestations and insistence that he was fine, just a little bruised and banged up, an ambulance was called to the scene so they could transport him to the emergency room at the nearest hospital, the Hi-Desert Medical Center, in Joshua Tree. Since Matt had been unconscious for a few minutes following the impact, the on-set doctor was insistent he be checked out in case there was a concussion, or worse, some kind of serious brain injury.

Matt complained incessantly as the paramedics strapped him down on the gurney and wheeled him off.

Before he was lifted into the back of the ambulance, Roy Heller and the stunt coordinator, Frank, rushed in.

"Matt, what happened? Why didn't you stop?" Roy asked.

"I tried, something went wrong with the brakes. I was pumping them like mad, but the car wouldn't slow down. I swerved to avoid the tree and flipped the car."

Poppy caught Roy and Frank exchanging concerned looks.

She had planned on accompanying Matt to the hospital, but she was practically body-checked by their hysterical and sobbing client Danika Delgado, who was devastated and emotionally distraught over the accident, blaming the director, the stunt team, the mechanics, everyone except herself, who had so brazenly and irresponsibly encouraged Matt to get behind the wheel and do the stunt himself in the first place.

Danika climbed into the back of the ambulance with Matt, clutching his hand and dramatically promising him she would stay by his side and make sure he got the best care possible for his recovery. Matt, for his part, seemed to be his usual jovial self and looked like he was enjoying the shower of attention he was receiving from his beautiful co-star.

Poppy decided Matt had enough people fussing over him and so she stayed behind on the set to try to figure out exactly what went wrong. Violet determined that her grandson Wyatt had been exposed to enough violence and trauma for one day and drove him home although Wyatt didn't want to go and thought the crash was awesome and Matt was so cool and was just like the hero in his favorite movie, *Baby Driver*.

The director, Trent, who no doubt was now suddenly fearing a lawsuit, vanished into thin air after calling a wrap for the day. The stunt guys and mechanics got to work inspecting the smoking wreckage of the car in order to zero in on the reason why the brakes didn't work. Poppy hung around, hoping to get some answers for herself.

It didn't take long.

She watched as Roy conferred with Frank, who was visibly upset and shaken as he explained what one of his mechanics had discovered. Roy had a disturbed look on his face, occasionally glancing over at Poppy, who was now dying of curiosity.

When Roy and Frank finished their conversation and Frank went back to the totaled car, Poppy made a beeline for Roy. She opened her mouth to ask what they had found, but didn't even get the chance to speak.

"It was no accident," Roy said soberly.

"*What*?" Poppy gasped.

"Somebody cut the brake line. It was intentional."

"But who would—?"

"Frank is still trying to find out who was the last mechanic to work on the car, but one of his guys, Jesse, they call him Speedy, he's suddenly gone AWOL. Nobody can find him."

"Do you think he was the one who tampered with the car?"

Roy shrugged. "Frank isn't sure. But Speedy just joined the crew recently so none of the guys know a whole lot about him." Roy paused. "Other than the fact that he was recommended for the job by Chase Ehrens."

Poppy's mouth dropped open. "*Chase*?"

"Yes. Chase worked with Speedy on his last movie and spoke very highly of him to Frank, said he was an excellent mechanic, and would be a good hire."

Poppy shook her head, stunned. "I knew Chase was upset when he got fired, but attempted murder?"

"I'm not saying Speedy sabotaged the brakes, or that Chase put him up to it, all I'm saying is it looks a little suspicious."

But it made perfect sense.

Chase blamed Matt for Hal Greenwood kicking him off the picture. If he wanted to exact some kind of revenge, enlisting the aid of a friend who had access to the car Matt would be driving was the perfect way to do it.

It was almost too much to grasp.

Poppy asked Roy to drive her to the hospital so she could check on Matt, and he happily obliged after she rejected his offer to fly her there in his helicopter. She was not about to create a spectacle. A lift in his Land Rover would be just fine.

By the time they reached the Hi-Desert Medical Center, Roy received a call from Frank, telling him that once Hal Greenwood had heard what had happened, he immediately called the cops, who put out an APB with Speedy's car make and license plate. Speedy was pulled over on the 10 freeway, heading east toward Arizona, no doubt Texas-bound to his hometown of El Paso. He was brought back to Joshua Tree for questioning. After a mere twenty-five minutes of claiming ignorance of any wrongdoing, Speedy finally caved and admitted that it was indeed Chase who had pressured him to damage the brake line so Matt would crash the car, ruining the shot. But they had never intended to kill Matt, just shake him up a bit and get back at him for getting Chase fired.

Poppy and Roy raced through the emergency room doors of the Hi-Desert Medical Center and then marched down a corridor to the waiting room where they were greeted by Danika, who was no longer convulsing and shedding tears.

"Where's Matt?" Poppy asked, worried.

"He's still in with the doctor. Have you heard about Chase?" Danika asked, breathless.

Poppy nodded. "The police are out now trying to track him down so they can arrest him."

"It's outrageous! I don't believe a word of what they're saying. Chase would never do something like that!"

Poppy was aghast over Danika's sudden and fervent knee-jerk defense of Chase Ehrens, but she had little appetite for a confrontation, not with Matt's condition still up in the air, and so she just kept her mouth shut.

Danika, however, did not. "I bet that mechanic, Speedy, installed a defective part, or was negligent with the maintenance, and just pointed the finger at Chase in order to cover up his own incompetence!"

Roy couldn't take it anymore. He stepped forward, his face reddened with anger. "The brake line was deliberately cut."

That did not seem to convince Danika at all. She just waved him off, rather disrespectfully. "Then someone's trying to set him up."

Roy was about to lay into her when Poppy tugged on his jacket, signaling him to back off for now. He complied but still kept glaring at the young actress.

"My only concern at the moment is Matt's well-being. Did they say anything when they took him in?" Poppy asked.

Danika sighed. "I told you, he is still with the doctor. I'm sure we will hear something soon. He looked fine to me. He was joking with the nurse as they wheeled him away," she said dismissively. "Look, I need to call my agent. I can't be near even a hint of scandal and risk losing any branded endorsements."

She hustled off down the corridor, her eyes glued to her phone.

Poppy was seeing a whole new side of their client, one she did not find likable at all. But she quickly brushed her concerns aside when the doctor finally emerged, looking for any relative waiting to hear about Matt Cameron aka Matt Flowers.

Poppy hurried over to the short, pudgy doctor of Indian descent. "Yes, I'm Poppy Harmon . . . Matt's partner."

The doctor cocked an eyebrow, assuming partner meant romantic partner, somewhat surprised by the vast age difference.

Poppy wisely chose to ignore the judgment. "How is he?"

"The MRI showed no signs of any bruising or bleeding in the brain. He's just got some scrapes and cuts. He's young. He'll bounce back in no time. Just no more dangerous driving."

"I'll make sure of that, Doctor," Poppy said with a huge sigh of relief, determined to make it her personal mission to prevent Matt from blithely putting himself in harm's way again.

Chapter 14

Poppy was not surprised to find out that late the previous evening a highway patrolman had pulled over a speeding Jaguar on the 10 freeway heading west to Los Angeles, and when the officer ran the license and registration, she was informed the driver's name was Chase Ehrens and there was a warrant out for his arrest.

Poppy had been confident that it would not take long for the law to catch up with the arrogant movie actor after Speedy's confession. But what did surprise her was at his arraignment the following day at the Larson Justice Center in Indio, where Chase pleaded not guilty to the charge of attempted murder in the first degree, the judge had granted him bail in the amount of five hundred thousand dollars due in no small part to his high-priced lawyers who tossed out arguments like no priors, no history of violence, well respected in his industry. Chase's manager promptly paid the bail money and the accused was now free until his trial in three months' time.

And now on the set of *Palm Springs Weekend* in the wide open range of Joshua Tree National Park where Poppy and Matt were keeping watch over their client, Danika was still fiercely defending Chase, refusing to believe he had had anything to do with causing the crash that had nearly killed Matt. She had cornered the two of them at craft services where they had stopped for coffee. The gaffer was still discussing the lighting plan with the cinematographer so they still had plenty of time before Danika would be called to the set to shoot the scene.

"I know he has a hot temper at times, and can be a handful, but he is basically a good guy. I wouldn't be defending him so vehemently if I didn't believe it in my heart," Danika said to Poppy and Matt, both of whom remained thoroughly unconvinced.

"A legal process has begun, Danika, so why don't we wait and see how that plays out first," Poppy said diplomatically.

"No!" Danika shouted, stomping her foot. "You don't understand. Prosecutors chomp at the bit to go after famous defendants. It's a way to make a name for themselves, get rich writing books and scoring gigs as TV pundits. It's a racket and it's disgusting!"

Matt stayed uncharacteristically quiet.

Poppy was confused as to why Danika was badgering them about Chase's court case. "What is it you think we can do, Danika?"

"Matt can talk to the prosecutor, refuse to testify, ask them to drop the charges," she said with a straight face.

"Drop the charges? Seriously, even if he wanted to do

that, and I would strongly advise him against it, the prosecutor doesn't have to listen to him. I'm sure they feel they already have enough evidence to win the case, plain and simple. A plea from Matt will not change that."

"What's the harm in him at least trying?" Danika whined. "Matt, I thought you cared about me. . . ."

Poppy could feel her face burning up with rage. This spoiled young actress was so obviously, so shamelessly trying to manipulate him.

"I do . . ." Matt said. "It's just that—"

Poppy could not take anymore. "Chase is going to stand trial for nearly killing Matt, whether he personally sabotaged those brakes or had someone else do it. There is no point in discussing this any further."

Danika reared back like a coiled snake, eyes blazing. There was a long moment of deadening silence before she hissed, "I don't like your tone, Ms. Harmon. As a matter of fact, I no longer feel comfortable having you near me." She whipped around to Matt and hissed, "Matt, if you want to continue working for me, I need you to fire her."

Poppy suppressed a smile.

Matt cleared his throat and looked sheepishly at Danika. "The thing is, technically I work for Poppy. *She* is the boss."

"What?" Danika cried. "But I thought . . ."

"The Flowers in the Desert Flowers Detective Agency doesn't actually stand for Matt Flowers. The three founders are named after flowers, Poppy, Iris, and Violet."

Danika was thunderstruck. The idea of three women old enough to be Matt's grandmothers as his bosses was utterly inconceivable. She took some time to process all of this before addressing Matt again. "And so you refuse to do as I wish, even though I'm paying you a lot of money?"

Matt slowly nodded.

"Then you're fired. All of you. I want you off the set now, or I'm going to call security and have you escorted off," she snarled before stalking away.

"What do you think she's going to do when she finds out we're stuck here as actors with contracts and aren't going anywhere?" Matt asked Poppy.

"It's going to make for a very awkward day," Poppy said, chuckling.

"I thought she really liked me," Matt said wistfully. "And now I find out she was only interested in Chase all along, and was just using me to make him jealous. She gets off on toying with men, playing them off each other."

"I feel as if this is all my fault. I encouraged you to pursue a relationship with her. How could I have been so wrong?" Poppy said with despair.

Matt hugged her. "You couldn't have known. At least Danika proved one thing. She's a decent actress. She had us all fooled."

Greta Van Damm suddenly blew on the set, panicked eyes scanning the area, clearly disturbed by something.

Poppy and Matt exchanged curious glances and wandered over to her. Before they had a chance to speak, she zeroed in on them. "Have you seen Hal?"

"No," Matt said. "Is something wrong?"

She didn't bother answering him. Instead, she made a mad dash over to Trent, who had now joined the conversation between the gaffer and cinematographer. "Hal drove out here ahead of me, his car is in the crew lot, so he's around here somewhere but I can't find him."

Trent sighed, irked by Greta's interruption. "I haven't seen him. Maybe he's visiting with one of the actors in their trailer."

Greta suddenly registered a look of alarm. "Well, that would be a disaster in the making, now wouldn't it?"

Trent finally saw the implication of Hal Greenwood somewhere on the loose unsupervised. "Yes, I suppose you're right."

"So why don't you have the assistant director call all the PAs and have them spread out and find him."

"Got it," Trent said, hustling off to find his AD, who was at the moment nowhere in sight.

"Why do you think everybody is so nervous?" Matt asked.

"Hal Greenwood's reputation has been an open secret in Hollywood for years," Poppy said before adding bluntly, "He's a sexual predator."

"Oh . . ." Matt whispered, wide-eyed.

"From what I heard from some of my old friends still working in the business, there is a long list of actresses who have worked for Greenwood over the years, all of whom were bought off with fat settlements and silenced by ironclad nondisclosure agreements."

A thought abruptly popped into Poppy's head. "You stay here, I'm going to go check on Danika."

"What for? She dismissed us."

"I know, but if Hal Greenwood is on the prowl, I'd feel much better knowing he's not trying to worm his way into her trailer. I'd never forgive myself if anything happened to her."

Poppy scurried off toward the row of trailers that housed the cast located several hundred feet from the main set and opposite the rest of the trailers for makeup, hair, wardrobe, and production. Since today's schedule did not involve any crowd scenes, the cast area was almost deserted. Poppy glanced around for any sign of Hal, but found none. When she reached the first trailer, the biggest one reserved for the star, she stepped up on the rickety stairs attached to the aluminum-sided trailer and rapped on the door with Danika's name printed in the middle of a yellow star.

There was no answer.

Poppy tried again, knocking her fist harder against the metal door. "Danika? Are you in there? It's me, Poppy. I need to speak with you!"

Still no answer.

Suddenly from behind her, she heard someone say, "I don't think she's in there."

Poppy spun around to find Timothy, the production assistant. "What makes you say that?"

"I mean, she could be. Maybe she's got headphones on listening to music, but when I brought Mr. Greenwood by just a few minutes ago, she didn't answer."

Poppy's heart nearly jumped in her throat. "You brought Hal here to Danika's trailer?"

"Yup, he wanted to see her about something. He knocked and knocked but she never opened the door. He finally got frustrated and stormed off mad."

Worried, Poppy whacked on the door a few more times.

Still nothing.

She tried the door handle.

It was unlocked.

She wasn't sure if she should just barge in, especially

if Danika was napping, or with someone, or just wanted to be left alone. But it was not as if Poppy was in any danger of displeasing her client; the girl had just fired her.

So she just went for it and swung open the door.

The lights were on inside the roomy trailer and the TV was broadcasting the E! Entertainment channel and some fluffy report on Lizzo's upcoming concert tour.

Poppy's eyes scoured the room until they settled on someone lying on top of the bed. She instantly recognized the cute patterned strapless T-shirt dress Danika had been wearing when they last saw her. There was a pillow over her face, which caused a dreaded feeling of déjà vu deep within Poppy.

Timothy called from outside the trailer, "Is everything okay in there?"

Poppy raced over and removed the pillow and tossed it to the floor. Danika's empty, glassy eyes stared up at Poppy. Her mouth was open and contorted as if she had been screaming at the top of her lungs as someone snuffed the life out of her with the pillow.

Everything was definitely not okay.

Because Danika Delgado was unmistakably dead.

Chapter 15

Poppy had been so shaken and unsettled by her stumbling upon the lifeless body of Danika Delgado sprawled out with a pillow over her face that she had nearly fainted dead on the spot. Matt swooped in to catch her and half escorted, half carried her out of the trailer while Greta Van Damm, who was quickly called to the scene by Timothy the production assistant, took charge and called 911.

Matt gently led Poppy over to a nearby director's chair and had her sit down. She took deep breaths, trying to calm herself. This was highly unusual for her to react in such a dramatic way. After all, this was not the first time she had seen a dead body let alone a crime scene in the time since opening the Desert Flowers Detective Agency. But it was the strong sense of déjà vu that was overwhelming her, and Matt quickly picked up on it.

"What is it, Poppy? What has you so spooked?" Matt asked, clasping her hand, trying to offer her some comfort.

Poppy shook her head. "I'd rather not talk about it."

"But—"

"Please, Matt. Not now."

Her tone was firm and Matt relented and asked no further questions. Poppy knew she would have to explain everything at some point, but was not emotionally prepared to do so just yet.

Remarkably, the police arrived within twenty minutes followed closely by the county forensics team. The set was swarming with law enforcement, and Poppy recognized the head honcho running the entire show immediately. Detective Lamar Jordan, primary detective with the Riverside County Central Homicide Unit. He was tall, handsome, African American, outspoken, and charismatic. Poppy had met him on a number of occasions, and although she could not claim that the detective was outwardly hostile toward her, he certainly did not appreciate her recurring presence at the crime scenes he was called in to investigate.

Poppy watched with a sense of dread as Detective Jordan questioned Timothy about who it was who discovered the body. Timothy turned, pointing in Poppy's direction. When Jordan's eyes fell upon her, he audibly groaned. He then shook his head and sternly marched over to where Poppy was sitting with Matt.

"Hello, Detective Jordan," Poppy said tentatively.

"Poppy Harmon," Lamar said, rolling his eyes. "Of course you're here."

"It's always nice to see you," Poppy said. "I wish just once it would not be under such tragic circumstances."

"Me too, believe me," he said, stone-faced. "Now, would you mind telling me what you're doing here?"

Matt, who didn't appreciate Jordan's dismissive attitude toward Poppy, interjected, "Poppy is playing a role in the movie they're shooting."

Jordan turned his head toward Poppy and arched an eyebrow. "You're acting again?"

"Yes," Matt answered for her. "We're both in it."

Jordan chuckled derisively. "Matt Flowers. The Hercule Poirot of the Coachella Valley. My wife reads of your exciting exploits in the *Desert Sun*. I think she may even have a little crush on you."

Matt could not help but crack a smile, flattered.

"So you're strictly actors and not here in any official capacity as private investigators?"

They both hesitated before Poppy answered, "No, that's not exactly true. Danika Delgado hired us to find a stalker who has been harassing her."

"I suspected as much," Jordan said, sighing.

"His name is Byron Savage," Poppy continued. "And we have found a home address in Desert Hot Springs. You really should look into him because he has crashed the set before and—"

Jordan cut her off. "Yes, I know. And according to the crew we've already talked to, security has been tightened considerably since then. The guard swears no one outside of the cast and crew working today has been anywhere near the victim. We'll check it out, but it's unlikely this stalker is actually responsible for murdering Ms. Delgado."

A chill ran through Poppy's body.

Jordan noticed Poppy slightly trembling. "Are you okay, Ms. Harmon?"

"Yes," Poppy whispered, obviously disturbed.

"Something you want to tell me?" Jordan asked.

Poppy raised her eyes to meet his and said firmly, "No."

She needed to process what was now racing through her mind before she could seriously consider discussing it with anyone, even the detective looking into Danika's murder.

"All right then, that's all for now, but you can bet I'll be in touch with more questions," Jordan said firmly.

"And we will certainly be available at any time to answer them, Detective Jordan," Poppy said, forcing a smile.

Jordan shook his head one more time and walked away.

"Not our biggest fan," Matt remarked.

"He just doesn't like us sticking our noses into police business, making his job harder."

"But maybe if we all try working together . . ."

"Detective Jordan doesn't strike me as a team player."

Matt sighed. "I somehow feel this is all my fault."

Poppy sprang to her feet. "Matt, no . . ."

"I should have stuck by her side, even after she fired us, and then maybe this would never have happened."

"You heard the detective. The set was locked down. We thought she was safe," Poppy insisted.

"But she wasn't. And that's on me."

"I will not allow you to take the blame for this, Matt, but if it makes you feel any better, we can push forward and try to find out who—"

"There you are!" Hal Greenwood bellowed as he hustled his hefty frame toward them with Greta chasing after him. "I just heard you two are not really actors!"

"Well, I have a People's Choice Award that would help argue that point," Poppy balked.

Hal turned to Matt. "I thought you were a security guard, not a private detective!" Hal bellowed.

"Danika hired them," Greta calmly explained. "To find her stalker."

"So *Danika* was paying them?" Hal growled.

Greta hesitated. "Not exactly. There was a clause in her contract for added security, if necessary, and so—"

"I'm bankrolling these two clowns? Well, okay, if they work for me, then I can fire them!" Hal yelled at Greta before turning back to Poppy and Matt. "You're fired!"

"Twice in one day," Matt said under his breath.

Greta quietly said, "Hal, they still have contracts as actors—"

"It doesn't matter! I'm shutting down production until this whole ugly mess is figured out. If and when we start up again, it will be with an entirely new cast!"

And then Hal angrily waddled off, his face as red as a ripe tomato, followed on his heels by his loyal lieutenant, Greta.

Poppy and Matt exchanged resigned looks. Poppy's comeback and Matt's big break were both now officially kaput.

Chapter 16

Linda Appleton.

Poppy sat back in her chair in front of the desktop computer in the garage office, stunned.

She stared at the name again, making sure she had read the name right.

Sure enough, there it was in black-and-white on a news Web site.

Linda Appleton.

She had known the woman a long time ago.

And memories of that awful day way back in the mid-1980s when Linda had so tragically died suddenly came flooding back.

Poppy swiftly grabbed her phone and called to arrange an emergency meeting at the Desert Flowers Agency with her partners. Violet and Matt were already en route to the office. Iris was on the golf course and grumbled about having to cut her game short, but reluctantly agreed to come right away.

When they were all assembled, curious to know what was so important, Violet handed out cups of coffee to everyone as Poppy took the floor and solemnly addressed them.

"I've stumbled upon a possible development in the Danika Delgado murder I need to share with you," Poppy said, visibly rattled.

"Poppy, you look pale, perhaps you should sit down," Violet suggested, worried.

Poppy waved her off. "I'm fine, Violet."

"What is it?" Matt asked, concerned.

Poppy took a sip of her coffee, her hand slightly shaking, before setting the cup down and continuing. "When I happened upon Danika's body in her trailer the other day, I was struck by the crime scene, a woman's lifeless corpse with a pillow covering her face . . ." Poppy took a deep breath before pressing on, ". . . because it was eerily similar to a string of unsolved murders that occurred in Los Angeles back in the nineteen eighties during the time I was starring on *Jack Colt*."

"Oh my . . ." Violet gasped.

"Yes! Of course!" Iris cried, slapping her knee. She turned to Violet and Matt. "I was in Germany at the time but I remember reading all about it in the papers."

"The murders got a lot of press coverage because the three victims were all pretty young actresses working in Hollywood," Poppy explained. "They were all asphyxiated with a pillow and left in their beds, and so the perpetrator became known as—"

"The Pillow Talk Killer!" Iris shouted.

Poppy nodded gravely.

Matt leaned forward. "Did they ever catch the guy?"

"No," Poppy said. "There was mass hysteria in Hollywood, every young starlet was living in fear during that period, scared that they might be next. At the time, I was living in a friend's guest house and so I moved to a more secure high-rise in Westwood with a couple of girlfriends. We figured there would be safety in numbers."

"Wow, how have I not heard about any of this?" Matt wondered.

"Were you even born yet?" Iris asked sharply.

Matt shook his head.

"Then case closed on that!" Iris snapped.

"There was a massive investigation, the FBI was called in, but in the end, the killer was never caught. They could not even be certain the murders were carried out by the same person. There was a theory floating around that maybe the second two murders were copycat killings," Poppy said.

"Since they were actresses just like you, did you happen to know any of the victims?" Matt asked.

"One. We had gotten acquainted at a few casting offices where we both auditioned for small roles on the big shows at the time, *Dynasty*, *The A-Team*, *Scarecrow and Mrs. King*, this was a couple years before I got cast in *Jack Colt*. But I remember how shocked I was to hear on the news a few years later that she had been the third victim."

"Then she must have been the last victim," Iris said. "The killings stopped after three," Iris said.

"Yes, she was. Her name was Linda Appleton," Poppy said.

"Linda Appleton," Violet said, scratching her chin. "I don't think I have heard of her."

"She never did any consequential role, maybe a tooth-paste commercial and a tiny walk-on role on *The Dukes of Hazzard*, if I recall correctly," Poppy said. "Of course there is no telling what she might have become if her life hadn't been cut so short."

There was silence in the office.

Poppy could feel her emotions bubbling to the surface, tears starting to pool in her eyes, but she managed to keep it all in check.

"I hadn't thought of Linda in years, not until I discovered Danika's body. I would not allow myself to believe there was any connection between the two murders despite the similar crime scenes. How could I? Those murders occurred almost forty years ago, but then today . . ."

Poppy hesitated.

"What, Poppy?" Violet asked gently.

Another deep breath, and then Poppy forced herself to go on. "Today I was reading Danika's obituary online and there was a mention of her grandmother and the notorious circumstances surrounding her death."

"Linda Appleton!" Matt gasped.

"*What*?" Iris howled. "That cannot be a coincidence!"

"Do you think the killer has come out of retirement after all these years?" Violet asked.

Poppy shrugged. "Who knows? But there is an obvious connection, and I intend to find out exactly what it is."

"Count me in!" Matt said, jumping to his feet.

"Poppy, what can we do? I'm sure the police are well aware that Danika is . . . *was* Linda Appleton's grand-daughter, and are already investigating," Violet said.

"I'm sure they are," Poppy said matter-of-factly, "But that does not mean we have to sit idly by and wait for them to find the answers."

"It's just such a violent and disturbing case," Violet said, scrunching up her nose with distaste. "I do not think the Desert Flowers Detective Agency should be in the business of hunting for serial killers. It's too dangerous and gives me the willies."

"I agree with Violet for once," Iris huffed. "Let the police and FBI handle it. This is way above our pay grade."

"I understand completely," Poppy said. "If you two want to sit this one out, I absolutely respect your decision. But this is personal to me, and so I hope you respect *my* decision to launch my own probe."

Matt put an arm around Poppy. "Don't you worry, Poppy, I'll be your wingman on this."

"Thank you, Matt."

Violet's bottom lip quivered, upset that she might be letting Poppy down. Iris noticed and rolled her eyes with a heavy sigh. "I knew you would cave, Violet! You are such a wet noodle!" Iris turned to Poppy. "We are a team. We will do this together."

"Group hug!" Matt cried happily.

They all stared at him, but then gave up and embraced as a group.

Poppy exhaled, full of relief knowing that she would not be alone in this because she instinctively felt in her gut that she was going to need all the help she could get.

Chapter 17

Sherie Rogers.
Theresa Brooks.

Linda Appleton.

Poppy sat on her couch, which was still wrapped in the movers' plastic, cradling her laptop, staring at the names of the three victims of the notorious Pillow Talk Killer. She knew when she had returned home from the office she should have got cracking unpacking boxes and setting up her new home, but she couldn't help herself. She fired up her computer and started googling old articles from the 1980s detailing the horrific exploits of the Pillow Talk Killer. The haunting memories of that tense and frightening time came flooding back in Poppy's mind as she scrolled down through the vintage news coverage of the panic sweeping Hollywood, the pressure on the police to find the killer, the added security at all the studios in order to protect their stars.

Poppy's eyes pooled with tears as she came across photos of the three victims: Sherie from the Bronx, a warm smile, gorgeous afro, and smooth chocolate skin; Theresa from Port St. Lucie, Florida—freckled face, long brown hair, a twinkle in her eye; and then there was Linda, the only one Poppy ever had any personal contact with, a beautiful blonde with a fluffy haircut popularized by Heather Locklear, who had the envious distinction at the time of starring in not one but two hit TV shows on ABC, *Dynasty* and *TJ Hooker*. Poppy could not help but think, *If they had been lucky enough to survive, where would they be today*? It was such a travesty that their lives had been so cruelly snuffed out.

Another fact kept insidiously creeping into Poppy's mind, and she simply could not shake it. She had for years buried the "what if" scenario, refusing to tell anyone how close she had been to becoming victim number three of the Pillow Talk Killer instead of Linda Appleton.

It had so disturbed her, so rocked her to her core, that just the idea of revisiting the sequence of events had always been too traumatic for her. But now, unfortunately, having been the one who had found Danika dead in her trailer, Poppy could no longer ignore it.

Staring at those pictures, those three young, beautiful women in their prime on her computer screen, Poppy seemed to slowly drift away and slip back in time to that specific moment in her life, arguably a high point. She was single, on top of the world, banking fifteen grand a week on a top twenty–rated network TV show, featured on the cover of *TV Guide* magazine during that month of July with her impossibly handsome co-star Rod Harper, playfully chewing on his necktie and beaming into the camera while he smiled lovingly at her. Her life was far from perfect. When was anyone's life ever really perfect? But it was a heady time, and she was enjoying a dizzying height of success. Which was why what unexpectedly happened one steaming hot night a week after the Fourth of July in the City of Angels would suddenly change everything.

Hollywood, California
July 11, 1985

Poppy casually thumbed through her dog-eared script as she sat in the makeup chair while Dolly, a perky, blond zaftig woman fond of bright pink lipstick and a matching bow in her hair finished adding a little blush to her cheeks. It had been a long day and she was relieved they only had one more scene to shoot before the company wrapped for the day.

"I hear Linda and Joan are fighting again," Dolly announced breathlessly.

"Oh, yeah?" Poppy said, half-interested. The rumors of feuding between two of TV's top stars, Linda Evans and Joan Collins of the megahit prime time soap Dynasty *had become old news, but Poppy didn't want to appear rude and not engage with the excitable, gossipy Dolly. "What's got them going this time?"*

"Well, my girlfriend Connie works over there in the wardrobe department and apparently yesterday they were shooting another one of those catfight scenes. Seriously, how many of those can they do? A pillow fight, thrashing around in the lily pond, it's getting old. Anyway, yesterday during rehearsal Linda jabbed Joan in the eye and she finally put her foot down and stormed off the set and threatened to quit the show if Linda wasn't fired, as if that

would ever happen. Joan stewed in her dressing room the whole afternoon and they had to rewrite the entire scene. Aaron Spelling even had to come down to the set to play peacemaker."

"I'm glad we don't have that kind of drama on this set," Poppy said.

Rod could be a handful sometimes, showing up hung-over on occasion after partying too hard the night before and sometimes feeling the need to assert his masculinity by demanding he be allowed to perform his own stunts even after he tore a ligament by insisting he do a jump off a moving car himself, but other than that there were no misbehaving divas to contend with on Jack Colt. For Poppy's part, she was just happy to have a regular acting gig and had no desire to cause any trouble. When she was on the set she was in her happy place. But they did work her hard, and today she was anxious to go home and sink into a luxurious bubble bath in the Hollywood Hills guest house she was renting.

"Eyes up," Dolly instructed.

Poppy looked toward the ceiling as Dolly applied some mascara while humming her favorite song of the moment, Madonna's big hit "Material Girl." Dolly stepped back and inspected her work, then moved aside so Poppy could get a good look at herself in the mirror.

Dolly tapped her chin with the eyeliner as she placed her other hand on her hip. "Well, hello, gorgeous."

"I look tired," Poppy moaned.

"They'll fix it in post," Dolly cracked.

"Wouldn't it be wonderful if one day they could actually do that?" Poppy said, laughing.

The door opened, and another blonde breezed into the trailer. Tinseltown was teeming with blondes, a few even *natural, but this girl had very dark roots so she was probably not among the minority. This girl, Pam, was jaw-droppingly beautiful and seemed very sweet even though she was playing the guest role of a hardened, heartless criminal by the name of Bloody Mary, who had shot two guards while breaking her murderous boyfriend out of prison.*

"Are you ready for me yet?" Pam asked.

"Perfect timing, I'm just about done with Poppy," Dolly said. "Come on in and take a seat."

"Thank you," Pam said, smiling as she sat down in the chair next to Poppy. "Have you all seen the new James Bond movie yet?"

"No, I haven't had time," Poppy answered. "What's it called?"

Pam began fluffing her own hair. "A View to a Kill."

"I saw it," Dolly sighed. "It was long. But Grace Jones was good in it. Frankly, I like the song better than the movie."

"Tanya Roberts was the Bond girl," Pam said dismissively. "I would have been so much better."

Poppy suddenly remembered that Pam had made a splash her first week moving to Hollywood from Boise, Idaho, when she was literally plucked off a movie line and screen-tested for Charlie's Angels *to replace Shelley Hack, who had been unceremoniously fired after the fourth season. Although she came close to snagging the coveted role, the producers ultimately had gone with another actress—Tanya Roberts. Poppy was certain that Pam's career disappointment was coloring her opinion. Ms. Roberts could have delivered a performance on the scale of Sissy Spacek, Jessica Lange, or Meryl Streep, and Pam still would have thought she was lackluster.*

There was a knock at the door of the trailer and a chubby, scruffy-faced, curly-haired, eager kid in his early twenties pushed his way inside. "Ms. Harmon, they're ready for you on set."

Poppy stood up. "Thank you, Dolly. See you out there, Pam."

Dolly gave her a friendly wave as she got to work on primping Pam for the scene.

The rotund young production assistant held the door open for her and then hustled alongside Poppy as they hurried toward the set in silence.

Finally the kid seemed to work up the nerve to speak. "You were very good in that last scene, Ms. Harmon."

"Oh, thank you . . ."

Poppy stopped midsentence. She could never remember the kid's name. Was it Henry? Hank? She felt terrible. He had been working on the show for a couple of weeks already and she was usually good at memorizing everyone's names on the crew. He was waiting for her to say it so she just took a stab in the dark. ". . . Hank."

"Harold," the kid corrected her with a grin. "Harold Lawson."

At least he did not appear to be insulted by her memory lapse.

Searching for another topic to discuss, Harold asked Poppy if she had read the paper this morning to which she replied she hadn't. Harold then went on breathlessly about how the police were still frantically searching for the man known as the Pillow Talk Killer, how he smothered his two victims, at least so far, and how he had probably seen both of them on television.

"There hasn't been a crime that's gripped LA so much

since the Manson murders back in 1969," Harold said. "It's all anyone is talking about."

Harold continued his dissertation, recounting to Poppy his disconcerting knowledge of the crime scenes and how the killer had so far left no clues that might lead to his capture.

"He's a cunning SOB," Harold remarked.

Poppy tensed, then smiled, and said gently, "Harold, I'm sorry, can we talk about something else?"

"Of course," he said, chastised. "I'm sorry, I didn't mean to upset you."

She felt bad cutting him off. But she also found the entire conversation utterly distasteful, and it was souring her mood, and she needed to focus on her performance in the upcoming scene.

Mercifully, Harold switched topics to the weather and the impending heatwave that was going to melt Los Angeles by the weekend.

They arrived on the set of a remote cabin in the woods where Poppy's character, Daphne, was being held hostage by two escaped convicts, Butch and Smitty, and Butch's girlfriend, the aforementioned Bloody Mary played by Pam. The well-known character actor Norman Alden was in the Butch role and a young up-and-coming newcomer fresh from New York and Stella Adler's acting workshops, Kevin, was playing Smitty. Kevin was a heartbreaker, handsome face, playful brown eyes, a boyish grin and a gym-toned body. He had been shamelessly flirting with Poppy all week, which she admittedly enjoyed but did not take too seriously. As hard as Kevin tried, Poppy chose not to give him the time of day. Mostly because as much as she tried to deny it, her heart was elsewhere, specifi-

cally her co-star Rod Harper. During the audition process for Jack Colt, *she had had a mild crush, figuring every girl auditioning probably developed one on Rod. When she got cast in the part and they began shooting the show, the crush morphed into full-blown romantic feelings. And now, as they entered their second season of the show, Poppy just did her best to keep her feelings under wraps. Rod, after all, was an infamous man about town, found most weekends cavorting with the Playboy bunnies at Hugh Hefner's mansion. He certainly was not relationship material, and Poppy had long made peace with that.*

Still, when they were posing for that TV Guide *cover, he had been so focused on her, so interested. A small part of her could not help but suspect the feeling might, just might, be mutual. Of course, she would never be brave enough to come out and ask him. If she was wrong, it could harm the chemistry they shared and alter the dynamic of their working relationship. She just could not take that chance.*

Pam soon appeared and they all waited for Jack to finally burst out of his dressing room. After a ten-minute wait with Poppy yawning and checking her watch, fearing Jack's tardiness would lead to them shooting the scene late into the night, Jack finally sauntered onto the set, ready to shoot. He was in military-style cargo pants, shirtless, and brandishing an intimidating prop knife. The scene they were about to shoot was the typical "Jack rescues Daphne" scene, she in peril, he flying in at the last second to save her. They had done this scene in a number of variations about a dozen times already, but the viewers loved it. As a self-avowed feminist, Poppy cringed at the sexism of her role, but today, at least she got to fight back, according to the script, by slinging hot coffee in

Bloody Mary's face when Jack blows through the door in a surprise attack.

A couple of crew members hosed Jack down since in the previous scene, shot a few days earlier on location in Big Bear, Jack emerged from the lake near the cabin like a Navy Seal, the knife between his teeth, muscles flexing, ready for action. He crawled on the ground so as not to be seen, taking point outside the cabin's kitchen window, where an eagle-eyed Daphne spotted him. He signaled her to be ready while she was preparing a pot of hot coffee for her captors and now was the time for the final confrontation.

The director didn't bother to discuss the scene with the principals since they had done it so many times. He just dropped down in his director's chair waiting for camera speed and lethargically called, "Action!"

Pam, determined to win an Emmy for her bold turn as a malevolent bad girl, stormed over to Poppy and grabbed her by the arm, snarling, "What's taking so long with that coffee, sweet cakes? Are you harvesting the beans yourself, or what?"

Poppy shook her arm free. "I think we'd all be a lot happier if you tried a little decaf, sweet cakes."

Butch and Smitty snickered at the joke, which infuriated Pam/Bloody Mary.

Pam glared at Poppy, grabbing her arm again and squeezing it tight. "Get cute with me, and you can get hurt, got it?"

There was a knocking sound outside the cabin.

Smitty, alarmed, jumped out of his chair. "What was that?"

"What?" Butch growled.

"That noise. Somebody's out there!" Smitty cried.

"*Relax, will ya? Nobody knows we're here,*" Butch sighed.

"*I'm tellin' ya, Butch, I heard something,*" Smitty insisted.

"*Fine, if you think there's somebody out there, go check it out for yourself then,*" Butch said, tossing him a gun, which Smitty fumbled on the catch.

"*Careful,*" Smitty whined. "*I nearly shot my toe off.*"

Butch ignored him.

Smitty huffily marched over to the door and swung it open. Standing there in all his Rambo glory was Jack, who struck with a punch in the face. Smitty doubled over and Jack kneed him in the groin. Smitty flopped down to the floor, writhing.

Butch, now alerted, struggled to stand up as Jack dove at him and they rolled around on the floor. Pam started for the gun Smitty had dropped and that was Poppy's cue to hurl the scalding pot of hot coffee at Bloody Mary, drenching her. Pam covered her face with her hands, spasming and screaming, like a true Method actress. After a brief scuffle, Jack managed to finish off Butch so the only two left standing were Jack and Daphne.

"*Oh, Jack!*" Poppy exclaimed, like she had so many times before, and ran to Jack where he embraced her, holding her tightly against his bare chest, muscles glistening.

"*It's okay, Daph, I'm here . . .*"

"*And cut!*" the director said listlessly. "*Great. Moving on to coverage.*"

Now they would repeat the scene multiple times for different angles and close-ups, at least another two or three hours of work.

Jack still held Poppy tightly against his chest.

"He said cut, Rod, you can let go now," Poppy said.

"Do I have to?"

Poppy giggled, then wanted to kick herself. Really? Did she have to giggle like a high school cheerleader in the arms of the star quarterback? It was downright embarrassing.

"When are we finally going to go for that drink, Poppy, just the two of us?" Rod asked, grinning.

"Oh, please, you are such a tease," Poppy scolded as she tried to extricate herself from his embrace, which caused him to just hold on tighter.

"Haven't you made me wait long enough?" Rod asked, fake pouting. "Come on, don't you find the scent of my manly sweat irresistible?"

Poppy scrunched up her nose, laughing.

He finally let go when the stunt coordinator approached him with a note on the choreographed fight scene with Butch.

Poppy tried not to stare at him.

Bloody Mary suddenly appeared at her right shoulder. "He's dreamy, isn't he?"

The question didn't surprise Poppy. She was very well aware of the fact that millions of women found Rod Harper to be breathtakingly sexy, but she was not about to let on that she was one of them. "Who, Rod? I think of him like a brother."

"You're kidding," Pam said, a disbelieving look on her face. "You two have never hit the sack?"

"No, absolutely not," Poppy said.

"Well, I'll be sure to let you know what you're missing."

"What do you mean?"

"He asked me out this morning. We're getting together

at his place later after we wrap. I'm so excited to see his house. I hear Humphrey Bogart used to own it before he married Lauren Bacall."

Pam pranced off excitedly, leaving Poppy behind, standing on the set alone. She kept a firm smile on her face, but she was devastated, and after the director announced a fifteen-minute break while they reset the scene, she slinked back to her dressing room, hoping that until she was finally alone, she would not cry.

Chapter 18

Poppy was halfway back to her dressing room after wrapping for the day, eager to shed Daphne's tight-fitting costume specifically designed to accentuate her curvaceous figure, don some casual street clothes, and head home to unwind with a long luxurious bubble bath and a glass of Chardonnay, when she was intercepted by Rod. He managed to corner her in the hallway of the cavernous soundstage, and stood so close to her she could smell his pungent body odor from all the running and brawling he had done in the scene they had just shot. She couldn't help but crinkle her nose slightly. Rod picked up on it immediately.

He lifted his arm and sniffed. "Yeah, I know, I'm a little rancid and need a shower." Then with a lascivious smile, he added, "Care to join me?"

Usually she would just laugh off his suggestive com-

ments, but today she was in no mood to do so. "Not today, Rod."

She made a move to circle around him, but he quickly stepped to the right, blocking her path. "Come on, it's been a long day, for both of us, why don't we freshen up and meet for a drink to wind down?"

Poppy gave him a puzzled look. "Tonight?"

Rod nodded. "My treat. How about the Roosevelt, in the bar, one hour?"

"What about Pam?"

Rod took a step back, lips pursed, stumped. "Who?"

"Pam, the actress playing Bloody Mary. We've been working with her all week," Poppy reminded him.

A light bulb seemed to go off in his head but it didn't appear to be very bright. "Oh, her. What about her?"

"She told me you two had plans together later."

Rod was genuinely perplexed. "She did?"

"Yes."

Rod shrugged. "Well, she may have mentioned meeting up at some point earlier, but it was nothing definitive, and I would much rather spend time with you, to be honest."

At this point, Poppy did not know what to think.

Pam had been so excited and eager to share her upcoming romantic rendezvous with Rod to everyone within earshot.

Had she been lying?

Rod barely seemed to even know who she was.

It was becoming clear that perhaps Pam had at least been exaggerating her chemistry with Rod, if not downright lying about it.

Still, Poppy had learned to be cautious when it came

*to her charismatic co-star, fearing his lothario-like ten-
dencies would eventually come back to bite her.*

"The thing is, Rod, I'm really tired tonight—"

*He instantly put a finger to her lips. "Please, Poppy,
we've both been promising to spend more time together
outside of work, but we never seem to get around to it.
Let's just grab a drink and relax." He could sense Poppy's
hesitation. "Come on, gorgeous, just one drink . . ."*

His eyes twinkled.

She hated it when they did that.

*Because she found herself weakening, like the hapless
subject of a master hypnotist. If there was one thing about
Rod Harper that a good deal of the female population in
America knew; it was that he could be overpoweringly intoxicating.*

Like 190 proof.

*Poppy, lost in those beautiful eyes, could not help but
finally succumb. "One drink?"*

*Rod nodded, delighted, and then playfully grabbed
Poppy's pinky finger with his own. "One drink, I swear,
pinky promise."*

Poppy laughed, slapping his hand away.

"Should I pick you up at your place?" Rod asked.

*"No, I'll meet you there," Poppy said before pinching
her nose with her thumb and forefinger. "Now, for everybody's sake, please go take that shower."*

*Rod sniffed himself again. "Is it that bad? You sure it's
just not my natural manly scent?" He raised his arm,
which sent Poppy scurrying away, down the hall to her
dressing room. She could hear Rod chuckle as he headed
off in the opposite direction.*

As Poppy passed one of the guest star dressing rooms,

*she overheard Pam talking on the phone to a friend about
her plans with Rod Harper later that evening. Poppy debated whether or not she should tell Pam that Rod had no
intention of meeting her later, that to be generous, they
had somehow gotten their signals crossed, but she decided to stay out of it. If Pam was telling everyone she
and Rod were involved romantically or otherwise, that
was her business. And it was Rod's job, not Poppy's, to
make that clear to Pam. Poppy continued on to her own
dressing room to change and head home to get ready before meeting Rod.*

Poppy glanced at her watch.

10:09 PM.

She had left the studio at eight o'clock and after a
quick change at home, she had arrived at the iconic Roosevelt Hotel bar in Hollywood just a few minutes past
nine. Rod had said he wanted to meet at the bar in one
hour. That was now over an hour ago. She stared at the
mostly melted ice in her glass wondering if she should
order another drink and give him a little more time.
Poppy's mood had not yet soured. Anything could have
delayed Rod. Perhaps the director had approached him
as he was leaving with some script changes, or a few au-
tograph hounds had descended upon him when he
stopped to gas up his Corvette at the Mobil station in his
neighborhood. She was optimistic by nature, but not
naive, and right now Rod was testing that steady opti-
mism.

She was sitting at the end of the bar, swirling around
the tiny chunks of what was left of the ice with a green
plastic stirrer, when the young, handsome bartender

swung around to her side of the bar. "Another vodka soda?"

Poppy covered the top of her glass with her hand. "No, I'm good, thank you."

The bartender gave her a rueful smile.

Please, God, no pity from the bartender.

He knew she was waiting for someone.

When a gentleman earlier had made a move to sit down on the stool next to her, she had politely informed him that she was meeting someone and was saving the seat for him. The man apologized and sat down a few stools away from her. The bartender had overheard and so now, almost an hour later, he was assuming she had been stood up.

And maybe she had been.

But Rod had been so insistent.

Perhaps he had been in a car accident.

As she thought about it, she wanted to kick herself.

Why did she always try to make excuses for him? She knew there had been no car accident. Rod was just being Rod. He would show up at some point, full of excuses. And she knew she would forgive him as she always did, and then go home and promise herself she would not fall for his charms ever again, even if it was just to keep peace and calm on the set of Jack Colt.

The bartender appeared again and set down a vodka soda with a wedge of lime in front of her.

Poppy sat up straight on her barstool, confused. "I'm sorry, I thought I said I didn't want another."

"You did," the bartender said amiably.

"Well, I hope this isn't a free cocktail because you feel sorry for me that my date is so far a no-show."

The bartender shook his head. "It's not from me. It's

from that gentleman over there." He stepped aside and gestured toward a good-looking blond man, mid-thirties, in a tan corduroy sports coat, white shirt, and bright red tie. The man smiled and waved nervously over to Poppy. She picked up the drink, toasted him, and took a sip. The bartender scooted off to attend to several people who clustered around his serving station wanting to order something.

Poppy never knew what to do in these kinds of situations. The man continued smiling at her, perhaps psyching himself up to get up and walk over and introduce himself. She prayed he would not. She was not in the right frame of mind for idle chitchat. She simply wanted to grab her purse and get out of there and drive home, silently cursing Rod Harper the whole way.

The blond man swallowed the rest of his beer, slammed the mug down on top of the bar, and hopped off his stool.

Poppy hoped he was just going to the men's room or leaving the bar altogether, but no such luck. He circled around and walked right up to her.

"I probably shouldn't have stopped and just kept going," he said sheepishly.

"I beg your pardon?"

"Well, I can tell by the sense of dread on your face that you do not have the slightest interest in talking to me."

"That's not true," Poppy lied.

"Really? I'm pretty good at reading faces."

"It's not you . . ."

"Yeah, usually when a woman tells you that, you can be sure it most definitely is."

"I'm sorry, I don't mean to be rude. . . ."

"Translation, please go away before I reach for my pepper spray," the man joked.

Poppy smiled.

"Oh my God . . ." the man gasped.

"What?"

"That smile of yours . . . it's breathtaking."

Poppy found herself rolling her eyes.

"I know, my wife says I could fill a book with all my cornball clichés that fail to impress women."

A wave of relief washed over Poppy.

He was married.

"Don't be so hard on yourself," Poppy said, looking at him for the first time.

He was more handsome up close. Piercing green eyes. A cute pair of dimples. Perfect white teeth. And again, married. So no threat. Why not invite him to join her while she nursed the drink he had just bought for her. And so she did.

He seized the opportunity to slide onto the stool next to her and continue their conversation.

"Don," he said extending a hand.

"Poppy, Poppy Harmon," she said taking it.

Don proved to be a talker. The wife he referred to turned out to be his ex-wife so Poppy's guard went up again. She also found it odd that he never provided a last name. But he was engaging and pleasant and definitely eye-catching enough that Poppy didn't worry about it too much. He was a salesman from Phoenix, in town on business hawking some kind of medical device he described in detail, but unfortunately Poppy's mind wandered through most of it. She sipped her drink, successfully enlisting her acting skills to pretend she was interested and he seemed to buy her performance.

Don had not been aware Poppy was an actress by trade, nor had he ever watched Jack Colt *since he spent* most of the time on the road for his job and not watching much television. A lot of men told her they had never heard of Jack Colt when, of course, they had and probably seen a number of episodes. They didn't want her believing they were chasing after her just because she was famous and had some money to her name. But Poppy actually believed Don, he seemed genuine in his surprise that she was in a network TV show.

Still, there was something off about him and she could not pinpoint exactly what was bothering her.

He was exceedingly polite, respectful, and again, strikingly attractive. And so she did not immediately shut him down when he suggested they take their conversation up to his room and have another drink.

Poppy had no doubt that Don was on the hunt for more than just having a nightcap with her. And she was feeling so low, now two hours after she was supposed to meet Rod here, that she briefly considered accepting his invitation. But she knew she could not make a rash decision to basically have a sexual encounter with a complete stranger based on her faltering self-esteem in this particular moment. That would be a disaster.

And so she calmly downed the rest of her cocktail, put the empty glass down on the coaster in front of her, and smiled at Don. "Thank you, Don, but I think it's time for me to go home."

His eyes could not conceal his disappointment, but he was enough of a gentleman to accept the rejection gracefully. "Poppy, it has been a pleasure. . . ." He took her hand and kissed the top of it.

"Good night," she said, smiling. She nodded to the bartender and was heading for the exit when she noticed a boozy, bleary-eyed, buxom woman at the opposite end *of the bar. She had obviously been there for some time. She recognized her as an actress she had seen at a few casting offices around town when they were both auditioning for the same part, but Poppy could not remember her name.*

Poppy acknowledged the woman with a brief smile, but the woman did not return it. She was too busy zeroing in on Don. Poppy glanced back to see Don returning the woman's gaze, and as Poppy turned the corner, she saw Don get up and join the woman.

Don was clearly on the prowl, determined to get lucky. And if it was not going to be Poppy, he would find someone else.

She had clearly made the right choice.

However, at the time she had no clue that it was a choice that possibly saved her life.

Chapter 19

There was no call from Rod on Poppy's answering machine when she got home, and no word from him when her alarm went off early the next morning. She hastily dressed and hurried out to her car in order to make her call time at the studio. When she arrived, parking in her usual space, she spotted Rod leaning against his Corvette, amiably chatting with guest star Pam, playfully twirling her long blond hair around with his finger. Pam giggled and cooed, hanging on his every word, and then, when he thought no one was looking, Rod leaned in and planted a brief kiss on her lips. Pam nearly lost her balance she was so woozy from his touch.

Poppy could feel her cheeks reddening. She felt foolish and embarrassed and ashamed of herself for once again giving in to Rod Harper's charms and then getting burned. She promised herself it would never, ever happen again. As she marched past Rod and Pam toward the sound-

stage, eyes fixed straight ahead, she could hear Rod calling after her. She kept going, ignoring him, until he managed to run and catch up to her.

"Poppy, wait . . ." he shouted as he grabbed her arm to slow her down. "What's the big hurry?"

She silently centered herself, then spun around to face him. "I need to get to makeup and hair, Rod. What is it?"

He reared back a bit, surprised by her huffy tone. "I just wanted to apologize again for having to bail on you last night."

"Again? What do you mean, apologize again? I never heard a word from you last night," she snapped.

"I left a message on your answering machine. Didn't you get it?"

"No, Rod, I didn't," Poppy sighed, so tired of hearing his lame excuses.

"That's weird," Rod said, genuinely perplexed. "I could have sworn I dialed the right number. It sounded like your voice on the recording."

Poppy wheeled around to walk away from him, but he jogged ahead of her and positioned himself in front of her, stopping her in her tracks. "Coppola's in town meeting with actors to star in his next film. He's already got Kathleen Turner attached, it's a great script, Peggy Sue Got Married. My agent says Nicolas Cage is in the running and will probably get it, but Coppola wanted to sit down with me personally. He only had an hour to meet me for a drink before flying to New York so I had to get right over to TriStar. I called you on my car phone on the way over to say I had to cancel."

Poppy studied him, not sure if he was truly being honest or just delivering another one of his performances.

"Please, Poppy, I know I left a message. Maybe something's wrong with your answering machine."

There was nothing wrong with her answering machine.

She was fairly certain he had been so excited about the last-minute meeting, so eager to impress the legendary director, he had plum forgot to call her and cancel, and was now trying to cover for himself. Rod would always be Rod. And she knew she could never change him. So in order to keep the peace in their working relationship, she once more would give him the benefit of the doubt.

"How did it go?"

Rod shrugged. *"I thought we hit it off, and he was very complimentary of my acting, but I may be a little too old for the part. The character, Charlie, is supposed to be a senior in high school."*

"Oh . . ." Poppy whispered.

"I know, it might be a stretch, but he promised to keep me in mind for any future projects down the road if this doesn't work out, so it was definitely worth it to take the meeting."

"That's great news," Poppy said, forcing a smile.

"Can we try again tonight?" Rod asked, hopefully.

Before she could answer, Pam interrupted them, slightly pouting for having been ditched by Rod so he could chase after Poppy. *"Excuse me, Rod, my manager is having a little soiree tonight at his house in Beachwood, and I was wondering, depending on what time we wrap, if you'd like to come with me?"*

Rod frowned. *"Sorry, doll, Poppy and I were just talking about—"*

Poppy quickly interjected, *"Tonight is not good for me, Rod, so feel free to go to that cocktail party with Pam."*

Pam, whose whole body had stiffened in front of Poppy when she first approached, was quickly put at ease and smiled sweetly at her.

"Now, I really need to get my face and hair done. See you both on set," Poppy said, finally managing to escape, determined to keep her guard up from here on out when it came to the skirt-chasing Rod Harper.

When Poppy entered the hair and makeup trailer, Dolly was glued to a portable television set next to the counter. There were a few stylists and assistants all gathered around, listening intently to a news report.

Poppy had made a move to sit down in one of the chairs in front of the giant mirror when she stopped cold at the sound of the TV news reporter's voice. "Police say they are fairly certain this is not a copycat crime, but that the Pillow Talk Killer has struck again, for a third time in the past four months."

Poppy gasped. "There's been another murder?"

Dolly glanced back at Poppy. "She was found in her bed by her roommate this morning, a pillow over her face."

Poppy joined the others over by the TV as the reporter continued. "The victim's name is Linda Appleton, an up-and-coming actress who has appeared in small roles in several film and television productions including The Dukes of Hazzard.*"*

There was a photo of the aspiring actress on the TV screen.

Poppy suddenly felt dizzy.

It was her.

The tipsy woman she had seen at the bar last night.

The one her admirer had focused in on after she rejected him.

Poppy, a bit wobbly, grabbed onto Dolly's arm for support.

"Everything okay, hon?" Dolly asked, concerned.

Poppy nodded slightly and then said hoarsely, "I'll be back. I need to make a quick call."

She stumbled to her dressing room and shut the door. She picked up the phone and called her agent, Diane Lipton, a tough-as-nails battle-ax who had been guiding her career for the past five years. She was also the first person Poppy called in a crisis. Diane's assistant cheerfully asked Poppy to please hold as Diane was finishing up another call.

Poppy's mind furiously flashed with images from the night before, Linda Appleton at the bar, the salesman from somewhere, she couldn't recall, eyeing her as Poppy left, getting up from his barstool to go join her.

Was he the last person to see Linda Appleton alive?

What if the salesman was actually the Pillow Talk Killer trolling the bars searching for his next victim?

What if Poppy had agreed to his proposition and gone with him up to his hotel room? Would she have been the killer's next victim? She shuddered at the thought.

Suddenly a voice made gravelly by too many cigarettes came on the line. "What's up? Don Juan having a category five star tantrum on the set?"

Don Juan.

That's what Diane always called Rod.

Don.

That was it!

The name of the salesman at the Roosevelt Bar.

"I know you're still there, I can hear you breathing," Diane said, shuffling papers in the background.

"I'm sorry, it's just that, I don't know how to say this,

Diane, but I think I may have encountered the Pillow Talk Killer last night," Poppy said solemnly.

This got Diane's attention.

She spewed out a litany of four-letter expletives before demanding a more detailed explanation.

As Poppy quickly filled her in, Diane was unusually quiet on the other end of the phone. When she finished, there was a few more moments of silence and then another loud expletive.

"Should I go to the police?" Poppy asked.

"What the hell for?" Diane howled.

"To tell them what I know."

"How can you be sure this sales guy is the killer?"

"I'm not. But any information I can give might help with the investigation."

"Sure, if you want to do that."

Poppy could sense Diane's reluctance.

"You don't think I should?"

"Look, I would never suggest you not do the right thing, but it's not like you're an eyewitness to the actual murder, you just saw the victim out in public, and some random guy trying to start up a conversation."

"It seems pretty important."

"Then call them. It's the right thing to do, I guess. I would just hate for you to get caught up in all this, and it somehow adversely affect your career."

Now this got Poppy's attention. "How is that possible?"

"I don't know, I'm just thinking out loud, but it could taint you, the Enquirer *would have a field day tying you to this whole Pillow Talk Killer mess, and you know how the studios hate even the whiff of a scandal."*

"Scandal? But I'm just relaying what I saw."

"Poppy, I support whatever you're going to do. Now I have to take this call."

That meant a more important client was on the other line.

There was a click.

She put down the phone and pondered Diane's advice.

And instantly tossed it aside.

Poppy was not going to hide potentially key information just for the sake of her career. She picked up the phone again and dialed the operator for the number of the LAPD tip line.

What she did not know at the time was that her phone call would be all for naught because the Pillow Talk Killer would never be caught.

Chapter 20

"My husband was most definitely *not* the Pillow Talk Killer," Rosemarie Carter sniffed as she dabbed her ruddy, heavily rouged face with a tissue in an effort to sop up the tears streaming down her cheeks.

"I'm sorry," Poppy said somberly. "I know this must be difficult for you to talk about."

Poppy, Iris, and Violet huddled around Rosemarie Carter's small table with its stained red-and-white-checkered tablecloth in a cramped alcove. The sun streaming through the windows brightened what was otherwise a drab, threadbare kitchen with worn appliances and a scuffed, smudged floor in desperate need of mopping. Poppy glanced over at Iris, whose nose was scrunched up in distaste at the musty, squalid surroundings. Poppy tried signaling her to stop, but Iris failed to pick up on her cue. Violet, however, gamely drank the coffee Rosemarie had offered them when they first arrived and pretended not to notice how unkempt the house was. As for Rosemarie herself, she appeared to have long given up on making herself look presentable, drowning in a shopworn wool sweater despite the hot temperature outside, a faded blue housedress, and slippers. Her hair was matted and unwashed. In fact, her only attempt to gussy herself up for company was the slabs of rouge on both her cheeks, which was incongruous with the rest of her dowdy appearance. Perhaps it was out of habit from when she was a younger woman, or a half-hearted attempt to paint over the cracks of time that were rapidly taking over her face. But the effect was disconcerting, a little too Baby Jane.

What had brought Poppy, Iris, and Violet to this rundown neighborhood in Indio today was the crack investigative work of Iris's grandson Wyatt, who when presented with the name "Don" by Poppy, the man she had witnessed approaching Linda Appleton at the Roosevelt on the night she was murdered, took only five minutes to come up with a full name from his online research.

"Don Carter," Wyatt had said at the garage office, pointing to a black-and-white photo on his computer screen. "Is that the guy, Poppy?"

"Yes, that's him," Poppy said, shuddering. "After I phoned the police, I heard they brought him in for questioning. After that, I tried to move on and didn't closely follow the case. I read something later on, how although he had been a focus of the investigation, an arrest was never made."

Wyatt nodded. "Yup. And according to this *Vanity Fair* article I found written about the murders back in 2005, since the killer was never caught, there was a cloud of suspicion around Carter for the rest of his life."

"He died?" Poppy asked.

"Way back in 1994."

"Oh . . ." Poppy murmured.

"But his wife is still alive and she's living right here in the Coachella Valley. I found her home address in Indio from public records."

Poppy had been hesitant to call the woman and possibly reopen old wounds, but she was determined to find out if Danika's death was in any way connected to the original Pillow Talk Killer murder spree that had plagued Hollywood in the 1980s. At this point, Rosemarie Carter was her only lead and so Poppy called her. As expected, Rosemarie initially resisted Poppy's request to meet, especially since she made it crystal clear she did not want to talk about the horrific crimes that had engulfed her husband all those years ago. The past, along with her husband, was long ago dead and buried.

But when Rosemarie realized Poppy was the Poppy Harmon from the old *Jack Colt* show, she wavered, as if the idea of a TV actress swinging by for coffee and a chat would be some kind of novelty, a way to brighten up an otherwise dull day. She had told Poppy that she could stop by for a visit in the morning before eleven and stay for thirty minutes tops because Rosemarie had to take her dachshund, Shelby, to the vet in Palm Desert at noon. Iris and Violet did not like the idea of Poppy driving out alone to a remote house in Indio to see a woman who might have been married to a serial killer and known about it, and so they had insisted on accompanying her.

And so here the three of them were, sipping bitter coffee and eating stale sugar cookies in a ramshackle house with an unkempt, oddly mannered woman whose late husband had been a prime suspect in the murders.

Rosemarie finished dabbing her face and crumpled the tissue up in her hand, squeezing it tightly. "I never knew Don was mixed up in any of that horrible mess, not until we were married, and some reporter came poking around, asking me questions about how it felt to be sleeping in the same bed as a murderer! It was awful! I had no idea what he was talking about. I confronted Don that day when he got home from work, and he finally admitted that he had been with that Appleton woman on the night she was killed, but when she left his hotel room, she was very much alive."

"When did you and your late husband meet?" Violet asked gently.

"In 1989, years after the murders. Don said he didn't tell me about being a suspect in a homicide investigation because he loved me so much, and was afraid I might be scared off. But I wouldn't have been. I loved him too much, and there was no way in my mind that he could be in anyway depraved or violent. I trusted him. He was a good man who just happened to be in the wrong place at the wrong time."

Poppy studied Rosemarie's clownish face, which despite her efforts with a massive amount of rouge to cover it up, managed to convey a sense of trustworthiness.

Iris, whose arms were stiffly folded across her chest, was not as inclined to believe what Rosemarie was saying. Violet, on the other hand, offered Rosemarie an encouraging smile, which went a long way in keeping her calm as she spoke of her dear departed husband.

"Apparently it was an anonymous tip from some actress he had met that got the police after Don. I'd sure as hell like to know who it was," Rosemarie spat out.

Poppy swallowed hard as Iris and Violet threw her nervous glances. Poppy remained steady, choosing not to share the information with Rosemarie that the actress in question was at present sitting at her kitchen table, because she did not want Rosemarie abruptly shutting down the conversation and ordering them out. Instead, she decided to breeze right past it. "So your husband did admit leaving the bar with Ms. Appleton?"

Rosemarie nodded sedately. "Yes. He never lied about that. They went to his room for a nightcap, and then, well, he was divorced from his first wife at the time, nobody should blame him for wanting to be . . . social. Anyway, after they, you know, finished, she went home. And that's where she was killed. In her home. Not Don's hotel room. I never understood why people thought Don could have done it. The desk clerk at the hotel said he saw Don leave right after the Appleton girl, like he was following her, but Don was a smoker and he just went out for a pack of cigarettes. Of course, the desk clerk was on his break when Don came back and didn't see him. It was a nightmare. Don spent the rest of his life denying he was in any way involved, trying to set the record straight, but because the cops never found the killer, there was always that constant suspicion hanging around him. I can't tell you how many crank calls we used to get, asking if the Pillow Talk Killer was at home, saying Don was going to burn in hell. We had to change our number every six months. The stress finally took its toll on poor Don, and he died of a heart attack nine years later. I was devastated, of course, but I remember thinking, finally he'll get some peace."

There was absolute quiet in the kitchen broken only by

Rosemarie's sniffles. She raised the wadded-up tissue in her hand and began wiping her face again.

Poppy finally stood up. "We've taken up enough of your time, Rosemarie. Thank you for the coffee and cookies. And I hope everything turns out fine for Shelby at the vet." She glanced over at the dachshund, who was snoozing in a quilted doggie bed next to the refrigerator.

Rosemarie nodded, thanked them for coming by, but did not make a move to show them to the door. Poppy turned and left through the kitchen door, which led to a walkway to the street as Iris and Violet followed suit.

After they all piled into Iris's car and were driving away, Violet, who sat in the back, reached over and gingerly touched Poppy's shoulder. "I know what you're thinking, and I want you to stop it."

Poppy swiveled her head around. "What are you talking about, Violet?"

"You are feeling guilty about calling the police to report Don Carter all those years ago. You somehow feel it's your fault he died, and that is simply nonsense!" Iris barked, hands gripping the steering wheel as she kept her eyes fixed on the road.

"How do you two know me so well?" Poppy sighed.

"Because we're your best friends," Violet piped in. "And just to be clear, you absolutely did the right thing. What if Don *had* been the killer and you didn't make that call? Who knows how many more poor girls he might have gone after? Better safe than sorry!"

"But I ruined his life. . . ." Poppy whispered, consumed with guilt.

It would take a long time for her to come to grips with what she had done, how her actions had changed the course of Don Carter's life. In her mind, the best way for her to cope now was to find out who smothered Danika Delgado to death because there was a very real possibility that this killer was the same one who had rampaged Hollywood over thirty-six years ago. And if she did find him, then perhaps she might find some belated justice for Don Carter, not to mention his first three victims.

Chapter 21

The house was located at the end of a dusty, deserted road on the outskirts of Desert Hot Springs. The structure appeared to be unstable and teetering, on the verge of collapse if suddenly buffeted by the stiff valley winds. There was a cracked window and large chips of stucco missing. A 2008 Toyota Corolla was parked out front and the license plate matched what Wyatt had found in the DMV records.

"Looks like we found him," Matt said as he and Poppy both hopped out of his Prius and made their way toward the tiny house, which was actually more of a shack. They were about fifty feet from the front door when it was suddenly flung open and a young man emerged holding a rifle.

He cocked it. "Don't come any closer!"

Poppy instantly recognized the man. The beady eyes. The beak nose. Acne-scarred complexion. Greasy black hair. This was the obsessive man who had cornered Danika in the gym before they spooked him and he managed to run off. This was Byron Savage.

Byron aimed the rifle in Matt's direction. "I know who you are! You're the guy who tried to beat me up!"

Matt slowly raised his hands in the air. "To be fair, you were accosting a friend of mine."

"I wasn't accosting anybody! I was just trying to tell her how much she meant to me! And then you had to show up and ruin everything!"

Matt took a small step forward. "Look, would you mind putting the gun down so we can talk—?"

Byron fired a shot that slammed into the ground, kicking up a cloud of dirt near Matt, who stood frozen in place.

"I said, don't come any closer!"

Matt nodded, hands still in the air, as Poppy hovered just behind him, still in shock from the sudden gunshot.

"Now turn around and get in your car and leave, and there won't be any more trouble!" Byron yelled, waving the rifle around haphazardly, but still aiming in their general direction.

Matt kept his eyes fixed on the barrel of the gun as it moved around. "Okay, we'll go, but if you won't talk to us, you better be prepared to talk to the police."

"Why? I didn't do anything!" Byron protested.

"You stalked an actress, trespassed on a film set, physically held her against her will—" Matt said slowly, deliberately, taking another tiny step forward without thinking.

Another shot fired in the dirt to the right of Matt. More dust kicked up causing Matt to cough. Matt and Poppy did not dare to make another move. Byron stamped his foot, frustrated. "You're twisting around what happened! I just wanted to meet Danika in person. I figured if she got to know me, she'd see how devoted I am to her, how much I care about her . . ."

"Maybe if you explain it to us, we can go to the police and tell them what really happened so you won't have to," Matt suggested.

Byron mulled this over before aiming his rifle right between Matt's eyes. "Is this some kind of trick?"

"No trick, I promise," Matt said, raising his hands over his head even higher, still standing in front of Poppy, shielding her from any flying bullets.

Byron finally lowered his gun, pointing the barrel toward the wooden porch steps. Then he waved for them to come inside.

Matt started walking toward the house.

"Matt, no!" Poppy whispered under her breath.

"I'll be okay. But you better stay out here," Matt said, locking eyes with Byron like a hunter would with a wild animal, trying to read whether it might suddenly spring forward and attack. Byron, at this point, however, appeared rather docile and almost welcoming.

"I will not allow you to go inside there alone," Poppy said, following on his heels.

Byron opened the door and ushered them inside, making sure to leave the rifle perched next to the door outside so his guests would not be so jumpy.

Once they crossed the threshold, Poppy's eyes were instantly drawn to a corner in the living room with a pristine glass case filled with framed photos of Danika Delgado, prayer candles, publicity stills, memorabilia, a small tablet playing her YouTube videos on a loop. It was so impressive and well kept and in direct contrast to the rest of the house, with its ripped, ratty furniture and stained wall-paper. The place was more downtrodden than Rose-marie Carter's house. But the shrine was almost majestic. Matt inhaled sharply once he noticed it.

Byron beamed proudly. "It brings me great comfort during this sad time. I sit in front of it for hours and pre-tend she's still with us."

Both Poppy and Matt declined to comment.

Byron gestured toward the couch. "Would you like to sit down?"

Poppy glanced over and saw a spring protruding up through the worn upholstery of the lumpy cushion. She swung back around and smiled. "No, thank you, I prefer standing."

Byron shrugged. "Suit yourself. I feel so lucky that I was able to find Danika and have a real moment with her before she . . ." Tears pooled in Byron's eyes. "I can't even talk about it."

Poppy and Matt exchanged curious glances. Byron seemed genuinely broken up over the fact Danika was dead. Although it could all still be a well-orchestrated act to throw suspicion off himself.

"Byron, how did you manage to track down Danika at the resort where she was shooting her movie?" Poppy asked gently.

"Oh, that was easy!" Byron excitedly said, snapping out of his melancholy mood. "I follow her on Instagram. She was posting selfies and videos all the time. Of course, she would never be stupid enough to come out and say where she was, I mean, that would draw out all the crazies, but she made sure I had the right clues!"

"How did she do that?" Matt wondered.

"I studied the reflections in the pools of her eyes," Byron said, impressed with himself.

Matt's mouth dropped open. "You what?"

"I could see what she was seeing. When she took photos outside, I could spot a street sign, and the mountains in the background, so I knew which direction she was facing. She never came out and said the name of the resort, but once I had a rough idea of the neighborhood, I studied the videos she posted in her room and researched resorts in the area that matched the decor on their Web sites. Once I had the right place, then I just used Google Maps to pinpoint her exact location. After that, getting inside was a piece of cake."

Poppy and Matt stared slack-jawed at Byron.

He was nothing if not resourceful.

Byron gazed longingly at one of the photos in his glass-encased shrine. "It was so beautiful when we finally came together, like two lost souls reunited, so perfect . . ." His smile slowly faded and he glared at Matt. "Until you forced us apart."

"After you ran off, did you try to come back? Maybe in disguise?" Matt pressed.

Byron shook his head, baffled by the suggestion. "No . . ."

"You strike me as a very determined kid," Matt noted. "You didn't follow the production to Joshua Tree, find a way to sneak on the set undetected, find Danika in her trailer, and when she screamed for help, you grabbed a pillow off the bed and smothered her cries?"

Poppy shifted nervously. She could tell Matt was riling Byron up again, and she feared he might try to go for his rifle.

"No, I did not!" Byron shouted. "I told you, I would never hurt a hair on her head! I loved her! I loved her!"

Byron dissolved into tears, covering his face with his long bony fingers.

"What the hell is going on here?" a man bellowed from behind them.

Poppy and Matt spun around to see a hulking biker-type with long black hair, big mustache, muscles, shirtless except for a ripped jean vest, and tattoos all over his arms and chest. Sunglasses shielded his eyes. He was a foot and a half taller than Matt and brooded in the doorway. Fear swept through Poppy as her instincts cried out that this man was dangerous.

Byron lowered his hands from his face and sniffed. "Axel, you're home early. . . ."

"You didn't hear me ride up on my bike?" Axel barked before resting his eyes on Poppy and Matt. "Who are these people, Mormon missionaries?"

Byron shook his head. "No, they came by to talk to me about Danika. . . ."

Axel's eyes narrowed. "You the police?"

"No," Matt said, clearing his throat. "Private investigators."

Axel did a slow burn.

Then he turned back to Byron, scowling, and seethed, "I told you not to talk to anyone."

Byron's whole body started to shake. "I know, but—"

"Zip it!" Axel yelled, jabbing a finger at Byron. "No more talking. Talking's going to get you thrown in jail. Trust me, little brother, these people are not your friends. Do you even know who they're working for? They could be trying to frame you for murder!"

"I-I don't think so—" Byron stuttered.

"I don't care what you think. I'm the one in charge around here," Axel said in a husky voice. Then he jabbed a finger toward Poppy and Matt. "I want you two out of here. Now."

Poppy and Matt quickly took their leave. Poppy squeezed past Axel first, flashing him the briefest of smiles, followed by Matt. But Axel extended one of his scuffed black riding boots out in front of Matt, tripping him up, and sending him hurtling to the wooden porch and driving a splinter up into the palm of his hand, causing him to wince in pain.

Axel stood over him menacingly. "Don't even think about coming back here."

Matt scrambled to his feet, gave him a quick nod, and then ran to catch up with Poppy, who was already waiting at Matt's car. A Harley-Davidson was parked with a kickstand a few feet behind the Prius. They both jumped inside. Matt made a point of locking the doors.

"I think he really wants to hurt us," Matt said, putting the gear in reverse.

"Well, please let's not stick around and give him the chance," Poppy cried, rummaging for some tissue in her purse and handing a wad to Matt. "Here, press this tissue against the gash to stop the bleeding."

Matt grabbed the tissue and clenched it in his hand, then pressed down on the accelerator, and the Prius backed up too fast and slammed into the Harley knocking it over, the aluminum frame crunching in the dirt upon impact.

Poppy swiveled around to see Axel standing on the porch, his face reddening with fury at the sight of his bike tipped over. "Go, Matt, go!"

Panicked, Matt slammed his foot down on the accelerator again, still in reverse, and hit the bike again, almost backing over it. Axel was now running toward them, eyes wild with fury.

Finally, with only seconds to spare before Axel was able to hurl himself on top of the hood, Matt managed to put the car in drive and speed away, leaving Axel choking in the dust.

Chapter 22

The strong, gusty Santa Ana winds started bearing down on the Coachella Valley as Matt and Poppy sped home on Gene Autry Trail from Desert Hot Springs, swirling up a dust storm so thick and heavy, Matt had to flip on the wipers to remove the sand from the windshield so he could see where he was going.

Poppy was about to suggest Matt pull off to the side of the road until the storm dissipated or at least calmed down, but before she had the chance, she heard a loud rumbling noise closing in on them from behind. She cranked her head around, trying to make out what it was but the whipping dust flying up from the surface obscured visibility.

Poppy turned back around to see Matt, his uninjured hand gripping the wheel, eyes fixed on the road, driving with extreme caution. Nothing was in front of them but wide open road from what they could see through the massive dust storm.

Suddenly Poppy heard the rumbling again and the next thing she knew it was now right outside the window. She could make out a man riding a motorcycle, zipping along on the passenger side of the Prius.

"Matt . . ." Poppy began warning him.

"I see him! There's another one coming up on my side!"

Poppy stared out the back window and saw a second bike with two men on it, roaring up fast. The man riding shotgun kicked his leg out and smashed one of the car's taillights with the heel of his boot.

Poppy whipped back around to see the bike outside her side swerve in close. A black leather-gloved fist smashed against the glass, causing it to crack and startle her.

"Hold on!" Matt yelled, slamming his foot down on the gas pedal, lurching them forward in a desperate attempt to lose the bikers.

"Matt, what's happening?" Poppy cried.

Matt didn't answer because he was solely focused on shaking their pursuers. It quickly dawned on Poppy that Axel was probably mad enough about Matt backing over his Harley that he had called in reinforcements from his biker gang in order to get revenge. In fact, the dust cleared enough for Poppy to recognize Axel as the one riding shotgun. The bike on Matt's side managed to speed up alongside the car, up close to Matt's window, where Axel leered at them, enjoying how much he was frightening them. The fat, bald, intimidating guy driving the bike swerved in, inches from colliding with the Prius, forcing

Matt to jerk the wheel. Poppy felt her whole body fly to the right. She was strapped down by the seat belt, but still banged her head against the cracked window.

"Are you okay?" Matt shouted, eyes still glued to the road.

"Yes, Matt, but please, slow down!"

"I can't! They're trying to run us off the road, and if that happens, there's no telling what they might do to us!"

His logic made perfect sense.

Matt then began cranking the wheel left and right, in quick jerky motions, forcing the bikes to pull out and give the car a wider berth. Then, without warning, an eighteen-wheeler appeared out of nowhere in front of them, horn blaring, heading straight at them. Poppy screamed as Matt realized he had drifted onto the wrong side of the road and was now on a head-on collision course with the big rig.

The motorcycles fell back, disappearing in the dust storm behind them. With seconds to spare, Matt wrenched the wheel as hard as he could and the Prius flew off the paved road into the desert sand, hurtling forward. In front of them was a giant billboard with a State Farm insurance advertisement. Poppy opened her mouth to scream, but nothing came out. She was in a state of shock. And unlike the ill-fated car stunt on the movie set where Matt had luckily avoided crashing into the Joshua tree by swerving at the last possible second and flipping the car over, in this moment there was not even time to do that before the Prius, in what felt like slow motion, slammed into one of the large metal columns that held up the billboard. The car crunched up like an accordion, airbags exploding open, glass shattering everywhere, and then everything went black.

Chapter 23

When Poppy slowly came to, she could feel a pair of hands untangling her from the strap of the seat belt and then grabbing her from underneath her arms, pulling her from the wreckage of the car. The next thing she knew she was lying flat on her back in a bed of sand. When she tried opening her eyes, the harsh light from the blazing desert sun caused her to squint and forced them to close again.

"Poppy, can you hear me?" Matt asked gently, slipping a hand behind her head and holding it so she was slightly upright.

Poppy nodded, although she wasn't quite sure. She wiggled her fingers and toes, which seemed to work fine, and then raised an arm up, covering her eyes with her forearm, and slowly began to sit up.

Matt immediately braced her back with the palm of his hand to steady her. "Are you okay?"

"I think so. . . ." Poppy mumbled before clutching Matt's other bloody hand tightly and using it to help haul herself to her feet.

"What happened to the bikers?" Poppy asked.

"They took off right after we crashed."

Matt noticed Poppy staring at the demolished Prius. "I know, can you believe it? Second car I destroyed in less than a week. Maybe I should rethink my dream of becoming a NASCAR driver."

"Where are we?" Poppy asked, glancing around at the swirling dust in the middle of nowhere.

"Somewhere between Desert Hot Springs and Palm Springs," Matt said.

Matt stared up at the State Farm billboard they crashed into with the slogan, LIKE A GOOD NEIGHBOR, STATE FARM IS THERE, and chuckled, "I sure hope they mean what they say."

Poppy appreciated Matt's attempt at a little levity in this traumatic situation as she looked around the wrecked car for her phone. Finding it on the floor of the passenger's side, she carefully removed it and tried to call 911.

After receiving a *Call Failed* message, Poppy held the phone up in the air trying to pick up a signal. "I'm not getting any service."

"Maybe we'll have better luck up on the main road," Matt said. As Poppy began trudging through the sand, Matt placed his hand on the small of her back to guide her. "Are you sure you're not injured?"

"I'm fine. What about you?"

"Bruised and scraped, same as last time, but otherwise fine," Matt said.

Once they clambered up the incline to the main road, Matt spotted a big SUV packed with high school kids speeding toward them. He jogged out in the middle of the road to wave them down, but the driver just blared his horn and swerved around him, music blasting from the radio, the other kids laughing.

Poppy glanced down at her phone.

She only had one bar of service, but tried calling 911 again. She waited a few moments, hoping for success, but then got another *Call Failed* message.

She looked back up in time to see Matt practically hurling himself in front of another oncoming car, this one a Mini Cooper with a woman in her seventies behind the wheel. Panicked, the woman nearly sped off the road herself in order to avoid hitting him, but managed to stop in the emergency lane. Trying not to scare the poor woman too much, Matt approached the car slowly, hands in the air so she wouldn't think he had some kind of weapon and was going to rob her, shouting at her that he just needed help calling a tow truck. The woman had to adjust her hearing aid a few times, but once that was done successfully, she was more than willing to help in the crisis. She even had a bottle of water in her car for Poppy and Matt to share while they waited, in addition to a working phone she lent to Poppy so she could finally call the police.

Poppy tried reaching Detective Jordan, but was told he was out of the office, and so she left him a detailed message recounting what had transpired after finding Byron Savage and paying him a visit.

Forty-five minutes later, a tow truck arrived and the cigar-chomping, sixty-something, grizzled driver who introduced himself as Mack went to work lifting what was left of the Prius onto the flatbed of his truck, while eyeing Poppy with prurient interest. She was so grateful he was

here helping them, however, she did not bother to shut
him down and call him out for his lewd looks and lecher-
ous winks and gestures. Still, when it came time for them
to climb into the front of his big rig, Poppy made sure
Matt sat in the middle so she would not be subjected to
Mack's wandering hands.

Mack drove them to the nearest mechanic, whom he'd
called earlier and given a heads-up that they were on their
way. The mechanic, a sweet-looking, older Mexican man,
cleaned the grease off his fingers with a gray rag, and
once the tow truck rolled to a stop outside his garage, circled around to inspect the damage to the Prius.

Poppy and Matt hopped out of the truck to join the mechanic, who introduced himself as Julio.

"How much time will you need to give us an estimate
on repairs so I can file a claim with the insurance company?" Matt asked the mechanic.

"I can tell you right now," Julio said flatly. "Won't cost
nothing."

Matt blinked at him. "Nothing? But there has to be at
least five, six thousand dollars—"

"Your car's totaled. There's no fixing it."

"Oh . . ." Matt groaned.

Mack slid up next to Poppy, who was focused on her
phone, which finally had a full five bars, and pressed a
piece of paper in her free hand. She reared back, startled.

"Sorry, didn't mean to scare you, just wanted to make
sure you had my number in case you ever want to give
me a call," Mack said with a wanton grin.

"Whatever for?" Poppy asked, genuinely perplexed.

"Come on, I noticed how you looked at me when I
drove you and your friend here. . . ."

He rested a beefy hand on her backside and she reached

around and grabbed his thumb and twisted it back, threatening to break it. He yelped in pain.

"I don't know what you think you saw, but you are wildly mistaken if you think—"

A call came in on Poppy's phone.

She glanced at the screen.

It was Detective Jordan returning her call.

She pointed an admonishing finger at Mack. "You're lucky I have to take this. Now, if you know what's good for you, you will keep your distance."

Mack, chastened, nodded and slowly began backing away.

Poppy wheeled away from him and put her phone to her ear. "Hello, Detective Jordan."

"How are you doing, Poppy?"

"I've had better days. Did you listen to my message?"

"Yes, I headed straight for Byron Savage's house the minute I got it, but I'm sorry to report he's no longer there. In fact, it looks like he left in a hurry."

"And his brother?"

"No sign of him or his buddies he corralled to run you off the road. They're probably off the grid now, lying low somewhere until things cool down."

"Did you put out an APB?"

"Already done."

"Thank you."

There was a brief pause before Detective Jordan spoke again. "Tell me, Poppy, what did you do to set this Axel guy off?"

"Besides accidentally adding a few dents to his Harley, he thought we were trying to pin Danika Delgado's murder on his little brother, but after talking to Byron, I'm not so sure he's the one who—"

Detective Jordan interrupted her. "If I ask you again to stay out of my active murder investigation, you might tell me you will in order to give me a little peace of mind, but you're not really going to do it, are you?"

Poppy weighed her answer carefully, then, in a clipped tone, said, "No, Detective, probably not."

"I didn't think so. But, hey, I appreciate your honesty." Click.

Poppy knew she had to answer the man's question truthfully, because Poppy Harmon was many things, some not flattering, but a liar was definitely not one of them.

Chapter 24

Village Fest, a street fair held every Thursday night in downtown Palm Springs was a popular attraction for both locals and tourists, where individuals and businesses sold food, handcrafted items, antiques, art, clothing, and jewelry. Poppy scanned the booths that lined both sides of the street, trying to locate a sign for Lulu's Scribblings. Lulu, the extra from the *Palm Springs Weekend* set whom Poppy had seen accepting a fat wad of cash from producer Greta Van Damm, was a sketch artist who drew comic caricatures of her subjects. Wyatt had done a quick Google search on just the first name Lulu. Other than a popular downtown restaurant with the same name, the only other local Lulu he found was Lulu Hopkins with a Web site for her artwork and a few Palm Springs discussion groups about Village Fest raving about her drawings. And so Poppy recruited Iris and Violet to accompany her to the popular street fair where she could track down Lulu and ask her questions about her interaction with Greta.

Violet had been distracted by a booth selling coconut-scented candles and Iris stopped at a kielbasa sausage stand that was handing out free samples, and so it was left to Poppy to soldier on with the search for Lulu. She had almost hiked up and down the entire stretch of street devoted to the fair when she finally spotted the bouncy blonde sitting in a rocking chair as an elderly man sat posing, his excited wife sneaking a peek of the sketch Lulu was working on, her eyes dancing with joy. Lulu finished and turned the canvas around to show the old man. The caricature reminded Poppy of the nearly blind cartoon character Mr. Magoo, but on closer inspection, the old man himself looked quite like Mr. Magoo. The man chuckled and his wife clapped her hands excitedly before reaching into her bag, which was flung over her shoulder, and handing Lulu a twenty-dollar bill.

Lulu stuffed the money into a tin box and the couple sauntered away. Unfortunately, there were no other potential customers waiting. She simply could not compete with the adjoining booth to her left, Joe's Pet Paintings, which was attracting a much larger crowd, eager to immortalize their beloved cats and dogs and even parrots in a pop art–style painting. Joe also offered free dog biscuits along with free shipping, and so it was tough for someone like Lulu to compete.

As Poppy approached the booth, Lulu sat up, instantly recognizing her. "Poppy Harmon! What a lovely surprise!"

Poppy was surprised by the ebullient reaction given the two women had never formally met. "Hello, Lulu, I saw the drawing you did of that man who just left, and I must say, you're very talented."

Lulu preened with pride, thrusting out her ample bosom. "Why, thank you. Would you like one of yourself?"

Poppy was not partial to actual photographs of herself, even the more flattering ones, let alone a caricature, but she knew if she wanted to get information out of Lulu, the odds were better if she was hiring her services.

"Yes, I'd love one," Poppy cooed as she plopped down in a chair and struck a pose.

Lulu grabbed her pencil and began sketching feverishly while chattering away. "It was such a shame the production had to be shut down after, well, you know, what happened to poor Danika. I was so looking forward to being in a big-time Netflix movie. Of course, it's not like I had a major part or anything, like you, but it was going to be my first official IMDB credit, which is like practically being on the road to becoming a legitimate actress."

"Yes, it's all very sad," Poppy said soberly. "But at least you have this to fall back on until the next acting gig comes along."

Lulu scoffed as she continued scribbling. "This doesn't exactly pay the bills. It's more of a hobby at this point." She glanced over at Joe besieged by jubilant animal lovers signing up for one of his pet paintings. "I keep hoping that someday I get the kind of traffic he gets, but I know it takes time. It's a marathon not a sprint, right?"

"Absolutely," Poppy offered reassuringly. "And it's lucky you're able to pick up the occasional odd job in the meantime to pay the rent."

Lulu stopped sketching and looked up at Poppy, perplexed. "What gave you that idea? I actually live with my mother because I can't afford my own place right now."

"Oh . . . I'm sorry, I was under the impression that you were working part-time, or at least doing some freelance work for Greta Van Damm since I saw her giving you a stack of cash on the set before we shut down."

Lulu's face froze.

She was not sure how to proceed, and so she decided to just ignore what Poppy had left hanging out there and redirect her attention back to the caricature she was working on.

"I just assumed you were doing a job for her because you would have been paid by the payroll company for your extra work on the movie."

More uncomfortable silence.

Lulu glanced back up at Poppy, studying her features, then sketched some more.

Finally, after what felt like an interminable amount of time, but was perhaps maybe ten or fifteen seconds, Lulu said without looking up from her drawing, "You're right. That money was for something else. . . ."

"I'm sure it's none of my business."

"Right again," Lulu said, instantly regretting her sharp tone. "I'm sorry, that was rude, it's just that I can't talk about it."

"I understand."

After a few more minutes, Lulu finished the caricature. She set her pencil down and showed Poppy. "What do you think?"

Before Poppy could react, she heard giggles coming from behind her. She swiveled around to see Violet and Iris staring at the caricature of Poppy that Lulu held up in her hand.

"Oh, Poppy, it's wonderful!" Violet cooed.

"It looks exactly like you!" Iris cracked.

Poppy arched an eyebrow.

"I mean if you were a cartoon character," Iris added.

Poppy stood up. "How about you two each get one done of yourselves?"

"I do not need a silly drawing to remind me of my imperfections!" Iris snorted.

"Oh, come on, Iris, don't be such a spoilsport," Violet said. "And we don't need a cartoon sketch to remind us of your imperfections."

Iris's nostrils flared as she glared at Violet.

Poppy pulled three twenty-dollar bills from her purse and pressed them into the palm of Lulu's hand. "That's for all three sketches."

Lulu eagerly accepted the cash. "Thank you so much."

"Do you have time to do two more?" Poppy asked.

"Of course. Other than the man ahead of you, you're the only business I've had all night."

"Great," Poppy said, whirling around to Iris and Violet. "Now, who's going to go first?"

Iris shoved Violet forward.

Violet sat down in the chair and tried adopting a sexy pouty pose and said pleadingly, "If you can, make me look like Betty Boop or Jessica Rabbit rather than Marge Simpson."

"I'll try my best," Lulu promised.

As she began doodling Violet, Poppy noticed some worry lines forming on Lulu's face. She could tell Lulu was worrying about her abrupt manner earlier when Poppy had brought up Greta Van Damm.

Lulu focused on Violet's face and added some more

details to her drawing before stopping. "Poppy, I hope you're not mad at me for before. I would hate to upset you, especially since you've been so generous, buying three sketches."

"I just want to support you, a fellow actor. . . ." Poppy said in a soothing tone.

Lulu perked up. The fact that Poppy Harmon had just referred to her as "a fellow actor" seemed to be a big boon to her morale. Suddenly they were more than just acquaintances, they were peers, and it bought Poppy an over-flowing abundance of good will.

"And I don't expect you to tell me something if you don't want to," Poppy said firmly.

Lulu scribbled furiously as she spoke. "It's not that I don't *want* to tell you, I just can't. I'm, like, legally bound not to say anything to anyone."

Poppy gave her a quizzical look.

"I signed a document," Lulu tried to explain. "A non . . ." She searched for the night words.

"Non-disclosure agreement?" Poppy offered.

"Yes! That's it! Greta had me sign one of those before she would give me any money."

That was all Poppy needed to hear.

She could surmise the rest herself.

Hal Greenwood had a long history of sexually harassing women on his film sets and at his production offices. Greta Van Damm's job was to keep the movies rolling at all costs in order to feed the bottom line. Even if that meant paying off actresses and pretty female extras targeted by Hal with big wads of cash and securing ironclad contracts designed to keep them quiet so the operation continued to run smoothly. She knew pressing Lulu for more details would be pointless. If she divulged any more, she could be sued, and Lulu clearly understood that.

But this latest revelation raised a very serious question in Poppy's mind. If Greta was forking over money to buy the silence of Hal's purported victims, what else could they be hiding?

Chapter 25

"I'm sorry, Ms. Van Damm is not in right now," the lovely, young, caramel-skinned Chrissy Teigen look-alike said from behind the reception desk at Hal Greenwood Productions located in a high-rise in Century City.

Matt flashed her a warm smile, planted his hands on top of the reception desk, and leaned forward. "Could you please check again, because we just saw her car in her reserved space down in the parking garage?"

Chrissy's own smile tightened and she spoke in a clipped, irritated tone. "I don't need to check again. She's *not* here."

"When do you expect her back?" Poppy asked, arms folded.

Chrissy hesitated, not sure how to respond. Then, she shrugged and just seemed to make things up as she went along. "She has back-to-back meetings at a couple of different studios, Universal and Disney, way in the Valley, so she probably won't even be back in the office today. She'll probably just go home from there."

"I see," Matt said, nodding before turning to Poppy. "I say we take our chances and wait here on the off chance she does drive back to the office, what do you say?"

Poppy plopped down on the expensive leather couch in the waiting area. "Sounds like a good plan to me."

Matt joined her, and they both sat staring at poor Chrissy, who was now at a loss as to how to get rid of them. Her phone chirped, she adjusted the headset she was wearing, and cleared her throat. "Hal Greenwood Productions, how may I direct your call?"

Poppy and Matt exchanged triumphant glances. They were not going to be summarily dismissed, not when they were reasonably certain Chrissy was lying and Greta Van Damm was at this very moment back there hiding from them in her office.

Matt called over to the receptionist once she had transferred the call. "Do you happen to have any water handy?"

"No," Chrissy said flatly, obviously having been instructed not to encourage these two to stick around for any extended length of time.

Matt flashed her another winning smile. Poppy could tell Chrissy, or whatever her real name was, was attracted to Matt, but she was fighting hard to maintain a sense of professionalism and to follow her orders from the higher-ups. Another phone call came through, which Chrissy answered. "Yes, Ms. Van—" Chrissy's eyes widened slightly as she stopped herself from announcing the caller's name. Poppy and Matt both perked up, assuming it was Greta calling from somewhere in the building. "Yes, what can I do for you?" Chrissy asked stiffly.

Poppy hoped that Chrissy was not one of the thousands of aspiring actresses working similar jobs in Los Angeles waiting for their big break to arrive because this pretty girl's acting skills were wanting.

Chrissy eyed Poppy and Matt nervously as she spoke to the caller. "Uh-huh . . . That's what I told them, but . . ." Chrissy lowered her voice to a whisper and mumbled into her mouthpiece, ". . . they won't leave. Should I call security?" Chrissy darted her eyes back and forth as she listened to her instructions. "Okay, I'll tell them." She ended the call and then addressed Poppy and Matt. "That was Ms. Van Damm. . . ."

"We never would've guessed," Poppy cracked.

The sarcasm flew right over Chrissy's head. "Anyway," she said breathlessly, "she told me to tell you that she will not be coming back to the office today after her meetings so there is no point in waiting around for her."

"Did you tell her just how important it is for us to speak to her?" Poppy huffed.

Chrissy nodded. "Yes. But I'm afraid she's very busy. You might want to try calling tomorrow."

Matt and Poppy had started to stand up when the elevator dinged, the door opened, and Hal Greenwood blew into the reception area, clutching a Starbucks cup, berating a wiry, young male assistant who chased behind him. "You're a useless moron, do you know that? I asked for sugar-free vanilla in my latte, this is regular vanilla. I'm not an idiot, I can taste the difference."

"I *asked* for sugar-free vanilla, the mistake must have happened on their end. . . ."

Hal hurled his cup at the male assistant, drenching his blue oxford shirt with hot coffee. The assistant had to bite down on his tongue to keep from yelping in pain. The cup bounced off the floor, splashing the rest of the contents all over the area rug. "Clean that up!" he barked at the assistant.

Chrissy Teigen sat upright, panicked, checking to make sure her desk was spotless, and then croaked, "Good afternoon, Mr. Greenwood, I hope you had a nice lunch."

He stopped, his ugly demeanor instantly melting away, and broke into a wolfish grin as he looked his receptionist up and down. "Why are you wearing that outfit, Julia? Are you trying to make me fall in love with you?"

Julia—the receptionist had a real name.

Before she could even respond, Hal was behind her and massaging her neck with his thick, pudgy, hairy-knuckled paws. She fought not to cringe at his touch.

Poppy could not help but audibly sigh with disgust.

Hal immediately glanced up to see where the sound was coming from. His face flushed with anger at the sight of Poppy and Matt. "What the hell are you two doing here?"

Matt jumped to his feet, never one to be intimidated. "Actually, we're here to see—"

"Forget it! I don't care! I want you two out of here!" Hal bellowed before spinning Julia around in her rolling chair and shouting down at her as she quite literally shrunk in her seat. "Why did you let them in here?"

"I d-d-didn't," she stammered. "They wouldn't leave and—"

"The last thing I need is a couple of private eyes poking around my business trying to dig up dirt on me or my people!" Hal pointed a fat finger at the phone on her desk. "Call security! If they don't leave voluntarily right now, I want them thrown out!"

"Yes, sir," Julia cried, her hands shaking as she frantically searched for the right number to press on her phone.

"We just want to talk to you and Greta about Lulu," Poppy said calmly.

Hal appeared genuinely perplexed. "Who?"

"You don't remember her name?" Poppy scoffed.

"Lucy?" Hal asked, sweat slowly forming on his furrowed brow.

"*Lulu*," Matt reiterated. "She was an extra on the set of *Palm Springs Weekend*."

"I don't know any Lulu!" Hal screamed before whirling back around to Julia again. "Did you call security yet? What's taking so long?"

"I-I am working on it," Julia said unsteadily, finally finding the correct button on her phone.

Hal barreled toward the door leading from the reception area to the production offices. When he tried the handle, it was locked.

"What are you waiting for, buzz me in! What the hell's wrong with you?" Hal shouted at the frazzled receptionist whom he had been shamelessly flirting with just two minutes earlier.

"I-I was calling security, wait, I will—" Julia murmured, her trembling hands finally managing to press the button to open the door.

"What? You can't do two things at once?" Hal barked.

Mercifully there was a buzz indicating the door was unlocked and Hal shoved it open and bustled into the back, the door slamming shut behind him.

Julia, who was now near tears, spoke in a jittery voice into her mouthpiece. "Yes, this is Julia on twelve. I need security up here immediately."

Poppy climbed to her feet and joined Matt. "You can relax, Julia. We're leaving."

Matt called for the elevator, which was already on the twelfth floor, and he and Poppy casually stepped inside. As the doors closed, Matt called out to Julia, "If you're not getting any combat pay for this war zone, I'd seriously consider finding a new job."

It was the best advice he could have given anyone working at Hal Greenwood Productions, especially an attractive young woman with admirable physical assets.

Poppy and Matt rode the elevator down to the parking garage where they spotted Greta Van Damm's car still parked in her reserved space. There was an empty visitor parking space at the end of the same row. Matt went to bring around his rental car and claim it so they could watch to see if and when Greta Van Damm believed they had finally gone and that it was safe to come down to her car and drive home unaccosted.

It was a long wait.

Matt slurped what was left of his Big Gulp and was now chewing on the ice. Poppy sat patiently in the passenger's seat, her bones tired, dreading the two-hour drive back to Palm Springs they would have to endure after finally confronting Greta Van Damm.

Three hours later, when seven o'clock rolled around, and there was still no sign of Greta, Matt suggested they hang it up and head home. But Poppy insisted they give it a little more time, and her instinct paid off. At seven forty-five, the parking garage elevator doors opened, and they spotted Greta Van Damm, phone clamped to her ear, a large Marc Jacobs crossbody bag flung around her shoulder, march straight for her car in her assigned space. Poppy and Matt immediately jumped out of the rental, a

Ford Fusion, and hurried over to intercept her. Greta heard
the rapid clicking of heels, sensing them coming up behind her, and spun around, almost striking a defensive pos-
ture. She groaned and lowered her guard when she saw
Poppy and Matt.

"You two just won't give up, will you?" Greta sighed.
"What can you possibly hope to gain by stalking me?"

"We had a very interesting conversation with Lulu
Hopkins," Poppy said sharply.

This got Greta's attention. She appeared to steel herself for what was about to come next. "I'm sorry, who?"
Greta asked lamely, her performance even more lackluster than the receptionist Julia's.

"The extra who I saw you pay off with a big wad of
cash," Poppy said, taking a step closer. "Or are you going
to deny that even happened?"

Greta's nervous eyes flicked back and forth between
Poppy and Matt. She was obviously agitated, then took a
deep breath and exhaled. "Lulu should not be talking to
anyone. She signed a legally binding NDA."

"How many other women out there have signed similar NDAs for Hal Greenwood Productions?" Matt asked.

Poppy could feel her anger rising and she could no
longer keep her thoughts bottled up inside of her. "The
idea of these NDAs designed to cover up Hal Greenwood's sexual misconduct is grotesque. But what I find
even more insidious, more revolting, Greta, is your bla-
tant complicity to protect a predator."

Greta's mouth dropped open in shock. "How dare
you!"

"Am I mistaken?" Poppy spit out. "Are you saying
you did not turn a blind eye to your boss's abhorrent be-

havior, that you did not play a critical role in covering it all up for the sake of the company's profit margin?"

"I-I don't have to stand here and take this," Greta sputtered as she fumbled in her bag for her car remote while hurrying toward her car.

Poppy and Matt did not chase after her, but stood in place, watching her run off, as Matt called out to her, "Did you do the same with Danika?"

Greta had just retrieved her remote and unlocked her Lexus when she stopped cold, stared at the ground a few moments, and then slowly turned back around to face Poppy and Matt. "Hal and I had nothing, repeat *nothing*, to do with that poor girl's murder, and if you dare to suggest otherwise, we will sue you for defamation."

"Okay, maybe *you* are innocent, but how can you be so sure about Hal? Were you with him on set at the time Danika was murdered?" Poppy asked.

Greta hesitated as she apparently went over the timetable in her mind, quickly realizing she could not vouch for her boss's whereabouts, and managed to squeak out a resigned, "No."

There was an icy silence.

Greta took a step toward them. "Look, I know Hal has his problems, and he's many things, a jerk, a bully, a misogynist, but a killer? That's ridiculous. I have to go."

Greta was so rattled she dropped her car remote and had to bend over and pick it up off the ground, trembling even worse than the poor receptionist's shaky hands back up on the twelfth floor. She glanced back at Poppy and Matt one more time, her eyes filled with fright, and then slid behind the wheel of her car and shut the door. The Lexus roared to life, the front and rear lights popping on, and Greta hastily backed out of the parking space to make a fast getaway. But her nerves obviously got the best of her, and she hit the gas a little too hard and banged right into the back of a BMW 750 parked directly across from her, smashing out both taillights.

Matt turned to Poppy and shook his head, grinning. "Looks like these car accidents are becoming an epidemic."

Chapter 26

Lynn Jordan loved posting photos on Instagram. She was one of those people, the kind Poppy could not understand, quite frankly, who relished social media, always keeping her friends, family and followers up-to-date on all of her various activities. There was Lynn shopping for avocados at a local farmer's market. Lynn with her yoga mat underneath her arm and a Starbucks coffee in hand on her way to a Bikram class. Lynn, doubled over laughing, as she tried discussing an embarrassing sex scene from this month's selection at her book club meeting. And it was with great interest that Poppy studied this morning's post. Lynn making breakfast for her loving husband, who was on his way to the gym. There was Lynn dishing out pancakes on a plate as her husband sat at the kitchen table behind her, a resigned expression on his face, as he glumly reached for his orange juice. It was obvious Detective Lamar Jordan did not appreciate his wife's savvy when it came to social media, but as an aspiring clothes designer, it was in Lynn's best interest to gain a public profile, so her husband more or less had to go along and accept it.

Poppy leaned back in her chair at the small kitchen table in her new house, amidst stacks of still-unpacked moving boxes, sipping her coffee, as she grinned knowingly at the tank top Detective Jordan was wearing with the logo for In-Shape gym. There was one location in Cathedral City, not too far from where the Jordans resided in Rancho Mirage. That had to be where he was going after breakfast. It was still early enough for him to squeeze in a quick workout before heading into the office.

Poppy jumped up from the table, ran to her bedroom, and whipped open her half-empty closet. She had only managed to hang about a third of her outfits, and quickly realized her own workout clothes were probably buried in one of the boxes stacked against the wall. She frantically began cutting them open one by one with a box cutter, and got lucky on the third one. There were a bunch of sweats and T-shirts and leggings and even a pair of unused Nike women's running shoes she had bought during the short time she had considered taking up jogging, which not surprisingly never materialized. Poppy quickly donned the appropriate attire, raced out of the house, hopped into her car, and drove straight to In-Shape.

After signing up for a guest pass, claiming to the sweet Latina girl at the front desk that she was still weighing options on what facility she was going to join full-time, it took all of forty-five seconds to zero in on Detective Jordan, in the same tank top he had been wearing in the Instagram photo, huffing and puffing on a treadmill, sweat pouring down his face, which he wiped away with a towel, his muscles glistening. Earbuds were nestled in the crevice of both his ears and his phone was perched on the display screen calculating his progress as he stared ahead, grim-faced, seemingly devoid of emotion.

The treadmills on either side of him were occupied, one with a bored-looking woman in her seventies who was checking out the butt of one of the male personal trainers doing squats on a nearby mat. On the other side was a young kid who had just started, increasing the speed of the belt until he was running full speed. Poppy figured her best chance was to wait for the woman to finish first. Sure enough, the same trainer she had been leering at ambled over and kissed her flirtatiously on the cheek before taking her hand and leading her off to her personal training session. Poppy made a beeline for the free treadmill and hopped on, taking a few minutes to figure out what buttons to press to get the damn thing going. Finally, she just pressed the manual button and the contraption whirred to life as the belt started to move and Poppy began walking at a leisurely pace.

She glanced over at Detective Jordan a few times, but he was so entrenched in his own thoughts he didn't notice her at first. Poppy decided to be a little less discreet. She began gesturing her hand toward him, slowly at first, then a little more forcefully, and when that still didn't get his attention, she started waving her arms spasmodically.

Jordan, finally alerted to the crazy woman on the treadmill next to him who appeared to be having some kind of seizure, jerked his head around to see Poppy smiling broadly at him. Confused, he reached up and took the buds out of his ears.

"Well, isn't this the wildest coincidence?" Poppy cooed.

"Good morning, Ms. Harmon," Jordan said gruffly. "I didn't know you were a member here."

"I just joined today!" Poppy said brightly, convincing herself this was mostly the truth and not a convenient fib. "I really want to try the cardio dance class, I hear it's loads of fun, but I thought I would start out slow and take a crack at this treadmill."

Jordan nodded with the thinnest of smiles and then put the buds back in his ears.

"What are you listening to?" Poppy yelled.

He didn't answer her, keeping his eyes straight ahead.

"What are you listening to?" Poppy repeated, louder.

He flicked his eyes over in her direction to see her talking, and then with a heavy sigh, he popped the buds out again. "I'm sorry?"

"I was just curious what you listen to while walking on the treadmill. I'm searching for suggestions."

"Oh, it's a podcast. They talk about famous unsolved murders in US history, and revisit them, looking for clues that might lead to them being solved."

"Wow, talk about taking your work home with you."

Detective Jordan cracked a slight smile. "I know, my wife says the same thing. She's always on me to listen to something lighter, like show tunes or comedy shows, but I don't know, the dark stuff kind of relaxes me in a weird way."

"Well, I certainly don't want to interrupt, I won't keep bothering you, I promise. . . ."

Jordan nodded gratefully, and was about to shove his earbuds back in when Poppy quickly blurted out, "But I was curious if you were able to find Byron Savage?"

Jordan did not seem surprised by Poppy's question, in fact he looked as if he had been expecting it. He dropped the earbuds in a plastic holder for keys and personal items and pressed a button to slow down the treadmill so he could talk.

"I'm afraid the trail's gone cold on him, for now anyway, but we still have an APB out on him, and we're hopeful someone will report something, and he'll turn up. We are a little closer on locating the brother, Axel. We arrested a couple of his biker friends for possession of some unregistered firearms, and after some intense questioning, they told us Axel may be hiding out with a girlfriend, well, one of them anyway, in Barstow."

"Barstow? He must really *not* want to be found!" Poppy joked.

Jordan chuckled.

Poppy considered it a triumph that she had managed to make the usually stone-faced detective crack a smile, if ever so slightly.

"There is someone else you should look into," Poppy said casually, not wanting to push him too much.

Jordan raised an eyebrow. "Oh?"

"Hal Greenwood."

"The movie producer?"

"Yes. My agency has obtained information—"

Detective Jordan wiped his face again with his towel and snickered, "Your agency . . . ?"

He still refused to take the Desert Flowers Agency seriously, but instead of taking umbrage, she allowed the comment to pass unchallenged.

"Yes," Poppy sighed. "Hal Greenwood has proven time and time again that he is a serial predator, making unwanted sexual advances on numerous actresses looking for a part, female assistants who just want to hang on to their job, any women who lack the power to stand up to him."

"And you think he might have been trying to come on to Danika Delgado?"

"I'm quite confident of the fact. He is undoubtedly three times her size. He might have made a pass at her in her trailer, and when she rejected him, he became angry and forced himself on her. When she started to scream for help, he could have pushed the pillow down over her face to silence her until she stopped breathing. Perhaps it was an accident or intentional."

"Sounds like an interesting theory, but I need proof, and you don't seem to have any," Jordan said, losing patience.

"Not yet," Poppy sniffed.

As dismissive as Jordan was, Poppy was satisfied she had at least planted the thought in his mind now, and hopefully that would mean Hal Greenwood would remain on the detective's radar during his investigation.

Poppy turned away from Jordan, pressed a button, and her treadmill came to a grinding halt. She stepped down and was about to walk away when Jordan called out, "That was quick."

She spun back around. "What?"

"Your workout. You done already?"

"I don't want to overdo it on my first day," Poppy said tightly.

Jordan grinned as he sopped his sweaty face and arms.

"What?" Poppy snapped.

"Nothing," Jordan said, looping the towel around his neck.

Poppy's eyes narrowed. "Do you think I only came here because I wanted to talk to you about Hal Greenwood?"

"I didn't say that."

"But you're thinking it!"

"Maybe," Jordan shrugged, still grinning.

There was no point in arguing with him any further because he was one hundred percent correct in his assessment. Poppy threw him an annoyed look and had started sauntering off when Jordan called out behind her, "I'll follow up. . . ."

Poppy swerved around, expectant. "Pardon me?"

Jordan was reaching maximum impact level and was running as fast as the kid on the treadmill next to him. "I'll look into Greenwood, I promise. . . ."

"Thank you, Detective," Poppy said, clasping her hands together, and headed out of the gym. Her leg muscles were already starting to feel sore.

Chapter 27

Outside the gym, as she approached her car on the far side of the packed parking lot, Poppy stopped short at the sight of a folded-up piece of paper lodged underneath the windshield wiper, flapping in the wind.

Please, not a parking ticket, Poppy thought, dreading the idea of having to pay a fine. But the only restricted spaces in the entire lot were clearly marked for the disabled, and this was definitely not one of those. Poppy marched over and reached for the paper, realizing this was not an official document of any kind, but rather a regular sheet of paper torn from a notebook. She wrenched it free from the wiper and unfolded it.

Mary Pickford Theatres
Bradley Cooper
10:45 AM
Back Row

The Mary Pickford was a state of the art cinema complex in Cathedral City, named after the late, great silent film actress. Poppy was a big fan of going to the movies there with Iris and Violet several times a month. She knew who Bradley Cooper was, an Oscar-nominated actor whom she found particularly moving in the *A Star Is Born* remake with Lady Gaga that had come out a few years ago. Poppy assumed "Bradley Cooper" must mean a film he was currently starring in, and that there was a 10:45 AM showing.

Poppy checked her watch.

It was already ten-thirty.

Poppy hastily jumped in her car, and sped along Date Palm Drive to Highway 111, veered right, and was pulling onto Pickfair Street within five minutes. Parking in the large adjacent structure, she hurriedly clicked along the pavement to the box office to purchase a ticket. Once inside, she bypassed the concession stand, although it wasn't easy, and checked the theatre number on her ticket. Nine. She followed the numbers down a long hallway until she located the right theatre, glanced around to see no one else around except for a lone uniformed employee vacuuming up some spilled popcorn in the hall, and then entered the theatre.

There were some coming attractions playing on the wide screen, and a smattering of people, mostly retirees, spread throughout the theatre. Poppy trudged up the steps to the back row, which was completely empty, and sat down in a large, plush leather seat close to the middle. Then she waited. After the last preview, the lights dimmed until it was completely dark except for the stair and floor lights so latecomers could see where they were going, and the feature began with the Universal Studios logo.

Poppy kept an eye out for anyone new entering the theatre as the credits unfurled with ominous, pulsating music. This was obviously not a comedy, but some kind of edge-of-your-seat thriller.

Poppy's eyes kept flicking toward the theatre entrance, but no new moviegoers arrived, and she was soon distracted by the story unfolding on the big screen, not to mention a shower scene with Mr. Cooper unabashedly in the nude.

He certainly is a fine specimen of a man, Poppy thought to herself, also grateful she had never been asked to do any kind of nude scene during her own short-lived acting career. Even if the role called for it, not gratuitous, tastefully done, she was not certain she would have had the guts to go through with it.

Poppy suddenly felt a presence next to her, and cranked her head around to see a handsome young man, late twenties to early thirties, sandy blond hair, sitting next to her, eyes glued to the movie, crinkling the paper bag of popcorn as he dug into it and shoveled handfuls of popped kernels into his mouth.

The young man did not turn and make eye contact with Poppy yet. He just sat next to her, quietly watching the movie except for the loud crunching sound from eating his popcorn.

Poppy had never seen him enter the theatre, which probably meant he had already been one of the people in their seats, and just stealthily moved up to the back row and next to Poppy once the movie started.

The action on the big screen was taking place at night, and so the theatre was nearly pitch-black. Poppy could not see the face of the man who was sitting next to her, but when the scene cut to the following morning, the wide screen filling up with bright, blinding daylight from the sun, the whole theatre seemed to illuminate, and Poppy was able to finally identify the man who had urgently summoned her to the Mary Pickford.

It was Fabian Granger.

The tenacious, dogged, camera-ready investigative reporter who Greta had unceremoniously kicked off the set of *Palm Springs Weekend* for trespassing.

"Thank you for meeting me," Fabian said in a hushed tone, eyes straight ahead, inhaling another handful of popcorn.

Poppy leaned over close to him and whispered, "Why all the subterfuge?"

Fabian scanned the theatre to make sure no one had moved to a seat closer to them in order to eavesdrop on their conversation.

"You need to be careful, people are watching you," he warned, wiping some greasy butter off the corner of his mouth with a wadded-up napkin in his hand.

"*Me*? Whatever for?" Poppy gasped.

"You've rattled a few monkey cages, and now the monkeys are upset and agitated," he said flatly.

"Hal Greenwood?" Poppy guessed.

Fabian nodded. "I just thought you should be aware. I'll give you my phone number in case anything else develops."

After exchanging phone numbers with Poppy, he started to get up to leave, but she reached out and grabbed his arm. "Wait, how do you know this?"

Fabian sat back down. "I have been working for months on an exposé of Hal Greenwood, and I've turned up a lot of deeply disturbing information. As I talked to people in his orbit, it got back to him and he started harassing me with phone calls, threatening to sue me for libel, spreading rumors about me to ruin my career, attacking my family, but I just kept my head down and kept going. . . ." A man a few rows down turned around in his seat and hissed, "Shhhh!"

Fabian lowered his voice. "When verbal threats didn't work, he hired some unsavory types to follow me around, and report back to him what I was up to. . . ."

"What kind of unsavory types?" Poppy whispered.

"A couple Ukrainian spies, hired by an Israeli private detective agency, real tough guys meant to intimidate me. I've been seeing them outside my LA apartment watching the building, tailing me when I'm driving around, keeping track of my movements. Last month, I found a GPS tracker attached to the undercarriage cover of my car."

"Oh my . . ." Poppy murmured. "And you think I'm now a target too?"

"Yes," Fabian said. "You set off a lot of alarm bells when you showed up at Greenwood's office yesterday. I have an inside source who tells me you're now on the list. Greenwood wants to find out what you know, and how bad it is for him."

Poppy leaned back in the comfy leather recliner and took all of this in, stunned. If Hal Greenwood was going to the trouble of having her followed, what lengths was he willing to go to make sure she did not find the truth? Was her life in danger? Was Matt's?

Poppy had many more questions, but Fabian was done with his stark warning and ready to go. He stood up to leave again, but knelt down next to Poppy, and with a darkened, dead serious expression whispered, "My source also has reason to believe your office has been bugged."

And then, in a flash, he shot back up to his feet, and dashed out of the theatre, leaving a flabbergasted Poppy behind.

Chapter 28

"Bugs? We do not have bugs! It is impossible!" Iris snorted disdainfully. "I had the exterminator come out and spray my whole house and this garage less than a month ago when I saw a cockroach in my dishwasher!"

Poppy, eyes widening, put a finger to her lips, frantically signaling Iris to stop talking.

But Iris missed the cue.

"Let me see this bug you found!" Iris insisted as she marched over to Wyatt, who quickly squeezed his fist shut and shook his head, fearing if she saw what was in his hand, she would further alert whoever was listening to what he had found.

Poppy had once again been duly impressed with Violet's grandson. When she had arrived at the office to find Matt and Wyatt playing a video game, she had written down on a piece of paper what Fabian Granger had told her. Poppy and Matt fumbled around, not sure what to even look for, but it had taken Wyatt less than a minute to locate a small square black device about an inch in diameter attached to the back of his desktop computer, which was facing the wall and out of sight.

Matt, always eager to showcase his acting talent, leaned into the device and began rattling off all kinds of false information about how they were ready to give up on the Danika Delgado case, how Hal Greenwood was no longer a suspect in their minds due to lack of evidence, how they were ready to move on and look for an entirely new case to investigate.

That's when Iris blew in after her morning golf game and threatened to blow everything up. Poppy had tried to calmly explain what was happening, talking low enough so Iris could hear but not loud enough for her voice to be picked up on the transmitter. Her effort, however, only managed to thoroughly confuse Iris.

"Why are you whispering? I can barely hear you!" Iris shouted. "What is going on here? Why do all look so nervous? Why am I the only one talking?"

Matt finally bounded over and cupped a hand over Iris's ear and whispered to her that they had found a bug planted in the office.

That did little to clarify matters.

And now Iris was skulking about the office, checking corners and desktops and inspecting the counter in the kitchenette, determined to find exactly where these insects were overrunning the office. "I told Violet not to leave food out when she made peanut butter and jelly sandwiches for Wyatt while he was working!"

Giving up, Poppy marched over and opened one of the kitchenette cupboards, grabbed a tall glass, and filled it with water. Then, she crossed the room to Wyatt and held it up. Wyatt opened his fist, revealing the black device in the palm of his hand. Iris opened her mouth in surprise, but Matt zipped up behind her and clapped a hand over her mouth to silence her. Wyatt dropped the device into the water where it floated to the bottom of the glass.

Matt released Iris, who wiped her mouth.

"Your hand smells fishy!" Iris barked.

"I had tuna for lunch," Matt said, chagrined.

"What is going on here?" Iris demanded to know.

Poppy set the glass down on Wyatt's desk. "Is it safe to speak freely now, Wyatt?"

"Yeah, I'm pretty sure that thing's short-circuited out by now," Wyatt said.

"Hal Greenwood had someone working for him plant a listening device here in our office," Matt said.

"*What*?" Iris gasped. "Why would he do that?"

"Because he's worried stiff about what we might find out about him, which just makes me want to push ahead even harder," Poppy said, folding her arms, determined. "I've known men like Hal Greenwood most of my life, especially during the years I was working as an actress in Hollywood, and believe me, nothing would give me greater pleasure than to nail that bastard to the wall."

Matt raised an eyebrow, fascinated by the fury in Poppy's tone.

Iris turned to Wyatt. "How long do you think he has had us under surveillance?"

Wyatt shrugged. "I don't know, but it's a pretty sophisticated piece of equipment. That's the smallest wireless transmitter I've ever seen. It's highly sensitive and can pick up a whisper from something like thirty-five feet away. There is a tiny SIM card in it so all you have to do is send a text from your cell phone number to the device, then it knows you. You can place it anywhere and call it any-time to listen to surrounding sounds from anywhere on your phone. No rings, beeps, or clicks to tip off the target."

"And how do you know so much about it?" Poppy in-quired.

"Come on, Poppy, haven't you figured it out yet? I'm really, *really* smart," Wyatt cracked.

"And half your Internet history are spy gadget Web sites. You're like a mini James Bond," Matt said.

Suddenly the door to the garage office flew open and Violet breezed in. "Hi, everyone, what did I miss?"

"The office was bugged!" Wyatt excitedly told his grand-mother.

"Well, it's no wonder, I have begged Iris countless times to keep up with her housecleaning," Violet sighed. "I even told her if she just invested in a mop and a bottle of Clorox, I'd do it myself. I really don't mind. If you let it go too long, that's when you can start to see an infestation."

"Don't be daft, Violet, he's not talking about those kinds of bugs! We found a listening device! Someone has been eavesdropping on our private conversations!" Iris groaned, completely forgetting she had just made the exact assumption only moments earlier.

"Oh, dear," Violet said with a furrowed brow as she undoubtedly recounted in her mind every possible embar-rassing conversation she might have had in the office over the past few days.

Poppy noticed something oddly different about Violet and asked, "Have you done something with your hair?"

"Yes," Violet said, brightening. "The girl at the salon called the style Stacked Ash Layers. Is it gray? Is it blond? You'll never know with this expertly blended ash-toned hue. She did a lovely job, don't you think?"

"Very chic," Matt agreed.

Iris stepped forward, suspicious. "That's very unlike you to experiment with a new hairstyle. You won't even eat a bagel if it isn't plain. What is going on?"

"Nothing," Violet said, her face slowly turning crimson. She was a terrible fibber.

"And where were you last night?" Iris asked brusquely. "I tried calling you four times and you never picked up or returned my calls!"

"I . . . I had a date," Violet muttered.

This revelation stopped the presses.

"You what?" Iris gasped, obviously convinced she had misheard what Violet had said the first time.

"If you must know, I met a man square-dancing at the club the other evening, and he asked me out to dinner," Violet said quickly. "And so last night he took me to John Henry's for dinner and it was quite lovely."

They all stared at her in disbelief.

"This is why I didn't say anything, so I could avoid this exact situation with all your mouths dropped open in shock. Is it so hard to believe a man would show interest in me anymore?"

"Of course not!" Matt exclaimed. "You're a beautiful, vibrant, dynamic woman, Violet!"

"Please, let's not get carried away," Iris remarked.

"What's his name? What does he look like?" Poppy asked.

"His name is Phil, he's a retired history professor from Boise, Idaho—"

"So he is boring," Iris said.

"Iris, *please*!" Poppy scolded before whirling back around to Violet. "Do you have a picture?"

Violet rummaged for her phone in her bag. "Why, yes,

I had the waiter take one of us while we were sharing a dessert, a key lime pie cheesecake, it was to die for." Violet tapped her phone and brought up the photo and held it out for all of them to see.

It was an adorable picture of Violet and Phil both diving their forks into the cheesecake, laughing, at a corner table amidst the lush greenery on the patio of this popular Palm Springs staple. What was striking was just how handsome and sexy Phil was, at least a decade younger than Violet, probably early to mid-fifties.

"This picture doesn't do him justice," Violet said.

Poppy gasped. "It *doesn't*?"

How could it be possible that Phil was even more good-looking in person?

"He's quite the stud, Violet, congratulations," Matt said.

"Am I going to have to call him Grandpa?" Wyatt asked.

"No, dear, of course not!" Violet laughed.

Iris grabbed the phone, inspecting the photo. "What does he want from you?"

Violet sighed. "Nothing, Iris. He just enjoys my company. He said, and these are his words not mine, 'You're a scintillating conversationalist, Violet.'"

"And no one else finds that highly suspicious?" Iris balked.

"Don't be offended by Iris, Violet, she's just jealous," Poppy joked.

"I know," Violet said, elated. "And it feels *so* good!"

Iris threw her hands up in surrender.

Poppy's phone buzzed.

It was Sam.

"Speaking of dinner dates. Excuse me," Poppy said.

"I'm going to take this outside." Poppy hurried out the door to Iris's backyard and answered the call. "Hi, Sam."

"Hey, beautiful," Sam said hoarsely.

"Is everything all right? You sound strange."

"I was wondering if we could postpone dinner tonight . . . ?"

"Of course. Are you sick? Are you running a fever?"

"No, just feeling a little off, that's all. Don't worry. I'll be fine."

Poppy sensed something was definitely wrong, but like most bullheaded men who refused to show weakness, Sam was trying to act like his normal upbeat, jocular self.

"Where are you, Big Bear?"

"Yes."

"Would you like me to come up there and check on you?"

Sam chuckled. "Poppy, there is no need for you to drive an hour and a half up a mountain when I'll probably be asleep in an hour. I'm well-stocked with Tylenol and canned soup, so I'm good."

Poppy hesitated. If there was one thing about Sam Emerson that she was sure about, it was that he was strong. But despite the calm, reassuring words coming out of his mouth, she could not ignore the overwhelming sense of dread building up in the pit of her stomach.

Still, she had to take him at his word.

"Okay, take care of yourself, I'll call you first thing in the morning to see how you're doing."

"Sounds good."

And then he hung up.

Rather abruptly, in fact.

And her sense of dread was not going away.

Chapter 29

As Poppy and Matt entered John Henry's Cafe through the side patio entrance, Poppy couldn't help but notice Matt wincing slightly, his body no doubt still hurting from having been in two separate car crashes in a matter of a few days.

"Are you in pain?" Poppy asked, full of concern.

Matt placed a reassuring hand on her arm. "A little, but don't worry, I'll be doing handstands in no time, not that I ever did them before."

Poppy chuckled. "I appreciate you filling in for Sam tonight as my dinner companion."

"What happened to him?"

Poppy shrugged. "I'm not sure. He didn't sound like himself when we spoke, but you know Sam, he's the last person willing to open up about what's going on with him."

"Poppy!"

Poppy turned to see Alfredo, the handsome, charming, fortyish owner of John Henry, who had started out as a busboy and worked his way up the ladder before buying the restaurant from the founding owner, a testament to the American dream.

Poppy hugged Alfredo. "Thanks for squeezing us in tonight, Alfredo."

"Anything for you. Follow me, we have a table for two tucked in the corner, very romantic," he said, leading them along past bustling waiters carrying food and taking orders, busboys cleaning off empty tables, diners eating, drinking, and chattering at a litany of white-clothed tables.

"Well, my request for something romantic is now off the table for tonight. My date couldn't make it. This is my business associate Matt Flowers," Poppy said.

"Ah, the famous Matt Flowers. I've read a lot about you. You've made quite the impression around here," Alfredo said as he stopped at a small table and gestured for them to have a seat. "I'll send over some escargot and baked brie on the house," he said with a wink.

"You're too good to us, Alfredo, thank you," Poppy cooed, blowing him a kiss, which he mimed catching and tapping against his cheek. He hustled off to attend to his other customers while Poppy picked up a menu to peruse the specials.

Matt glanced around the patio. "He's got a good business going here. Hey, did you get the idea to come here because Violet mentioned she had dinner here last night with her new beau?"

"Not exactly," Poppy said, eyes fixed on her menu.

Matt suddenly sprang to attention. "Hey, isn't that—?"

Poppy followed Matt's gaze over to a table on the opposite side of the patio, just outside the covered dining room where Detective Lamar Jordan and his wife, Lynn, were having dinner. He was devouring a breaded pork chop while she daintily picked at a macadamia nut–encrusted sole.

"What a coincidence," Matt remarked.

"Not really," Poppy muttered.

Matt snapped to attention. "So you knew they were going to be here tonight?"

"I may have been tipped off by Mrs. Jordan's Instagram post. She loves to tell everyone everything she's doing and everything she's planning to do. It's proven to be very helpful."

Matt flashed a sly smile. "Well, then, it would be rude of us not to go over and say hello." He jumped up, and ever the chivalrous gentleman, scuttled around and helped pull out Poppy's chair so she could stand up. Then, arm in arm, they traipsed over to Detective Jordan and his wife.

"Hello, this is a surprise," Poppy said, beaming.

Detective Jordan was just raising his fork, about to pop a piece of his pork chop into his mouth, when he suddenly stopped halfway as he looked up from the table to see Poppy and Matt.

"Is it?" Jordan snarled.

"What are the odds of us running into each other again so soon after the last time?" Poppy asked, feigning innocence.

"Are you intentionally following me around, Ms. Harmon?" Jordan asked, a tension in his tone.

Poppy mustered up a slightly hurt look. "What? No, my business partner Matt and I just happened to arrive here for dinner and saw you across the patio, and so we thought . . . I'm sorry if we disturbed you."

209 POPPY HARMON AND THE PILLOW TALK KILLER

"Lamar, why are you being impolite?" Lynn snapped before flashing her own radiant smile and sticking out her hand. "Lynn Jordan. I'm a huge fan of yours, Ms. Harmon. When I was a kid watching you on *Jack Colt*, I begged my mother to take me to her hairdresser's so I could get the same style that you had on your show!"

"Oh, how sweet!" Poppy cooed.

Lynn caught her husband rolling his eyes and kicked him under the table. Lamar dropped his fork, then, aggravated, scooped up his glass of wine and guzzled what was left of it.

"We're going to need another bottle," he murmured.

"Lamar, stop it," Lynn scolded.

"This is Matt Flowers," Poppy said to Lynn, who went to shake his hand, but Matt caught it and planted a kiss on it.

Poppy wanted to signal him he was taking it too far, but she had learned a long time ago there was no reeling Matt back in once he was committed to charming any woman, or man for that matter. Luckily Lynn fell for his unabashed gallantry hook, line, and sinker.

Lamar flagged down the waiter and picked up the empty bottle of wine, signaling him to bring another.

Lynn threw him a judgmental look and muttered, "Looks like I will be driving us home tonight."

Lamar sighed. "Lynn, don't be fooled. It's no coincidence that they're here. Ms. Harmon tends to show up wherever I am when she is in need of information on my cases that she also happens to be investigating."

"That sounds a bit paranoid to me," Lynn sniffed. "How does she manage to track you down wherever you are?"

"I don't know, maybe if you didn't tell the whole world where we are all the time on Instagram—"

"Oh, so it's *my* fault?" Lynn growled.

"How's the sole? I was thinking of ordering it for my entree," Matt offered in an unsuccessful bid to break the tension.

There was a long pause.

"Well, enjoy the rest of your dinner," Poppy said.

Poppy and Matt turned to go.

"Wait," Lynn said before they left. She glared at her husband. "Why don't you tell them what you told me during our appetizer course?"

Detective Jordan stared at his wife blankly. "What?"

"About Hal Greenwood," Lynn sighed, annoyed.

Poppy's ears instantly pricked up.

She wanted to give Lynn Jordan a big, loving hug, but resisted, keeping her cool so as not to prove too eager to lap up whatever information Jordan had to share.

Lynn sat back in her chair and folded her arms, eyes locked on her husband. "Look, Lamar, it's not like you're in competition with the Desert Flowers Agency. What's wrong with offering a few details if it helps both of you?"

"Because the police are not in the habit of sharing our intelligence and evidence with just anyone—"

Lynn abruptly cut him off. "She's not just *anyone*. She's Poppy Harmon, and she was a role model to me growing up, and from what I have heard recently, she now helps people in need around here so I don't see what possible harm could come from simply relaying what you know."

Lamar Jordan dealt with enough drama and misery in his daily line of work, so his utmost priority at home was to keep the peace. And that was about to work to Poppy's advantage.

"Fine," Jordan sighed before pivoting around in his chair toward Poppy and Matt. "Hal Greenwood has an alibi for Danika Delgado's murder. I checked it out. It's solid."

"Where was he?" Matt asked.

"One of the production assistants, Tommy . . ."

"Timothy," Poppy corrected him.

"Yeah, him. He claimed that when Hal Greenwood arrived on the set in Joshua Tree on the day of the murder, he demanded to see Ms. Delgado. Timothy took him to her trailer where she was supposed to be. They knocked a few times but she didn't answer. So he left. That was before you came around and discovered the body."

"Yes, we know, but couldn't Hal have doubled back on his own between the time Timothy escorted him to the trailer and the time Poppy found the body?" Matt asked.

Jordan shook his head. "No, because right after he left Timothy, he jumped on a conference call with the director and producer of another film he has in preproduction. I have phone records and witnesses to back it all up. It would have been impossible for him to sneak back to Danika's trailer, break in, and suffocate her with that pillow before or after he was on that call."

"So he didn't do it," Poppy murmured. "I was so certain that he was the one. . . ."

"What about Chase Ehrens?" Matt asked somberly.

"Missing," Jordan said quietly.

"Missing?" Poppy gasped.

"After he posted bail, he up and disappeared. Neither his agent nor his manager have been in contact with him since and his landlord says he hasn't been back to his apartment in days. I've got a couple of my detectives working on locating him but so far no luck."

"Maybe you should assign Poppy to the task force since she is apparently so good at tracking people down," Lynn joked.

Detective Jordan failed to see the humor.

"And still no word on Byron Savage?" Poppy asked, frustrated.

"Nope. But don't worry, we'll find him eventually."

Poppy nodded appreciatively, but was truly worried. How would they ever solve Danika Delgado's murder if the strongest suspects just kept vanishing off the face of the earth?

Chapter 30

I know who killed Danika Delgado.
Parker Hotel. Room 12.
Come ASAP.

Poppy stared at the text on her phone. She recognized the number. It was the one given to her by Fabian Granger when they had exchanged phone numbers at the Mary Pickford. Matt had dropped her off after dinner, and Poppy had barely unlocked the door of her house and stepped inside, exhausted and ready for bed, when she'd received the urgent text from Fabian.

Poppy considered texting back, or calling him, but she knew it was risky. Hal Greenwood's operatives could have already hacked her phone, or Fabian's phone, and might be following their communication in real time. No, it was probably safer if she followed his instructions and drove herself over to the Parker immediately.

Poppy turned back around, marched outside to her car parked in the driveway, and drove to the elegant Parker Hotel just off Highway 111 near the border of Palm Springs and Cathedral City. She parked on the street and headed into the lobby where a bright-eyed, sun-kissed, perky hotel clerk awaited her behind the opulent reception desk.

"Can you please direct me to room twelve?" Poppy asked.

"That's one of our poolside rooms. Just follow the path outside past Norma's, and you'll see signs pointing you in the right direction," the bubbly girl answered.

"Thank you."

Poppy continued on outside, past the brightly colored open-air terrace restaurant Norma's, which was still serving a few guests, and quickly spotted a sign that led her to a long hallway with doors leading to the room.

When she reached number twelve, she knocked but there was no answer. She tried again. This time a little more forcefully. The third time she pounded on it with her fist, startling a couple returning from a night out on the town. They were a little tipsy and eyed her suspiciously, the husband nodding as he passed, "Good evening."

"Good evening," Poppy responded with a smile.

The couple moved on down the hall and let themselves into a room on the end. When they were safely inside, Poppy tried the door handle to room twelve. It was locked. Then she remembered the clerk saying the room was a poolside room. Perhaps there was another way in on the opposite side.

She scurried back to where she had come from, circled

around to see a petite aqua gem of a pool with soothing lighting, one of several on the property, and counted the bougainvillea patios until she got to the one she assumed was number twelve. She glanced around to make sure no one was watching her. There was an older couple in the pool smooching and not paying any attention. No one else was around. She quietly tiptoed over to the sliding glass door. When she reached for the handle, she realized it was already open and the curtains inside were wafting in the soft night breeze. Poppy pulled them aside and entered the room, which was dimly lit and eerily quiet.

"Fabian?"

No answer.

"Fabian, are you here?"

Nothing.

She had thrown caution to the wind by coming here, but now she felt a nervous twinge. Perhaps this had been a mistake. She was about to turn around and hightail it out of there when she noticed a flickering light coming from the bathroom. The door was wide open. She slowly, cautiously stepped toward it until she was close enough to see a mason jar candle burning on the tiled sink. There was a strong vanilla scent. Her eyes fell upon the bathtub, which was filled with foamy white bubbles that covered the top of the water. Instinctively, she slowly walked over, reached down with her hand, and began clearing the bubbles off to the side until she could see the haunting, dead eyes of Fabian Granger staring up at her from underneath the water. Poppy reared back, screaming, slipping on the wet floor and landing hard on her bum.

She scrambled to her feet and ran out of the bathroom just as the doorbell to the room rang. She raced over and whipped it open to reveal a portly young smiling waiter with a rolling room service cart and a plate covered with a metal tin, a bottle of Pinot Noir, a wineglass, and utensils rolled into a cloth napkin.

He started to push his way inside with a friendly wave when Poppy threw herself in front of the cart, and cried, "There is a dead body in the bathtub! Call nine-one-one!"

The startled waiter's smile quickly faded and he grabbed his phone from his back pocket and fumbled to make the call.

Poppy was feeling faint from the shock of discovering poor Fabian Granger dead, and had to sit down on the couch in the living area to collect herself.

Within ten minutes, the room was crawling with police officers. Poppy cringed when Detective Jordan swept inside, conferring with a couple of his subordinates, a man and a woman, not yet spotting her.

"Who discovered the body?" Jordan asked gruffly.

The female detective pointed at Poppy sitting stiffly on the couch, hoping that if she did not move and pretended to be invisible, she would not be noticed.

No such luck.

"You have got to be kidding me!" Jordan roared.

"Do you know her?" the male detective asked.

"I'm afraid so," Jordan spit out. "She just stalked me and my wife while we were having a nice dinner out, and now, once again, she turns up at another murder scene!"

"*Another* murder scene?" the female detective asked, incredulous.

"Don't get me started!" Jordan bellowed.

Poppy knew at this point she was going to be in for a very long night.

Chapter 31

Poppy yawned and rubbed her eyes while sitting at her kitchen table, sipping coffee, holding her cell phone out in front of her, the speakerphone enabled. "You're going to have to repeat that."

"I'm afraid our installation team will be unable to complete the job today," the representative from Smart House Security said, trying to remain chipper.

Poppy sighed, agitated. "Why not?"

"We overbooked. I swear to you, this *never* happens," the girl promised.

"Well, it just did," Poppy said through clenched teeth. She was dead tired, having not arrived home until after three in the morning due to exhausting questioning from Detective Jordan at the Parker Hotel crime scene. Then, she had to set the alarm for six-thirty in order to be up in time to greet Smart House Security, which was scheduled to install her new home security system, but now was a no-show.

Poppy had waited over an hour before calling the company to find out what was going on. After another fifteen minutes on hold, a representative had finally gotten on the line. She cheerfully announced her name was Britney, and explained how excited she was to help Poppy with whatever she needed. But after a few clicks on her keyboard, Britney somberly delivered the bad news that her guys would not be coming today.

Then it was back to perky. "We have an appointment open in three weeks, how does Thursday the tenth sound to you?"

"It doesn't sound good to me at all, Britney," Poppy seethed. "This appointment today has been on the books for weeks. It's very important to me I get this done. I scheduled this security alarm installation before I even moved into the house."

Poppy wanted to explain why she was so eager to have peace of mind, knowing her new house was wired and being monitored by all the emergency services. How she was supremely uncomfortable with the local press excitedly documenting her purchase of this house, because of its pedigree and the fact that Poppy herself passed as a "celebrity buyer," someone who had enjoyed a modicum of Hollywood success, if ever so briefly. It was enough to warrant an article in the real estate section of the *Desert Sun*. And then there was the run-in with Byron Savage and his brutish brother Axel. Both were currently on the run, off the grid, free to show up out of nowhere and strike at any moment. She wouldn't feel safe until she had a direct line to the police in case anyone tried to break in to frighten her, terrorize her, or worse, as Axel had so ominously promised. She wanted to stress to this cheery young woman that if anything bad happened to Poppy between now and Thursday the tenth, then Smart House Security would be responsible.

But true to form, in the end, Poppy kept all that information to herself because she knew the young woman was just doing her job, and frankly, Poppy relating her fears would probably not do much good. She would just be seen as some paranoid old woman from Britney's millennial vantage point.

"I can put you on a waiting list in case we have a cancellation between now and the tenth," Britney offered.

"Yes, fine, do that," Poppy huffed.

Poppy's phone buzzed.

It was Sam.

"Great. You're all set," Britney said. "Now would you like to fill out a survey online about how your experience was with us today?"

"Believe me when I tell you this, Britney, you do not want me to do that. Good-bye," Poppy said, ending the call and answering Sam's. "Hi, Sam."

"Hey, beautiful."

Poppy grimaced. Always the flirt to be sure, but there was a detectable strain in Sam's voice.

He coughed and cleared his throat. "I just wanted to apologize again for breaking our date. I'm sorry if I ruined your evening."

"Sam, you cancelling was a disappointment, but it was a far cry from the cataclysmic event that really ruined my evening."

"You got me curious."

Poppy just did not have the energy to breathlessly recount her stumbling across the dead body of Fabian Granger in a bathtub at the Parker. Nor would Sam be shocked by that news, given her escalating habit of coming into close proximity with recent corpses. No, she was not going to go there, at least for now. "Never mind. I'm safe and sound, that's all that matters. How are you feeling, any better?"

"I wish I could say yes, but after we spoke on the phone yesterday, things took a little turn for the worse."

"Oh no. Did you go see a doctor?"

"Yeah, eventually. And now I have a full-time staff looking after me."

Poppy crinkled her nose, confused. "What do you mean?"

"I'm in the hospital."

Poppy gasped. "*What*?"

"Apparently I had a heart attack," he said, disconcertingly calm. "I had been feeling weird all day, and then last night I felt chest pains, shortness of breath. I was going to drive myself to the emergency room, but then I thought better of it and called an ambulance."

"*Sam* . . ." Poppy gasped, already looking for her bag with her car keys so she could drive herself up to Big Bear pronto. "I'm on my way."

"Poppy, you don't have to do that. It's nothing serious," Sam said.

"Don't be *that* man, Sam," Poppy admonished.

"What man?"

"The kind of man who downplays everything, pretends he's got everything under control when he is actually in a very serious situation . . ."

Sam remained silent on the other end of the call.

"What hospital are you in?"

"Bear Valley Community Hospital. Pretty much the only one up here," he said.

"Hold on. I'm coming to you."

"Thank you," he said quietly.

Poppy jumped in her car and raced on the 10 freeway to Calimesa where she exited onto CA-38 in San Bernardino County, continuing on up the mountain to Big Bear. She made it in less than two hours. Her GPS got her to the hospital, and after parking, she was at the admitting desk. A receptionist directed her up to the second floor where Sam was recuperating.

When Poppy burst into his room, she stopped in her tracks at the sight of him. He looked thinner, weak, pale. It was so startling because she had only known Sam Emerson as a rough-riding, macho, strong-as-nails cowboy.

It was a dramatic change.

Sam seemed to notice her troubled reaction.

"The doc gave me two stents to open up the blockage. Says I'll be as good as new in a few weeks so you can stop worrying."

Poppy employed her acting skills to quickly cover up her obvious dismay and project a more lighthearted tone. "I'm sure you're a terrible patient," she teased.

"That's not true. The nurses say I've been a dream," he said, trying to sit up in bed. He winced, obviously in pain, and eased himself back down, hoping Poppy hadn't noticed.

But of course she had.

"Oh, I'm certain the nurses have been dreaming about you. You're a serial flirter."

"Whatever gets me an extra Jell-O," he said, smiling.

There was a brief silence before Poppy reached out

and squeezed Sam's hand. "I wish you had called me earlier."

He nodded. "I didn't want to worry you." Then, still holding hands, he shakily raised them up to his lips and softly kissed the back of Poppy's hand. "But I'm glad you're here."

Poppy was floored. For Sam to freely admit that much, well, he might as well have proposed to her. That's how rare it was for Sam Emerson to show any overt emotion.

She was touched by it, and thankful that she was by his bedside now, too, because she knew he was going to need her support now more than ever. Her biggest fear at the moment was just how much Sam might be downplaying the current state of his health.

She wanted a blunt conversation with his doctor as soon as she could get one.

Chapter 32

Poppy spent the rest of the day running errands for Sam, picking up his mail at his remote house in the woods, buying some magazines and paperback westerns for him to pass the time with and a box of his favorite cookies at a nearby bakery, before walking up and down the halls of the hospital in search of Sam's doctor to get a realistic idea of what they were facing regarding Sam's overall recovery. She finally managed to corner Dr. Brad Levin by the elevator.

"Are you Mrs. Emerson?" Dr. Levin asked.

"No," Poppy said quickly.

"Then I'm afraid if you are not family, I can't discuss Mr. Emerson's condition—"

"I'm his sister!"

Dr. Levin eyed her suspiciously. "Sister?"

"What, you don't believe me?" Poppy asked evenly, an indignant look on her face. The actress was always prepared to deliver a convincing performance in a pinch, especially in an emergency.

Luckily Dr. Levin was not in the mood to argue given his busy schedule.

"My apologies," he said before launching into a detailed explanation of exactly what happened with Sam's heart.

As he talked, Poppy sized the doctor up, his baby face and boyish demeanor doing nothing to assuage her fear that Sam might be under the care of someone not even old enough to vote. But her mind was quickly put at ease by Dr. Levin's meticulous description of Sam's coronary blockage that resulted in the attack, how he had inserted two stents after an angioplasty in order to help keep the blood flowing and the artery from narrowing again, how he was going to prescribe a regimen of anti-platelet drugs and clot-busting medications for him to strictly follow in the months ahead. Dr. Levin may have looked like he was twelve years old, but he came off as exceedingly knowledgeable and competent.

"Will you be looking after him once we discharge him?" Dr. Levin asked.

The question surprised Poppy.

She had never imagined Sam might need home care.

Would he even allow her to move in and play nurse?

Probably not.

Sam could be frustratingly stubborn.

But that was a discussion for later.

"Yes," Poppy answered. She thanked the doctor and walked back to Sam's room where she found him cracking open a William W. Johnstone gunslinging novel.

He smiled warmly at her as she entered. "They say they're going to keep me here a couple more days, to monitor me and make sure there are no complications from my surgery, so you don't have to stick around."

"I know I don't have to," Poppy said. "I want to."

"Seriously, I appreciate all you've done, but I don't want to be a burden, and I know you're very busy right now investigating a case."

"Sam, you're a lot more important to me than any case. . . ."

Sam shifted uncomfortably in his bed. She knew he despised being vulnerable or dependent on anyone. In his mind it was of utmost importance to project strength, and he was not going to allow a pesky little heart attack to chip away at that image. "Doc says the worst is over, I don't need to be fussed over . . ."

Poppy sighed.

Frustratingly stubborn, indeed.

She decided to let him win this battle.

For now.

But the war was far from over.

Sam was going to allow her to help him through this heavy ordeal, whether he wanted her to or not.

"Fine," Poppy said. "If you have everything you need, I'll drive back to Palm Springs and we will pick up this conversation when I return tomorrow morning."

"Tomorrow? You don't have to come back here—"

"*Tomorrow*," she said firmly.

Sam shrugged and threw his hands up in the air.

Poppy marched over, planted a firm kiss on his lips, which he most certainly enjoyed, and then spun around and left the room, stopping at the nurses' station to leave her contact information in case there was any sudden change in Sam's condition.

Within minutes, she was back in her car driving down

the mountain. Matt had texted her earlier when she was at Sam's house to alert her to the breaking news—Fabian Granger's death had unsurprisingly been officially ruled a homicide. He did not down too many sleeping pills or drink too much liquor and accidentally drown in the tub. Someone had deliberately and cruelly held him under the water until his lungs had been filled with bathwater and he was dead. Now, on speakerphone, they were formulating a plan on how to proceed.

"I was thinking we could meet at the Parker Hotel where it happened, maybe get a look at who came in and who left the hotel during the time of the murder, if they'll let us watch the security footage," Matt suggested.

"I'm sure the police have already beaten us to the punch," Poppy said, carefully maneuvering around a slow-moving Mercedes on the long, winding, downhill road.

"Yeah, but who knows? Maybe we'll pick up something they missed."

He had a point.

There was no harm in double-checking.

Matt's gusto and thoroughness was about to pay off in dividends.

They met in the lobby of the Parker two hours later and approached the reception desk, this time manned by a handsome young, wiry Latino man who practically lit up like a Christmas tree when Poppy and Matt approached. "Good afternoon. Checking in?"

Poppy stood back, allowing Matt to take the lead since the receptionist couldn't tear his eyes off the exceedingly good-looking man who was accompanying her.

Matt's eyes fell upon the receptionist's name tag pinned to his chest. "Matt Flowers, private investigator, it's a pleasure to meet you, *Gustavo*." Matt let the name roll slowly off his tongue as he locked eyes with the receptionist, who for a moment was stricken mute. Matt gestured toward Poppy. "This is my assistant, Poppy Harmon."

Gustavo didn't even bother to look at Poppy; instead his puppy-dog eyes remained firmly glued on Matt's handsome face. As Matt explained why they were here, how they were investigating the Fabian Granger murder, how a brief look at the hotel's security cam footage would be immeasurably helpful, Poppy began to assume from Gustavo's troubled expression that even Matt's considerable charm might not be enough this time.

"I don't know . . . I'd have to ask the manager, and I'm not sure he would want me to—"

Matt reached out and gently placed a hand on top of Gustavo's, which was resting on the check-in desk counter. "I understand. The last thing I would want to happen is for you to get into any kind of trouble. I'd feel terribly guilty." Then he lightly patted Gustavo's hand. Poppy saw a slight shiver rushing through Gustavo, who glanced around to see if his manager was anywhere in the vicinity. Satisfied, Gustavo leaned closer to Matt and said in a whisper, "I can't let you back there where we keep the footage, but I could download it on my iPad and show you out here."

"You would do that for *me*?" Matt asked, a hand on his heart.

Gustavo nodded with a conspiratorial smile.

And a lot more, I'm sure, Poppy thought.

For a straight man, Matt was a master at the seduction of gay men.

"I have a feeling we're going to be lifelong friends, Gustavo," Matt purred.

"I'm going to hold you to it," Gustavo giggled, lighting up again with the force of not just any Christmas tree, but the one towering every year in the middle of Rockefeller Center. "Be right back."

Gustavo flew out a door marked EMPLOYEES ONLY.

"Impressive," Poppy said, shaking her head. "Do you find it at all tiring handling all the unrequited crushes these countless girls and boys seem to have on you?"

Matt tossed her a knowing smile. "Oh, please, Poppy, I know you had your own long line of admirers back in the heyday of your acting career, still do from what I can tell."

"Perhaps, but you are a master, when called upon, at using it to your advantage. I'm afraid that's a skill I sorely lack."

"I can teach you," Matt eagerly offered. "It's all in the eye contact."

Poppy let loose with a throaty laugh.

He was being sincere not boastful, but Poppy still found it amusing.

The door opened and a chastened Gustavo returned, clutching his iPad. Behind him was a stern-looking much older man, in his sixties, *Ralph* printed on his name tag along with *Hotel Manager*.

Poppy swallowed hard.

It was clear Gustavo had been caught downloading the security footage onto his iPad.

Ralph pushed in front of Gustavo, who flashed Matt an apologetic frown. "I'm sorry, but it is against hotel policy for us to hand out our security footage to just *anyone* to watch. Gustavo should have known that."

"I'm sorry. Matt Flowers, private investigator," Matt chimed in, thrusting out his hand to shake.

Ralph limply accepted it, clearly nowhere near as enthralled with Matt as Gustavo had been. No, Ralph could not have been less impressed and it was becoming increasingly clear that their efforts to see the footage were about to be curtailed.

Until . . .

Ralph finally noticed Poppy.

Matt was still prattling on about how deeply personal this case was to him, how he only wanted to assist the police and not get in their way, but all of his entreaties fell on deaf ears because Ralph the hotel manager was now solely focused on Poppy.

Or Daphne, Poppy's character on *Jack Colt*.

Ralph's eyes flickered back and forth, and Poppy wondered if he was trying to place her from somewhere, not quite remembering where he knew her from, but that notion was quickly dispelled.

"I was such a huge fan of yours," Ralph announced, practically drooling.

"Why, thank you," Poppy said, almost with a Southern drawl, which she couldn't explain. She just wanted to come off as friendly.

"My wife is never going to believe this. She's always joking that I'd rather be married to you because I still watch old episodes of *Jack Colt* on MeTV when I'm feeling down and need to lift my spirits. Rhonda, that's my wife, likes you, too, mostly from that perfume ad you did in the late seventies." Ralph gestured toward Matt. "He with you?"

"Yes, he's my associate," Poppy answered.

"You mean, you're a private detective, too? Are you kidding me? You played a detective's secretary on TV back in the day, and now you're one in real life? That is so awesome!" Ralph barreled out from behind the reception desk, waving his phone. "Do you mind if I get a selfie? My wife is going to die!"

"Of course," Poppy said cheerfully.

Matt offered to take it, but Ralph waved him off, preferring to snap it himself. Once he got one he was satisfied with, Ralph hurried over and snatched the iPad out of Gustavo's hand before hustling back over to Poppy's side. "Rules are made to be broken and all that, right?"

"We're so grateful for your help, Ralph," Poppy purred, even more seductively than Matt.

Matt, standing next to Poppy, whispered under his breath, "I don't need to teach you a damn thing."

Ralph thrust the iPad in front of them and began playing the footage. "Cops went over this with a fine-tooth comb. We only found one person entering the hotel, besides yourself, Ms. Harmon, who was not a registered guest." Ralph fast-forwarded through the footage. "The police had no idea who this guy was, and the girl on duty at reception didn't even remember seeing him, but the camera picked him up entering around eight-thirty and leaving again around eight-forty-five." Ralph tapped the screen to stop the footage. "There he is. Recognize him?"

Ralph held the iPad up in front of him.

Poppy and Matt stared hard at the footage.

Matt crinkled his nose. "I feel like I've seen him before, but I don't know where."

"You have seen him before," Poppy said solemnly.

"Who is he?" Matt asked.

"That's Violet's new boyfriend."

Chapter 33

"I don't understand," Violet muttered softly while sitting on the plush sofa at the Desert Flowers garage office, knees together, hands clasped resting on top of them, while staring wide-eyed at Poppy and Matt, who stood across from her, both with pained expressions on their faces.

"What's not to understand? Your boyfriend is a fake just as I suspected!" Iris snorted from the kitchen area as she poured herself a glass of white wine.

"We don't know that for sure, Iris, so stop saying that," Poppy scolded. Then she turned and said gently to Violet, "Do you have any idea what he might have been doing at the Parker on the night I found Fabian Granger dead?"

Violet shook her head vigorously. "No. But I cannot believe that Phil had anything to do with something so horrid—"

"When was the last time you spoke to him?" Matt asked.

"The day after we had dinner. I texted him to say what a lovely time I had at John Henry's and he texted back and said he agreed and was looking forward to doing it again soon," Violet said.

"Maybe you should call him now and make another plan to get together, you know, to see if he's for real or not," Wyatt suggested, sitting at his desk in front of his computer, swiveling around in circles on his stool, chewing on a candy bar.

Matt nodded. "That's not a bad idea, Violet."

Violet hesitated. "I don't know. . . ."

She was scared. Scared they would turn out to be right about this Phil they had never heard of until just a few days ago. It would be humiliating and heartbreaking for her.

Poppy walked over and sat down next to Violet, lightly touching her arm. "It's the only way to be absolutely certain his intentions are noble, Violet."

Violet sighed, still not sure. She glanced over at her grandson, who was wiping some chocolate off his face with the palm of his hand before lapping it up with his tongue.

"Better to know now than later," Iris said, folding her arms. "It is like ripping off a Band-Aid. It is going to hurt no matter what, but better to do it fast and get it over with, rather than slow and making the pain last longer."

Poppy threw Iris an annoyed look as Iris casually sipped her wine.

Resolute, Violet picked up her phone off the coffee table in front of her and made the call. She put the phone to her ear, waiting a few moments for Phil to answer.

Slowly, Violet's face began to fall. Then her whole body sagged.

Poppy leaned forward, concerned. "Violet, what is it?"

Violet's lips were now trembling as she handed the phone over to Poppy, who turned on the speaker so they all could hear an operator report in a robotic tone, "*The number you are calling is no longer in service.*"

"Oh, dear," Poppy mumbled.

Violet stared helplessly into space, not moving.

"I'm so sorry, Violet," Matt said earnestly.

Something dawned on Violet and she was drawn back from her trance. "But he also gave me his home address in Palm Desert when we exchanged contact information. Why would he do that if he was just using me to keep tabs on us for Hal Greenwood, or God only knows what other reason?"

Wyatt hopped off his stool and scurried over to his grandmother. He held out his hand for the phone. "Is the address in your phone, Grandma?"

"Yes," Violet whispered. "It's under McKellan. Phil McKellan."

Poppy relinquished the phone to Wyatt, who raced back to his computer and speedily tapped on his computer keys. A Google Earth map popped up on his screen as he zoomed in on an image of the North America continent, then the state of California, Riverside County, the city of Palm Desert, then an exact neighborhood. He scanned a street, stopping at what appeared to be an empty lot on the corner. Then, he slowly swiveled around to face Violet. "You've been ghosted, Grandma."

"What?" Violet sniffled.

"The address he gave you doesn't even exist."

Violet dropped her head. She had expected this, but

hearing it out loud seemed to only make it worse. "I feel like such a damn fool."

Poppy grabbed Violet's hand and squeezed it. "Do not blame yourself for this, Violet. Something like this could have happened to any one of us."

The moment it flew out of her mouth Poppy cranked her head around in Iris's direction to stop her from commenting, but of course, it was too late.

"Not me," Iris grunted.

"Not helping!" Poppy snapped.

Chapter 34

The last place Poppy had ever imagined she would be was back on the set of *Palm Springs Weekend* in the heart of Joshua Tree National Park. But a surprising call from Greta Van Damm the evening before had confirmed the rumors that she had been hearing all day that Hal Greenwood Productions had found a suitable replacement for the late, lamented Danika Delgado, and the decision had been officially made to forge ahead on the movie, finish the remaining scenes left to shoot, and then go back and reshoot the scenes already in the can involving Danika's character with the new actress.

Poppy had honestly assumed the whole project would be shelved after Danika's murder, and the millions of dollars already spent would be written off as a loss. She was even more stunned to discover that the producers wanted both Poppy and Matt to return and finish the handful of scenes they had left to film. After hanging up with a very cold, remote, yet professional Greta, Poppy immediately got Matt on the phone, who was decidedly more enthusiastic about returning to the set.

Carpooling with Matt to Joshua Tree the following morning, Poppy had placed a call to Detective Jordan to bring him up to speed on what little information they had about Phil McKellan, whom they had clearly identified on the Parker Hotel's security footage, and whom they suspected had bugged their office using Violet as his way to get inside. It wasn't much. But it was something. Naturally, Detective Jordan had declined to take Poppy's call, but the desk sergeant who took the message did at least sound mildly intrigued.

After parking her car at a base camp, Poppy and Matt hustled into a van and were transported about a half mile to the set. They had barely had time to get a cup of coffee at the craft services table and find the makeup trailer when they suddenly heard a man yelling at the top of his lungs.

"What the hell are they doing here?"

Poppy and Matt spun around, coffee in hand, dumbstruck as they saw Hal Greenwood in all his blustery, full-tilt rage, pointing a pudgy finger directly at them.

"I want them off my set! Somebody call security!"

Nobody moved.

Everyone was still in shock from the sudden, unexpected outburst.

Hal, his face as red as a ripened tomato, sweat dribbling down his chubby cheeks, stomped his feet in the desert sand like a petulant child, still pointing his finger at Poppy and Matt. "I fired you two! That means you're trespassing and subject to arrest! And let me tell you, I'm gonna love seeing those smug, sanctimonious faces of yours behind bars!"

Poppy didn't feel like she was being smug or sanctimonious. In fact, she was more confused than anything else. But she was not about to budge. She was going to stand her ground against this bully, at least until someone explained to her why they had been dragged back to the set if they were not wanted.

"Hal! Hal! Wait!" Greta called breathlessly as she scurried onto the set and physically placed herself as a barrier between her mercurial boss and Poppy and Matt. "I asked them to come."

"You *what*?" Hal wailed.

Greta stopped momentarily to catch her breath, a hand over her rapidly beating heart, and pressed on. "Can we go talk somewhere privately so I can explain?"

"No! You can tell me right here!" Hal roared.

Greta glanced around at the small crowd, cast and crew, all gathered around, eyes glued to the big boss's meltdown. "Okay," she sighed, shrugging, figuring there was probably relatively little harm in letting everyone hear the truth. "The insurance company is covering the cost of recasting and reshooting the scenes with Danika that we lost, but not any additional scenes. I talked to Netflix and they're happy with all the other dailies so it wouldn't be financially prudent to let any more cast members go at this point—"

"I don't care! I'll cover the damn costs myself!" Hal erupted.

"We're already over budget," Greta pleaded. "They only have a couple of scenes left and then they will be done."

Hal sputtered and fumed and swore to himself some more, but in the end, he knew his right-hand man, or woman, was making the correct call. "Fine," he muttered before pointing his finger again at Poppy and Matt while yelling in Greta's direction. "But I want their scenes done today, you hear me, today, and then I want them gone!"

"Yes, Hal, I can arrange that," Greta promised, relief in her voice.

Hal stormed off, still seething, and Greta made a bee-line over to Poppy and Matt.

"I have never felt more welcome," Poppy cracked.

"I'm sorry about that. Hal is still a little rattled over you showing up at our office in LA unannounced and insinuating that he had something to do with Danika's murder."

Neither Poppy nor Matt had any intention of disavowing those suspicions and Greta bristled at their stony silence. But then, she quickly shifted back into producer mode, her primary mission to keep the peace and the production on track.

"Anyway, I appreciate you both keeping your commitment and coming back to wrap your scenes. Given how Hal has treated you both, a lot of actors would have stayed away. If there is anything you need, just let me know," Greta said with a tight smile.

Before they could respond, Greta was off like a shot, ready to put out more fires.

"I suspect it's going to be a very long day," Poppy sighed.

"At least it won't be boring," Matt chuckled before something caught his eye. "Not boring at all."

Poppy followed his gaze to the opposite side of the craft service table where a statuesque girl with a striking resemblance to Danika, smooth caramel skin, jet-black hair, beautiful and even doe-eyed from a distance. But as they approached, Poppy noticed up close a roughness around the edges. She was draped in a pink bathrobe that hung open just enough, on purpose Poppy suspected, to flaunt her ample breasts. A few crew members stopped what they were doing to gape at her as she hummed to herself and perused a platter of fresh fruit. As she settled upon a piece of melon and popped it into her mouth, the juice dribbling down her chin, there was almost an audible heavy sigh from her gaggle of male fans on the set watching her.

She circled around the table and made a point of walking up to Poppy and Matt. "Hi, I'm the new girl."

"Matt Flowers." He pumped her hand, a silly grin on his face. He made no effort to introduce Poppy as he was so distracted by this absolute vision of loveliness.

"And I'm just a random person standing next to him," Poppy said, elbowing Matt in the rib cage.

"Oh, where are my manners? This is Poppy . . ."

"Harmon," Poppy said, rolling her eyes at Matt.

"Joselyn Tremblay," the girl said, breaking into a smile wide enough to compete with Farrah Fawcett on her famous poster from the 1970s. Joselyn wasted no time in giving them her full, unabridged biography, growing up in Santa Fe, the daughter of a painter and a sculptor, her strong Native American heritage, how she competed for Miss Teen USA representing her home state of New Mexico, how that led to modeling jobs and a few local commercials before she followed her boyfriend, an aspiring screenwriter, to Hollywood, how he dumped her after they arrived, how she struggled getting acting gigs, almost becoming homeless and was living out of her car before scoring a guest spot on the *One Day at a Time* reboot, how that led to other jobs, but nothing as high profile and potentially career boosting as this lead role in *Palm Springs Weekend*.

Poppy, hoping her oral history was finally coming to an end, opened her mouth to excuse herself so she could go get made up for her first scene, but the girl continued talking unabated. "I can't tell you what a big break this is. I auditioned the first time around, and not to toot my own horn, but I nailed it. I thought I had it in the bag. Hal loved me, Netflix loved me, I was packing my bags for Palm Springs, but then my manager called with the bad news. They decided to go with a name. Danika was a big social media star with millions of followers. How could I compete with that? I was so crushed. But it's funny how things work out."

"*Funny*?" Poppy asked warily.

"I don't mean funny, *funny*, it's tragic that Danika died and all that, but I always knew deep down inside that this part belonged to me. From the moment I first auditioned. Even after Danika got cast and the film started shooting, I couldn't accept that I was not going to play the role . . . and then . . . well, it worked out in the end, like it was supposed to. . . ."

Poppy stared at Joselyn, wondering if she had any idea how awful she was coming across, so callous, as if a woman's murder was just a fortuitous stepping-stone to her ultimate goal of becoming a movie star.

Joselyn must have noticed Poppy's and Matt's horrified expressions because she efficiently erased her smile and said with a dash of false compassion, "But poor Danika . . ." Then her megawatt Farrah smile was back.

"Anyway, it's nice meeting you both. I'm really looking forward to working together."

And then she bounced away, still commanding the admiring stares of the mostly male crew setting up the next shot.

"Man, I thought she was the most beautiful woman I had ever laid eyes on for a moment there, and then she started talking," Matt said, shaking his head.

Poppy could not help but be reminded of that old actor saying, "I would kill for that part," which in this case she suspected might not be just an old saying after all.

Chapter 35

Poppy made her way down the aluminum steps of the makeup trailer, her face freshly painted and her hair fussed over and sprayed firmly into place. In one hand she clutched a rolled-up copy of her script and in the other her phone, pressed to her ear as she waited, on hold.

Finally, a woman came on the line. "Bear Valley Community Hospital, how may I direct your call?"

"Yes, hello, I have been trying to reach Sam Emerson's room, but he hasn't been picking up."

"Who?"

"Sam Emerson," Poppy said, louder.

"Hold on."

She heard computer keys clicking as the receptionist typed. "I'll connect you now."

"No! You don't understand. I have been calling the room and there has been no answer—"

The receptionist was suddenly gone.

The line rang and rang.

Still no answer.

Poppy sighed, frustrated. She hung up and called the hospital again.

"Bear Valley Community Hospital, how may I direct your call?"

Poppy couldn't tell if it was the same woman as before. This one's voice sounded like it had a faint Southern accent. She was going to have to assume this was a whole new person and she would have to start all over again.

"My name is Poppy Harmon. My boyfriend, Sam Emerson, is a patient in your hospital. I have been calling his room, but there has been no answer and I'm very worried—"

"What's the name again?"

Poppy sighed. "Sam Emerson." Then she added quickly, "Please don't transfer me to his room, no one is there to pick up. He had a very serious heart attack, and I am worried he's not in his room in bed and—"

"They may have taken him down for some tests," this more helpful receptionist suggested.

"Can you check for me, please? I want to be sure nothing's wrong."

Silence.

Poppy could feel the woman's annoyance coming through the phone.

"Hold please," she said abruptly, then got off the line.

Someone tapped Poppy on the shoulder.

It was Timothy, the PA. "Hey, Poppy, we're going to need you on set in five minutes."

"Thank you, Timothy."

He trotted off, and Poppy stood, phone still clamped to her ear, waiting impatiently, working hard to not allow her mind to go to a worst-case-scenario situation.

Sam was going to be fine.

Back to normal in no time.

Or a new kind of normal.

She heard some kind of a scuffle happening on the opposite side of the makeup trailer. Voices murmuring. She lowered the phone and was about to wander around to see what was going on when a nurse came on the line.

"Are you the one trying to find Sam Emerson?" Her voice was much kinder, more accommodating, understanding.

"Yes, he's not in his room."

"That's because he terrorized the nursing staff until he was allowed to take a walk outside."

"That sounds like Sam," Poppy chuckled.

"He should be back in his room in about ten or fifteen minutes." The nurse's calm, serene tone put Poppy immediately at ease.

"Thank you."

"You're welcome. And just so you know, the doctor delivered some good news today. Mr. Emerson might be discharged on Thursday depending on the results of his EKG tomorrow."

"That's wonderful," Poppy said, relieved.

The fracas on the other side of the trailer was getting louder, more intense. Poppy pushed a finger in her free ear to drown out the noise.

Before hanging up, the nurse said, "May I ask, are you his significant other?"

That was such a complicated question, but there was no point in trying to work it out on the phone with a busy health-care provider who had much more important things to tend to, so Poppy simply replied, "Yes."

"He's going to need someone looking after him when he gets home, so you might want to think about making arrangements to have someone check on him, either yourself, or a family member."

"I will do it," Poppy said.

She wasn't exactly sure how that would work with Sam all the way up in Big Bear and her down in Palm Springs. But she would figure it out.

Poppy ended the call, still distracted by the commotion on the other side of the trailer. She marched around and stopped in her tracks at the sight of Hal Greenwood, his massive bulk pressed up against his newest star, Joselyn Tremblay, pinning her to the side of the trailer. His paws were all over her, a couple of his fat fingers working to undo her blouse. Joselyn struggled to free herself from his grasp, but kept a pleasant smile on her face, as if she did not want to upset him, but clearly there was distress written all over her face.

"Now, Hal, don't be a naughty boy . . ." she pleaded.

"I can't keep my hands off you, you're so beautiful . . ."

Poppy was not about to let this poor young woman become the latest victim of this revolting lech. She raised her script that was rolled up in her hand, waving it at Hal. "Excuse me, Hal, sorry to interrupt, but I would like to discuss this scene we're about to shoot with you."

Hal tore his lustful, roving eyes off Joselyn and fixed them angrily upon Poppy, the last person he wanted to see right now. "What?"

He loosened his grip on Joselyn, who seized the opportunity to slip away from him and keep a safe distance.

Poppy continued, pretending to be oblivious to what

she had just witnessed. "There is a line in the script that doesn't make any sense to me and I'm curious to get your thoughts on how I should play it."

Hal exploded with a spew of expletives that Poppy calmly ignored. Finally, when he finished ticking off just about every four-letter word in the English language, he bellowed, "I am not the director of this movie! If you have a problem with the line, go talk to the Brit! Now leave me alone!"

Poppy, however, did not budge, which just infuriated him even more. He knew it would be impossible to try foisting himself on Joselyn again, especially in front of Poppy, so clasping his fleshy hands together, almost as if to beg, he asked Joselyn, "Maybe we can continue this in your trailer where it's more private?"

Joselyn feigned immense disappointment. "As much as I would love to, Hal, I'm in the next scene with Poppy."

Poppy could almost see the steam rising off the top of Hal Greenwood's head, his lewd, crude, unwanted efforts stymied. Without another word, Hal stormed off.

Poppy had expected Joselyn to dissolve into tears on the spot, having been through such a ghastly ordeal, but instead, she was almost robotically placid. She gave Poppy a wan smile.

Poppy stepped forward, concerned. "Are you all right?"

"I'm fine," Joselyn reassured her.

"What just happened now is not only disgusting and unacceptable, it's illegal."

Joselyn shrugged. "Just part of the job, I guess."

Poppy reared back, stunned. "No, Joselyn, it most definitely is not. Hal Greenwood has a notorious reputation for this kind of thing, and should be held accountable."

Joselyn considered this rather apathetically, then with another shrug, said, "Maybe, but he's the big boss who can make or break careers, so what can I do?"

Poppy could not believe how blasé this girl was acting after such a traumatic ordeal. "You can do plenty. You can report his abominable behavior to the Screen Actors Guild. They will protect you."

Joselyn considered Poppy's recommendation briefly then summarily rejected it. "No, I don't think so."

"Why not?"

"Because like I told you before, I have worked too hard to get here, and I'm not going to ruin everything now by being some kind of whistleblower. . . ."

"He can't be allowed to get away with this!"

"Forget it. I have too much riding on this. And if you go blabbing to SAG or anyone else about what you saw, I'll deny it."

"But Joselyn—"

"Mind your own business, Poppy," Joselyn warned before flipping a switch and returning to her perky, upbeat self again. "See you on set."

And then she happily flounced away, as if nothing had happened, leaving Poppy simmering with anger and feeling utterly helpless.

Chapter 36

Every bone in her body ached as Poppy pulled up in front of Matt's house to drop him off. It was closing in on nine in the evening after clocking in a long twelve-hour day on the set, not including the drive time to and from Joshua Tree. Matt, who was barely thirty, had weathered the grueling day far better than Poppy, who had swung through a Starbucks drive-thru that was trying to close for the night for a desperately needed shot of caffeine on their way back to Palm Springs. She didn't care that she would be up and buzzing most of the night because she only had one more scene left to shoot and that was not scheduled for another few days, leaving her free tomorrow. Greta had asked them both not to tell Hal they were coming back for one more day in order to avoid another one of his temper tantrums on set, and Poppy and Matt agreed.

Matt shifted in the passenger seat, turning toward

Poppy. "I gotta admit, despite all the drama with Hal and everything, I had an awesome day today. I love playing this part."

"That's one of us," Poppy cracked.

"But you were great, you're such a talent, Poppy, you never should have quit acting."

"Leaving Hollywood was the best decision I ever made. Marrying Chester. Moving to Palm Springs. Getting involved in charity work. Traveling. I had a lot of happy years before Chester died and I found out he had been frittering away our savings, but that doesn't take away from the life we created together."

Matt nodded, although it was obvious to Poppy he did not really understand where she was coming from. He was young, his whole life was ahead of him, and he was far more ambitious than Poppy had ever been. It was only a matter of time before career opportunities would take Matt away from her. There was no doubt in her mind despite his adamant denials that at some point very soon, perhaps after the release of *Palm Springs Weekend*, when the whole world saw Matt in a substantial film role, he would finally ditch the Matt Flowers persona he had created for Poppy, Iris, and Violet to jump-start their private investigations business, and follow his true calling to become a working actor in Hollywood. It was sad to think about. But she was going to enjoy the remaining time left that she had with him, this man young enough to be her son, who had so unexpectedly wormed his way into her heart.

"Well, good night," Matt said, leaning in to give her a sweet peck on the cheek. "I'll see you at the office tomorrow."

"Not too early, get some rest. It's been a very long day." Poppy was saying it more for herself than Matt.

There was no way she would make it to the office until at least the late morning hours.

Matt jumped out of Poppy's car, crouched down to give her a wink, and then slammed the door shut, jogging up the driveway to his front door.

Poppy put the gear into drive and was about to pull away when her phone rang.

It was Sam calling.

She shifted back into park and picked up her phone.

"Hi, Sam."

"The nurses tell me there is a very nice lady who has been calling a lot, and that I should feel lucky to have someone who cares so much," Sam drawled, a bit drowsy but in good spirits.

Poppy smiled to herself. "How are you feeling tonight?"

"All right, I guess. But I'll feel a whole lot better when I ditch these tubes and this lumpy hospital bed, and can go home and chow down on some real food, not this tasteless slop they serve up here."

"I want to talk to you about that. . . ."

"You planning on making me a home-cooked meal when I get sprung?"

"Yes, we can discuss that, but I'm talking about you going home. I've been thinking about it and I believe it would be best if you—"

A crash startled Poppy, who jolted upright in her car seat. She glanced in the direction of the sound, Matt's house, but at first saw nothing. The front door was wide open and the lights were on inside, but there was no sign of Matt.

"Poppy?" Sam asked, wondering about the dead air on the phone.

Poppy pressed the button to lower the driver's-side

window when she heard the faint sound of grunting. Then, suddenly she saw Matt through the front window of his house grappling with another man who was dressed all in black and a stocking mask pulled over his head. They crashed into a floor lamp, knocking it over as they both battled to get the upper hand.

"Poppy, are you there?"

"Sam, I have to call you back!" Poppy screamed, dropping her phone on the passenger seat and struggling to free herself from her seat belt before springing out of the car. Despite her weary bones, she sprinted up the drive-way and into the house where the man had just taken a roundhouse punch at Matt, clocking him on the chin and sending him hurtling to the floor. As he went down, Matt, who gripped a fistful of the man's shirt, nearly tore half the sleeve off. The brute then began viciously kicking Matt in the rib cage, nearly beating him senseless.

Poppy screeched at the top of her lungs, leaping onto the man's back, surprising him.

"What the—?" he exclaimed, his knees buckling.

Poppy wrapped her legs around his waist and started to pummel him on the head to slow him down. But the sudden attack only seemed to rile him up even more, and with a burst of strength he wheeled around and slammed Poppy against the wall, her breath whooshing out of her, as she sank to the floor, dizzy and dazed, her eyes on Matt, who was crumpled up, moaning.

The assailant bolted out the door. Poppy crawled to the window just in time to see the black-clad attacker vanish into the darkness of the night. Then, on her hands and knees, she crawled over to Matt, who was on his side, and gently rolled him over on his back so he was looking up at her.

"Matt, are you okay?"

"Yeah, the dude caught me off guard. He must have been hiding in the bushes, lying in wait. I had just unlocked the door and was halfway inside the house, turning the lights on when all of a sudden he came out of nowhere and pounced."

"Do you have any idea who it was?"

"Not with that stocking over his face."

Poppy nodded slightly, discouraged.

"But when I tore part of his shirt off, I got a good look at his arm. The guy had some kind of tattoo. Very colorful and unique. Kind of reminded me of a Pink Floyd album."

Poppy cocked an eyebrow. "How are you even old enough to know who Pink Floyd is?"

"My dad was a huge music lover. He schooled me on all the great seventies bands," Matt chuckled, wincing in pain, clutching his rib cage as he tried to stand up.

"Here, let me help you," Poppy said, gripping him underneath his arm as he hauled himself to his feet, holding tight until he was able to steady himself.

"Two car wrecks. Three physical assaults. I'm beginning to think somebody up there doesn't like me," Matt joked before turning to Poppy. "Thanks for coming to my rescue. You're a real badass, Poppy Harmon."

Poppy brushed him off with a wave of her hand. She was far more concerned with discovering the identity of this brutal thug with the arm tattoo, and if his violent attack on Matt had any connection to the murders of Danika Delgado and Fabian Granger. Was this some kind of warning? Or was the bushwhacker intent on a more permanent result, like wanting to make sure when he was done, Matt Flowers would be dead?

Chapter 37

"It had this triangle in space with a rainbow off to the side that you could see through some kind of brick wall that had been partially torn down," Matt described to Wyatt, who sat at his computer in the Desert Flowers office, intently digitally re-creating the image from Matt's memory on his screen.

"The triangle was a little smaller," Matt said as Wyatt began shrinking the image. "Yeah, that's more like it."

"That looks ridiculous!" Iris snorted. "Who would be dumb enough to have that put on his arm?"

"Whoever attacked me must be a Pink Floyd fan, too. That looks like some kind of odd mash-up of two of their most popular albums, *Dark Side of the Moon* and *The Wall*," Matt said.

Wyatt added a few finishing touches and then wheeled back in his office chair so they could all get a good look. "How's that?"

"Perfect," Matt beamed. "Kid, you're a genius."

"Now that we have the tattoo, what do we do with it?" Violet asked.

"I can run a Google image search to see if any tattoo shops in the area have that same design or something similar on their Web site. It's pretty elaborate and well done, so I'm hoping an artist would like to showcase it. Maybe we'll get lucky. Give me a few minutes," Wyatt said, swiveling back around to get started.

"I'm just so proud of him," Violet gushed.

"We have a devotee to seventies psychedelic rock. Well, I suppose that's something," Poppy sighed. "At least it's more than we had last night."

Violet put on a pot of coffee and the team took a break as Wyatt worked furiously to come up with some useful information. Before she even had a chance to pour cream into Iris's cup, Wyatt was spinning back around in his chair, a triumphant look on his face.

"Off-Melrose Tattoo Shop," he cried.

"Where's that?" Violet asked, handing Iris her coffee.

"Off Melrose!" Iris snapped. "Where do you think?"

Violet narrowed her eyes, perturbed. "I mean, what city?"

"I'm assuming LA," Matt answered.

Wyatt nodded. "I traced the image and found maybe six or seven shops in the country that specialize in that signature style, but only one located in California. And the shop in LA is the only one with the exact same image, triangle, rainbow, wall and all."

"That's got to be the place!" Matt said, clapping his hands together.

"The owner of the shop who does most of the tattoo

designs is a woman named Kale," Wyatt said, bringing up an image of a raven-haired, ghostly pale creature with heavy mascara and a lip ring, wearing a black tank top and sporting arm sleeves of tattoos from her shoulder blades to her wrists.

"*Kale*? That's a name?" Iris laughed. "What are the names of her parents, Romaine and Butter?"

Matt, leaning over Wyatt to read the text underneath her photo on the shop's Web site, said, "Apparently she's quite well respected in the tattoo community." He whipped around to Poppy. "You up for another road trip to LA?"

Poppy did not even have to answer him. She just grabbed her purse and they hurried out, promising to be back by mid-afternoon. Traffic was light on the 10 freeway, and when they arrived in Los Angeles, and parked on a side street across from the Off-Melrose Tattoo Shop, it was just opening for the day. Poppy checked her watch. It was going on noon. Artists, from her experience, were rarely early risers.

Poppy and Matt scurried across the street and entered the ramshackle store to find Kale sweeping the floor with a broom and dustpan. She didn't even look up at them. "Have a seat, I'll be right with you."

Poppy and Matt plopped down in a pair of rickety plastic chairs and perused photos of Kale's past work hanging on the walls. Matt spotted a framed photo of the Pink Floyd–inspired design toward the end of the wall near the restroom and nudged Poppy, gesturing toward it.

Kale took her sweet time. After dumping the dust bunnies in a bin, she disappeared inside her office to make a phone call. The front door swung open and a young man in his early twenties, rail thin, drawn face, tired eyes, with spiky blond hair and a ring of thorns tattooed around both biceps, ambled in, carrying a Starbucks cup. He glanced at Poppy and Matt. "Kale here?"

"Yes, she's in the back," Poppy said politely. "She told us to wait."

The young man nodded, then strolled past them and down to the office. Poppy assumed he must work at the shop. She managed to pick up bits and pieces of the conversation between Kale and this kid, recounting their previous evening, hanging at some dive bar, partying too much, Kale complaining of a massive hangover. Poppy impatiently checked her watch, but Matt gently placed a hand over her wrist, signaling her that Kale was finally coming out to deal with them. The kid stayed in the office.

"Which one of you is here for a tattoo?" Kale asked.

Poppy stood up. "Actually, neither of us. We were wondering if you could answer a few questions."

"And who are you?" Kale asked suspiciously.

"Poppy Harmon. This is Matt Flowers. We're from the Desert Flowers Detective Agency."

Kale was suddenly on guard. "Detectives?"

"Yes," Poppy said, pulling the printed image of the tattoo Wyatt had re-created out of her purse. "We were hoping you could tell us who—"

"I'm backed up with appointments today so I'm sorry I can't help you," Kale said evenly.

Poppy glanced around the shop incredulously. "But there is no one here."

Kale shrugged. "Believe me, there's going to be a line outside around the block in about five minutes."

"Well, this won't take long—"

Kale cut her off. "Sorry."

Poppy sighed, frustrated.

"How much?" Matt suddenly asked.

"For what?"

"A tattoo," he answered.

"Depends on what kind and how big. Small ones start at a hundred and fifty."

"Done. I'd like to get one."

Poppy's jaw nearly hit the floor.

Matt did not strike her as the tattoo type.

"Poppy, why don't you leave me here, go do some shopping, and come back in a little while when I'm done," Matt said before whispering under his breath, "I got this."

"Okay," Poppy said, hesitating, and then she left the shop. She drove around the city for an hour, stopping at a few clothing stores on Rodeo Drive in Beverly Hills, establishments she had frequented regularly during her time as a TV actress but now scoffing at the exorbitant price tags, killing time before returning to the Melrose area. The streets were much busier now, and Poppy had a challenging time finding a parking space, but after paying the meter for an hour, she returned to the shop.

Kale had been right. There was now a line out the door with people waiting to get tattooed. She entered the shop to see Matt sitting in a chair with his shirt off as Kale busily drew a design on his upper left arm with her inks and needles. Poppy could see Matt wincing in pain a couple of times but otherwise maintaining a brave face. He had always told her he had a very low threshold for pain.

Kale finished her work finally, and stepped back and inspected it, satisfied.

Matt nodded appreciatively, then stood up and reached for his wallet in the back of his pants.

Poppy could not see the design as he was turned away from her.

Matt showed Kale the printed image of the Pink Floyd tattoo. Apparently now with a fresh sale, she was more open to answering questions.

"Yeah, I've done that design a few times," Kale said.

"Do you keep records? Can I have their names?" Matt asked.

Kale burst out laughing. "Are you kidding me? Look around. We're a small operation. I don't keep tabs on everybody who comes in here. I only remember tattoos, not faces."

The spiky blond-haired kid emerged from the office and looked briefly at the image Matt was still holding up for Kale. "Unless they're famous, like that one guy."

Poppy snapped to attention. "What do you mean? Did someone famous come in here and get that particular tattoo?"

"Yeah, remember, Kale? I mean he's not that big of a deal, not like it was Ryan Reynolds or somebody like that, but I've seen this guy in a couple of movies. What did he say his name was?"

"I don't remember," Kale said, thoroughly disinterested.

Poppy tried an educated guess. "Chase Ehrens?"

The blond kid brightened. "Yeah, him! How did you know?"

"Zip it, will you?" Kale barked at the young man before turning to Poppy and spitting out, "I don't feel comfortable discussing my clients. They have a right to privacy."

"Kale, we're looking for Chase Ehrens because he physically attacked me, tried to kill me, and there is a strong possibility he may have had something to do with the murder of Danika Delgado."

"I love her! She's so hot!" the kid cried before realizing the inappropriateness of his comment. "I mean was. That was a real sad story."

A light went on in Kale. She may have been trying to stay true to her professional ethics, but there was a hint of empathy at the mention of Danika. "He was in here recently with his girlfriend, or at least I assumed she was his girlfriend. I had never heard of him, but a few of the customers were buzzing about him being in the shop. When we were done, I remember thinking how odd it was he let his girlfriend pay for the tattoo. I mean, if he was such a big movie star like everybody said, why not pay for it himself?"

"Did she pay cash?" Poppy asked.

Kale shook her head. "No, I think she used a credit card."

"Then you must have a record of her name."

Kale wavered, not quite prepared to be that helpful.

Matt opened his wallet. "How much do I owe you?"

"A hundred and fifty."

Matt handed her two one-hundred-dollar bills.

"I'll get you some change."

"No, keep it," Matt said, locking eyes with her.

Kale finally relented. She took the bills and slid them into the register before asking, "So is this Chase guy really as bad as you say?"

Vigorous nods from both Poppy and Matt.

Kale reluctantly got onto her desktop computer and scrolled down a bit before she came up with a name.

Tracy Watson.

Her zip code to verify was 92202.

Somewhere very close to Palm Springs, California.

Poppy was confident Wyatt could locate her.

They thanked Kale and left the shop, walking a few blocks to where Poppy had found a parking space for her car.

Matt turned to Poppy with a grin. "You haven't asked to see it."

"See what?" Poppy asked, perplexed.

"My tattoo!"

"Oh . . . I'm not sure I want to."

Matt lifted the sleeve of his shirt to reveal three small flowers on his bicep.

Poppy chuckled. "What made you choose flowers?"

"Not just any flowers. Take a closer look. There's a poppy, a violet, and an iris."

Poppy erupted in laughter. "I guess now you're stuck with us forever."

Chapter 38

Matt knocked on the door of the ramshackle crack den of a little house in a dusty, downtrodden, eerily quiet neighborhood in Indio. He had slicked back his hair and was decked out in a crisp short-sleeve white shirt, black tie, black pants, and black patent leather shoes. He clutched a book in one hand. He waited a few moments, then knocked again. Finally, the door opened to reveal a tiny wisp of a woman with flat blond hair, golden brown skin from laying out in the sun all day, sporting a revealing halter top and cut-off jean shorts. She was barefoot.

"Hello, ma'am, how are you doing today?" Matt asked brightly.

She gave him the once-over. "Fine."

"I'm Elder Flowers, and what is your name?"

"Tracy."

"Hello, Tracy, nice to meet you."

"Don't you guys usually travel in pairs?"

"I'm sorry?"

"You're a Mormon missionary, right? I thought there is always supposed to be two of you knocking on doors, you know, so you can tag-team your marks."

"Oh," Matt said, momentarily caught off guard. "Elder Covey is under the weather today, so it's just me."

"Is Elder Covey as cute as you are?"

"I . . . I don't know . . ."

"Aren't you going to ask me if I feel God hears and answers my prayers?"

"Yes, that was one of my questions," Matt said, fumbling with the book, checking a note inside where he had written down some questions. "Also, if there was another book that spoke of Christ, would you be open to reading it?"

"You're new at this, aren't you, Elder Flowers?" Tracy chuckled.

Matt nodded. "It's my first day."

"And the other guy got sick, and left you all on your own?"

"Yes, I'm afraid so."

"Well, you're doing great, for your first day. You had me at hello," she purred.

Poppy, who was hiding off to the side of the house behind Detective Jordan and a few of his men, safely out of view, shook her head and sighed. This girl was utterly shameless. An unabashed flirt.

"I'm sure you've had a lot of doors slammed in your face today," she said.

"More than I can count."

She reached out and took hold of his tie, playing with it. "Well, I would love nothing more than to invite you in and see everything you have to offer me. . . ."

Matt took a deep breath.

"But unfortunately, I'm not alone," she sighed, furtively glancing back inside the house.

"Oh, is your husband at home? Perhaps he would like to join us to discuss the doctrines and principles of the gospel of—"

Tracy held up a hand to stop him. "He's not as open to new things like I am," she sighed, dropping his tie, devouring Matt's worked-out body with her eyes.

"Tracy, what the hell? I told you to get rid of whoever was at the door!" a man's booming voice bellowed.

Poppy tugged on Detective Jordan's jacket and nodded.

She knew that voice.

It was Chase Ehrens.

Tracy stepped a bit farther outside and whispered to Matt, "Maybe you could come back tomorrow. My boyfriend won't be here and then we could—"

Suddenly without warning Chase appeared in the doorway behind Tracy and barked, "Whatever you're selling, we're not interested!"

He roughly grabbed Tracy by the shoulders and shoved her back inside the house before his eyes fell upon Matt's face and instantly widened with recognition. "You! What are you doing—?" He took in Matt's outfit and book. "What is this?"

Tracy pushed her way forward. "He's harmless, Chase. He's just one of those Jesus freaks who go door to door and—"

Chase reached out and grabbed Matt by the shirt. "He's a detective, you stupid—"

Suddenly Detective Jordan called out, "Chase Ehrens,

this is Detective Lamar Jordan, you're under arrest. Step outside with your hands in the air!"

Chase froze in place for a moment, still clutching the poly-cotton blend of Matt's crisp clean white shirt. Then he gave Matt a hard shove sending him stumbling back, whipped around, and made a run for it back inside the house, colliding with Tracy and knocking her to the floor. Matt hurtled forward, chasing after him as Jordan and his men, with Poppy bringing up the rear, ran to catch up to them. Poppy stopped to kneel down and check on Tracy, who was grasping her arm in pain from the fall.

"Who are you? What's happening?"

"It's probably best you stay out of it, dear," Poppy said, springing to her feet and hurrying through the house after them. When she got to a sliding glass door that led to a mostly gravel backyard with overgrown palm trees and a tiny pool filled with algae and debris, she was just in time to see Matt close the distance on Chase, who was running for a wooden side gate to escape. When Chase stopped long enough to open the gate, Matt flung himself on Chase's back to stop him. The two men grappled, punching and kicking each other, locked in a strange embrace until Chase lost his balance and fell into the pool, dragging Matt with him. Poppy cringed at the idea of poor Matt in that dirty, foul, contaminated water, and prayed he wouldn't catch some kind of awful disease.

When the two men both splashed to the surface, panting and coughing, Detective Jordan stood at the edge of the pool, gun drawn, flanked by his men. Jordan signaled two of them to grab Chase by the arms and haul him out of the pool. One of the officers wrenched Chase's arms behind him and snapped on a pair of handcuffs while the other read him his rights.

Matt crawled out of the pool on his own as Poppy rushed over to him.

"Matt, are you all right?" Poppy cried.

"Yeah, but my shirt is ruined. He tore it when he grabbed me and my Bible is soaking wet. I was going to save this costume in case I was ever cast in a production of *Book of Mormon*."

Poppy laughed heartily and reached out to Matt but stopped short of touching him. He gave her a curious look. She shrugged apologetically. "I don't want to catch anything you might have picked up in that nasty pool."

Tracy suddenly appeared in the sliding glass doorway, and seemed almost resigned to her boyfriend being carted off by the police. "Does this have anything to do with Danika Delgado?"

Before they could answer, Chase was screaming at the top of his lungs while being led away. "I didn't touch a hair on her head! I'm innocent! They're trying to frame me!"

Whether that was true or not, Poppy was just happy Chase Ehrens was finally off the street, because whatever charges awaited him, there was enough evidence for at least one of them to be the attempted murder of Matt.

Chapter 39

As Poppy stared at Wyatt's computer screen at the garage office, she thought she might be watching a trailer for some kind of war movie with fierce-looking men and women clad in military fatigues running around carrying guns, engaging in hand-to-hand combat, racing through the desert in high-tech vans. At the end of the thirty-second video, the brave men and women posed heroically, staring at the camera with dead-serious looks on their faces, arms folded, like an unbeatable superhero team line-up in the latest Marvel or DC blockbuster. An animated logo of a coiled snake popped up on the screen accompanied by a man's commanding voice-over, "Cobra Security Force International . . . We're there when you need us!"

Wyatt froze the image on the entire team of military operatives as they all gave a thumbs-up at the same time.

Poppy, who had been leaning down just above Wyatt's shoulder, stood upright. "What am I watching?"

Wyatt swiveled around in his office chair. "It's a commercial I found on YouTube for a high-tech private security firm. According to their Web site, they specialize in highly confidential and effective security-related services for governments, multinational corporations, and prominent individuals from corporate billionaires and royalty to Hollywood celebrities. They have offices in Los Angeles, New York, London, and Dubai with operatives, mostly elite forces types, dispatched all over the world ready and willing to face a wide variety of imminent dangers to keep you safe."

Poppy nodded. "Perhaps a better question would be, *why* am I watching this?"

Violet, who had been sitting on the couch knitting a sweater, put her needles and fabric down and joined them at the computer. "Because of him," she said, pointing her finger at one of the Cobra team now frozen on the screen with their thumbs in the air. He was in the back row, a big, hulking, handsome man in full battle dress.

Poppy squinted to get a good look at him. "Who is he?"

"That's Sarge," Wyatt said. "There's a better picture of him on his profile page on the Cobra International Web site," Wyatt said, clicking out of the video and opening the Cobra home page. Sarge's biography popped up with a professional headshot.

Poppy studied the photo. "That's . . ."

"Phil McKellan. Apparently he lied to me about what he did for a living. He's actually some kind of soldier of fortune who works for this security firm. I feel like such a fool believing anything he told me," Violet lamented.

Poppy was just grateful Iris was not around to dish out another "I told you so" to Violet, who was doing a decent enough job on her own of beating herself up. "You have to stop blaming yourself, Violet."

"I am not a confrontational person by nature, but I swear if I ever see that man again, I will give him a good verbal thrashing!" Violet spit out, almost surprising herself with her outburst.

That was about as rough as Violet Hogan would ever get given her usual sweet, unruffled demeanor, which frankly was what Poppy loved most about her.

Poppy turned back to Wyatt. "How did you find him?"

Violet smiled at her cherished grandson. "He took the bugging equipment we found here in the office thanks to the tip you got from that poor journalist Fabian Granger, may he rest in peace, and traced it to a spy store in New York."

"They're the only place in the country that carries this brand of surveillance equipment," Wyatt explained. "I called the store and talked to the clerk, but he wouldn't give out any customer information, so I went to the shop's online store and they had ads boasting about all the high-profile security companies, including Cobra, who purchased equipment from them. So I just started researching the various companies until I came across this commercial."

"He had seen the selfie of me and Phil because I had posted it on my Facebook page . . . Wyatt *liked* it . . . I got over fifty likes on that one photo. Doris Cosgrove even left a comment that she was so jealous I had snared such a handsome boyfriend . . . I mean, as awful as he turned out to be, you have to admit Phil is a very good-looking man. . . ."

"I recognized the similarity between Sarge on the commercial and Grandma's boyfriend Phil from the photo on Facebook, so I called her to come in and confirm it was the same guy. . . ."

"Which it is, obviously," Violet said. "Gosh, you know, I have a feeling, it's just a feeling, but my grandson is so talented and such a true genius, I'm going to go out on a limb and predict that someday he will get some kind of prestigious award, you know, like the Presidential Medal of Freedom."

"Can we think a little bigger, Grandma? I mean it sounds nice, but even Rush Limbaugh got one of those," Wyatt groaned.

Poppy gazed at the still image on the computer screen as her mind raced. She needed a plan to find evidence of a direct connection between Hal Greenwood, whom she suspected wanted to spy on them, and Cobra Security Force International.

And although unlike Matt, she had been reticent about doing any undercover work since starting this private investigation business, there was a character she had developed years ago for an improv class, Claire St. Clair, a spoiled rich heiress with her own cosmetics company, who might be the perfect force of nature to establish that direct connection.

Chapter 40

"Mrs. St. Clair, sorry to keep you waiting," the tall muscled bronzed man with a buzz cut said as he entered the large conference room on the twenty-sixth floor of a towering high-rise in Downtown Los Angeles.

"Just Claire, I don't want to be confused with my mother," Poppy said, standing up in her multi-pink-checked boucle Brooks Brothers suit she had kept stored in her closet for a very special occasion. Poppy was not a particular fan of pink, but it seemed an appropriate choice for Claire St. Clair, the ridiculously successful makeup maven character she had not trotted out since a stage benefit for breast cancer way back in the early 1990s.

"Of course. This is Ty Hardy and Chava Levy. Ty is a highly decorated Army helicopter pilot who served in both Iraq and Afghanistan, and Chava is former Mossad. They're two of my top operatives." The big boss stuck out his hand, disregarding the new social norm of simple elbow bumping. Poppy nevertheless accepted it and they shook hands. The top dog in the room, the big stud with the buzz cut, was Dan LeVoie, American businessman and former Navy SEAL who had founded Cobra and felt this meeting important enough to run it himself.

Wyatt's Web site must have worked like a charm. The best way to make an impression on the Cobra principals, Wyatt determined, was to quickly build a Web site touting St. Clair's billion-dollar share of the cosmetics company. He even built in links to fake stock prices and news articles, even doctoring Poppy's photo on various magazine covers. He was so detailed and thorough, incorporating glowing fake testimonials from world-famous figures such as Kylie Jenner, Taylor Swift, Jennifer Lawrence, even Meghan Markle, he could fool even the smartest CEOs that St. Clair Cosmetics was a real thing and a big deal.

Poppy had remained skeptical. Fooling a world-renowned security firm seemed, well, foolish, but remarkably it had worked. An underling had probably been assigned to check out the company to see if it was legit, and been fooled by Wyatt's impressive handiwork. And so here they were, Poppy, Matt, and Violet inside the lion's den, ready to mix it up.

"May I introduce my executive assistant, Violet Hogan, and my head of security, Matt Cameron," Poppy said.

She had decided to use Matt's real name since Flowers might set off alarm bells in Dan LeVoie's mind about the Desert Flowers Detective Agency, which they obviously had under surveillance. Since these three were high up in the firm, it quickly became clear they were not out on the street following the marks around, bugging offices and homes themselves, and so the likelihood of Dan, Ty, and Chava recognizing any of them was remote.

"Nice to meet you all, please, have a seat," Dan said, gesturing for them to sit down, which they did. Dan and his team followed. Coffee and cookies had been set out, but no one in the room decided at the moment to partake.

Dan eyed Matt curiously. "Head of security? I didn't think you would need a bodyguard in your line of work."

"You'd be surprised. The cosmetics industry is a very cutthroat business," Poppy said.

"Good to know," Dan said, nodding with a smile. "How can we help you today, Mrs. . . . I mean, Claire?"

"Well, I'm not going to assume you know what's going on in the world of makeup and perfumes, so I'll try to bring you up to speed as quickly as I can," Poppy said, reaching into her Valentino leather satchel bag in raspberry pink, extracting a pink perfume bottle in the shape of a woman's high heel, and setting it down on the conference table.

"My company is about to release our newest fragrance, Cinderella, a floral bouquet of rose and jasmine with a touch of vanilla, simply divine, here let me show you. . . ."

Dan, Ty, and Chava sat across the table, dumbfounded at what she wanted them to do. Ty glanced at Chava since she was the lone woman in their group, expecting her to take the bottle and spray some on her neck, but Chava was definitely not the type that wore perfume of any kind so she sat back in her chair and folded her arms defiantly. Finally, Dan glared at Ty and he reluctantly reached his arm out, wrist up, so Poppy could spray some on him. He took a whiff and nodded approvingly, then raised his arm in front of Dan so he could awkwardly smell the fragrance, too.

"Nice," Dan said.

"Thank you. I worked very hard to find the right balance," Poppy cooed. "As you are probably aware, there is rampant corporate espionage in the cosmetics industry."

Dan cocked an eyebrow. "No, I actually wasn't aware. . . ."

"I can assure you there is, and I have heard through my own contacts that Maybelline is about to unveil this exact scent with this same bottle design, same shape but in crystal, in two weeks, beating our own release by a matter of days! It's virtually impossible for two competing companies to come up with the exact same idea. There has to be a spy in my organization."

Dan leaned forward, elbows on the table. "And you want us to ferret him or her out?"

"Not only that, I want you to conduct a wide-range surveillance of Maybelline because I want a full accounting of everyone involved in this theft for when I sue," Poppy said forcefully. "I assume you can do that?"

Dan cracked a smile. "Oh, yes, we can do that. For the right price."

"I hate discussing money, that's what I have Violet for, she handles all that, which leaves me unencumbered so I can freely nurture my creativity."

"Of course," Dan said, widening his smile as he began seeing dollar signs.

Suddenly the door to the conference room burst open, and a man breezed in.

"Sorry, I was on the phone with another client," the man said before turning to the group assembled.

"This is Phil McKellan, another associate. He heads

up our surveillance unit, so I'm sure you're going to want to talk to him."

Phil took one look at Violet and blanched. He opened his mouth to say something but no words came out.

"Phil, you okay?" Dan asked, slightly concerned.

Violet stood up to confront him, her whole body shaking.

Phil started backing out of the conference room. "Excuse me, I need to go. . . ." He didn't even bother waiting until he could come up with something. He just turned and bolted.

"Don't you dare walk out on me!" Violet shrieked, running around the table and out the door after him.

Poppy turned back and smiled at the stunned faces of Dan, Ty, and Chava. "They obviously know each other."

"Apparently," Dan said, utterly confused.

Poppy jumped to her feet. "Violet can be a little highstrung. I should probably go check on her to see what all the fuss is about. Matt, why don't you walk Dan and his team through our security protocol, maybe they can identify any soft spots that may have made us vulnerable to a mole. Sound good?"

"Happy to, Claire," Matt said, although he would be making it up as he went along.

"I'll be right back," Poppy said, scooting out of the conference room, stopping at the secretary's cubicle just outside.

Before Poppy had a chance to ask, the secretary pointed down the hall. "They went that way."

"Thank you," Poppy said, hurrying off, the high heels of her pink Jimmy Choos squishing into the thick gray carpet. She rounded the corner to find Violet hovering outside a door. "Is he in there?"

"Yes, he thinks the fact that it's a men's room is going to stop me from following him!" Violet scoffed.

"So why are you still out here?"

"It's a men's room," Violet moaned.

Poppy admired Violet's shyness, but Poppy herself was never one to be deterred. She grabbed Violet by the hand and together they barged into the bathroom.

Phil stood near the urinals, facing them, astonished they were in the building let alone the men's bathroom.

Finding her voice, Violet finally stepped forward in front of Poppy and cried, "How dare you? How dare you toy with my emotions like that! How can you be so thoughtless and cruel?"

Before Phil could respond, the door to one of the stalls opened and a small man with thick glasses meekly poked his head out to see if it was safe to come out. "I just need to wash my hands, if that's okay."

"Hurry up!" Violet snapped.

Startled, the man scooted over to a basin and turned the water on, pumping soap in his hands, scrubbing as fast as he possibly could. He glanced over at Phil, who was frozen like a statue. "I'm going to need your expense report by the end of the day, Phil, otherwise I can't cut you a check until next week."

Phil nodded nervously. "Got it, Stu."

The accounting guy finished, then tore off a paper towel from the dispenser, quickly drying off before cautiously moving around Poppy and Violet with a polite nod and escaping out the door.

When he was gone, Violet angrily folded her arms. "Well, I'm waiting! How many other women have you pretended to be interested in, raising their hopes that this time it might be the real thing, then coldly and callously deserting them after you got what you wanted?"

Poppy gently touched Violet's arm. "Honey, since time is of the essence and we're going to be thrown out of here in a matter of minutes, maybe we should focus on the more pressing issue?"

"What's more pressing than my heartbreak?"

"I would never diminish what you're going through, Violet, but there is the matter of why Phil was seen on the Parker Hotel's security cameras loitering in the lobby the night Fabian Granger was found drowned in his bathtub."

"Oh, yes, well, I suppose murder does trump my fragile emotional state," Violet agreed before spinning back and spitting out in Phil's direction, "But that in no way lets you off the hook for what you did to me!"

Phil took a tentative step forward. "For the record, I had nothing to do with what happened to that reporter."

Poppy studied him closely. "Then why were you there?"

Phil hesitated.

"We already know you must be working for Hal Greenwood," Poppy said. "You might as well come clean."

Phil glanced at Violet, who was still steaming. Fearing what might happen if he made her even more upset, Phil finally relented and said, "Greenwood hired Cobra to spy on Granger and find out how much he knew about the sexual harassment claims against him, hoping to somehow stop him from writing about them. He was desperate. He also widened our mission after Danika Delgado's murder to also keep tabs on your agency because he was worried about what you might find."

"That Hal Greenwood is a murderer?" Poppy asked.

Phil sighed. "No. You know that can't be true. He has

an airtight alibi. He was on a conference call. If we ever seriously thought Hal Greenwood suffocated that poor girl, we would instantly drop him as a client and contact the authorities. Greenwood was obsessed with his reputation. His sole purpose for hiring us was to keep ahead of any scandal that might break wide open."

"And so that's why you showed up for square dancing at the senior center and tried to sweep me off my feet!" Violet wailed, a humiliated look on her face. "It was all just a ploy to get close to me so you could lift my office key and duplicate it and plant your bugging devices!"

Phil nodded solemnly and muttered, "Yes."

Violet walked up to him, eyes blazing. She waited for him to look at her, and then she raised her hand and slapped him hard across the face.

"Violet!" Poppy cried.

Phil rubbed his cheek with his hand. "No, I deserved that."

Violet stepped away from Phil until she was next to Poppy.

Phil lowered his hand. His cheek was slightly red from the slap and he continued, "I went to hang out at the Parker just to make sure Granger didn't go anywhere, and to follow him if he did leave. That was my assignment. Keep watch, but make no contact. I never went to his room, I never saw him, I never touched him. You can check out the hallway cameras outside Granger's room and the one pointed at the patio near the pool. You'll never see me anywhere near there. I was hanging around the lobby exit the whole time."

Phil waited for Poppy or Violet to say something, but neither spoke.

He took a deep breath. "I'm not a killer . . ." Then,

after thinking about it, "At least not anymore. I used to be a Green Beret, and that kind of came with the job."

Violet shuddered.

Phil softened, took another small step toward her. "Violet, for what it's worth, I hated dropping contact with you. It's the worst part of this job. To be honest, I found you utterly charming and fun to be with during our brief time together. And if circumstances were different—"

Violet shot a hand up to stop him.

She didn't want to hear anymore.

She turned on her heel and fled the bathroom.

"You can tell your boss Claire St. Clair will be taking her business elsewhere," Poppy sniffed before turning and chasing after her friend.

As the door closed behind her, she overheard Phil say to himself, "Who?"

Chapter 41

Poppy could not help but feel a bit garish in her bright pink suit that she had worn to play the part of Claire St. Clair as she burst through the doors of Bear Valley Community Hospital in Big Bear, California. When she, Matt, and Violet had decided to trek to Los Angeles to look into Cobra Security Force International, Poppy had insisted they take two cars since she had received word from a nurse that Sam would be discharged later in the afternoon once his doctor officially signed off.

Sending Matt and Violet back to the desert in his rental, Poppy had zipped up the winding roads to the top of Big Bear Mountain and arrived just before six in the evening. Clicking down the hallway in her heels, she stopped at a nurses' station and asked where she could find Sam Emerson. A distracted male nurse, manning two phone calls at the same time, and an impatient doctor, waiting on some paperwork, gestured toward Sam's room down the hall. Poppy thanked him, and marched down to the open door where Sam, fully dressed, sitting in a wheelchair by the bed, was arguing with a short, stout, stern-looking nurse in blue scrubs who appeared to not appreciate Sam's aggravated tone.

"Look, I feel fine," Sam said gruffly. "What's so bad about calling a taxi to drive me home?"

"Because it's against hospital policy as I have already explained to you, three times, Mr. Emerson. You need to be driven by a friend or family member, and that's all there is to it."

"Well, that's just ridiculous," Sam spat out. "What if I just *say* the cab driver's an old army buddy?"

The irked nurse vigorously shook her head. "That won't work."

"Why not?" Sam sighed.

"Because now I know you'd be lying. Am I going to have to call the doctor, who is a very busy man, and have him come here just so he can talk some sense into you?"

Poppy stepped into the room. "There's no need for that. The friend or family member has finally arrived."

Sam and the nurse turned to Poppy, both surprised by the shiny pink suit she was wearing. There was a silence as they both took the whole look in.

"I know, I know, I look like a walking stick of bubble gum," Poppy sighed.

"I was going to say you look beautiful," Sam said with a sly grin.

"Hallelujah! The man finally said something *nice*," the nurse cracked. "I was beginning to wonder if he was even capable!"

Sam shot her an annoyed look. "Don't start with me, Nurse Ratched."

"He can get a little irritable and depressed when he feels confined and trapped," Poppy explained. "He's like a wild horse that needs to run free. I'm sorry if he's given you any trouble."

"Oh, we've kept him in line as best we can," the nurse said.

"Don't talk about me as if I'm not here!" Sam barked, gripping the sides of the wheelchair and starting to struggle to his feet.

The nurse grabbed him by the shoulders and shoved him back down. "Oh, no you don't. Until the doctor says you can go, you're not getting out of that chair."

"I feel like Papillon on Devil's Island. There is no escape!" Sam bellowed.

The nurse, who was probably in her early thirties, gave him a quizzical look. "That must be one of those old man references."

"You really are working my last nerve, lady," Sam seethed.

"Good, it'll keep your blood pumping and your heart rate up," the nurse said before turning to Poppy. "Let me call the doctor, and then, if there is a God, you can finally take him off our hands." She turned back to face Sam and patted him on top of the head. "Sit tight, Mr. Emerson."

Sam swatted the nurse's hand away from his head. She chuckled and ambled out of the room.

Poppy folded her arms and tried not to crack a smile. "Sounds like you've been a naughty boy."

"Well, if they're going to treat me like a child, then I'm going to act like one. Let's get the hell out of here. I've been here long enough. I hate hospitals."

Poppy had never seen Sam so anxious and uncomfortable, but she was not going to allow him to run roughshod over the dedicated and hardworking nursing staff. "No, you do as the nurse says. They've done a remarkable job. You look a thousand times healthier than when I saw you last."

Sam grumbled something unintelligible, which Poppy ignored. She sat down on the bed to wait for the nurse to return. Sam rattled on about all the things he needed to do like chop wood for his fire, replace a cracked window pane on the cabin, fix the broken starter motor on his car. Poppy just nodded politely and let him go on.

When the nurse returned, she did not look happy. "I'm afraid the doctor wants to keep you one more night."

Sam nearly jumped out of his wheelchair. "*What*?"

The nurse grinned. "Just kidding. You're good to go."

"You nearly gave me another heart attack!" Sam snapped.

"Please, nobody wants that. We're already so close to finally getting rid of you."

Poppy couldn't suppress a chuckle.

"Yeah, she's a real Ellen DeGeneres, this one," Sam said.

"He's all yours," the nurse said. "Good luck."

"Don't worry, I'll whip him into shape once I get him home," Poppy promised.

Poppy positioned herself behind the wheelchair and pushed Sam out of the room and down the hall.

An orderly appeared to take over for Poppy. "Allow me, ma'am."

"Oh, that's okay . . ."

"Hospital policy," he insisted.

Poppy shrugged and allowed the cute young orderly to take her place and push Sam's wheelchair.

"They got a policy for *everything* around here!" Sam bellowed.

"Don't forget to write!" the nurse yelled as she laughed and returned to her station.

"Don't hold your breath!" Sam yelled back, then shifting in the chair as the orderly wheeled him into the elevator, he turned to Poppy. "You don't have to hang around my place playing nursemaid, I'll be fine on my own."

"I was never going to stay at your cabin," Poppy said.

"Oh, I thought you said . . ."

"You're coming to my place."

"What? No! You don't have to take me all the way back to Palm Springs with you, that's crazy."

"It's already settled. I've been by your cabin and packed you a bag. You have everything you need, and what you don't have, I can pick up for you."

"Poppy, I'm not an invalid. . . ."

"Now you listen to me, Sam Emerson, maybe you think you can get away with torturing the nurses with your miserable behavior, but I will not tolerate it, do you hear me?"

Sam, startled by her unusually stern tone, glanced up at the orderly behind him, who was trying to suppress a grin.

The elevator dinged and the doors opened. Before the orderly could wheel Sam out, Poppy stepped in front of the wheelchair, blocking their way. "You had a heart attack, Sam. You need ample time to recover. And you can't be doing it all alone in some remote cabin in the woods. I won't hear of it. So you're moving in with me for a few weeks, whether you like it or not. And if you give me any trouble, I will call Nurse Ratched up here to come by and help me keep you in line. Do you understand?"

Sam, speechless, nodded.

"Now the first thing we're going to do when we get to my house is write a nice thank-you card to all the good people who worked so hard taking care of you," Poppy said, flicking her eyes to the orderly, who was now smiling ear from ear, impressed. "Starting with . . ."

"Rodrigo, ma'am" he said.

"Starting with Rodrigo. Thank you."

Rodrigo nodded appreciatively and began to help Sam stand up, but Sam waved him off, preferring to do it himself.

Rodrigo grabbed the handles of the wheelchair and turned to go back inside. "You take care, Mr. Emerson."

Sam grunted a reply.

"He's usually much nicer, just wait until he makes a full recovery, you won't recognize him," Poppy called out to Rodrigo the orderly.

Poppy slid her arm through Sam's to give him support. He flinched but didn't pull away.

"I know, you like to be the big, strapping, strong man all the time, and you will be again, trust me," Poppy said. "Just give it some time."

"I just hate having to rely on other people to take care of me," Sam whispered.

As they arrived at Poppy's car and she gently assisted Sam into the passenger seat, his body stiff and bones creaky, Poppy tried to cheer him up. "If it makes you feel any better, you are doing me a big favor."

"How's that?" Sam asked, insisting on locking the seat belt into place without any help.

"The security company I hired still has not installed my burglar alarm and so I feel a lot safer having you around."

Sam laughed. "You really don't have to say that."

"I will say anything that will get you down off this mountain and into bed at my house."

Sam cocked an eyebrow, intrigued.

"That did not come out right," Poppy said, cheeks reddening.

"What are you talking about? You just gave me all the incentive I need to will myself back to perfect health. It's all about having something to look forward to," Sam said with a wink.

And then Poppy slammed the car door shut on him.

Chapter 42

After preparing Sam a heart-healthy meal of salmon, sautéed garlic spinach, and mashed potatoes, washed down with one glass of Chardonnay, although she suspected Sam snuck a second glass while she was in the kitchen loading the dishwasher, Poppy prepared the guest room for Sam. She changed the sheets on the bed, provided him towels, and made sure his bathroom was fully stocked with all the necessary toiletries.

Sam remarked that Poppy was a shoo-in for a five-star review on TripAdvisor. As Sam undressed, Poppy headed to the kitchen to fetch him a glass of water so he could take his sleeping pill. Since his heart attack, Sam had been tossing and turning at night, unable to sleep for any long stretches, and so his doctor had prescribed him a pill to knock him out, and it had been mercifully working the past few nights.

When she returned with the water, she couldn't help

but notice Sam's hand shaking as he gratefully took the glass from her and popped the pill into his mouth before chasing it down with the water. She could tell he was still in a fragile state, and his recovery was going to take longer than Sam was willing to admit, especially since he had already been chattering on at dinner about going hunting with some buddies back up in Big Bear next week. Poppy chose not to argue with him except to say quietly, "We shall see. . . ."

Sam smirked at the comment.

Poppy glanced around the room. "Do you have everything you need?"

"Almost," he said playfully, wrapping his arms around her waist.

"There will be plenty of time for that once you have fully recovered," Poppy said, extricating herself from his grip. "Which is what you need to focus on right now."

"Is that why I'm banished to the guest room?"

"Yes, as a matter of fact. We're just asking for trouble if you sleep in the main suite with me," Poppy laughed.

Sam yawned.

The pill was starting to take effect.

Sam looked at the turned-down bed. "Where's the mint on my pillow?"

To his surprise, Poppy was ready for him. She carefully placed a chocolate mint wrapped in green foil on his white pillowcase.

He shook his head, smiling, then gave her a gentle kiss on the lips. "I appreciate all you're doing, Poppy. I know I'm a big imposition. . . ."

"Nonsense. I love having you here. Now get some sleep and I will see you in the morning," she said.

"Yes, ma'am," he said, chuckling, plopping down on

the edge of the bed as Poppy walked out and closed the door behind her.

The dishwasher was running in the kitchen and she turned on the TV in the living room to watch the local news and Stephen Colbert, making sure to keep the volume low so she would not keep Sam awake, although his sleeping pill was apparently quite potent. Sam had told her a 7.2 earthquake would probably not even rouse him.

Poppy sat down on the couch, half listening to the news as she scrolled through her e-mail on her iPad. Her eyes got heavy and she yawned a few times so she set the tablet down on the coffee table and stretched out on the couch, falling asleep to Colbert's opening monologue.

She had no idea how long she had been out when a crash jolted her awake. She sprung up from the couch. The sound had come from the patio. She reached for the remote and muted the volume on the TV and then stood still, listening.

All was quiet.

She made her way down the hall and pressed her ear to Sam's door. She could hear him lightly snoring. Then she headed for the kitchen where the dishwasher had long finished its cycle. She flipped on the lights outside on the patio and peered through the window to see one of her potted plants on the cement floor, smashed to bits. She knew the neighbors' black cat, Oswald, had been making a habit of hanging out on her patio ever since Poppy had moved in. She craned her neck to see if she could spot him sprinting across the street toward home, but saw nothing.

Poppy crossed to the side door and stepped out onto the patio. There was no strong wind whipping about that might have knocked the plant off the sill, or any sign of a coyote sniffing around for an unsuspecting cat to snatch and escape with back into the desert night. She had been warned that coyotes often turned up in the neighborhood, hungry and on the hunt. She was about to go get her broom and dustpan to sweep up the dirt on the patio, but then decided it was late, and she was tired. It could wait until morning.

She turned toward the door and stopped suddenly in her tracks. A man stood in the shadows just out of the light, watching her from only a few feet away.

"Who are you?"

He hesitated, not wanting to reveal himself just yet.

"I said, who are you? What are you doing here?"

Finally, he took a tentative step into the light.

It was Byron Savage.

Danika Delgado's persistent and dangerous stalker.

Poppy gasped, stumbling back, and opened her mouth to scream for help.

Byron rushed forward, grabbing her around the waist and clamping a hand tightly over her mouth to silence her. He then backed her up against the wall, pressing himself against her and holding her in place. Poppy struggled mightily, but knew she was no match for this much younger, much stronger man.

"Please," he hissed. "Please don't scream."

Poppy, panicked, wriggling and twisting, trying to bite his hand, but he held her firmly in place until she began to realize he had complete control over her, at least for now.

"I'm not here to hurt you. I just want to talk to you."

She didn't trust him.

She knew what he was capable of, what his brother was capable of, and it frightened her that he had tracked her down at her home, no surprise since anyone with access to the local Palm Springs real estate news would know where she lived, and with no security system in place yet.

"I promise I am not going to hurt you, Ms. Harmon. If I let you go, will you at least hear me out?"

Poppy, resigned, nodded.

He waited a few seconds, just to make sure she wasn't going to try to run, then slowly removed his hand and took a small step back.

"You have some nerve showing up here after what your brother and his pals did to me and my associate," Poppy spit out.

"I know, in his own way, he was just trying to protect me . . ."

"By attempting to *kill* us?"

"Axel has a short fuse. He doesn't think things through like he should."

"And you do? You stalked a young actress, an actress who is now dead, by the way."

"That's why I'm here. I want to help you. I can't go to the police with what I know because they'll arrest me, and I can't go to jail, I would never survive it."

Poppy managed to calm down and listen to what the young man had to say, but remaining alert in case he suddenly changed his mind and attacked her.

"After you came to my house, thinking I was the one who killed Danika, I've been wanting to tell someone, anyone, what I heard because I loved Danika, I wouldn't have harmed her in any way, not in a million years. But I may know who did."

"Go on," Poppy said quietly.

Byron took a deep breath, then continued. "That day when I crashed the set, trying to find Danika so I could tell her in person how much she meant to me, I saw the producer, that fat guy, the one who has won all the Oscars . . ."

"Hal Greenwood."

"Yeah, him. I saw him threatening Danika. He had her cornered near her trailer, and he was practically on top of her, and she looked so scared as he was yelling at her."

"What was he yelling at her about?"

"I couldn't hear everything, but I did pick up a few things. Like how her career would be over if she claimed he had been inappropriate with her, stuff like that."

That seemed to line up with everything Poppy knew about Greenwood at this point so she tended to believe Byron's story.

"It made me so mad hearing him talk to Danika that way, I was ready to explode. I was just about to storm over there and rescue her, thinking maybe she would see me as some kind of hero, when a couple of crew members walked by and Hal backed off immediately so they wouldn't see him intimidating her. Danika took that opportunity to slip away from him and run off. That's when I decided to follow her to the gym, to make sure she was safe."

That was a crock. It was obvious Byron was far more interested in getting Danika alone to profess his undying love than to check and make sure she was safe from Hal Greenwood. But that didn't take away from what he saw.

The problem was Greenwood had an alibi on the day she was murdered.

However, she was not about to share this key piece of information with Byron. She was not going to risk setting him off.

"I know you are investigating Danika's murder so I thought you'd want to know."

"You should go now."

"Please, just give me a ten-minute head start before you call the police. . . ."

"Get out of here, Byron."

Byron nodded, then dashed away, across the street and into the darkness. Only then did Poppy breathe again. She had never been so scared in her life.

She contemplated calling the police, or waking Sam, but ultimately decided to do neither. She was reasonably certain Byron had not been the one to suffocate Danika, he seemed sincere. Hal, on the other hand, continued to haunt her. She knew intellectually that he could not have been Danika's killer, but instinctively she suspected he was a lot more involved than he was letting on. He could have easily hired someone to do his dirty work for him.

No, Poppy was hardly done with Hal Greenwood.

Chapter 43

"You have some nerve showing up here!" Iris spit out, enraged.

"Iris, please, let the man speak," Poppy implored.

Violet just sat on the couch, mouth agape, staring at Phil McKellan, who stood near the door to the garage office, eyes full of shame. Matt was on the couch beside Violet, his arm slung protectively around her. Wyatt sat at his desk, his head toggling back and forth between Phil and Iris, who appeared as if she was about to lunge at him like a cougar defending her cubs against a marauding grizzly bear.

"I have absolutely no interest in hearing what this man has to say," Iris snorted, pointing an accusing finger at Phil. "Not after the disgraceful way he treated poor Violet!"

"You're right," Phil muttered. "I acted terribly."

"Violet is a remarkable, beautiful woman who deserves better than to have some lying, unscrupulous, two-faced scoundrel stomping all over her emotions," Iris bellowed.

Phil nodded his head sorrowfully. "I know, I know. . . ."

Everyone in the room, especially Violet, was surprised at the voraciousness of Iris's defense of her friend, but they should not have been. Although Iris had a tendency to be outspoken and blunt, sometimes to the point of hurting someone's feelings, she was a fiercely loyal friend and would never tolerate anyone else mistreating one of her own, especially someone she considered vulnerable and too trusting such as Violet.

"So turn around and walk out that door, and do not ever come back here again!" Iris insisted.

Phil held a brown string-tied folder in one hand as he nervously tapped it with his index finger. "I just need for you to see this." He tossed the folder down on the coffee table in front of Violet and Matt.

"What is that?" Violet asked quietly.

"A dossier."

"On what?" Matt asked.

"Hal Greenwood."

"I don't understand," Poppy said.

Phil addressed Poppy but kept his eyes laser-focused on Violet. "First of all, I feel terrible about what went down with Violet. I admit, I went to that square dance at the senior center for the express purpose of meeting her and getting close to her so we could keep tabs on your agency and what you were up to. I saw it as just part of the job, my latest assignment . . ." His voice trailed off.

Violet stared down at the floor, unwilling to make eye contact with him. Matt slid in closer to her while still glaring at Phil, silently warning him to keep his distance.

"Mission accomplished," Iris sneered. "Do you expect us to applaud you for a job well done?"

"What I didn't expect was how much I would like her and enjoy spending time with her. I was conflicted. I couldn't tell her who I was, and what I was doing, or I would have been fired, but I also didn't want to mislead her so when the truth finally did come out she would think my feelings for her were not genuine."

"Well, it is a little too late for that. The damage has been done," Iris said, folding her arms. "Right, Violet?"

Violet ignored her. "What are you trying to say, Phil?"

"I was besotted from the moment I met you, and I am so deeply sorry for the pain I caused. In my own inept thinking, I believed that once my job was done, I could continue seeing you, and you would never have to know the truth about *why* we met."

"If that's true, why did you ghost her?" Matt asked.

"I had to, at least for a little while, I was being watched at the company, I couldn't afford any missteps, but I was always going to come back and try to pick up where we left things off."

"I do not believe a word you are saying!" Iris snapped.

"You're entitled to believe whatever you want," Phil said, before turning toward Violet. "What matters to me is what Violet thinks."

"I don't know . . ." Violet whispered.

"And your peace offering is a dossier on Hal Greenwood?" Poppy asked, confused.

"Look, I know you've been investigating Greenwood," Phil said.

"Of course you know! You have been *spying* on us!" Iris exclaimed.

"True, but I also know Greenwood's got an airtight alibi for the Danika Delgado murder."

Matt shrugged. "So what? He could have hired someone to do his dirty work, a thug from Cobra perhaps, someone like you to shut her up before word got out that he was harassing her."

"Okay, I deserved that, but you're wrong. I would never do something so vile, and that's not the kind of company I work for either. Once we compiled this file on Greenwood, we dropped him as a client."

"Why? What's in there?" Poppy asked, pointing to the dossier on the coffee table.

"There is a lot of truth to the rumors out there about him. He's scum and not worth our time," Phil said. "There is stuff in there that dates all the way back to his childhood. It's a complete picture of the man, and it's not pretty. And having worked for the guy, I'm now convinced even if he didn't commit the murder, he's somehow connected to it."

There was a long silence.

He was echoing Poppy's own suspicions.

Phil was done, but he made no move to leave.

Poppy finally decided to take charge of getting him out. "Thank you, Phil. We'll look it over."

Phil took a step toward Violet and said quickly, "I texted you my new number, Violet. Feel free to use it . . . But I understand if you decide to leave things where they are."

Violet's lip quivered. She didn't know what to make of him, if he was being sincere, not sure she could ever trust him again. She simply managed to croak out, "Okay."

That was all he was going to get at this point.

"Thanks for your time," he mumbled, and then headed out the door.

Poppy walked over and picked up the dossier and began untying the string to open it. Phil McKellan had a gut feeling about Hal Greenwood, and so did Poppy, and for what it was worth, so did Byron Savage. Hopefully whatever was in this envelope would finally provide some answers.

Chapter 44

When it became clear that Poppy and her Desert Flowers team would be working late poring over the information in the dossier Phil McKellan had left behind, Poppy put in a call to Sam to check up on him and make sure he was taken care of until she was able to get home.

"There is some cold chicken in the fridge, and enough veggies in the crisper to make yourself a salad, and there might be some cookies in the pantry, hopefully not too stale."

"I'll wait up for you," Sam said.

"Don't be ridiculous. There is no telling how long I'm going to be stuck here."

"Any wine left?"

"You should not be drinking."

"They say red wine is good for the heart."

"I'm never sure if it's the doctors saying that or the wine industry," Poppy said. "If you must, just one glass."

"That's no fun."

"And don't forget to take your sleeping pill."

"Yes, dear," Sam cracked.

"What was that?" Poppy snorted.

"What?"

"*Dear*? You've been at my house one day and already we're acting like an old married couple."

"I know, it's kind of fun, isn't it?" Sam joked.

"And don't overexert yourself. You're supposed to be taking it easy."

"I'll try not to get too excited lying on your couch watching Anderson Cooper tell me what's going on in the world."

"Good-bye, *sweetheart*," Poppy said, grinning.

"Later, *pumpkin*."

Poppy laughed as she ended the call.

In order to give the team an energy boost, Iris had offered to make a Starbucks run before they closed for the day.

"How thoughtful, thank you, Iris," Violet cooed.

"I am a thoughtful person, Violet," Iris said before scooting out the door.

Poppy knew Iris was more interested in getting out of the claustrophobic office and into some fresh air than doing a selfless act and treating everyone to shots of espresso to keep them awake. That left Poppy, Violet, Matt, and Wyatt to sift through the pages in the dossier.

The first batch of pages mostly contained information about Hal Greenwood that they already knew, past lawsuits and depositions both as plaintiff and defendant.

Greenwood had a litigious nature and enough money to drag things out in a court for years until he usually won or got a settlement. There were a lot of disgruntled screen-writers who sued when he stole their ideas, and directors he fired who were supposed to get final cut on their films according to their contracts, and then there were the flood of NDAs, non-disclosure agreements signed by hundreds of actresses, assistants, masseuses, and cocktail waitresses over his long thirty-five-year career, almost too many to count.

Poppy rifled through stacks of pages, choosing to focus on Greenwood's earlier years, before he hit it big, to see if there might be something about him they had missed, a key event that could provide a clue to how he evolved into the monster he ultimately became. That's when she spotted a name that stood out to her.

Harold Lawson.

That's the name Hal went by during his first few years in Hollywood. It made sense. Hal was short for Harold. But why Lawson? Why not Greenwood? She delved a lit-tle deeper into the file, turning up a hometown newspaper article from the time when local boy done good Harold Lawson, now Hal Greenwood, was producing his first in-dependent feature film in the late 1980s. According to the article, Lawson was Hal's father's name. Greenwood was his mother's maiden name. Why did he feel the need to change it? Did Hal Greenwood strike him as more of a Hollywood power player than Harold Lawson?

Maybe.

Then something hit Poppy.

Like a fast-moving freight train.

She gasped out loud.

Matt, Violet, and Wyatt all stopped what they were doing.

"What? What is it?" Violet asked.

"It could be nothing, but . . ."

Matt leaned forward. "But what?"

"Ever since I found Danika in her trailer with that pillow over her face, I began recalling my time in Hollywood when I first became aware of the Pillow Talk Killer, and it was on the set of *Jack Colt*, actually on the day I believe I almost became his next victim . . . and, no it can't be . . ."

"*What*?" Wyatt yelled.

"There was this young production assistant, and I could never remember his name, and so he told me it was Harold, and I made a promise to myself not to forget it."

Matt's mind clicked. "Hal. Do you think that PA was really Hal Greenwood?"

"He could be. I remember Harold was about the same height and build, it was just so long ago."

Wyatt plucked a piece of paper out of the pile. "According to this old article from *Entertainment Weekly* back in 1996 when he was pushing one of his films for a Best Picture Oscar, Greenwood told the reporter that he began his career as a production assistant on a number of top-rated television shows including *Dukes of Hazzard*, the last season of *Hart to Hart* and, wait for it, *Jack Colt, PI*!"

"As I recall, one of the victims had played a bit role on *The Dukes of Hazzard*," Poppy exclaimed.

"It's got to be him!" Matt cried, clapping his hands together.

Wyatt jumped off his stool next to his computer and

shuffled over to Poppy, who had sat down on the couch, her mind racing. "Do you have a photo of him when he was younger?"

Poppy shook her head. "No, why would I . . . ?" Then she shot back up to her feet. "Wait! I remember Rod Harper recently posted on Facebook an old cast and crew photo from the show on one of those Throwback Thursdays and so it's possible he might be in that!"

Wyatt scrambled back to his computer and quickly brought up Rod's Facebook page, scrolling down until he found the photo. He zoomed in close so Poppy could see everyone's faces. It took a few moments, but then she pointed at a chubby young man with frizzy hair in the back row. "There! That's him!"

"Hold on," Wyatt said. He isolated Harold in the photo and blew it up to maximum size making sure not to blur it.

Violet put a hand on Wyatt's shoulder. "Wyatt, honey, do you still have that computer program where you can age someone digitally—"

"Way ahead of you, Grandma," Wyatt said.

Within seconds, he had aged the photo of Harold about thirty or forty years, and the result was an exact double of a contemporary Hal Greenwood.

"It's definitely him," Matt said before patting Wyatt on the back. "Good work, kid."

"I remember him escorting me to the set and going on and on about the murders, the crime scenes, the beautiful victims," Poppy recounted. "It was almost as if he was boasting about how much he knew."

Violet trembled. "Do you think Hal Greenwood, or Harold Lawson may have been—?"

"The killer? He was so young and inexperienced. I didn't take his interest in the murders seriously at all. And then I had that run-in with Don Carter on the same night Linda Appleton became the third victim, and I was so convinced it had to be him, and so were the police, I forgot all about Harold . . . or Hal."

Poppy knew Hal could not have killed Danika Delgado. But what if the killer on the loose now in the present was a copycat, and Hal Greenwood had been the *first* Pillow Talk Killer back in the 1980s?

The thought was enough to make Poppy shudder.

Chapter 45

Poppy had noticed the black Mercedes parked across the street from her house when she pulled into her driveway, but didn't think much of it until she was at her front door, slipping the key into the lock, and heard a rustling sound behind her. She spun around, hand raised in self-defense. There was no one there. She had to laugh at herself. What was with the hand? She had no karate training whatsoever. What was she going to do, crack a neck with it? That usually worked on *Charlie's Angels,* which she watched religiously when she was a young actress just starting out in LA and stayed home most nights because she hardly knew anyone in town.

Poppy had started turning back toward the door when she heard the sound again, this time coming from her right. She whipped her head around to see a bulky man partially hidden in the shadows of her curve-leaf yucca plants, his feet trampling her carefully arranged colorful succulents.

He held out a chubby hand. "Don't panic, I'm not here to hurt you."

"That's the second time I've heard that this week," Poppy growled, recognizing the man's voice. "You should not be here, Hal." Her stomach flip-flopped. First Byron Savage. Now Hal Greenwood. Two people she did not trust or feel safe around. Especially Hal, given what had come to light about him only an hour earlier.

Hal stepped tentatively out of the shadows of the tall yucca plants. His appearance did nothing to calm Poppy's heart, which was trying to pound its way out of her chest.

Hal looked wild-eyed, nervous, slightly unhinged.

"I just want to talk to you," Hal tried to assure her.

"Then you should call the office and make an appointment, like you expect everyone else to do for you," Poppy sniffed.

"I heard what you did, you and your associates, crashing the Cobra offices pretending to be some kind of cosmetics queen. That takes a lot of balls," Hal said.

"You sound impressed."

"Maybe a little," Hal sneered.

"Now please, get back in your Mercedes and go home. I have no interest in talking to you here like this."

Hal didn't budge. "What kind of game are you playing? You know I had nothing to do with Danika Delgado's murder, I have an airtight alibi."

"What about Fabian Granger?" Poppy asked.

"If I had been at the Parker someone would have seen me. I'm famous, or I would have turned up on the security camera at some point, but I didn't," he said. "I didn't because I was never there. I'm innocent. So would you please stop obsessing over tying me to these horrific murders? Can you do me that one favor, *please*?"

"Maybe you're not responsible for those murders, but what about the others?"

"What the hell are you talking about?" Hal bellowed.

"There is no statute of limitations for murder so any cold case can still be solved and the killer brought to justice. You've produced enough crime movies to know that, Harold."

He almost missed it.

He was about to argue some more when something in his brain suddenly clicked and his mouth dropped open.

"What did you just call me?"

"Harold, that's your name, isn't it? Harold Lawson?"

"How did you—?"

She could see the wave of panic rising up from inside him.

He took a minute to collect himself.

Then, Hal took a deep breath, and smiled. "Nobody's called me by that name in years. I may have underestimated your detective skills. I really didn't think you'd remember me."

"I didn't. Not at first. But it came back. Who would have guessed the great Hollywood producer Hal Greenwood started out as our ambitious, socially awkward production assistant who was so keenly interested in all the gory aspects of the Pillow Talk Killer murders?"

Hal flinched slightly. "Wow, good memory."

"It's been hard to forget that particular day, no matter how hard I've tried. Why did you change your name?"

"I was focused on becoming a power player. I never thought Harold would ever command much respect, especially since Harold the PA was treated like dirt most of the time. Although I have to admit, you were always very nice to me."

Poppy ignored the compliment. "So it wasn't because you *had* to change it?"

"I know what you're implying and you're dead wrong," Hal sighed. "I don't know why you are so hung up on me being the Pillow Talk Killer. I wasn't him then, I'm not him now. So get over it. We all know the real guy was Donald Carter. He was at the Roosevelt that night with you and Linda Appleton. He bought you a drink after Rod stood you up, you were pegged as his next victim until you ran off at the last minute, and so the killer had no choice but to redirect his attention toward poor unsuspecting Linda. . . ."

Poppy's already racing heart nearly jumped into her throat. "How did you know Rod Harper stood me up that night?"

"Oh, come on, everyone knows that. It was all over the news the day after it happened," Hal argued.

"Yes, except the part about Rod standing me up. That was never mentioned in the press."

"Of course it was," Hal said warily.

"I'm quite sure the police did not share that detail with reporters at my request, and I know I never told anyone because the last thing I wanted was to fan the flames in the media with endless, breathless stories about me and Rod."

"Well, what can I say, it's out there!" Hal yelled.

Poppy studied Hal, whose fleshy face was red and sweaty. "You only know because you followed me to the Roosevelt that night. You were watching me the whole time. Donald Carter wasn't the Pillow Talk Killer. *You* were!"

Hal knew he had been caught. His eyes darted back and forth nervously. Finally, he sighed heavily. There was no point in continuing to lie. Poppy knew everything. "I was never going to hurt you. I overheard Rod on the phone getting that last-minute audition. I knew he was going to be a no-show so I went to the Roosevelt and hung out in a booth in the back, hoping to swoop in at the last minute once you realized Rod wasn't coming, maybe offer a comforting shoulder, or . . ."

"It *never* would have happened!" Poppy snapped.

"You fled the bar so fast, I didn't even get my chance. And then I saw Linda. Sweet, beautiful Linda. But before I could work up the nerve to go talk to her, Don Carter was all over her, and the next thing I knew they were heading up to his hotel room. I hung out at the bar a while longer, and when I finally got up to leave, I saw Linda coming down in the elevator on her way home. . . ."

Poppy knew what had happened next. "You felt so rejected, so angry, that all those violent urges rose up inside you again, and so you followed her home and . . ." Poppy couldn't finish the rest of her thought, the image so disturbing. She cleared her head and continued. "After the police became convinced that Donald Carter was guilty of the three murders, you changed your name, tried to bury that side of yourself, start fresh, focus on becoming a famous producer. And you succeeded beyond your wildest dreams. You got exactly what you came to Hollywood for, respect, money, and a feeling of indestructibility that led to you becoming an unapologetic sexual predator!"

Hal took a menacing step closer to Poppy. "What do you think is going to happen now?"

Poppy shot a hand forward, trying to keep him at arm's length away from her. "With what I know now, if I do a little more digging, well, like I said, there is no statute of limitations on murder."

She was trying to keep him focused on what she was saying and not what she was doing because she had managed to surreptitiously extract her phone from her coat pocket with her other hand, hide it behind her back, and was now struggling to dial 911, praying she was hitting the correct numbers blindly. She traced her finger back up the screen, hoping she would hit the number one twice and the call would mercifully go through when Hal suddenly noticed what she was doing and slapped the phone out of her hand. It clattered to the ground, the screen cracking.

Poppy pushed Hal away from her and then reeled around, twisting the key in the lock, attempting to get inside and shut the door behind her before Hal could get to her, but she was a fraction of a second too late. She almost had it closed when Hal hurled his huge body at the door, smashing his way into her house. Poppy kicked him in the shin and his tongue flapped out of his mouth, but he was operating on pure adrenaline now, and it failed to slow him down. He grabbed Poppy in a bear hug and they stumbled across the living room and fell down on the couch, Hal on top of her, his heavy weight immobilizing her, his beefy hands wrapped around her throat. Poppy opened her mouth to scream, but her windpipe was cut off and no sound came out.

Hal reached over for one of the throw pillows and jammed it over Poppy's face, violently trying to smother her to death and silence her for good. "This was always my favorite part," he hissed. "Up close and personal."

Poppy fought like mad but Hal was twice her size and almost three times her weight. She couldn't breathe and was becoming light-headed and desperate as the chilling thought that she was not going to somehow miraculously break free crept into her mind along with a feeling of utter hopelessness.

But then, she heard a thwack and Hal suddenly loosened his grip on the pillow. His body was pulled off her and there was a loud thud as it hit the floor. The pillow was then gently removed from her face and she was looking up at Sam's concerned face.

"Are you okay?" Sam asked, clasping her hand and helping her to sit up on the couch.

Poppy nodded, still trying to catch her breath.

"I was in the guest room, tossing and turning, unable to get to sleep when all of a sudden I heard this commotion in the living room, and I came out to see this rhinoceros on top of you, trying to kill you, so I grabbed the first thing I could find and whacked him the back of the head."

Poppy was on the verge of tears she was so relieved and grateful.

"By the way, sorry about your People's Choice Award."

Poppy was finally able to speak. "What?"

"I think there is a crack in it," Sam said pointing to her award on the floor next to Hal's prone body. She had won it back in the 1980s for her role on *Jack Colt.* It was in the first box she had unpacked and had finally come in handy.

Poppy tried to stand up, but she was still woozy. Sam put an arm around her to keep her steady.

"I thought for sure you'd be sound asleep and wouldn't hear anything," she said.

"I forgot to take my sleeping pill."

Poppy rested her head on Sam's shoulder, happy that his annoying habit of not obeying her instructions had just saved her life.

Chapter 46

Poppy shoved a dishrag into Hal Greenwood's mouth and secured it with gray duct tape when she tired of listening to him spew offensive four-letter words and empty threats to her well-being as Sam tied him to a kitchen chair with several electrical cords around his chest and legs before binding his wrists.

Hal squirmed and struggled through all his muffled screaming, but soon when it became abundantly clear it wasn't doing him any good, he finally slumped over, defeated as they all waited for Detective Jordan to arrive.

When the doorbell rang, Poppy sighed with relief and hurried to let the police in. But when she opened the door, she was surprised to find a short, wiry Latino man with spiky black hair and a big friendly smile standing there instead of Detective Jordan.

"Hi, I'm Willie from Smart House Security. You must

be . . ." He stopped to check his notes. "Ms. Poppy Harmon?"

"What are you doing here so late?" Poppy asked, peering around him to see his van with the Smart House logo parked out front.

"We had a last-minute cancellation. Didn't Britney call you?" Willie asked, slightly confused.

"No, she didn't."

Britney had not struck Poppy as a reliable brain trust from their previous conversation, but she refrained from further comment on her competence, or lack thereof.

"It's almost eleven o'clock at night," Poppy scolded, checking the time on her phone.

"Smart House Home Security is on call twenty-four seven to insure that your home is not vulnerable to any bad guys lurking about!" Willie proudly touted.

"Well, you're too late. My house has been invaded twice while I've been waiting for you people to show up and install my security system!" Poppy barked.

"Oh . . . I'm sorry to hear that," Willie said, flummoxed, before taking it upon himself to attempt to rectify the situation. "How about I give you a ten percent discount?"

"How about you call Britney and tell her she booked this appointment without even bothering to consult me?"

"I can see that now is not convenient, would you like to reschedule?"

"Yes, I would, Willie. I would like to reschedule with another home security company. Good night!"

Willie finally got the message, and with a hangdog look on his face, slowly turned around and shuffled back to his van just as a white Ford Focus arrived, followed by a couple of police squad cars, blue lights flashing. Detec-

tive Jordan jumped out of his Ford and gave Willie a curt
nod as he hurried up the walk toward Poppy. Four officers got out of the squad cars and followed Jordan as a
curious Willie hung back, watching all the action unfold.

"Where is he?" Jordan asked Poppy.

"In the kitchen," she said, opening the door all the way
to allow him and his officers inside the house.

At the sight of Jordan and his team of patrolmen, Hal's
whole body sagged, resigned to what was now happening.

Jordan knelt down and locked eyes with Hal Greenwood. "I'm going to dispense with the usual questioning
because it's pretty clear what happened here. I'm charg-
ing you with attempted murder for starters, then we'll be
adding more as we go. Now, I'm going to remove this
tape so my officers can read you your rights, and let me
stress, one of those rights is for you to remain silent, and
I would strongly suggest you pay close attention to that
one."

Hal glared at him defiantly.

Detective Jordan reached out with his fingers, got ahold
of the duct tape, and then roughly ripped it off, causing
Hal to wince and yelp. Since Hal was not a dumb man, he
wisely chose to follow Jordan's advice and kept his mouth
shut. A female officer, African American, husky build,
stepped forward as Sam untied the power cords.

"Stand up, please, sir," she ordered.

Hal had trouble lifting his bulk off the chair, but no
one made a move to assist him. He didn't seem to have
any fans in the room.

The officer had a blasé, seen-it-all-before look on her
face as she slapped a pair of handcuffs around Hal's thick

wrists. She began reading him his rights as she and two of the other officers escorted him out of the house to the squad car.

"He's the Pillow Talk Killer," Poppy exclaimed breathlessly to Detective Jordan. "The original, the one who started it all back in the nineteen eighties."

Jordan stared at her, surprised. "Are you serious?"

Poppy nodded. "He confessed to me and I'm willing to testify to that fact."

"But you don't think he had anything to do with the current murders?" Jordan asked.

Poppy shook her head. "There's no way."

"Maybe he's working with someone new," Jordan suggested. "Someone he's taken under his wing, a protégé who he has trained to do his dirty work for him."

"I suppose that's possible, but I'm not inclined to believe it," Poppy said. "Why would a killer prefer to just live vicariously through someone else instead of committing the murders himself? It doesn't make sense he would outsource his own violent behavior."

"Okay, what about Chase Ehrens? He's a dangerous guy with a volatile temper, he had a motive for Danika's murder, she dumped him, he got fired from her movie, and the good news is, we already have him in custody," Jordan said.

"Chase is a vile human being, and he should be in jail for a long time, but I'm just not certain he was the one who suffocated Danika, not without concrete evidence, and even if he did kill her, then who drowned Fabian Granger? There is so much more we don't know."

Jordan sighed, frustrated. He stayed another half hour taking statements from both Poppy and Sam. After finally ushering the detective out, Poppy turned to Sam. "You should be in bed."

"Are you kidding? After all that excitement, I feel like a new man," Sam said, grinning. "It's the first time I've felt this alive in a long time," Sam said, pounding his chest.

"Well, Tarzan, Jane here is very grateful for you swinging in on your vine to rescue me from the evil animal poacher, but now it's time for you to go back to the tree house with Cheetah and get some rest."

"Oh, come on," Sam scoffed. "Let's stay up and have a celebratory drink. Together we got the despicable Hal Greenwood off the streets."

Poppy knew it was a lost cause battling the overpowering charm of Sam Emerson. She was never going to win. She just threw her hands up in the air. "One drink!"

Chapter 47

"And . . . cut!" Trent called out in his haughty, superior-sounding British accent. "Thank you, everyone. That's a wrap here in Joshua Tree."

Matt bounded up to Poppy and gave her a hug. "Congratulations! You made it through. We both did."

"I can't say I'm not happy that my brief return to acting is over," Poppy chuckled. "You certainly seemed to have a much better time at this than I did."

"What can I say, I got the bug!" Matt said with a bright smile.

They had both just completed their final scene on the film, a simple group shot for the last big sequence in the movie; neither of them had any dialogue. It was customary for the director to announce an actor's completion on the film followed by applause from the rest of the cast and crew, but Trent had forgotten or willfully declined to mention Poppy and Matt. There would be no cake or tearful good-byes, and Poppy was fine with that. She did not relish any further attention on herself. She was eager to put this whole experience behind her, and prayed she did not embarrass herself in the final product, which would be released later in the year on Netflix.

The crew got to work breaking down the set. Although the company was done shooting in Joshua Tree, the production was now scheduled to move back to the resort with Joselyn to reshoot Danika's scenes that were already in the can.

The last twenty-four hours had been a whirlwind. Word of Hal Greenwood's arrest had leaked almost instantly, and headlines around the world blared that the infamous Pillow Talk Killer had finally been caught after almost forty years. Some less judicious reporters failed to mention that Greenwood had an alibi for the recent Danika Delgado murder, preferring to ignore the facts and pin the blame directly on him despite the lack of evidence. It was a better headline. CRAZED HOLLYWOOD SERIAL KILLER BROUGHT DOWN AFTER STAGING COMEBACK!

Despite the police stressing that they believed a killer was still at large, Hal Greenwood became the face of the new devil of the moment like Charles Manson. He was everywhere on TV and online. His lawyers cried, "Fake news!" But nobody really listened because Hal Greenwood looked the part of a depraved, privileged monster who felt entitled to prey upon those young women who showed so much promise, whose lives he had so insidiously cut short.

Poppy was understandably frustrated, too. The Desert Flowers Detective Agency got a few mentions in the press as having been key in exposing Hal Greenwood. A few journalists even picked up on Poppy's personal connection back in the 1980s and wrote breathlessly about her forty-year struggle to find the killer of her dear friends, the original three victims, even though in reality, Poppy only knew one just in passing.

Poppy and Matt had both been surprised when they received phone calls from Trent's assistant director asking them to report to the Joshua Tree set at 5:00 AM for makeup and hair so they could shoot their final scene. They had assumed the film would be inevitably delayed once more after Hal's arrest and impending arraignment. But the investors had decided otherwise. They refused to be deterred any longer. They had already lost millions from the initial production shutdown after Danika's death; they were not going to lose another cent. A meeting was hastily called, and in a unanimous decision, the production was placed under the guiding hand of Hal's loyal sidekick, Greta Van Damm. In an e-mail to the cast and crew, Greta trumpeted that the production would move full steam ahead and finish on time and on budget, or rather the revised budget with an additional two million to cover the costly delays and overruns.

"Hey, I'm going to go say good-bye to Joselyn before we head home. Meet you in your trailer?" Matt said to Poppy.

"Fine," Poppy answered.

Matt hustled off and Poppy fixed her attention on Trent. He was busy flagging down Greta, who appeared to be on the phone with her office back in LA.

Poppy started approaching Trent. She didn't know what she was going to say, but she knew she should at least thank him for believing in her, fighting to cast her in the part when there was a lot of pressure on him to use a bigger name. She just hoped she had not disappointed the up-and-coming director. As she moved toward them, Greta finally got off her call and Trent was suddenly in her face, aggressively wagging a finger at her.

Greta appeared slightly stunned, slowly backing away from him, a distasteful, annoyed look on her face. Poppy stopped a few feet away from them, and was able to overhear bits of their conversation.

"I was in her trailer giving her direction on an upcoming scene and that's when Joselyn noticed him staring at us through the window. He must have been using an apple box to stand on so he could get a good view!" Trent spat out angrily.

Greta dismissively mimed air quotes with her fingers and sneered, "*Direction*?"

"Yeah, we are shooting a movie and she is my leading lady! That's what I do. Give direction!" Trent huffed.

Greta folded her arms and smirked skeptically. "Yes, you've proven time and time again you're a *hands-on* director."

"What the hell is that supposed to mean?"

"You know what it means, Trent. I don't have to explain it to you."

Trent swatted away an annoying fly buzzing around him and then focused on Greta again. "Look, it doesn't matter what we were actually doing. That doesn't give your creepy son the right to play Peeping Tom. This shoot has had enough problems and you certainly don't need your new star slapping you with a lawsuit."

The word *lawsuit* finally got Greta's attention. "I'll talk to him, okay?"

"Thank you," Trent sighed.

Greta stalked off, clearly rattled.

Trent watched her go and Poppy stepped forward. "Trent?"

The director spun around and growled, "What?"

His pinched face softened a bit at the sight of his former childhood crush.

Poppy smiled. "I know it's been a bumpy ride, but I appreciate all you've done, giving me this chance . . ."

"You were great. We were lucky to have you. You really classed up my movie," he said, slightly rushed. He gave her a quick peck on the cheek and was about to move on.

Poppy stepped in front of him, blocking his hasty exit. "I couldn't help but overhear. I didn't know Greta had a son."

"Yeah, she strong-armed me into hiring him. I only agreed because I figured if I gave her a win, she'd have to cave on some of my casting choices, like you, for instance, so I guess it all worked out in the end."

"What does her son do on the set?" Poppy asked, looking around.

Trent raised an eyebrow. "It's Timothy."

Poppy stumbled back, floored. "The PA?"

"Yes. I thought you knew."

"No, I-I had no idea. . . ."

"Have you ever really talked to him? He's a strange bird, that one. I got a weird vibe from him on the day he started. And now it turns out he's a pervert just like his dad."

"His *dad*? Who is his father?"

Trent glanced around to make sure Greta was nowhere in sight, then leaned in closer. "Well, nobody knows for sure, but there has been a rumor going around that Hal Greenwood is the father."

Poppy let out an audible gasp.

Trent nodded knowingly. "I heard a few in the know call him 'Little Hal.'"

Chapter 48

Armed with this startling, disturbing, potentially game-changing new information, Poppy knew she had to catch Greta before she left the set back to LA. A grip packing up some cables pointed Poppy in the direction of the base camp parking lot where he had last seen Greta heading. Poppy made a mad dash in hot pursuit, but was stopped in her tracks at the sight of Iris and Violet lumbering toward her, Violet wildly waving at her and shouting, "Poppy! Poppy!"

"What are you two doing here?" Poppy asked, utterly confused.

"The last time I was here with Wyatt, watching the car chase scene, which of course ended so badly for Matt, anyway I met that handsome helicopter pilot . . ."

"Roy Heller," Iris almost sang, clearly smitten.

"Yes, Roy," Violet sighed.

"He is a very attractive man," Iris cooed, as much as Iris was capable of cooing.

"He most certainly is, that swagger of his is just so manly," Violet agreed, turning back to Poppy. "Anyway, Roy was kind enough to invite me and Wyatt for a ride in his helicopter once the film wrapped here in Joshua Tree. Wyatt was so disappointed he had school today and couldn't join us, which is why Iris insisted on coming along to take his place."

"But, Iris, you're afraid of heights," Poppy remarked.

Iris shrugged. "I will be fine. I trust Roy to keep me safe." She turned to Violet. "And for the record, Violet, you already have one man, that corporate spy Phil McKellan, drooling all over you so why not be a good friend and let me sit up front in the co-pilot's seat with Roy?"

"But it was *me* he personally invited, not you—" Violet began to argue before Poppy pushed past them.

"I've already flown around with Roy in his helicopter so you two go on and have fun. I need to find Greta. . . ."

Poppy scurried off. Behind her, Violet called after her, "Is everything all right?"

There was no time to explain. She kept going.

As she neared the base camp, Poppy spotted Greta's car pulling out of the parking lot toward the paved road leading out of the park. She practically threw herself in front of the vehicle in order to stop it. Greta slammed down on the brakes and the car jerked to a halt. She rolled down the driver's-side window as Poppy approached.

"Are you crazy? I nearly hit you," Greta snapped.

"I just wanted to have a quick word with you before you left," Poppy said calmly.

Greta eyed her warily. Poppy could tell she had little

interest in engaging in any kind of conversation with her, but then Greta softened a little and said, "I suppose I should thank you. It's because of you Hal is behind bars. He's finally going to pay for his depraved, unspeakable actions back in the nineteen eighties. Those poor women are finally going to get some justice."

Poppy stared at Greta stone-faced, which made her uncomfortable as she pressed on. "I just want to make perfectly clear to you, Poppy, I had no idea Hal Greenwood was the Pillow Talk Killer back then. I never in a million years would have partnered with him, worked side by side for all those years. . . ."

Poppy held her tongue, resisting the urge to remind Greta that although she may have been clueless about Hal's past as a serial killer, she had spent years covering up his gross sexual misconduct.

History would judge her role in those crimes.

"As satisfying as it is to know Linda Appleton and the others will finally get justice, I'm just frustrated we haven't been able to find the Pillow Talk Killer 2.0, the one on the loose now, ready and able to strike again at any moment. Danika, and perhaps Fabian Granger, are still waiting for their justice," Poppy said.

Greta studied Poppy, then almost as if brushing her off, said, "Well, I have faith that the police will find him or her eventually. It took forty years to finally expose Hal."

Greta gripped the steering wheel, pressed down on the gas, and slowly started to drive away when Poppy grabbed ahold of the rearview mirror, almost running alongside the car. "It's remarkable how similar the MOs of both killers are, Hal in the eighties and the one now. . . ."

Greta kept her eyes fixed ahead, speeding up some

more, hoping Poppy would let go of the mirror and fall away so she could finally escape this conversation.

Unable to keep up, Poppy finally released her grip on the mirror and the car raced ahead of her, kicking up dust and sand. Poppy cupped her hands to her mouth and shouted, "It's almost as if they both share the same DNA!"

The car screeched to a stop, engine idling.

Behind the wheel, Greta sat motionless.

Poppy slowly, methodically walked back up to the driver's-side window, instantly noticing the stricken look on Greta's face.

"Whatever wild, unprovable theories you may want to throw out there doesn't make them true," Greta huffed.

"I had no idea Timothy was your son."

Greta flinched but kept her cool. "It's hardly a secret. Everyone on the crew knows. You just didn't ask."

"You two look nothing alike," Poppy noted, her eyes falling on Greta's white-knuckled grip on the steering wheel. "Does he take after his *father*?"

Greta flinched again, this time more noticeably. She let go of the wheel, flopped back in her seat, and sighed. "Look, there is no point in dancing around it. You obviously already know Hal is Timothy's father."

Poppy nodded solemnly.

"The result of a messy, drunken encounter at the Cannes Film Festival over twenty years ago. Hal made it perfectly clear he had no interest in being a father and I respected that. I raised Timothy all on my own. I suppose I should give Hal credit for continuing to work with me, encouraging me to produce his films that made me quite a lot of money I could use to support my son. But other than a financial boost, Hal was definitely out of the picture when it came to Timothy."

"Does Timothy know who his father is?"

"Yes. I tried to keep it from him, but he was too determined to find out and figured it out on his own. I admit Timothy takes after Hal in many ways, and has some challenging emotional issues, but he most certainly is *not* a killer!"

"You didn't know Hal Greenwood was a killer until yesterday," Poppy said quietly.

"Timothy has nothing to do with the Pillow Talk Killer, and if you try to pin blame, or even associate his name with any of these awful crimes, I will sue you with a vengeance," Greta warned. "Believe me, I have the means to do it, so leave my son alone!" Greta cried as she stomped on the gas and peeled away.

Poppy watched her disappear in a cloud of dust. She could tell Greta was shaken because she simply could not even face the possibility that she might be wrong about her son. Hal had an airtight alibi for Danika's murder, but as far as she knew, Timothy did not.

Poppy hurried back to her trailer where Matt had told her he would meet her after saying his good-byes to Joselyn and the crew. She clattered up the metal steps and inside to pack up her things, barely making it past the door when it slammed shut behind her and a hand roughly grabbed her by the arm and spun her around.

It was Timothy, brandishing a Glock pistol in one hand while squeezing her arm so tight with the other it began to cut off her circulation. His eyes were dark and menacing, and the malevolent sneer on his face chilled her to the bone.

Chapter 49

Timothy forcefully shoved Poppy down on the hard, uncomfortable couch and took a step back, the pistol pointed directly at her.

Poppy took a deep breath. "Timothy, what are you doing with a gun? Why would you—?"

"Stop! Just stop!" he barked. "My mother called me from her car and told me all about the wild rumors you were spreading about me. She warned me to steer clear of you, but I knew I had to deal with you myself, once and for all."

"Then it *was* you, you smothered Danika with that pillow."

"She trusted me. I offered to run lines with her and she let me in her trailer when no one else was around. It was so easy."

"Why? Why did you do it?" Poppy cried, her eyes fixed on the pistol aimed straight at her face.

Timothy's eyes seemed to glaze over as his mind wandered back to another time. "When I was a kid, I always felt so lost and alone, my mother did her best to raise me, but she was always working and didn't have much time for me, and not knowing who my father was consumed me. Every time I watched a TV show or the news and saw some random guy I'd think, is that my father? Could that be him? Whenever I'd ask my mother, she'd brush it off. Finally she told me my father was dead just to get me to shut up, but deep down I knew she was lying."

"When did you find out about Hal Greenwood?" Poppy asked gently, not wanting to rile him up any more than he already was.

"About five years ago. Can you imagine my surprise? My mother's boss? He'd been in my life the whole time and she kept it hidden from me, I was completely in the dark! She didn't even list his name on my birth certificate, she just said 'father unknown.' But my grandmother knew the truth, and on her deathbed, she couldn't stand to see how tortured I was about not knowing who my father was, and so she confessed everything. I was so angry. It took me a long time to forgive my mother."

"So you reached out to Hal and he rejected you?" Poppy asked. It was a guess. But an educated one knowing the kind of man Hal Greenwood was.

"He adamantly denied it. I told him I wasn't trying to get any money or anything like that, but he didn't care. He just kicked me out of his office and threatened that if I ever brought it up again, he'd fire my mother. But that didn't stop me from wanting to know more about him. I became obsessed, I did a deep dive into his past, where he came from, how he became the success he is today . . . and along the way I stumbled across the Pillow Talk mur-

ders back in the nineteen eighties, and suddenly everything came into focus. . . ."

Poppy stared at him, confused. "How?"

"My whole childhood, especially when I was a teen-
ager, I had these violent thoughts, these urges to kill in
order to release all the anger pent up inside me. Whenever these thoughts crept into my mind, I'd try to suppress them, but the older I got, the more frequently they
came, and it was like I was at war with myself on the inside. When I found a link between Hal and the Pillow
Talk murders, it was like a eureka moment."

"You finally found a connection with your father,"
Poppy said solemnly.

"What is it they say, the apple doesn't fall far from the
tree? I was ecstatic, I finally had an explanation for what
was going on with me, it was simple genetics."

"That is an extreme oversimplification," Poppy snapped,
shaking her head. "Just because you share DNA with someone who has committed murder, that doesn't give you an
excuse to do the same!"

Timothy thrust the gun out, inflamed. "You don't know
anything! Don't you see? We're now bonded, inextrica-
bly linked, forever! Father and son!"

"You're deluded if you believe that he will somehow
be *proud* of you for this! Hal Greenwood is a raging, im-
moral narcissist! He won't care that you were trying to
impress him by following in his footsteps! He only cares
about himself, and right now he's not thinking about you,
he's only thinking about how he's going to get out of
spending the rest of his life in prison for those ghastly
murders he committed forty years ago!"

"You're wrong!" Timothy shouted.

"And your mother? Did she know what you did to Danika?"

"Of course not. She would have been horrified. It was best to keep her in the dark, like she kept me in the dark all those years."

"Why Danika? What did she ever do to you?"

"She was the exact same type of victim as the ones my father went after. She fit the profile. Simple as that. Anyone on the set could see how attracted he was to her. I knew if he had been younger like me, Danika would have been his perfect victim so I chose her. I wanted to feel what he felt all those years ago, the adrenaline, the thrill. . . ."

His cold assessment sent chills through Poppy.

She was desperate to cry out or try to knock the gun out of his hand and make a run for it, but she knew that was a risky proposition, especially since Timothy was now a self-confessed killer. She was trapped, unsure how she was going to get out of this predicament. She needed to keep Timothy talking until she could figure out a plan to escape.

"And then you targeted Fabian Granger because he somehow found out about you?"

"Yeah, I felt bad about that, but I had no choice. He had been poking around the set, asking questions, and somehow he discovered my true identity, that I was Hal Greenwood's bastard son. What a scoop, right? Well, I couldn't let that get out into the public, because it might raise suspicions about Hal and me and the Pillow Talk Killer, and so I needed to silence him. Permanently."

"How did you get past the hotel's security cameras?"

"That was a breeze. I pilfered a waiter uniform from a supply closet and grabbed a room service cart so nobody would question seeing me roaming the halls. I told a chambermaid that Mr. Granger had told me to let myself in with his dinner but I had forgotten my master card key, and so she was kind enough to let me in. I found him in the bathtub. He had his eyes closed, listening to a podcast, and so he never saw it coming."

The real waiter arrived with his dinner later, after Poppy had arrived and discovered the body.

Suddenly the door to the trailer flew open, and an unsuspecting Matt bounded inside. His eyes fell upon the gun in Timothy's hand and he stopped short. Timothy quickly pressed the gun to his temple.

"Come inside and shut the door," Timothy ordered.

Matt did as instructed. He looked at Poppy. "Are you all right?"

Poppy nodded, although it was impossible to conceal her cold-sweat terror.

Timothy had come prepared. He had some rope and zip ties in a plastic bag and ordered Poppy at gunpoint to bind Matt. Once she was finished and Matt was secured, Timothy went to work tying up Poppy, forcing them both back down on the couch side by side, his Glock pistol still trained on them.

"How about we go sightseeing in Joshua Tree Park? The views are so stark and dramatic, and there are so many hidden places where no one would ever find a body . . . or two," he said with a smug smile and a curt laugh.

Poppy and Matt exchanged tense looks as Timothy took the wheel of the mobile trailer and drove them away from base camp and into the vast, empty, foreboding desert.

Chapter 50

As the mobile home trailer barreled deeper into the heart of Joshua Tree National Park, Timothy swerved off the paved road and headed straight into the harsh, unforgiving hot desert farther and farther away from any signs of civilization. Poppy had no illusions as to what his plan was. He was going to take them as far out as possible, shoot them dead, then hide their bodies where they would probably never be found by anyone except a few wild animals that would hungrily feast upon their carcasses. It was a chilling fate, and Poppy was silently kicking herself for allowing herself and Matt to get caught up in this horrifying situation.

As Poppy and Matt sat side by side on the couch, hands and feet bound, shoulders bumping into each other from the sharp hairpin turns of the mobile trailer as it sped along, Poppy leaned in and whispered to Matt, "I'm so sorry about all this, Matt."

He gave her a puzzled look. "Sorry for what?"

"I feel like this is all my fault. You just wanted to be an actor and I forced you into this pretend role of a detective, and now it's going to end up getting you killed."

"Don't be ridiculous," Matt scoffed. "I knew what I was signing up for."

"No matter what happens, Matt, I want you to know how much I care for you, how much you've changed my life for the better. . . ."

"You're not saying that just because you think we're going to die today, are you?" Matt cracked.

"Of course not," Poppy said.

"Good, because I'm going to remind you of those words when we get out of this," Matt said, peering up front where Timothy was in the front cab driving the trailer, eyes glued to the desert in front of him.

Matt began twisting his wrists in a circular motion.

"What are you doing? The zip ties are too tight. You'll never wriggle free," Poppy sighed.

"There's a trick to zip ties," he said in a hushed tone. "When he had you tie me up, I knew there was a way to clench my fists with my palms facing down, which makes my wrists bigger and creates a little room to slip out. Since we've been talking, I unclenched my wrists so they faced inward and started to work my way out, thumbs first."

Matt checked on Timothy again, whose back was still to them, and then triumphantly held up the warped zip ties that had been locked around his hands. "Voilà."

"How did you learn that?"

"I used to watch a lot of YouTube videos in between acting auditions. And I do mean *a lot*."

Matt got to work freeing Poppy, and within seconds, she was free and rubbing the red marks on her own wrists. Matt put a finger to his lips, signaling her to keep quiet, and then he noiselessly crouched down, and slowly made his way up to the cab in the front of the mobile home. Poppy nervously watched him as he crawled up behind the driver's seat, steeled himself, then popped up and lunged at Timothy, wrapping an arm around his throat. Timothy croaked in surprise, his foot slamming down on the gas pedal, the mobile home lurching forward, sending Poppy slamming to the floor of the trailer.

Matt struggled with Timothy, choking him, as Timothy's arms flailed as he released his grip on the steering wheel. The trailer swung from side to side, out of control. Poppy grabbed ahold of the table leg which was bolted into the floor and held on with all her might as Matt and Timothy battled up front.

Then, suddenly she felt the entire vehicle flip up and over, and Poppy closed her eyes as cupboards flew open and dishes and glassware came flying out. She held on to the table leg for dear life as the upended trailer finally skidded to a stop.

There was utter silence for about a minute as Poppy slowly opened her eyes to survey the damage. The whole trailer was on its side. She heard Matt groaning but could not immediately see him.

"Matt! Matt!" Poppy cried. "Are you all right?"

"Yeah, I'll live," he moaned. "I think."

Poppy clambered to her hands and knees and made her way up to find Matt attending to Timothy, who was sprawled out across the front seats, unconscious, a deep gash in his forehead.

"He cracked his head against the windshield when we flipped over. He's out cold," Matt said.

"This is the third vehicle in a week you've destroyed," Poppy playfully admonished. "But thank God, this time it was to save our lives."

Matt grinned, then climbed over Timothy's body and kicked open the passenger's-side door, which was facing up, allowing Poppy to crawl out. Matt followed behind her, and once they were outside the air-conditioned mobile home, it quickly became apparent they were in the middle of nowhere, a blinding, unrelenting sun beating down on them with stifling temperatures well above a hundred degrees and still rising.

"My bag is in the trailer with my phone," Poppy said.

Matt pulled his own phone out of his pocket. The screen was smashed but it appeared to still be working. He held the phone up in the air. "Nope. No service."

"Then we're stuck here," Poppy said, suddenly worried. "With no one around for miles."

Matt turned around and climbed back inside the trailer. Poppy could hear him rummaging around.

"What are you doing?"

He didn't answer at first, but emerged a few seconds later. "I was hoping to find some bottled water in the minifridge, but no such luck."

"They probably didn't bother restocking since we wrapped shooting in the desert and were doing a company move back to the resort," Poppy sighed.

"What do we do now?" Matt asked, blocking out the sun with his hand as he scanned the vast, endless desert.

Poppy walked around to the back of the trailer. "We can follow the tire tracks back to the main road."

"That has to be at least a ten-mile walk. In this heat, with no water, we'll never make it," Matt said solemnly.

Poppy didn't respond.

She knew they had no other choice.

When the same thought finally hit Matt, they grabbed each other's hands and began the long, brutal trek back to where they had come from under the scorching sun and nothing around for miles.

Chapter 51

Poppy followed behind Matt as they staggered through the endless sand past rock formations and cacti, the wind, which had started to pick up, whistling and gusting. Poppy had brought along a neck scarf which she used to mask her face from the grit and dust. Her mouth was dry, she felt light-headed, no doubt from dehydration, and as far as the eye could see, there was nothing ahead of them but cracked land, crumbling rock, and mountains in the far distance that never seemed to get any closer. She wasn't sure how much longer she could go on, and began contemplating a scenario where she would find some cover behind a rock where she could find respite from the harsh sunlight and rest awhile, allowing Matt to continue on ahead to seek help unencumbered by her. She had not reached that desperate point yet, but she was getting awfully close.

Her impractical shoes were not designed for desert

trekking and her ankles throbbed with pain, but taking them off and walking barefoot was not an option because the dry baked earth would sear the soles of her feet.

The cutting wind suddenly picked up speed, battering them relentlessly. Poppy stumbled and fell to the ground, covered in dust, and licked her cracked lips to try to moisten them, even a little bit. Through the blinding sandstorm, she could see Matt running back to get her, grabbing her hand, hauling her to her feet, then leading her forward until they reached a large rock near what looked like a dry creek, circling around it and ducking down together.

Matt huddled with Poppy, grabbing ahold of her scarf, which looked like it might loosen and fly away from her face, holding it in place to protect her. They crouched next to each other, clinging to each other for what felt like hours, but was only a few minutes until the sandstorm subsided and there was a heavy silence.

"Sit tight, I'll be right back," Matt said, standing up and circling back around the rock.

Poppy closed her eyes and her head drooped forward. She pretended she was back in her brand-new house cooking Sam dinner. She was grateful that the shadow of the rock was at least offering some shelter from the unrelenting rays of the sun. She was sitting quietly, meditating, trying hard to focus on the task at hand, surviving this journey, when she heard a strange sound.

A rattling.

Poppy froze, holding her breath.

She opened her eyes and found herself face-to-face with a long, thick rattlesnake, only inches from her feet. Its triangular head raised, its catlike pupils locked on Poppy, the brown-, gray-, and rust-colored scales curled up, the end of the tail vibrating with a stark warning. Poppy stifled a scream, trying not to move a muscle, hoping the snake might just slither around her and go on its merry way. But the rattler had already identified Poppy as a threat and was rearing back to strike. She knew if the snake bit her with its poisonous fangs all the way out in the middle of nowhere, she would be a goner.

The snake sprang forward and Poppy cried out in shock, shutting her eyes, fearing the worst. But then, in a split second, she heard a loud pop. And all was quiet again. The rattling sound had stopped. She opened her eyes to see the snake's carcass splayed in front of her, mere inches from her right foot. Matt was a few feet away, gripping Timothy's Glock pistol.

"When I went back into the trailer to find us some water, I figured it would be a good idea to bring the kid's gun along just in case," Matt said.

Poppy could barely speak her mouth was so dry, but she managed to get out a sincere "Thank you."

"The sandstorm pretty much erased the tire tracks so we no longer know which way is the main road," Matt said, frowning. "But our best bet is to follow the sun in the west and hope it takes us to some kind of road where we can flag down a car."

Poppy nodded and climbed to her feet as Matt gently took her by the elbow to steady her, and they continued walking. Another hour passed as they slogged through the dirt and sand. Several times Poppy resisted the urge to ask Matt if they could stop and rest, maybe wait until the sun set and the high temperatures began to drop. But stuck out in the desert in the middle of night with all kinds of wild animals was not exactly a preferred option.

The only choice was to plow ahead.

Poppy's ears perked up at a faint sound.

Was it another snake?

She scanned the ground around her fearfully, but there was nothing.

"Do you hear that?" Matt asked.

"Yes, what is it?"

Matt shook his head. "I don't know."

The sound grew in volume.

It wasn't a rattling, but more like a chopping.

Whup. Whup. Whup.

Matt pointed at something in the sky.

It was dark and blurry, but Poppy thought it might be a bird of some kind. Or a desert illusion. After all, she was feeling faint from lack of water and might just be hallucinating. But Matt saw it, too, and then he frantically began waving his arms, trying to catch its attention.

Poppy rubbed her eyes and the image finally came into focus. It was a helicopter. For a moment, Poppy thought the chopper was going to fly overhead, oblivious to them, but then after passing them, it descended from the sky and landed on the flat desert surface a few hundred feet away from them.

Matt bolted forward, still flapping his arms as if he couldn't believe the pilot had spotted them. Poppy followed as fast as she could in her weakened state.

She saw Roy Heller jump out of the helicopter followed by Iris and Violet. Matt gratefully pumped Roy's hand as Iris and Violet joyfully raced over to Poppy, pulling her into a group hug as Poppy sobbed, so grateful to have made it out of this ordeal alive.

Finally, they broke apart.

"We were out for a joyride and saw your dressing-room trailer on its side from way up in the air, and thought you had been killed in a terrible accident. We were so panicked. Roy landed the helicopter, and that's when we found Timothy barely conscious, and surmised what had happened," Iris explained.

"Oh, Poppy, we were so worried!" Violet cried. "But Roy was confident all along that we would find you."

Roy pushed past them and enveloped Poppy in an unexpected hug. "Actually I had my brave face on. I'd be lying if I said I wasn't a little concerned. I'm happy to see you alive, gorgeous." He reached in to kiss her. Poppy instinctively turned her head and his lips landed squarely on her cheek.

Iris's face blanched, but she remained uncharacteristically quiet.

Roy stepped back. "Sorry, too forward?"

Poppy nodded with an apologetic smile.

"She's got a fella waiting for her at home," Matt said.

"I see," Roy said. "Well, let's not keep him waiting."

He gently put an arm around Poppy and escorted her back toward the helicopter with Matt leading the way and Iris and Violet falling in behind them.

"Is he better-looking than me?" Roy joked.

"I'm not answering that," Poppy sighed.

Then Roy got serious. "Do you love him?"

Poppy thought about it.

"Yes, yes I do."

It was the first time she had admitted it out loud to anyone, and it felt good.

It felt right.

Chapter 52

As Poppy stood at the island of her new kitchen tossing a salad in a large glass bowl with her tongs, she felt a pair of hands sliding around her waist, gently pulling her back into a strong chest as a face began nuzzling her neck.

"I can feel your heart beating," Poppy said, setting down the tongs. "So I guess it must be working again."

Sam spun her around and kissed her on the lips.

She could smell a hint of garlic.

"You snuck a piece of garlic bread while I was getting dressed, didn't you?"

Sam shrugged. "Maybe. I'm not admitting to anything."

He cupped a hand around her neck and drew her closer, kissing her again, this time more passionately.

She stepped away, putting a hand up to stop the foreplay before it got too out of hand. "We have guests arriving any minute now."

"I know. I saw the table set for four. What a shame. I'm only here one more night so I was hoping we might enjoy a romantic dinner for two," Sam whined.

"There will be plenty of time for those later. According to your doctor, you'll be kicking around a while longer."

"Yeah, but after such a major event like a heart attack, aren't I supposed to be living my best life every day, or something like that?"

"You are. You're helping me entertain some friends. That's your best life, at least for tonight."

Sam chuckled. Poppy opened the oven to check on her eggplant parmesan bubbling in a glass casserole dish, then she shut the door and went to open a bottle of Pinot Noir to let it breathe.

"The best part of my time here is finally getting out of that sad, lonely guest room and into the main bedroom last night. It's done wonders for my recovery."

"Yes, well, you can just keep that little detail to yourself when our guests arrive," Poppy warned.

"I'm going to miss seeing your beautiful face every day. It's going to be hard going back to the way things were, you here in Palm Springs, me up in Big Bear."

Poppy began piling the garlic bread into a basket. "We'll adjust, we have before."

"But things won't be the same . . ." Sam's voice trailed off as he seemed to become melancholy.

Poppy stopped what she was doing. "What do you mean?"

Sam shrugged. "This thing, the heart thing, well, it's changed me. How could it not? The guy I used to be . . ."

"You mean the big, strong, stoic cowboy who taught me how to fire a gun in his backyard? That was an image, Sam, your image, that you've projected to the world for as long as I've known you. But that's not the Sam Emerson I know, the one who cries at all those YouTube videos where soldiers come home from overseas and surprise their kids at school, or when police officers and firefighters stand outside a hospital applauding the health-care workers who worked so hard and were so overwhelmed during the pandemic, the one who was man enough to know he needed help after a traumatic health scare. I never wanted Sam Emerson, Marlboro Man. No, this Sam, the Sam right here, is the man I've fallen in . . ." She abruptly stopped herself. She could see Sam's eyes widening in surprise and anticipation. It was too late now. She had admitted it out loud already to a stranger she hardly knew, she might as well say it outright to the man in question. ". . . fallen in love with."

Sam kissed her again. "I love you, too."

Now that they had both finally said it out loud, Poppy felt an enormous release of pressure. There would be no more guessing. Sam was going to be around for a while. She had to admit to herself that she was going to miss seeing him in her house every day. After the dramatic events that had unfolded during the previous month and their aftermath, time just flew by. Poppy had been caring for Sam for over three weeks now, and he was finally well enough to go home and look after himself. But nothing is permanent and Poppy suspected that maybe, just maybe, Sam might be back in her new house sometime in the foreseeable future. Except the next time, strong and healthy and able to change a burned-out bulb in the carriage light above her garage door. Not that she saw the man that she loved as a glorified handyman, but it certainly didn't hurt.

The highly publicized arrest of Hal Greenwood and his copycat son Timothy was still raging like a California wildfire through news cycles and social media and their trials were not even scheduled to begin for at least a year. Poppy tried ignoring all the hysteria and hoopla but couldn't avoid the onslaught of press announcements heralding the exploitation of the Pillow Talk Killer. Already a TV movie called *Like Father, Like Son* was in development at Lifetime. Donald Carter's wife, Rosemarie, Danika's stalker, Byron Savage, and Hal's longtime personal assistant had all scored major book deals for big bucks. As for Poppy's comeback role in *Palm Springs Weekend*, Netflix was taking full advantage of the film's sudden notoriety with a major fall rollout with millions in ads and promotion. Poppy just held her breath, mentally preparing for the onslaught to come, hoping to keep as low a profile as possible until all the intense interest mercifully subsided.

Unfortunately for Joselyn, the actress who had resumed the leading role following Danika's murder, her rising star was already sputtering out. Word came from the editing room that she was a decidedly lackluster presence, failing to match the charismatic heights of her predecessor, the far more talented Danika Delgado. According to the director Trent Dodsworth-Jones, who gave an interview in *Entertainment Weekly* about the upcoming film, the true star to watch was the previously unknown Matt Flowers, Trent's new discovery and muse who he promised had delivered a star-making performance. True to form, at least on the outside Matt shrugged off the accolades, claiming it was just engineered publicity for the movie. But Poppy could tell that on the inside he was bouncing off the walls like an excited kid on Christmas morning. Although Matt continued assuring Poppy that he was loyal to the Desert Flowers Detective Agency, Poppy knew it was easy for him to say that with the film still on the horizon. What Matt's future held beyond the film's release, well, only time would tell.

The doorbell rang.

Sam sighed, frustrated. "All right, you win, let's play host and hostess. Is it Iris and this new fella she can't stop talking about?"

"Roy Heller, speaking of macho hero types," Poppy laughed. "No, Iris is still working on that particular project."

"Then who is it?"

Poppy smiled knowingly and walked out of the kitchen, Sam following her. She went to the front door and swung it open. Violet and Phil McKellan stood there, Phil clutching a bottle of red wine, which he handed to Poppy.

"Thank you, come in," Poppy said, stepping aside and ushering them into the foyer. "Sam, you know Violet, and this is Phil McKellan."

"Pleasure," Sam said, extending a hand.

"Nice to meet you, Sam," Phil said, smiling.

Violet appeared as if she was ready to burst with joy.

It had been a long time since she had dated a man.

And after an admittedly rough start with Phil, Violet had done a lot of soul searching, and with Poppy and Iris's urging, she had decided to give the guy a second chance.

It was a smart decision.

The two looked blissfully happy together and a perfect fit.

"Make yourselves at home. What can I get you to drink, Phil?" Poppy asked.

"Glass of red wine would be nice, whatever's open," he said.

"Me too," Violet piped in.

As Poppy headed for the kitchen, she heard Sam ask, "So, how did you two meet?"

Poppy smiled to herself.

It was going to be an interesting night.

Private Investigator Poppy Harmon can see through the charms of Southern California's trickiest criminals. But when she and the Desert Flowers Detective Agency go up against a dashing dating show murderer, they may have finally met their match!

While sidekick Matt Flowers shoots a film abroad, Poppy dusts off her own acting chops to break up a Gen Z crime ring targeting seniors in Palm Springs. Tanya Cook and her gal pals have been swindling susceptible residents for all they're worth—until the gang meets Poppy undercover. Yet with the case cracked, the desert heat is on full blast as new terrors take the lead . . .

Poppy's already sweating over a menacing mystery stalker when a shocking death proves she's in serious danger. As suspicions fall once again on Tanya, finding answers may mean pulling off the most challenging performance of her career . . .

Now, with Poppy's unknown stalker rumored to be posing as one of several bachelors on a glitzy reality series, a disguised Poppy must reveal his true identity on set before he realizes hers. Does Poppy have what it takes to catch the cold blooded killer in time for the season finale . . . or should she start planning for her funeral?

Please turn the page for an exciting sneak peek of Lee Hollis's next Poppy Harmon mystery POPPY HARMON AND THE BACKSTABBING BACHELOR coming soon wherever print and e-books are sold!

Chapter 1

Poppy Harmon was having a devil of a time operating her electric wheelchair. When she pushed the joystick forward, the wheels seemed to veer right, not straight ahead, and she banged into a wall in the hallway after maneuvering out of the bedroom, trying to steer herself toward the living room.

Poppy sighed.

She was never going to get the hang of this.

She tried cranking the knob to the left, but only managed to drive the wheelchair away from one wall and crash it into the opposite one. The noise alerted someone in the kitchen, and within seconds a young woman in her twenties with long, straight black hair, emerald green eyes, and a bright smile that mostly disguised a somewhat hardened face suddenly appeared in front of her.

"Oh, you're up. How was your nap?"

"Fine," Poppy spit out, frowning, continuing to push the knob forward but getting nowhere. "I hate this new wheelchair. My old one was a lot easier to operate."

"Here, allow me," the young woman said, slipping behind Poppy and manually pushing the wheelchair by the handles out to the living room and parking it in front of the large flat-screen TV hanging on the wall. "I have some tomato soup heating up on the stove for your lunch. Would you like Ritz crackers or Saltines to go with it? I have both."

"Saltines, please," Poppy answered gruffly.

"Coming right up," the woman said before snatching up the remote and turning on the TV. "Now you just relax and watch your British Bake Off show, and lunch will be ready in just a few minutes."

She bounded back to the kitchen.

Once she was gone, Poppy adjusted the itchy, stringy gray wig she was wearing; straightened her burgundy housecoat; and checked out her face in a wall mirror across from her. The retired Tony Award–winning Broadway makeup artist the Desert Flowers Detective Agency had hired to transform Poppy into a ninety-two-year-old woman had done an incredibly convincing job using liquid latex, eyeliner, and face paint. Poppy looked at least thirty years older than her actual age.

And more importantly, Tanya Cook, the self-described "professional home care nurse" who'd answered her ad to help out with shopping, errands, meals, and to administer medications, was totally buying the disguise.

Poppy heard a thump.

It had come from down the hall, the small guest bedroom that she had set up as her office.

Poppy tried to pick up the remote off the coffee table to lower the television volume, but couldn't quite reach it. She stretched her fingers as far as they would go, but the remote was still about an inch away from her grasp. Frustrated, Poppy swiveled her head around to make sure Tanya had not wandered back into the living room, and then, with lightning speed, she jumped out of the wheelchair, grabbed the remote, and quickly sat back down. She muted the TV and waited.

Sure enough, she heard another thump.

Poppy pulled back on the joystick, the wheelchair rolled in reverse, and then she buzzed back down the hall. The door to the guest room was closed. She leaned forward, turned the handle, and pushed the door open, surprised to find two more young women, both around Tanya's age, and just as pretty. One was blond and the other auburn haired. The blonde was seated at a desk meticulously going through drawers while the other one held a half-filled plastic garbage bag that she appeared to be stuffing with valuables.

"Who are you? What are you doing here?" Poppy cried.

The two girls froze in place, not quite sure what to do.

Tanya appeared in a flash. She stepped in front of Poppy's wheelchair and knelt down so they were at eye level, a reassuring smile on her face. "There's no cause for concern. These are my friends, Bella and Kylie. I invited them over to help tidy up the house. Don't you want your lovely home to be nice and clean for when your grandkids come to visit?"

"I suppose so," Poppy said. "How much is this going to cost me? I used to do my own housework. . . ."

"Oh no, Edna, this is included in the service. You don't have to pay anything extra. I am just here to make things easier for you."

Poppy nodded. She had momentarily forgotten her cover name was Edna Greenblatt, so she was grateful that Tanya had just reminded her. She smiled warmly at the two nervous-looking women in the office. "Thank you, girls. I may have some gingersnap cookies in the kitchen. Would you like one?"

They exchanged quick glances, and then the one with the garbage bag, Bella, shook her head and muttered, "No, we're fine."

Tanya firmly gripped the handles of the wheelchair and rolled Poppy out of the room and back down the hall. "Come on, Edna, time to eat your soup."

"I spotted some dust bunnies underneath the desk. Do you think they can sweep those up, too?" Poppy asked.

"Of course, the whole house will be spotless when they're done, I promise," Tanya said, parking Poppy back in front of the TV in the living room. "Now stay put while I finish preparing your lunch tray."

Poppy detected a slight annoyance in Tanya's tone. She was obviously getting tired of being nice to this high-maintenance old crow.

Because the fact of the matter was Tanya was no professional home care nurse. Tanya Cook and her two cohorts, Bella and Kylie, were professional criminals, allegedly running a massive financial fraud and theft scheme by infiltrating the homes of susceptible senior citizens and gaining access to their bank passwords, cash, checks, credit cards, valuables, and personal documents. Basically bleeding their victims dry right in their own homes! Tanya would scout out a vulnerable target, someone in need of in-home care; apply for the job with forged credentials; then show up at the door with a friendly smile and a promise to take good care of them. She would play nursemaid for about a week, gaining the trust of her charge before bringing in her two accomplices to rob the unsuspecting senior blind, even insidiously redirecting social security direct deposits to a dummy bank account.

Their last mark, however, a feisty widow by the name of Cecile LaCrosse, an eighty-nine-year-old battle-ax who unfortunately fell victim to the scam, was not about to let them get away with it. And so she brought in Poppy and her crew at the Desert Flowers Detective Agency to set up a sting and bring this evil coven of Gen Z witches down.

Poppy, along with her two partners, Iris Becker and Violet Hogan, took a very personal interest in this particular case because they felt a strong kinship with the victims. Although still in their sixties, they knew it was only a matter of time before they themselves might be confused, defenseless elderly victims preyed upon by opportunistic, heartless swindlers.

And so Poppy had insisted that she pose as an elderly widow, drawing on her years of acting experience from when she was a starlet in the 1980s, in order to bust up this enterprising, depraved crime ring.

And so far she had played it to perfection.

Tanya was confident enough after only three days of playing nursemaid to bring in her two sidekicks to finish the job by pillaging poor Edna Greenblatt's home until she was left with nothing but her electric wheelchair, which had a mind of its own.

Tanya appeared with a wooden tray and set it down in front of Poppy. "I garnished the soup with a few garlic croutons. My own grandmother used to love the extra kick."

"It looks lovely," Poppy said, picking up the spoon with a shaky hand and scooping some up, making sure to dribble a little on her housecoat just to be convincing.

"Can I get you anything else?" Tanya asked.

"Oh, no, dear, you've done quite enough," Poppy said with a thin, knowing smile.

And she meant it.

Tanya and her friends had certainly done enough.

And they were about to discover just how "done" they actually were.

Chapter 2

Violet's loud, piercing, high-pitched voice of concern blasted through Poppy's ear. "Poppy, Poppy, what's happening in there? Are you okay?"

Poppy dropped her spoon on the tray and raised her hand to adjust the small earbud resting in the crevice of her right ear, and urgently whispered into the tiny microphone that had been pinned on the inside of her housecoat, "Violet, turn down the volume on your mic, you're going to burst my eardrum!"

"Oh, sorry," Violet said, lowering her voice. "Iris, how do you adjust the volume on this thing?"

"Here, let me do it," Iris snapped.

There was a pause.

"Hello? Hello? Is this better?" Violet bellowed, even more deafening than before.

Poppy sighed. "No, she just made you even louder."

"Hold on," Violet said.

Poppy could hear her two friends and partners bickering in the background away from the microphone that they were using to communicate with Poppy.

"Is that better?" Violet asked, almost whispering.

"Yes, much," Poppy said.

"Who are you talking to?"

The stern voice came from directly behind her. Poppy used her joystick to turn her electric wheelchair around.

Tanya stood staring at her, a plate of gingersnap cookies in her hand.

"What?" Poppy asked innocently.

"I heard you whispering to somebody," Tanya said suspiciously, eyes darting around to see if anyone else was in the room before returning her mistrustful gaze back to her charge. "Who was it?"

Her tone was unsettlingly sinister.

"Abe," Poppy said softly.

"Who's Abe?"

"My late husband. He comes to talk to me every now and then," Poppy said with a sad, drawn face. "I miss him so much. He would have loved this tomato soup." Poppy picked up her spoon to take another sip, making sure to get a garlic crouton. As she slurped and crunched, Tanya seemed to size her up, ultimately opting to believe her story, then held out the plate of gingersnaps toward her.

"Cookie?"

Poppy slowly reached out with her trembling hand and took a cookie, then shoved it into her mouth and talked with her mouth full. "Yummy."

"I'm going to see if Bella and Kylie would like one," Tanya said, turning around to head down the hall, but stopping at the window. "Have you noticed that van parked across the street?"

"What van?" Poppy asked innocently.

"Desert Florists," Tanya said, staring out the window.

Poppy swallowed hard.

The van had been rented by the Desert Flowers Detective Agency. They had slapped on a fake florist shop decal on the side so as not to arouse suspicion. Inside were Violet and Iris, keeping a careful watch over the house. However, they had underestimated how smart and observant Tanya Cook could be.

"If they're just here to deliver flowers to a house in the neighborhood, it's taking them a really long time," Tanya said warily, checking her wristwatch. "It's been there since I arrived this morning."

"Oh, that van is parked there all the time," Poppy quickly explained. "It belongs to one of the neighbors. That's his business. He's always leaving it there and getting a ticket because he forgets to move it on street-cleaning day."

Tanya peered at the van a few more seconds before deciding to buy Poppy's on-the-spot made-up explanation. She then continued on down the hall with her tray of cookies.

"Is everyone in place?" Poppy whispered.

There was silence.

"Violet?" Poppy asked.

Still nothing.

She had lost communication.

Either her earpiece battery had suddenly died, or there was a problem with the transmitter in the van.

"Violet?"

"I'm here, Poppy, I accidentally hit the mute button! Sorry! Yes, we're ready, it's go time!"

"I knew I should have been in charge of the communication equipment!" Iris snorted.

Poppy braced herself just as Tanya returned from the guest bedroom/office with her empty plate. Something outside caught her eye and she raced back to the front window in time to see a uniformed police officer ducking down and circling around the house. Tanya gasped, her mouth dropping open in surprise. She quickly found her voice and started yelling, "Cops!"

Bella and Kylie came crashing out of the guest room, Kylie holding a stuffed garbage bag in her arms.

"Are you serious?" Bella asked nervously.

"Yes!" Tanya cried. "I just saw one sneaking around the side of the house! Run!"

Bella sprinted toward the kitchen, Kylie following close behind but weighed down with the bag. She finally let go of it and it dropped to the floor with a thud as she raced to catch up with Bella.

Poppy heard a man yell, "Police! Put your hands up!"

Tanya's eyes popped open in surprise and she made a mad dash for the front door. Poppy, anticipating the move, jammed the joystick of her wheelchair all the way forward, full speed, and whizzed over in front of the door, blocking her escape.

"What are you doing? Out of my way, old woman!" Tanya screeched, furious, struggling to get around her.

Poppy sprang up to her feet and forcefully pushed Tanya back.

The miraculous sudden strength and agility of the ninety-two-year-old stymied Tanya briefly, but she was still not to be deterred. She charged forward, trying to physically shove Poppy out of the way. Poppy held her ground, knowing she was no match for the young, physically fit girl, but determined to keep her from getting away. Poppy and Tanya grappled, Tanya trying to scratch Poppy's face with her nails in the hope she might release her grip, but as Tanya withdrew her nails, she was stunned to find latex hanging off them, not blood.

"What the—?"

Two uniformed cops suddenly bolted into the living room from the back door off the kitchen, their guns drawn.

"It's over, Tanya!" One of the cops yelled.

She shuddered at the mention of her name because she knew at this moment this had all been a sting.

A con job.

And she had willfully, stupidly, walked right into it.

Tanya slowly raised her hands in the air while glaring defiantly at Poppy, who busily wiped the old-age makeup off her face with the napkin from her lunch tray.

One of the cops, a boyish, inexperienced one, struggled to unhook a pair of handcuffs from his belt loop. Finally, he glanced apprehensively over at his more seasoned partner. "Sarge?"

The older cop sighed, and assisted him in releasing the handcuffs from the officer's belt so he could snap them on Tanya's wrists.

Once her face was free of powder and latex and added wrinkles, Poppy removed her gray wig.

Tanya gaped at her, undoubtedly kicking herself for so easily buying into her now obvious disguise.

The older cop studied Poppy, then stepped forward with a big smile. "Hey, I know you . . ."

The younger cop snapped to attention and stared at Poppy, still clueless. "You do?"

"*Jack Colt, PI*!" Sarge crowed, slapping his forehead. "You're Daphne, Jack's secretary!"

The younger cop still appeared totally confused. "Who?"

"The TV show, it was on in the nineteen eighties!" Sarge exclaimed.

"I wasn't born until nineteen ninety-seven," the younger cop said.

Both Poppy and Sarge chose to ignore him.

Sarge was almost giddy. "Detective Jordan said he had recruited an actress to help with this operation. I just never imagined it would be *you*! This is so cool!"

Of course, Poppy knew that it was she who had contacted Detective Jordan, bringing him into the case, not the other way around, but why clarify such things and potentially bruise Jordan's fragile ego?

"I am a private investigator these days," Poppy felt the need to explain.

"Wait, a *real* one? Are you joking?" Sarge asked, still beaming from ear to ear.

Poppy nodded shyly.

Sarge fumbled for his phone. "Hey, do you mind if I get a selfie with you? My poker buddies are never going to believe this!"

Poppy did not feel this moment was appropriate for that kind of thing, but she also did not want to disappoint a fan.

Sarge basically bodychecked a handcuffed Tanya out of the way to get to Poppy.

"Maybe I should read this woman her rights first, Sarge," the younger cop quietly suggested.

"That can wait, kid, hold on a sec," Sarge barked before holding his phone up and beaming while snapping a photo. He checked it and frowned. "It's a little blurry. Do you mind if I take another one?"

"No, not at all," Poppy said, keeping one eye on Tanya, who glowered at her menacingly.

Sarge tried again, this time satisfied. "Thank you, Daphne, you made my day!"

"Of course," Poppy said, grabbing the handles of the wheelchair and pushing it out of the way so the officers could escort Tanya Cook outside to their waiting squad car.

The young officer gripped Tanya by the arm to lead her out, but she refused to budge, her eyes angrily fixed on Poppy. "So you're telling me, the cops recruited some washed-up, old has-been Hollywood *star* to take us down?"

Sarge nodded. "Yeah, and unfortunately for you, it worked like a charm, didn't it?"

Tanya sneered and looked dismissively at Poppy. "Why bother with the old lady makeup? You're already old enough to be my grandmother."

Poppy bristled on the inside, but was not about to show any emotion on the surface to give this she-devil the satisfaction. Instead, she calmly replied, "Yes, Tanya, you may have many more years ahead of you in life than I do, but a lot of them will no doubt be spent behind bars . . . so there's that."

Poppy opened the front door, allowing the two officers to leave with Tanya, who looked as if she wanted to smack Poppy right across the face but couldn't because her hands were handcuffed behind her back, so instead, she just raised her head high contemptuously and began to softly whistle the children's nursery rhyme "Twinkle, Twinkle, Little Star."

Poppy scoffed at Tanya's labored attempts to ridicule her Hollywood past. But given what was about to come, that unfortunately would turn out to be a very grave and dangerous mistake.